The Murders at Clarion Castle
A Homefront Sleuths Cozy Mystery
Anna Elliott and Charles Veley

Wilton Press

This is a work of fiction. Names, characters, organisations, places, events, and incidents are either products of the authors' imagination or are used fictitiously.

Text copyright © 2025 by Anna Elliott and Charles Veley. All rights reserved.

No part of this book may be reproduced, or stored in a retrieval system, or transmitted in any form or by any means, electronic, mechanical, photocopying, recording, or otherwise, without the express written permission of the authors.

Contact the authors at the Sherlock and Lucy series website: SherlockAndLucy.com

Contents

Epigraph	VII
Prologue: August 1941	VIII
1. Evie	1
2. Dorothy	7
3. Evie	11
4. Harry	16
5. Evie	21
6. Harry	27
7. Alice	33
8. Harry	39
9. Harry	46
10. Katherine	52
11. Harry	58
12. Evie	63
13. Harry	67
14. Evie	73
15. Harry	75
16. Harry	79

17.	Harry	84
18.	Harry	93
19.	Alice	97
20.	Katherine	103
21.	Katherine	109
22.	Alice	114
23.	Evie	121
24.	Harry	127
25.	Dorothy	134
26.	Alice	139
27.	Dorothy	146
28.	Harry	149
29.	Dorothy	155
30.	Blake	160
31.	Harry	165
32.	Harry	172
33.	Evie	177
34.	Harry	182
35.	Harry	188
36.	Evie	194
37.	Dorothy	200
38.	Dorothy	206
39.	Alice	210
40.	Katherine	216

41.	Harry	221
42.	Harry	226
43.	Evie	233
44.	Harry	240
45.	Evie	244
46.	Harry	246
47.	Evie	250
48.	Evie	254
49.	Katherine	256
50.	Harry	261
51.	Alice	265
52.	Harry	270
53.	Alice	274
54.	Dorothy	281
55.	Harry	284
56.	Dorothy	289
57.	Evie	293
58.	Dorothy	296
59.	Evie	299
60.	Harry	304
61.	Harry	310
62.	Alice	314
63.	Evie	318
64.	Evie	321

65.	Evie	325
66.	Harry	328
67.	Historical Notes	333
68.	A Note to Readers	337
69.	Also by Anna Elliott and Charles Veley	338

Epigraph

"Never give in, never give in, never, never, never, never—in nothing, great or small, large or petty—never give in except to convictions of honour and good sense. Never yield to force; never yield to the apparently overwhelming might of the enemy."

- Sir Winston S. Churchill, in a speech given at Harrow School on October 29, 1941.

Prologue: August 1941

Evie drifted slowly towards consciousness, as though emerging from a thick fog. She tried to open her eyes, but her lids felt weighted with a dull heaviness that filled her head. Her body was stiff, her muscles aching as though she hadn't moved in hours, and a faint smell lingered in her nose and in the back of her throat: something chemical and sweet.

The scent brought back a fleeting memory—less a memory, really, than a sense of dread or danger or . . .

The memory hovered, just out of reach, but the unsettling sense of dread remained, making her pulse skip and quicken. What had happened to her?

Even her thoughts felt sluggish and slow. But as she bobbed closer to the surface of full consciousness— like a swimmer rising through deep, dark water— she realised that she could hear a man's voice speaking somewhere nearby.

"Is she awake yet?"

No. Evie's heart jolted against her ribcage and her eyes flew open. No. She had to be unconscious, still, and dreaming this.

Paul was dead, shot down by a German fighter plane while flying a mission for the RAF. He couldn't be somewhere close by, speaking in what sounded like the next room—

A woman's voice answered. "Not yet. I looked in on her about half an hour ago and she was still unconscious. Hans used a lot of the chloroform. It could be hours yet before it wears off."

Evie frowned. She knew the woman's voice, too, although for the moment she couldn't place it. But she'd heard it somewhere, and recently at that—

"I need to leave soon." The man's voice spoke again. Paul's voice. It was Paul's voice; Evie was certain of it. And with that certainty came an avalanche of memories in a sudden, pulse-pounding rush:

Her visit to Paul's parents' house in Greenwich.

Finding the door ajar.

Entering— and then being attacked from behind and then—nothing.

Now she was lying on a bare mattress in a dingy, windowless little room. Evie tried to sit up, but her muscles were uncoordinated and unsteady, and her head swam with dizziness. She had to content herself with letting her gaze sweep the place, taking rapid stock of her surroundings.

Greyish paint peeling on the walls. The smell of must and damp that pervaded a place when it had been left empty for too long. Floors that were covered in a thick layer of grime and dust.

And Paul speaking in the next room to the woman Evie had thought was his mother . . . but who in fact must be nothing of the kind.

Almost immediately, other pieces of the puzzle fell into place with the impact of concrete blocks being slapped together to form a barricade. But although the full implications left Evie breathless and with a cold, hollow feeling spreading out from under her ribcage, the pattern those puzzle pieces made was dazzlingly plain.

"I'll just go in and make sure there's nothing she might use to escape," Paul said.

The walls in this place must be practically paper thin. His words came through quite clearly.

"Of course there isn't!" the woman sounded indignant. "There's not so much as a stray matchstick. We made sure of that before we put her in there. And besides, the door's locked."

Paul laughed shortly. "You don't know her. I've seen her disarm a man using nothing but a loaf of stale bread, and pick a lock with a bent hairpin."

Evie supposed it was gratifying—if unfortunate—to hear that Paul wasn't likely to underestimate her abilities. But the next moment she heard a step in the passage outside of her door, and the rattle of a key in the lock.

She had barely a split second to drop back down on the mattress, close her eyes and force her breathing into the deep, even rhythm of sleep.

Then she heard the door swing open.

Paul stood in the open doorway, looking at her for a long moment. Evie didn't dare risk opening her eyes by so much as a sliver, but she could feel the weight of his gaze.

Then his voice said, softly, "Evie?"

Evie's mind spun, flipping through the possibilities. With anyone else, she might try feigning unconsciousness. But Paul knew her. They'd spent weeks sleeping side by side as they escaped German-occupied France, and then they'd been married, even if only for a short few months before word had reached her of Paul's death.

There were a good many words she would have liked to use to describe Paul at this moment. But—also unfortunately for her—stupid would never be one of them.

Evie didn't trust herself to put on an act good enough to fool Paul. So she let her head turn restlessly on the pillow and moaned faintly, as though she were just waking up.

"Evie?" Paul took a few more steps into the room.

Evie let her eyes flicker open.

Paul was standing within arm's reach of the bed. Alive.

Chapter 1
Evie

Evie didn't even have to feign her gasp of shock.

Until this moment, some deeply buried part of her must not have entirely believed that this wasn't some fantastical, chloroform-induced dream. But it was truly Paul who stood before her now. He was as handsome as ever, his golden-fair hair swept back from his forehead, his rugged, masculine face clean-shaven, and his blue eyes alert.

Evie should have been angry— or terrified— or both. But as she stared at him, she heard herself suddenly laugh out loud.

Paul frowned. He'd never liked being laughed at. "What's funny?"

Evie had no doubt that he would like the honest answer— *you're alive and a traitorous, murdering German spy, which means that now I don't have to feel guilty about having fallen in love with another man*— even less than he liked her laughter. So she quickly turned the laugh into a soft, wondering smile. "Nothing, it's just . . . you're alive! It's like a miracle!"

Paul's expression cleared. "Nothing particularly miraculous, just some careful staging on the part of the military higher-ups."

"Yes, of course." Evie drew in her breath, trying to force herself to think clearly, past every last lingering shred of the drugged haze. Back during her days with the French resistance, she'd enjoyed the missions that called for her to play a part— whether her role was that of an elderly flower vendor who slipped hidden messages to allies into bouquets of flowers or a young widow whose black cloak and veil concealed the guns she was smuggling past a German blockade.

The edge of danger had sharpened all her senses and even made each new role more fun.

This wouldn't be fun now. But it would probably be the most challenging bit of play acting she'd ever performed in her life.

"You're Siegfried, aren't you?" Evie said. "I thought I'd recognised you on the beach last month, when you picked up the message at the dead drop!"

That night, she had crouched on the white chalk cliffs above Dover beach. She had watched a German agent row ashore from a U-boat out in the Channel to collect what he'd thought was a message from a fellow German spy.

At the time, Evie had tried to persuade herself that the figure couldn't possibly be Paul, despite the similarities in build and the characteristic way he'd moved. But maybe that was why the pieces had slid so quickly into place now: she'd suspected this for some time.

She went quickly on, before Paul could answer, fixing him with a look of smiling admiration. "Oh, Paul, that's so terribly brave of you! You've been pretending to work for the Germans. And all the time you've been playing the double agent, feeding what information you gathered to our side. I only wish that I'd known, or I would have done everything in my power to help you!"

Evie kept the look of admiration fixed on her face, even as she watched Paul's expression. She could almost see the calculations taking place behind his keen blue eyes.

On the one hand, there was the cruel impulse to rip her romantic illusions away entirely, let her know that if he was a double agent, his loyalties were entirely to the German side. Why had she never noticed before the cruelty that lurked behind Paul's ready smiles?

But on the other hand, Paul liked being adored, even worshipped. And he was practical enough to realise that she would be far easier to manipulate and control if he let her continue to believe him a hero.

He took her hand. "I would have told you if I could, darling. I wanted to, of course. But you know how strict the top brass is about secrecy in these matters. I was sworn not to tell a single soul."

"Of course." Evie had to exercise every last shred of her will not to yank her hand away from his. "I do understand. But why kidnap me now? I suppose the man and woman who pretended to be your parents are just two more agents?"

The hard, angry part of her— the one she was trying very hard to keep in check for the sake of the act she was putting on— enjoyed the momentarily blank look that came over Paul's face as he scrambled to come up with an explanation.

Then he lowered his voice, perching beside her on the edge of the bed. "They are agents, you're right. German agents. They work for me— or believe that they work for me— in my role as Siegfried. Our orders from Berlin were to capture you and interrogate you over the Fort Hardwick affair, to find out what you know about the SOE agents involved."

Evie thought of Mr Brown and the other agents of the Special Operations Executive who had saved both her life and the lives of countless other British civilians. She didn't doubt that Paul and his German paymasters would love to know their names and where to find them.

"I had to play along," Paul went on. "To make it appear I was fully complying with Berlin's directive. Although of course"— he smiled another of the smiles that Evie had once thought so boyish and charming and that now made her skin crawl— "I was glad of the excuse, since it gave me the chance to finally make myself known to you."

As spontaneous explanations went, it wasn't at all bad; Evie had to give him credit.

"Although I wasn't sure how glad you'd be to see me," Paul went on. Something hard-edged and far less charming crept into his tone. "You looked as though you were getting awfully friendly with that policeman. The one who plods around Crofter's Green, finding out who stole half a loaf of bread from Mr Bun the bakers."

Nigel. Evie went as cold as though her blood had just turned icy in her veins. Of course. Paul was the one who had shot at her and Nigel when they'd stood together, laughing in her kitchen. She'd asked herself over and over again why the shot had missed. But Paul hadn't intended to hit her. He probably had just lost his temper seeing her with Nigel, and fired off a round intended to frighten them.

Evie shrugged indifferently. Not just her own life but Nigel's depended on her ability to make the next part of her act convincing.

"You mean Inspector Brewster?" she said. "He's nice enough, I suppose. He's very British— and very conscientious about his job. He actually suspected me of being a German spy when I first came to Crofter's Green." That had the advantage of being entirely true. "I had to try to charm him a bit; otherwise he could have made life frightfully difficult for me— denying permits for the tea shop and all of that sort of thing." She tilted her head, smiling up into Paul's eyes. "Don't tell me you were jealous of a dull stick like Nigel Brewster. Do you really think I could care for anyone, after losing you?"

Paul's expression relaxed. He squeezed Evie's hand. "Of course not, darling." He laughed a little. "I've missed you so much, these past six months— just seeing you speaking to another man was almost enough to drive me mad."

He leaned forward. Evie's stomach clenched. If he kissed her, there was a sizable chance that she would actually be sick. Maybe she could blame the chloroform.

But at the last moment, a knock came on the door and a man's voice called out, "The car is downstairs waiting for you, sir."

Paul swore under his breath, but straightened and called back, "Yes, all right, I'll be there in a moment."

He turned to Evie, speaking in a rapid undertone. "I have to leave you here, a prisoner. Hans and Gerda— the agents whom you met as my supposed parents— think that they're in charge of making sure you don't escape. You understand, don't you?"

"Of course I do," Evie said. Relief made it easy to add the proper degree of fervour to her tone. "You have to keep up the act. I'll do everything I can to help."

"That's my girl." Paul squeezed her hand again and dropped a light kiss onto her forehead. "I'll be back as soon as I can, I promise."

Chapter 2
Dorothy

"Thank you for coming over," Dorothy told Harry Jenkins.

Tall, grey-haired, and solidly built, Harry looked every inch like the retired Scotland Yard inspector that he was. But he also had a reassuring, grandfatherly quality that Dorothy badly needed right now.

"That's all right," Harry said. "I drop by the Cozy Cup for tea and a biscuit around ten o'clock most mornings. No bother to come an hour earlier. Now, what seems to be the trouble?"

They were standing in the tea room of Evie's Cozy Cup, the village tea shop where Dorothy had been working for the past several months. In another few minutes, Dorothy was supposed to open the shop to the housewives who liked to stop in for a restoring cup, after battling to stretch their ration coupons as far as possible in the village shops.

Ordinarily, the Cozy Cup was a small, unspoiled bit of peace in a world that was torn up by the war raging across Europe and the rest of the world. The floors were polished oak that matched the exposed wooden beams running across the ceiling, and the walls were creamy white plaster, with shelves that held their array of teas and preserved jellies in glass jars.

People could sit at a table covered by a lace cloth and drink tea out of a blue Wedgewood cup and forget for a quarter of an hour or so that Hitler badly wanted to march his armies right across the Channel and over into Britain. Unless there was an air raid on, of course. They'd seen their share of raids and even had a few bombs fall not far away, so trying to forget only carried you so far. Still, the Cozy Cup was beautiful, and Dorothy loved coming in to wait tables and help with the baking every morning after she'd dropped her son Tommy off at school.

This morning, though, worry was a queasy wash in her stomach. "It's Evie," she told Harry. "She left a note for me yesterday, saying that she'd gone to visit Paul's parents. You know, her husband Paul who was killed last winter?"

Evie's husband had been an RAF pilot, whose plane had been shot down a month or two before Evie moved here to Crofter's Green.

Harry nodded. "Nigel mentioned she'd been to see them."

Dorothy held up a slip of paper. "Yesterday when I came in, I found this note, saying that she'd gone to Greenwich for the day and hoped I'd be able to manage the shop all right without her." Which Dorothy had. The Cozy Cup was doing good business, but things were never so busy that Dorothy couldn't handle things on her own. "She said she expected to be back last night, though,"

Dorothy went on. "But I came this morning to open up the shop and she wasn't here. She's not been back, either. I ran upstairs to check, and her bed hadn't been slept in. What's more, her handbag— the one she carries anytime she goes out— is still gone."

Dorothy nodded to the curtained-off stairs that led up to Evie's living quarters.

Harry frowned, pulling at his upper lip as he studied Evie's note. "Doesn't necessarily mean that there's anything wrong," he said. "Or rather, anything sinister," he corrected himself. "There's plenty that could have gone wrong, these days. There could have been a bombing raid last night that knocked out the railways around Greenwich and stopped the trains from running. Could have taken out the telephone lines, too, so that Evie couldn't 'phone and let you know she'd been held up."

"Yes." Dorothy couldn't disagree. But neither could she argue away the cold fear that had settled in the pit of her stomach. "But look at Evie's note. She was upset when she wrote it."

"How can you tell that?" Harry asked.

"I know how Evie's handwriting normally looks," Dorothy said. "Here." She picked up a notecard from the counter, the one where they kept their cash register. "Evie wrote this out for Mrs Phillips the other day. Mrs Phillips asked for Mrs Dean's recipe for hot cross buns." Mrs Dean had been Evie's grandmother and the original owner of the Cozy Cup. "And Evie said she'd have a hunt for it in amongst her grandmother's other recipes and have a copy waiting for Mrs Phillips to pick up today. Not that it matters, of course," Dorothy added. "But look. Do you see the way she's written *Hot Cross Buns* here at the top of the recipe? And the list of ingredients, too. *Milk, butter, sugar*. Her letters are all nice and neat and upright."

Evie had been a schoolteacher at a girls' boarding school over in France, and her handwriting was a beautiful copperplate script written in perfectly straight lines— not like Dorothy's, which tended to straggle all across the page.

"Now look at the note again," Dorothy said. "It's still Evie's writing; there's no doubt about that. But do you see how the letters are all a bit slanted, like she was writing in a hurry and just wanted to get the job over and done?"

Harry glanced at Dorothy with a faint smile. "You have got an eye for noticing details, haven't you?"

Dorothy's cheeks flushed. She'd never thought of herself as clever, not when she'd just barely scraped by with passing marks in school—

even if her husband Tom had always tried to tell her that she had better sense than a lot of their teachers. Still, it was a whole new experience to have a Scotland Yard inspector listening to what she had to say.

"I know it doesn't prove anything," Dorothy went on. "Evie could have been upset when she wrote this note to me just on account of it being a hard thing, visiting her dead husband's parents. But all the same, I don't know, I've just got a feeling that something's not right."

Harry nodded, his expression grave. "It's not as though we don't have just cause to worry in any case. We may have wrapped up the Judas Monk affair. But Siegfried is still out there, somewhere— and we already know that he has a grudge against Evie."

Dorothy shivered. Siegfried was the code name of a German agent who'd been at the back of a nasty business involving murder and spying— not to mention a Nazi plot to invade Britain by breaching the defences around Dover.

"Do you think Siegfried could have captured Evie?" Dorothy didn't even want to think about a possibility that was even worse: that he might have killed her. Right this moment, even as she and Harry stood in the Cozy Cup's pretty tea room, Evie might already be dead.

Harry patted her shoulder in the way Dorothy could remember her own father doing when she was growing up. "Evie's tough and she's smart. If Siegfried has tried anything on her, he'll get more than he bargained for, I can promise you that." He paused, frowning. "But still and all, let's get Alice and Blake and Nigel over here so that we can sort this properly. That's what we do, isn't it? We take care of our own."

Chapter 3
Evie

After Paul had gone, Evie shut her eyes, drew her feet up, and rested her forehead on her raised knees, forcing herself to take breath after long, shuddering breath.

She'd loved Paul. She'd loved him so much that when word of his death came, grief had felt like the jaws of some monstrous beast, trying to physically tear her apart. And now—

Now she had to take every last bit of the hurt and anger and pain and betrayal she was feeling, lock it up, and let it harden into determination to escape from this place. No, not just escape. She also had to make sure that Paul paid for all the French and British lives he'd taken.

Evie waited until her heartbeat had finally slowed and steadied and the blood no longer pounded in her ears. Then she stood up and began a slow circuit of the room that was her temporary prison. Not that she considered it very likely that she would find anything useful. The woman who had played the part of Paul's mother— the one he'd identified as Gerda— had assured Paul that they'd swept the room for anything that could possibly be used to help her escape. Still, anything she could deduce about the place where she was being held was a potential advantage that could be leveraged in her favour.

Besides, it gave her a distraction, something to focus on besides replaying every moment of her marriage to Paul and wondering what— if anything— of it had been real.

Her investigation didn't take long. The room was small, only about eight feet by ten feet, the walls dingy grey and the floorboards scuffed and heavily worn. The man who'd called to Paul through the door— Hans, presumably?— had said that a car was waiting downstairs, which meant that she had to be on an upper floor. But as she'd already observed, there were no windows, nothing that could tell her anything else about the building beyond the four square walls of this room. Was she in a townhouse? A flat? An abandoned farm cottage?

She couldn't hear anything from outside, no traffic noises, no rumble of aeroplanes or whistles of trains. Either she was somewhere extremely isolated, away from all such city noises, or else the walls of the place were exceptionally thick. Neither of which was a comforting thought.

Evie blew out a breath and turned her attention back to the room itself. Despite the generally shabby, dilapidated feel of the place, the door looked extremely solid, a heavy panel of age-darkened wood. She'd heard Paul slide at least one bolt into place after he left her, too, so there was no point in checking to see whether she was locked in.

There was no furniture, apart from the bed— which was only a bare mattress laid on top of a plain metal frame. No sheets or blankets at all.

Evie crouched down and peered under the bed without much hope of finding anything. The dust was thicker here, tickling Evie's nose so that she almost gave up. But then, way back at the join of the wall and the floor, she spied something that had rolled into a groove in the wooden floorboards. Lying flat, she stretched out her hand and managed to pull it out.

A pencil. Just the stub of one, really. But all the same, it might come in useful. Evie debated momentarily, then slid it down into her shoe. It wasn't particularly comfortable, but at least no one would be likely to find it and take it away.

Evie took one last look under the bed, but there was nothing else besides the dust. She sat upright, staring up at the bare electric bulb in the middle of the ceiling that provided the room's harsh yellow light. What time of day was it? For that matter, what day was it? She'd arrived in Greenwich and been chloroformed the same morning. Was it still the same day, or had she been unconscious right through the night?

If she had been gone overnight, someone back in Crofter's Green would surely have realised by now that she was missing. And she'd left a note for Dorothy, saying that she was going to visit Paul's parents in Greenwich. That would give Harry and Nigel a place to start searching for her. If they did start searching; if they didn't just assume that Evie had decided to extend her stay with Paul's parents. Or that she'd left Crofter's Green entirely.

Evie pressed her eyes shut. She had tried to leave without telling anyone. She'd thought that Siegfried might be a danger to anyone she cared about, and she'd been trying to protect Dorothy and Alice and all of the others from the danger of association with her.

She hadn't even known then just how right she was about the threat Siegfried— Paul— posed.

But that meant that she couldn't count on any of them coming to rescue her now. Not when she'd made an entire career out of keeping even her closest friends at arms' distance, not letting anyone share in her troubles or cares.

Evie had been managing to keep her fear largely at bay. But now threads of panic pulled tight in her chest at the thought of what Alice and Dorothy would think, if they believed that she had disappeared without a word of goodbye. They'd be so hurt, so disappointed in her.

And Nigel. Would he be hurt, too? Or would he only think that his initial estimation of her had been right after all, when he'd disliked and distrusted her almost on sight?

Evie gave herself a hard mental shake. Thinking like this was making her odds of escape exactly zero per cent more favourable, which meant these were entirely pointless questions to be worrying about right now.

She'd exhausted everything the room had to offer, but as she sat on the bare floorboards, trying to quiet the noise from her own churning thoughts, she realised that there was another noise coming from down below her. Specifically, a murmur of voices.

Evie lay down flat, pressing her ear against the floorboards. There were two voices, a man's and a woman's. For a moment, Evie couldn't make out the words at all. Then she realised that they were speaking in German.

She had to credit Gerda, the woman who had played the part of Paul's mother. Evie had visited with her for an entire afternoon and spoken twice more to her by telephone, and not once had she suspected that English wasn't her native language. Hans, who'd played Paul's father, hadn't spoken more than a dozen or so words throughout the entirety of Evie's visit.

At the time, Evie had just thought him either very shy or very dull.

She stopped herself before she could fall down the rabbit hole of berating herself for stupidity, and instead focused on what Gerda and Hans were saying to one another in the room below hers. She'd learned to speak fluent German of necessity during her Resistance work over in France, but the fact that the voices were muffled combined with the lingering effects of the chloroform made translating the words she was hearing now a far more laborious process.

Castle was the first word that she caught, spoken in Hans' deeper, guttural voice. Then a longer string of words that she couldn't make out, although she thought that she heard him say, *the factory*.

Evie heard a rattle as of pots and pans that blocked out part of Gerda's reply. Maybe the room down below was the kitchen? When Gerda's voice came through clearly, Evie heard her say, "— latest report was that the under-butler suspects. That is why Herr Siegfried has gone to make sure that he is taken care of."

Chapter 4
Harry

Harry Jenkins checked his pocket watch for the third time in as many minutes. The quiet ticking had always been a comfort to him throughout his years at Scotland Yard—a steady, reliable pulse in a world of chaos and uncertainty. Today, though, each tick felt like an accusation. Time passing. Evie still missing.

The kitchen at the Cozy Cup had seen many strategy sessions over the past few months, but none had begun with such a palpable sense of dread. Harry looked around at the grim faces gathered at Evie's worn oak table—their war room, as young Tommy, Dorothy's son, had once called it with innocent excitement. Now the phrase carried a more ominous weight.

"Thank you all for coming so quickly," Harry said, his voice steadier than he felt. "As Dorothy has explained, Evie went to Greenwich yesterday to visit her late husband's parents and hasn't returned."

Alice Greenleaf sat with her hands folded before her, the stillness of her posture betrayed only by the whiteness of her knuckles. "It's him, isn't it?" she asked quietly. "Siegfried."

The name hung in the air like a curse.

"We can't jump to conclusions," Harry replied, though the same fear had taken root in his own mind. "But given our recent... entanglements, we must consider the possibility."

Dorothy was busying herself making tea, her movements mechanical and precise—a mother's instinct to nurture, even as worry etched lines around her eyes. "I keep thinking," she said, not turning from the stove, "what if she needs us right now? What if she's—" She stopped, unable to finish the thought.

"She's alive," Blake Collins said firmly, his schoolteacher's certainty breaking through their gloom. Katherine sat beside him, her eyes darting nervously between the faces. Though Harry knew her memory remained fragmented, he also knew she'd developed a sisterly bond with Evie during her recovery. "Siegfried wouldn't risk killing her immediately. She has information he wants."

"That's hardly comforting, Blake," Harry said, though he appreciated the younger man's clear thinking.

The kitchen door swung open, and Detective Inspector Nigel Brewster stepped in, rain darkening his coat and hat. The weather had turned, as if reflecting their collective mood. Harry observed his nephew's expression carefully—Nigel had learned to mask his emotions as a policeman, but the tightness around his mouth spoke volumes about his feelings for Evie.

"I've made inquiries about train disruptions," Nigel announced, removing his hat. "No bombing raids near Greenwich last night, and the telephone exchanges are all operational."

"Which means she could have called," Dorothy said, setting the teapot down with an unintentional bang that made Katherine jump.

"We need to work methodically," Harry said, feeling his thoughts steadying with the familiar investigative rhythm. "First things first—where in Greenwich were Paul's parents supposed to be?"

The room fell silent.

"She never actually mentioned an address, did she?" Blake said slowly.

Dorothy shook her head. "Just Greenwich."

"Her bedroom," Alice suggested, rising from her chair. "She might have kept letters from them."

Harry nodded. "Good thinking, Alice. Dorothy, would you...?"

"I'll check," Dorothy said, already heading toward the curtained stairway.

While they waited, Blake spread out several scraps of paper on the table—remnants of the coded message they'd pieced together during the Judas Monk affair.

"These spell 'Clarion,'" he explained, his scholar's fingers arranging the fragments. "It might be referring to Clarion just up the road."

The village of Clarion was only about eight miles from Crofter's Green, Harry knew. But he didn't see what that had to do with Evie.

"You think it's connected to Evie's disappearance?" Nigel asked, scepticism clear in his voice.

"I don't believe in coincidences," Blake replied. "Not after everything we've seen."

Harry studied the scraps. "Clarion could be a code name for a covert operation, not just a place."

"Or it could mean both," Alice suggested quietly.

The sound of Dorothy's footsteps on the stairs silenced them. She returned clutching several envelopes, her expression a mixture of triumph and anxiety.

"Found them," she announced. "Three letters from Mrs Rebecca Harris, 42 Blackheath Road, Greenwich."

"That's our starting point," Harry said, rising to his feet with newfound determination. "Nigel, can you arrange transportation?"

Nigel nodded. "I'll use my Ford. Petrol rationing won't be an issue for official business."

"This isn't technically official police business," Harry reminded him gently.

Something hard flashed in Nigel's eyes. "It is if I say it is, Uncle."

Harry felt a surge of pride mixed with concern. His nephew was risking his position for Evie. He couldn't blame him; they all would risk everything for Evie.

"We can't all go," Harry said, looking around the table. "The shop needs to stay open—appearances must be maintained. If Siegfried has people watching, we can't alert them."

"I'll stay," Dorothy volunteered, though it clearly pained her. "Tom can come help this afternoon when he and Tommy are back from his rehabilitation walk."

"I should stay too," Katherine said softly. "I'd only slow you down." She squeezed Blake's hand. "Find her."

Blake nodded, his eyes bright with emotion.

"Alice, you have a knowledge of medicinal herbs that might prove useful if..." Harry couldn't finish the sentence.

"I'll prepare a kit," Alice said, understanding his unspoken concern.

"That leaves Harry, myself, and Blake," Nigel concluded, already calculating travel times in his head.

Harry looked at the clock on Evie's kitchen wall. "We leave in thirty minutes."

As the group dispersed to prepare, Harry remained at the table, studying the map Blake had brought. Greenwich to Clarion. What was the connection?

Alice paused beside him, her herb basket already in hand. "We'll find her, Harry," she said, her quiet voice holding more strength than her frame suggested.

"We have to," Harry replied, not looking up from the map. "Because if Siegfried has her..."

He didn't finish the thought. He didn't need to. They all understood.

Outside, the rain intensified, beating against the windows of the Cozy Cup like impatient fingers. Somewhere out there, Evie was waiting for them. Harry only hoped they wouldn't be too late.

As he folded the map, his eyes fell on a faded photograph pinned to Evie's kitchen board—all of them together after they'd completed the remodelling of the kitchen, Evie's smile bright and infectious in the centre of the group. The sight of it tightened Harry's chest with an emotion he couldn't quite name.

"Hold on, Evie," he whispered to the image. "We're coming."

Chapter 5
Evie

Evie woke with a lurch that sent blood pulsing out to the tips of her fingers. She hadn't intended to fall asleep at all, but exhaustion and the lingering remnants of the chloroform had won out, and she must have nodded off while lying down on the bare mattress. Now she sat bolt upright, realising in a flash that the sound that had awakened her was the rattle of the bolt outside her door.

Another cold lurch went through her at the thought that Paul might have returned.

But it wasn't Paul who came through the doorway after all, but Gerda, the woman whom Evie had first met in the guise of his mother.

In her role as Mrs John Harris, Gerda had seemed a completely average British housewife: a small, nondescript-looking woman of around sixty, with faded blue eyes and washed-out looking greyish blond hair set in stiff curls that sprang back in a kind of halo around her head. Evie could have seen her in a crowd of women waiting in a bus queue or doing the day's marketing and never looked at her twice.

Now her appearance hadn't changed in any outwardly identifiable way. She was dressed in a drab brown cotton housecoat with a pattern of small white flowers and carried a tray that held tea and toast. But when she looked at Evie, there was a kind of cold arrogance in her gaze that sent a fresh chill slithering across Evie's skin.

How to play this, though?

Ordinarily, Evie's first instinct was to refuse under any circumstances to show so much as a flicker of fear. But allowing Gerda to underestimate her could be an advantage— and just now, she was sadly in need of anything that could be counted in her favour.

So she allowed herself to gasp and shrink back at the sight of the older woman.

Gerda enjoyed that. Evie caught the small flicker of satisfaction in her pale eyes before she said, "You are awake."

Evie's skin crawled all over again at the thought that the older woman had looked in on her while she slept.

"What day is it?" she asked. She made her voice sound subdued, more than a little frightened.

Gerda seemed to hesitate, as though unwilling to dole out even that small crumb of information. But then she said, "It is the evening of August 1."

So Evie had been missing for about thirty-six hours. By now, possibly— surely?— Dorothy would have been alarmed to find that Evie wasn't there to open the Cozy Cup this morning.

Evie stopped herself before her thoughts could spiral in that direction again. She had to assume that she was entirely on her own, that any possibility of escape would depend on her own efforts and not those of anyone coming to save her.

Her tactics to make Gerda under-estimate her as a potential threat hadn't been entirely successful; the older woman remained standing in the doorway, well out of Evie's reach. "Do not imagine that you can try to overpower me," she said. Now that she wasn't bothering to play the part of an English housewife, Evie could hear the notes of a German accent in her words. "There is only one flight of stairs here, and Hans is standing at the top of them. He has a gun. He will not hesitate to shoot you, even if you manage to get past me."

Evie nodded. She didn't think getting past Gerda would in itself be an easy feat. The German woman might be slight, but she also had the tough, wiry kind of strength that would make her very difficult to overpower in any kind of close combat fight.

"Where is Paul?" Evie asked.

The contempt in Gerda's gaze intensified. "He has work to be done. A mission that is far more important than you."

A mission that presumably had to do with the castle, the factory, and the under-butler whom Paul had gone to take care of. But since Evie didn't want Gerda to suspect that she had overheard any of that, she kept silent.

The older woman set the tray down on the floor in the middle of the room. Evie eyed it, but made no move to pick up either the cracked teacup or the single slice of dry brown bread.

Gerda snorted. "You need not fear that the food and drink have been drugged. Herr Siegfried has given orders that so long as you behave yourself, you are not to be dosed with narcotics. He wishes your mind to be clear so that we may be sure that you are telling the truth when you are interrogated."

Evie had assumed there must be a reason that she was being held captive rather than being killed. But to hear it laid out so bluntly in Gerda's coldly accented tones made her stomach clench.

"Thank you." She couldn't keep the note of irony out of her tone.

Gerda's gaze narrowed, dislike showing plainly on her pinched, nondescript face.

"You need not think that he will show you any mercy, simply because you were once his wife," she said.

"Oh, I promise you, I don't think that."

Gerda seemed slightly taken aback by Evie's ready agreement, although the statement was nothing more than the simple truth. Evie

had already seen the cruel, soullessly empty look in Paul's blue eyes—
the same predatory look you might find in the eyes of a savage tiger or
a venomous snake.

He might have hidden it well during their marriage, but she didn't
for a single second think that he was a man capable of showing mercy
to anyone.

"Good," Gerda said at last.

Evie hesitated. But she couldn't see anything to be lost by asking
the question she had in mind. If Gerda repeated this conversation
to Paul— which she certainly would— he would only think she was
committed to playing her part as she'd promised she'd play it. Anger
at Paul for his betrayal would be natural, under the circumstances.

So she said, in a hard voice, "Do you know why he married me in
the first place?"

Gerda's upper lip curled. "For information, of course. He wished
to know about the inner workings of your Resistance group. You
had inflicted significant damages on our side, and that he could not
tolerate."

"But why me?" Evie asked. "I wasn't one of the leaders or even a
particularly crucial member of the unit."

She had carried out missions, but had never been the one to plan
them or give out orders. That role had belonged to Jean-Paul and
Andre, a pair of tough, middle-aged men who had served with the
French army in the Great War.

Gerda snorted again. "For exactly that reason. He wished to find
someone who was not important— a nobody. The resistance leaders
would be on their guard, and besides, most of them were men. He
needed a woman who would be easy to manipulate."

Which Evie had certainly been. She locked away the humiliation of
that fact as something else that she could take out and feel later.

"And you think you have his full confidence?" she asked Gerda. "I doubt you even know the details of whatever operation he's currently planning."

Gerda gave her a contemptuous look. "Really, given how Herr Siegfried described you, I had expected better things. Do you really imagine that you can trick me into revealing his assignment with so clumsy a trap as that? Of course I do not know every detail. I know what I need to know— and that is far more than you do or ever will. Unless he allows you to live long enough that you will read of it in the newspapers."

Evie straightened, glaring at Gerda as though determined not to give way or admit defeat. "I have friends, you know. They'll be searching for me. They'll find me, eventually."

Gerda gave a brief, dismissive jerk of her bony shoulders. "They will not find you all the way out here. And if they do, we will see them coming a mile away and be ready."

With that, she turned and went out, shutting the door behind her with a bang.

Evie exhaled a long, slow breath. Gerda might not be entirely stupid, but she could clearly be manipulated. It was one of the oldest tricks in the game of spy craft: set up an easy verbal trap for your opponent to fall into, so that when they avoided it, they would be so full of over-confidence that they stepped into your next more subtle trap without realising.

Gerda might not have revealed much, but she had in fact given Evie three small scraps of information:

1. Paul wasn't planning to keep her alive indefinitely. That wasn't good news, but since Evie had already assumed as much, she could simply use the fact as further motivation to escape from here.

2. Whatever Paul was planning, it was big enough to make national headlines. The way Gerda had said, *You will read of it in the newspapers* was enough to convince Evie that his assignment was no mere bombing of a bridge or even the sabotage of a local harbour's defences. If Paul's mission succeeded, she could be reasonably sure that it would strike Britain a crippling blow.

And 3. Wherever she was, it was somewhere entirely isolated. Gerda had said that anyone looking for Evie wouldn't find her all the way out here. Also not good news, but it was as well to know as much as she could about her situation before she tried to formulate any escape plans.

Evie leaned her head back against the wall behind her bed and stared at the solid, bolted door.

On Paul's side, he had the entire force of the Nazi war machine behind him and presumably almost unlimited resources to fund whatever he was plotting. While she had only her own ingenuity and whatever small bits of information she could pry out of Gerda.

Oh, and a pencil stub. Evie felt the small round, hard object she'd pushed into the bottom of her shoe. It might be pathetically small as advantages went, but it was still better than none at all.

Chapter 6
Harry

The semi-detached Edwardian brick house at 42 Blackheath Road looked exactly like its neighbours—dignified, respectable, and utterly unremarkable. Harry noted the wrought-iron railings, the large sash windows, and the protective sandbags piled against the doorway. A perfect camouflage for whatever might be happening inside.

"No answer," Nigel said after knocking for the third time, his knuckles white against the dark wood of the door. The grim set of his jawline had only grown more pronounced during their journey to Greenwich.

Harry placed a steadying hand on his nephew's shoulder. "Perhaps they've gone out."

"Or perhaps they never existed," Blake suggested quietly from behind them. "What if these 'parents' were just a fabrication to lure Evie here?"

Nigel's face hardened. Without another word, he stepped back, raised his foot, and drove his heel against the lock with surprising force. The door shuddered but held.

"Nigel!" Harry hissed, glancing anxiously at the neighbouring houses. "This is hardly procedure—"

But Nigel wasn't listening. He kicked again, and this time the lock splintered with a crack that seemed to echo down the quiet street. The door swung inward.

"Police business," Nigel muttered, more to himself than to Harry or Blake.

Harry sighed. His nephew's feelings for Evie were clouding his judgement—but Harry couldn't bring himself to object further. Not when Evie's life might hang in the balance.

The three men slipped inside, closing the broken door behind them as best they could.

The sitting room they entered was cluttered with furniture and knick-knacks—china dogs arranged in a neat row along a bookshelf, commemorative plates above the fireplace, small tables with doilies and vases. Everything meticulously arranged, yet somehow feeling staged rather than lived-in.

"It doesn't feel right," Blake whispered, scanning the room. "Too perfect. Like a museum."

Harry nodded, the hairs on the back of his neck standing up. In his years at Scotland Yard, he'd developed an instinct for places that had been deliberately set up to create an impression. This room felt exactly like that—a carefully constructed fiction.

"Check for signs of struggle," Harry instructed, trying to maintain some semblance of professional procedure. "But touch nothing unless necessary."

Nigel moved through the room with controlled urgency, his training temporarily overriding his emotion. Blake headed toward a small writing desk in the corner, while Harry examined the mantelpiece.

A silver-framed photograph caught his eye—a boy of about eleven in a school uniform. Handsome, light-haired, a confident tilt of the head, a carefree, nonchalant grin.

THE MURDERS AT CLARION CASTLE 29

And a nameplate, attached to the base of the frame.

"Paul Harris," Harry murmured, lifting the frame carefully.

Blake looked up. "Her husband?"

Harry nodded, a chill running through him. "Why would his supposed parents have only one photograph of their son? And why this one, from his childhood?"

"Uncle Harry," Nigel called from the doorway leading to what appeared to be a dining room. His voice had an uncharacteristic tremor. "You need to see this."

Harry pocketed the photograph frame—evidence, he told himself—and followed Nigel into the adjoining room.

The dining table was set for three, teacups still half-filled, a plate of cucumber sandwiches untouched. The scene looked eerily normal, as though the occupants had simply stepped away momentarily.

"There," Nigel said quietly, pointing to a small brown bottle that had rolled beneath the sideboard, and lay almost hidden by its shadow. He crouched down and carefully extracted it without touching the glass directly.

The label had been removed, but when Nigel cautiously uncorked it and wafted his hand above the opening, his face hardened. "Chloroform," he said, his voice tight with anger.

Harry took the bottle, holding it by its edges, and confirmed with a careful sniff. "They drugged her here," he said grimly. "Must have knocked the bottle over in their haste and didn't notice it roll away."

A few feet away, partially visible behind the leg of a chair, lay a plain white handkerchief. Blake spotted it and pointed silently. The cloth was crumpled, as though it had been used and discarded in a hurry.

"They would have pressed this over her face," Harry said, the professional detachment in his voice belied by the tremor in his hands as he carefully lifted the handkerchief with his pen. The sweet chemical smell still clung to the fabric.

The room seemed to drop several degrees in temperature. Blake, who had followed them in, let out a slow, controlled breath.

"So they drugged her," Blake said, the schoolteacher's analytical mind working through the scenario. "Invited her for tea, then rendered her unconscious."

"But who are 'they'?" Harry wondered aloud, surveying the room. "And where are they now? Where have they taken her?"

Nigel stood abruptly. "I'm going to check upstairs," he announced, already striding toward the hallway.

"Be careful," Harry called after him, unnecessarily. Despite his emotional state, Nigel was still a trained detective.

Harry continued his examination of the dining room, noting the fine layer of dust on the sideboard, the slightly yellowed lace curtains, the general air of a place not truly lived in. Blake was right—this wasn't a home. It was a stage set.

"The bedrooms are empty," Nigel reported, returning down the stairs. "Beds made up but no clothing in the wardrobes. No toiletries in the bathroom. Nobody lives here."

"A trap," Harry said, the evidence now unmistakable. "Set specifically for Evie."

"Siegfried," Blake murmured, the name falling into the quiet room like a stone into still water.

Nigel's face had gone deathly pale beneath his controlled exterior. "We need to contact Dorothy," he said. "See if there's been any word."

They found a telephone in the hall—another prop in this elaborate deception—and were surprised to discover it had a working dial tone. Nigel dialled quickly, the tendons in his hand standing out as he gripped the receiver.

Harry watched his nephew's face as he spoke briefly with Dorothy, asking for updates. Then Nigel's expression changed, his brows drawing together.

"When?" he demanded. "What exactly did he say?"

Harry and Blake exchanged glances.

"I understand," Nigel said finally. "Yes. We'll come straight away." He hung up the receiver with a deliberate gentleness that spoke of barely controlled emotion.

"What is it?" Harry asked, dreading the answer.

"There's been a murder," Nigel said, his voice eerily level.

Blake's eyes widened. "Who? Where?"

"My superintendent has been trying to reach me all morning," Nigel continued. "He's furious. Says I need to get there immediately." His brow furrowed. "To Clarion Castle."

Harry and Blake exchanged glances. That same word—"Clarion"—had appeared in the code fragments left behind by the German spy.

"It could be a coincidence," Harry said carefully, though his expression suggested he didn't believe it. "But you've got to go anyway, lad. You've got your orders."

Nigel nodded slowly. "Still, if Siegfried's spy ring and this Clarion murder are connected, some answers might be there." He hesitated. "And we have to believe the spy ring is connected with Evie's disappearance."

"So we're still doing our duty," Harry finished for him.

"I don't like leaving Greenwich without more answers," Blake said, glancing around the staged home once more.

"We don't have a choice," Nigel replied, already moving toward the door. "But we'll be back if we need to be. Right now, Clarion is our only lead."

As they stepped out of the house, the afternoon sun seemed suddenly mocking in its brightness. Harry patted his pocket, feeling the hard edges of the photograph frame.

"Hold on, Evie," he murmured, echoing his words from earlier that morning. "Just hold on."

The three men hurried back to Nigel's Ford, their faces grim with purpose. Behind them, the broken door of 42 Blackheath Road swung slightly in the summer breeze, the perfect façade now irrevocably shattered—much like their hopes for a simple resolution.

Chapter 7
Alice

Alice Greenleaf had always prided herself on her ability to keep calm and carry on. As the village herbalist, she'd learned that patience was as essential to her craft as any plant or potion. Waiting for herbs to grow, for tinctures to steep, for remedies to take effect—these things required an emotional detachment that most people never mastered.

But today, Alice couldn't keep still.

Her hands moved restlessly, arranging and rearranging the medicinal supplies she'd gathered on the kitchen table of the Cozy Cup. Yarrow for wounds, comfrey for bruises, valerian for sleep—if Evie was injured, Alice intended to be prepared. She refused to consider the possibility that her friend might be beyond the help of her herbs.

And Alice had hope. Harry and Blake were here, after Nigel had driven back from Greenwich and dropped them off. They would all think of a plan. Somehow.

"Nigel's just telephoned from the Ashford HQ. He's had his interview with his chief," Dorothy announced, entering the kitchen with Tom at her side. Tom's limp on his prosthetic leg was more evident today; the long rehabilitation walk must have taxed him. Behind them, Tommy clutched a paper aeroplane, his usual boundless energy subdued by the sombre atmosphere.

"And?" Harry asked, looking up from the map of Clarion he'd spread across Evie's oak table.

"He's proceeding directly to Clarion Castle," Dorothy reported. "His superintendent was quite determined that Nigel must lead the investigation. Apparently, it's a rather... significant ... murder."

"Who's the owner?" Harry asked.

"You'd know him if you'd lived here as long as we have," Alice said. "He's a millionaire who made his fortune in steel. His castle is really a mansion, chock-full of servants. Now and again you'll see one of his green Lagonda motor cars speeding around."

"He has four," Dorothy said. "His name is Walker."

"Did Nigel say who the victim was?" Blake asked, his arm protectively curved around Katherine's shoulders.

"Someone on the staff," Dorothy replied. "Nigel couldn't say more over the telephone."

Alice watched the shifting expressions around the table. She had always been observant—it came with being quiet—and now she read the fear and determination in every face. These people had become her family, and one of them was missing.

"We need to be methodical about this," Harry stated firmly, tapping his finger on the map. "Rushing in without a plan could cause more delay."

"And waste precious time that Evie might not have," Alice said softly, surprising herself with the edge in her voice.

All eyes turned to her. Alice rarely asserted herself in their discussions, preferring to offer quiet insights rather than forceful opinions. But Evie and Alice had been through a lot together during the past months, and had grown close. Despite Evie's insistence on striking out on her own and keeping her true feelings hidden.

"I'm sorry," she added quickly. "I didn't mean to snap."

"No, you're right," Harry conceded, his lined face softening. "Time is of the essence. But that's precisely why we can't afford missteps."

Tom lowered himself carefully into a chair, wincing slightly as he stretched his bad leg. "Should we involve the authorities? Beyond Nigel, I mean."

A heavy silence fell over the kitchen.

"I don't think we can," Blake said at last. "If Siegfried is behind this, he likely has informants within official channels. We've seen it before."

Katherine nodded, her pale face grave. Alice wondered whether this discussion had awakened more of her fragmented memories.

"Besides," Dorothy added, glancing at the curtained windows that separated them from the tea room, "we don't know who might be watching. If we suddenly close the shop or change our routines, we could alert Siegfried's people that we're onto them."

"So we maintain appearances," Harry concluded. "That's point one. Now, what's point two?"

Alice watched Tommy as he flew his paper aeroplane in small, careful circles. Children always seemed to sense when adults were troubled, she thought. Even play became cautious.

"We could split up," Tom suggested. "Some of us stay here to keep the shop running naturally, others go to Clarion."

"And do what, exactly?" Dorothy challenged, her maternal practicality asserting itself. "We can't just wander around the village asking if anyone's seen a kidnapped woman."

"Research first," Blake insisted, the schoolteacher evident in his tone. "We need to understand if there's a connection between Clarion and Siegfried before we act."

Alice's mind drifted to the last time Evie had gone out on her own—during the Ashford Auto Parts affair. Evie had managed to infiltrate the factory by posing as a new factory worker, gathering crucial intelligence.

"We could use a cover," Alice said, the idea crystallising as she spoke. "Like Evie did at Ashford. Get inside the castle somehow."

"As what?" Tom asked.

"Castle staff?" Alice suggested. "With one of them dead and Nigel questioning the others, they might need extra hands."

Harry's eyes brightened with approval. "We can ask Nigel to arrange it. If the castle owner will cooperate."

"Or I could pose as a journalist," Blake offered. "Covering the murder for a London paper."

Katherine squeezed his hand. "That would be dangerous."

"All of it is dangerous," Blake replied gently. "But Evie would do the same for any of us."

Alice knew he was right. When Blake and Tom had been kidnapped, Evie had risked everything to rescue them. They owed her no less.

"I think Harry should join Nigel at the castle first," Alice said, surprising herself again with her decisiveness. "See what he can learn officially, then telephone back with what we need to know."

"And I can start gathering information about the castle itself," Blake added. "Ownership, layout, staff, history—anything that might help us understand whether Siegfried might be involved."

Dorothy looked troubled. "I don't like the idea of any of us walking into a trap."

"I don't think we have much choice," Harry said grimly. "But Dorothy's right—we need to be careful. I'll go to Clarion immediately, assess the situation with Nigel, and then we'll formulate a plan."

"Meanwhile," Alice continued, "we maintain normal operations here. Katherine and I can help Dorothy to keep the shop running, and—"

She stopped as Tommy's paper aeroplane sailed across the table and landed directly on the spot marked "Clarion Castle" on Harry's map. The coincidence sent a chill through her.

"What is it, Tommy?" Dorothy asked her son.

The boy looked up solemnly. "Aunt Evie told me that paper aeroplanes always fly home if you make them right."

A lump formed in Alice's throat. To Tommy, this was perhaps a simple matter of rescue—go where Evie was, bring her home. But Alice had seen enough of war and espionage to know the reality would be far messier and more dangerous.

"We'll bring her home," Alice promised, meeting the child's eyes. "Just like your aeroplane found its way back."

Harry folded the map decisively. "I'll telephone the moment I know anything."

As Harry telephoned for a cab, Alice retreated to her small collection of the herbs she'd prepared for the contingencies she didn't want to imagine.

"Evie's strong, Alice," Dorothy said softly, appearing at her elbow.

Alice nodded, blinking back unexpected tears. "I know. But everyone has a breaking point."

"Then we'll just have to find her before she reaches hers," Dorothy replied with quiet determination.

Through the window, Alice could see the rain had stopped, but dark clouds still loomed on the horizon. A perfect metaphor, she thought, for what they now faced—a brief respite before the storm truly broke.

She watched Harry's retreating figure as he headed for his waiting cab. She found his careful steps somehow reassuring. despite the enormity of the task ahead.

"Be careful," she whispered, though he couldn't possibly hear her.

Behind her, the others had begun to move with renewed purpose. Blake was heading for the Crofter's Green library to learn more about the castle; Tom was taking Tommy home to Bramblewood Cottage. Dorothy and Katherine were arranging the tea room for the next wave of customers.

The Homefront Sleuths had faced danger before, Alice told herself.

She took a deep breath and returned to her herbs. If—when—they found Evie, she would be ready. Until then, all she could do was prepare and hope that somehow, despite the odds, their small band of amateurs could once again outwit one of Germany's most dangerous operatives.

And pray that Evie was indeed as strong as Dorothy believed.

Chapter 8
Harry

Harry Jenkins paid the cabbie and stood for a moment, taking in the sight before him. Clarion Castle loomed impressively at the top of a gently terraced hill, its brick and stone façade catching the afternoon sun with a warm, honeyed glow. Though the clouds threatened rain again, here on the estate grounds the air felt different somehow—cleaner, more rarified, as if the troubles of war could not quite penetrate this sanctuary of wealth and privilege.

The cab pulled away down the winding gravel drive, and Harry straightened his tie. The castle staff should be waiting for him. After he'd called for the cab at Evie's, he'd telephoned the Crofter's Green station house—the duty sergeant should have called the castle to give notice that Harry was coming.

He was suddenly conscious of his modest attire. He had dressed that morning expecting a quick meeting with Dorothy at the Cozy Cup, not a visit to one of Kent's grand estates. His practical brown tweed jacket and sensible shoes seemed shabby against the backdrop of such opulence.

He dismissed the thought. Evie was missing, possibly in grave danger, and a murder had been committed. It was time to get moving.

As Harry made his way up the drive, he couldn't help but notice the meticulously kept grounds. The gardens spread out on either side in geometric precision—clipped hedges, carefully tended flower beds, and immaculate lawns rolling down to what appeared to be a small ornamental lake in the distance. How the estate managed such perfection with the wartime shortage of gardeners was a mystery.

The castle itself wasn't at all what he'd expected. No medieval towers or crumbling battlements here. This was a grand manor house built of brick and stone, with symmetrical wings, tall mullioned windows, and ornate gables reaching up against the skyline. It spoke of wealth carefully cultivated over generations, of power comfortably worn. Up close, it was evident that the place was well-maintained, and had been for centuries.

Despite himself, Harry felt a stirring of patriotic pride. This was a piece of England worth protecting—this quiet grandeur, this testament to what his nation could create and preserve. Even as the thought crossed his mind, he chided himself for sentimentality. Beauty was no guarantee of virtue, as his years at Scotland Yard had taught him all too well.

At the impressive doorway, Harry pulled the bell chain and heard the distant chime echo within.

Sure enough, moments later, the heavy oak door swung open to reveal a pale-faced man in impeccable butler's livery. The butler was perhaps forty-five, Harry judged—alert, with a well-groomed pencil moustache, and trying very hard to appear composed despite the slight nervous flutter of his hands.

"Inspector Jenkins?" the man inquired, his accent carefully cultivated to match the surroundings.

"*Retired* inspector," Harry corrected automatically. "I'm here to—"
"Uncle Harry!"

Relief washed over Harry as Nigel appeared behind the butler, his police notebook clutched in one hand. His nephew looked frustrated but visibly brightened at Harry's arrival.

"Thank goodness," Nigel said, dismissing the butler with a nod. "Come in. Things are rather... complicated."

The entrance hall was magnificent—a soaring space stretching out before him in all directions, with a grand staircase sweeping upward, wood panelling gleaming with the patina of centuries, and a marble floor that reflected the light from enormous diamond-glazed windows. Beautiful landscape paintings lined the walls, as if to welcome visitors to a world of natural loveliness both inside and out.

What caught Harry's eye, however, was the incongruous splash of bright red in one corner of the hall—a telephone box, exactly like those found on London streets, complete with crown and frosted glass panels. It stood like a whimsical sculpture amid the grandeur, as out of place as a circus clown at a funeral.

"Odd touch, that," Harry murmured, nodding toward the telephone box.

"Mr Walker's idea of humour, apparently," Nigel replied in a low voice. "He has them installed in all his properties. Claims it reminds him of his humble beginnings, though between you and me, there was nothing humble about Bradford Walker's beginnings."

Nigel drew Harry aside, his voice dropping further. "He's in the east room," Nigel said, tension evident in his clipped tones. "He's pleasant enough, but not being terribly helpful. The body's been moved already—on his orders, before I arrived."

"Already?" Harry's eyebrows rose. "That's highly irregular."

"Everything about this case is irregular," Nigel replied grimly. "Come along. We shouldn't keep him waiting."

The east room proved to be another exercise in tasteful opulence—leather-bound books lining the walls, deep armchairs arranged around a marble fireplace, and tall windows offering views out to the surrounding countryside and the well-manicured slope which Harry had recently climbed. A drinks trolley gleamed with crystal decanters in one corner.

Bradford Walker rose from one of the armchairs as Harry and Nigel entered. He was a substantial man in his fifties, with the beginnings of a paunch straining against his expensive waistcoat and a florid complexion that spoke of good living. His suit was impeccably tailored, his shoes handmade, and his manner suggested the easy confidence of a man accustomed to getting his own way.

What struck Harry immediately, however, were Walker's eyes—unnaturally grey, almost colourless, like water over stones—and his left eyebrow, which arched permanently higher than its twin, giving him a perpetual look of imperious inquiry. The effect was oddly unsettling; even when Walker smiled and extended a large hand in greeting, that questioning eyebrow and those cold eyes seemed to be evaluating, calculating, measuring worth with merciless precision.

"Ah, another policeman," Walker boomed, extending a large hand. "Bradford Walker. Charmed to meet you, Inspector."

"Retired Inspector Harry Jenkins," Harry replied, taking the offered hand. Walker's grip was firm but not challenging—the handshake of a man who knew precisely how much pressure to apply in any given situation.

"As I've been telling Inspector Brewster," Walker continued, gesturing them to sit, "it's imperative that this matter be cleared up. And soon."

Harry settled into one of the armchairs, noting how the leather yielded perfectly to his weight. "How soon?" he asked mildly.

Walker's smile remained fixed, but something flickered behind his eyes. "I'm afraid I can't tell you."

"Why not?" Nigel pressed, leaning forward slightly.

"Government business," Walker replied, with the casual air of someone dropping a minor social bombshell. "Highest level. And there's something else."

Harry felt a familiar tightening in his stomach—the sensation that had guided him through countless investigations over the years. "Oh?"

Walker hesitated.

Nigel interjected, "Surely you can understand that we'll need full access if you want this cleared up."

Walker nodded sagely. "Yes, well, I'm afraid there will be things I can't tell you."

"What?" Nigel's professional composure slipped momentarily.

"Regrettable, I know, but—"

"Then I'd like to use that telephone you have in your entry hall," Harry interrupted, his voice calm but firm. "I will place a trunk call to London to a certain number, and you can trust me that you will soon have absolutely no restrictions for us."

He nodded to Nigel, whose eyes widened slightly in understanding.

Walker's affable expression faltered. "I beg your pardon?"

"I'll be calling the number of a gentleman named Mr Brown," Harry said, the name falling into the elegant room like a stone into still water. "After a previous case, I have it emblazoned in my mind. I believe he'll remember my name as well. We met less than a month ago in London at one of his offices. The outcome was satisfactory, memorable to me and, no doubt, memorable to him as well."

The steel magnate's face underwent a remarkable transformation. The overly-jovial host vanished, replaced by a calculating businessman assessing unexpected variables.

"Mr Brown," Walker repeated carefully. "I see. Perhaps we should discuss this more... openly. Jenkins, was it? Former Scotland Yard?"

"Twenty-six years," Harry confirmed. "And my nephew here is one of the finest detectives in Kent."

Walker studied them both for a long moment, then rose and crossed to the drinks trolley. "Whisky?"

"No, thank you," Harry and Nigel replied in unison.

"And I take it you know of Mr Brown," Harry said. "Just so you know, I'm perfectly willing to call him with you at my side. You can listen in to the conversation after I've introduced you."

"Won't be necessary," Walker said. He poured himself a generous measure and took a fortifying sip before turning back to them. "I do know the man himself. Had to deal with him before."

"Indeed?"

"So, first let's get to the murder business. The dead man was my under-butler, Vernon. Found early this morning in the wine cellar. Throat cut."

"And the body?" Nigel prompted.

"Removed to the estate's icehouse," Walker said defensively. "I have guests arriving two days from now. Important guests."

"I telephoned Canterbury," Nigel told Harry. "Two men from the police mortuary are guarding the ice house now."

Harry nodded. Then he turned to Walker. "How important are these guests?"

Walker glanced at the closed door, then lowered his voice. "Cabinet level. That's why this has to be resolved quickly and... discreetly."

Harry exchanged glances with Nigel. Cabinet ministers coming to Clarion Castle, a murdered servant, and somewhere in the background, possibly, the shadow of Siegfried and the missing Evie. The pieces were beginning to form a pattern, though it wasn't one Harry could feel good about.

"Mr Walker," Harry said carefully, "we'll need to see where the body was found, speak to your staff, and examine the victim."

"You have my permission."

"And as to that 'something else' you mentioned?"

Walker hesitated, weighing his options. Finally, he nodded. "Very well. Let me make the arrangements to address that other matter. Meanwhile, my under-butler will take you to visit the wine cellar. His name is Graves—you met him at the entry hall just now. While you're doing that, I'll have the staff assemble in our Minstrel's Hall—just across from where we are now. You can come back upstairs, look them over as a group, and then bring them back here one by one to question them individually. But I expect discretion, gentlemen. The staff all have their duties to perform, and this upcoming meeting simply cannot be disrupted."

As Walker rang for the under-butler to show them to the wine cellar, Harry caught Nigel's eye. The silent communication between them was clear: Walker was plainly going to 'make arrangements' —which likely meant telephoning Mr Brown— before divulging anything of the 'other matter' he had referenced.

To be expected, Harry supposed. Judging from the meticulous landscaping and the exquisite upkeep of the estate, Walker was no doubt a very particular and careful man.

But no doubt Mr Brown would reassure Walker, and full cooperation, whatever that was, would be forthcoming.

The question was whether they could solve this murder within the one day remaining before the arrival of the cabinet minister, and whether that would be soon enough to help Evie.

One thing was certain, though. Reinforcements would be required. As they headed for the wine cellar, Harry was already planning his call to the Cozy Cup, and the assignments he would have for the Sleuths.

Chapter 9
Harry

The staircase to the wine cellar descended in a tight spiral, the worn stone steps testifying to generations of servants making this same journey. A series of electric bulbs in iron cages cast pools of yellowish light at regular intervals, creating more shadows than illumination. Harry followed Graves down, with Nigel trailing behind them.

Simon Graves wore his dark hair slicked back with so much brilliantine that it seemed moulded to his skull. Despite his current agitation, his movements retained something studied about them—a self-consciousness, as if he were perpetually on stage.

"Just through here, gentlemen," Graves said, his voice carefully modulated. "The wine cellar proper."

They arrived at a heavy oak door banded with iron, its ancient hinges gleaming with regular oiling. Outside the door, a row of wooden crates lined the corridor, all bearing the stamp of various vineyards and shipping companies. A single wall sconce cast long, distorted shadows across the bottles visible through the slats.

Graves turned towards them as he reached for his key. His pencil-thin moustache appeared almost painted on, each hair precisely in place. Harry noticed a small scar bisecting his right eyebrow, giving that side of his face a permanently puzzled expression.

But there was fear now evident in his eyes.

He patted his pockets with increasing urgency. "I... that's odd. I seem to have misplaced my key." His scarred eyebrow twitched nervously. "Perhaps Mr Glenwood should assist us. He is the head butler, you know, and he was the one who discovered... who found Mr Vernon."

Nigel made a note in his book. "And when was that exactly, Mr Graves?"

"Early this morning. Before breakfast." Graves swallowed visibly. "If you'll excuse me, I'll fetch Mr Glenwood."

As Graves hurried back up the stairs, Harry knelt to examine one of the crates. "French. An old vintage," he murmured. "Walker likes his wine, it seems."

Glenwood's arrival was preceded by the measured sound of his footsteps. The head butler appeared, and Harry was immediately struck by his commanding presence. Tall and imposing at around sixty, Glenwood carried himself with a military bearing that spoke of discipline maintained over decades. His silver-white hair was immaculately groomed, not a strand out of place, and his face might have been carved from marble—all planes and angles, with deep-set eyes that seemed to miss nothing. When he spoke, his voice was pitched low but carried effortlessly through the confined space of the corridor.

"Inspector Jenkins. Inspector Brewster." Glenwood acknowledged them with a slight bow that betrayed no stiffness despite his age. "I understand you wish to examine the scene of the unfortunate incident."

"Mr Graves says you discovered the body," Harry prompted.

"Indeed." Glenwood's deep-set eyes betrayed no emotion. "I came down shortly after six this morning to select wines for the forthcoming dinner. The door was locked, which was unusual. I used my master key and found Vernon..." He paused almost imperceptibly. "I found

Vernon on the floor. Quite dead. Throat cut. There was a significant amount of blood."

"And then?" Nigel asked.

"I immediately informed Mr Walker. He decided, given the imminent wine delivery—he gestured to the assembled crates— and the... sensitivity of the forthcoming visit, that the body should be moved to the ice house."

"Who moved it?" Harry asked.

"Daniel Cooper and Jarrett Fenton, from the stables. Mr Walker felt staff from the outdoors would be less likely to gossip with the house staff." Glenwood's expression remained impassive, but Harry detected a slight disapproval in his tone.

"And these crates?" Harry gestured to the wooden boxes lining the corridor.

"Mr Walker ordered that the wine be delivered but not stored. He was concerned about preserving the scene for your examination." Glenwood withdrew a large brass key from his pocket. "Shall we?"

The heavy door swung open with a groan, revealing a cool, dimly lit space. A single overhead bulb cast a weak, spectral glow over the central area, leaving the corners shrouded in darkness. Their shadows seemed larger than life, shifting as they entered and flitting over stone walls lined with rack upon rack of bottles that gleamed dully in the inadequate light. The air held the musty scent of earth and cork, overlaid now with the metallic scent of blood.

Harry's eyes were drawn immediately to a dark stain on the flagstone floor. The blood had mostly dried to a rusty brown, but its pattern was unusual—a large pool with strange smears and disruptions, as if the body had been moved or had moved itself while it was still living.

Nigel squatted beside the stain, careful not to touch it. "Odd pattern," he murmured. "We'll need photographs."

"Indeed," Harry agreed, studying the disturbed edges of the bloodstain. His eyes tracked across the floor, noting scuff marks and what appeared to be the imprint of a hand—a bloody handprint that had been partially wiped away.

Then something caught his eye—a glint of metal beside the blood pool. Harry moved closer, careful not to disturb any evidence.

"What's this?" he asked, pointing to a thin folding knife resting at the edge of the dried blood.

Glenwood stepped forward cautiously. "That's one of our sommelier's knives, sir. French manufacture. It was left in place, untouched, when the men moved the body."

Harry bent lower to examine it without touching. The knife resembled a large folding switchblade of the type London gangsters favoured, only this one had a corkscrew built into the polished wooden handle. The blade was crusted with dried blood.

"May I?" Harry asked, pulling a handkerchief from his pocket. At Glenwood's nod, he carefully picked up the knife, wrapping it in the cloth.

"Where would this normally be kept?" Nigel asked, making another note in his book.

"In the butler's pantry, sir," Glenwood replied. "It's used for uncorking wines. The blade assists in removing the wax covering, and the corkscrew—"

"I understand that part," Harry cut him off. "Who has access to the butler's pantry?"

"Everyone on the staff, sir." Glenwood's face remained impassive. "Including Vernon. He may very well have had the knife with him when he went in to select a wine—or for whatever reason brought him in here, sir."

"Or someone else did," Harry murmured, re-wrapping the knife and handing it to Nigel, who placed it in an evidence bag.

Glenwood stood in the doorway, his imposing frame silhouetted against the light from the corridor. "Vernon was well-liked," he said. "A conscientious worker. Excellent knowledge of wines."

"Was he now?" Harry murmured, eyes still scanning the scene. "Any idea who might have wanted him dead, Mr Glenwood?"

"None whatsoever. It's unfathomable." The butler's voice betrayed no emotion, but Harry noticed his thumb moving unconsciously across his ring finger.

"We'll need to talk to everyone on staff," Nigel said, making notes. "And examine the body as soon as possible."

"Of course." Glenwood stood a little straighter. "If you're finished here for the moment, I can escort you to the ice house personally. I have the key, and it would be my duty to ensure you have proper access to everything you need for your investigation."

Harry took one last look at the disturbed bloodstain. Experience told him that something wasn't right about the scene—the blood pattern suggested movement after death, not the clean pool you'd expect from a straightforward throat-cutting.

"Let's lock up for now," he said to Nigel. "We'll have your photographer document everything properly."

As Glenwood secured the door, Harry noticed Simon Graves hovering at the top of the stairs, his face a study in barely contained panic. The under-butler's left hand trembled slightly as he brushed invisible lint from his impeccable jacket.

"Mr Graves seems rather affected by his colleague's death," Harry observed quietly to Glenwood as they climbed the stairs.

"Mr Graves is... sensitive," Glenwood replied, his voice neutral. "And Mr Vernon was his immediate superior. There may have been some professional tension."

Harry filed this information away as they emerged into the grand entrance hall. A few staff members were hovering around the entrance to the Minstrel's Hall. Soon more of the staff would be assembled, and eventually every person at Clarion Castle would be questioned, their stories examined for inconsistencies, their secrets prodded.

Eventually.

For now, he and Nigel would visit the ice house. Then Harry would telephone the Tea Shop and call in the reinforcements.

Somewhere in this grand house was a thread that would lead not only to Vernon's killer but possibly to Evie. There had to be.

Chapter 10
Katherine

"Are you all right?" Ellen Thorpe asked.

Katherine startled and almost dropped the pint glass she was drying with a dish rag. She and Ellen were doing the washing up in the kitchen of the King's Arms, the village pub in Crofter's Green.

The kitchen was tucked behind the main bar and not much larger than a scullery. A big coal stove blackened from years of use dominated one wall, and a single window let in just enough daylight to catch the glint of well-worn cutlery and stacks of chipped plates that lined the bare wooden shelves nailed onto the other walls for storage.

"Yes, fine," Katherine said. "Why?"

Ellen smiled a little. She was a plump, pretty young woman with blond hair and wide blue eyes that matched the flowers on the print cotton dress she was wearing.

"Because you've been wiping that same glass for the past five minutes. I think it's dry by now."

Katherine set the glass down on the draining board by the sink and pushed a stray lock of hair out of her eyes. The air in the kitchen was humid and thick with the scent of boiling vegetables, fried onions, and a hint of stewed meat—but only a hint, because of wartime rationing. The meals served here consisted mostly of vegetables like potatoes, carrots, and turnips, along with bread and dripping. Meat, when they could get any, was eked out in pies or stews and often padded with lentils or breadcrumbs to make it stretch into as many servings as could possibly be managed.

"I'm sorry," she told Ellen. "I'm probably not being much help today."

When Katherine had decided to stay in Crofter's Green a few weeks ago, Ellen was the one who had offered her a place to stay, in the flat above the King's Arms. And she'd also spoken to Mr Piggot, the manager, and persuaded him to give Katherine the job of helping out in the kitchen and occasionally serving customers out in the tap room.

"Don't apologise; I didn't mean to make you feel guilty!" Ellen told her. "I was just wondering if something was troubling you, that's all."

Katherine sighed. She'd known Ellen ever since they were girls together. Not that she remembered, except for an occasional flash here and there that was gone almost as soon as she tried to grasp hold of it.

Having what the doctors called retrograde amnesia was a strange and often maddening experience. Katherine had no idea whether in her past life— the life she couldn't remember— she would have qualified as a patient person. She knew that she'd worked as a librarian, even if she couldn't remember that, either, so it seemed somewhat likely. Now, though, she often found herself wishing that she could grab hold of her own brain and shake it and demand that it work properly.

Not that shaking her brain would help. A blow to the head during a London air raid was what had got her into this state in the first place, a little under a year ago— a state in which as far as her recollections were concerned, she might as well have been born again as a newborn baby. Everything before that date was a great, gaping blank, like a swath of impenetrable darkness— and when she did get a brief inkling of memory, the flash of light was so dim that even the Air Raid Wardens wouldn't count it as a threat to Blackout regulations.

But even if she couldn't call up any concrete memories of Ellen, Katherine still felt something of the same indefinable sense of familiarity with her that she did with Blake. Her conscious mind might not remember, but some other part of her, whether you wanted to call it her soul or her heart or her spirit, somehow did.

"I suppose I'm worried about Evie," she said. She'd already told Ellen that Evie had gone missing. "And Blake. He went to Greenwich with Harry and Nigel to see whether they could learn anything about where she might have been taken."

Ellen nodded, looking sober. "Of course you're worried," she said. "Anyone would be."

Ellen had lost her own sweetheart barely a month ago, now. She didn't talk about Donnie very much, but Katherine could see for herself the shadow of pain in Ellen's eyes and the way that even her smiles were a little sad.

Katherine looked around. She and Ellen were alone in the kitchen, and there was enough noise coming from the bar room that no one would overhear. But she still lowered her voice a little as she said, "They'll probably go to Clarion next. There's been a murder there."

"A murder?" Ellen sucked in a sharp breath, then frowned. "I wonder whether it has anything to do with the castle."

"There's a castle in Clarion?" Katherine asked.

"Yes, don't you—" Ellen stopped herself. "No, of course you don't remember. Sorry. Yes, Clarion Castle. It's not a real castle, not anymore. Not that I've ever been there." Ellen gave a wry laugh. "I'm nowhere near important enough to be invited to a grand estate. There was a story about it in the papers a few years back. There was a castle there from the days of the Conqueror, I think. But then a friend of King Henry the Eighth took it down to use the stones for building a new house somewhere else."

"Henry the Eighth? Really?" Katherine had read plenty of Shakespeare plays and history books during her time at St Thomas's hospital; there hadn't been very much else for her to do, when she wasn't volunteering in the wards.

"It's just a manor house, now," Ellen went on. "Built sometime in the 1500's, I think. But it's a grand place. The newspaper said they'd got a swimming pool inside the house! A swimming pool, can you imagine? Who would ever need a swimming pool indoors?"

"Probably the sort of person whose idea of roughing it is pouring their own champagne on the butler's day off," Katherine said.

Ellen laughed. Then she said, in a different tone, "I wanted to tell you." She drew in a breath. "I'm moving to Birmingham at the end of the month."

"Birmingham?"

Katherine tried to remember whether she knew— or had ever known— where that was. Another of the frustrations of having amnesia was how utterly sick she got of asking people to explain things that Dorothy's son Tommy would probably know quite well.

"Yes." Ellen dunked a soapy cup into the clean water to rinse it. "There's a Red Cross centre there where I can train for the VAD. After—" her voice caught a little. "After Donnie dying, I can't just stay here, working at the King's Arms day in and day out. I want to do something to help with the war effort. And I want... I just want to get right away. Away from here, where I'm always remembering."

Odd, Katherine thought, how she'd give almost anything to have her memories back, and so many other people she met thought that they wanted to forget. But she covered Ellen's hand with her own and gave her fingers a squeeze. "Of course. I understand. I'll miss you, but you'll be a wonderful VAD."

That was something Katherine actually didn't have to ask about, in addition to King Henry VIII.

Dozens of VAD— or Voluntary Aid Detachment— girls had worked at St Thomas's hospital, where Katherine had stayed before coming to Crofter's Green. The VAD was made up of volunteer civilian women who weren't fully trained nurses but supported military and civilian medical services, both on the front lines in Europe and here at home.

"Thank you." Ellen blinked and then smiled a little tearfully. "I'll miss you. But you'll write to me, won't you?"

"Of course I will! I'll give you all the local gossip."

"So you're really going to stay?" Ellen asked. She gave Katherine a curious glance. "You and Blake are going to be married, even if you don't remember him at all?"

"We haven't talked about an official date for a wedding. I think he's giving me time to get re-acquainted with him," Katherine said. "But . . .yes." Blake was the one solid anchor in her life, the one piece of the ongoing puzzle in her brain that entirely made sense. "I might not remember how I fell in love with him. But I know why I did. I knew that after talking to him for ten minutes."

Ellen's eyes misted over again.

"I'm sorry," Katherine said quickly. "I didn't mean to upset you."

"You didn't." Ellen shook her head. "I'm happy for you. Truly, I am. So are you going to go with him to Clarion, if he's helping to look into the murder there?"

"I—" Katherine stopped.

She hadn't thought about that. "I'd like to," she said slowly. She'd worry far less if she could actually be on the scene while Blake was taking part in the investigation. "But—"

"But what? Do you think Blake wouldn't let you come?" Ellen asked.

"Oh, no." Katherine didn't think it would ever occur to Blake to forbid her to do anything, or even try. He'd think the very idea that a man ought to have that kind of authority over his future wife completely illogical. "He'd never do that. I just don't know that I'd be able to help, and I wouldn't want to get in the way."

"You don't give yourself enough credit, Katherine," Ellen said. She set the dish she'd been drying down. "You're not so different now, you know. Even with amnesia, you're still the same person you always have been."

Blake had told her that, too, or something very like it. But Katherine still shook her head. "I want to believe that's true. But since I don't remember who I was before, how do I actually know?"

"Well, you were always kind before," Ellen said. "And generous. And funny, too. You're still all those things."

"Maybe— and thank you," Katherine said. "But that doesn't help much with solving a murder."

"You're clever, too; you always were. You knew all about books."

"Maybe, but—" Katherine stopped as a sudden idea struck her. "I don't suppose the newspaper article mentioned whether this Clarion Castle place has a library?"

"Oh, it does!" Ellen must have understood what was in Katherine's mind, because she brightened, sounding excited. "I remember reading that the steel magnate who owns the place has a collection of all sorts of rare books and manuscripts, some of them dating back to the days when the original castle was still standing."

Katherine nodded. Was this almost too easy— or just a kind of wink on the part of fate that her idea was meant to be? Either way, she said, "Then maybe I will be going to Clarion after all."

Chapter 11
Harry

The late afternoon sun slanted across the immaculate grounds as Harry, Nigel, and Glenwood made their way toward the rear of the castle. Harry checked his watch—nearly six o'clock. The day was slipping away, but with sunset not due until well after ten in the summer months, they still had plenty of daylight left.

"I must apologise if I should seem impatient," Glenwood said, his marble features showing the slightest hint of discomfort. "This unfortunate business and the impending interview with all the staff will completely disrupt Mrs Finch's preparations for Mr Walker's supper this evening, and it would be wonderful if we could resolve—"

"Murder tends to be inconvenient that way," Harry replied dryly.

As they approached, Harry noted two men in dark coats waiting beside a squat brick structure—the mortuary attendants from Canterbury that Nigel had summoned. They nodded respectfully as the party drew near.

Harry paused, taking in his surroundings. The castle grounds were enclosed by a perimeter wall, but its weathered grey stones stood far enough away that he could see beyond, to rolling hills and dense woodlands. An unpaved track wound its way through the countryside, disappearing into a copse of trees in the distance.

"What's that road there?" Harry asked, pointing.

"The Pilgrim's Way, sir," Glenwood replied. "It runs through the village of Clarion and continues northeast to Canterbury Cathedral and the shrine. Been there since medieval times, I believe."

Harry's gaze shifted to a looming grey stone structure within the perimeter wall—a stark contrast to the more elegant lines of the main house. Its weathered walls spoke of centuries gone by.

"And that?" Harry nodded toward the ancient structure.

"The original castle keep," Glenwood said. "Built some eight centuries ago."

"What's it used for now?"

"It's unused, sir," Glenwood replied, producing a large iron key and inserting it into the heavy oak door of the ice house. "Too damp and cold for comfort. Mr Walker had it structurally reinforced about five years ago, but otherwise the keep is padlocked and left to the tourists to admire from the outside."

The icehouse door swung open with a reluctant groan, releasing a wave of cold, stale air. Harry steeled himself as they stepped inside. The unpleasant odour of death mingled with the musty scent of the rarely used building.

"Frankly, we had to remove the ... remains from the wine cellar," Glenwood explained, reaching for a switch on the wall. "We thought of bringing in one of the electric freezers from the pantry, but Mrs Finch objected. With the impending dinner, she wanted no disturbance."

A single electric bulb flickered to life, casting a harsh yellow glow over the interior. The brick walls were thick, designed to keep in the cold when the building had been filled with winter ice in centuries past. In the centre of the floor lay a dark shape—Vernon's body, resting on a woollen blanket that had clearly been used as a makeshift stretcher.

Harry noted traces of sawdust on the floor and the distinctive footprints of two men—the stablemen who had carried in the body.

"Was anything removed from the body?" Harry asked, kneeling beside it.

"Nothing, sir," Glenwood replied, his face impassive. "I supervised the entire procedure."

Harry nodded and began his examination. Vernon's skin was ashen white, the pallor taking on a sickly yellow cast under the electric light. The wound on his throat was precise and deep—a single, decisive cut from left to right that had opened the carotid artery and windpipe in one efficient stroke. Harry noted the dark stains saturating the victim's shirt collar and upper chest. The pattern of the wound was entirely consistent with the sommelier's knife they had found beside the blood stains in the wine cellar.

The blanket, though, was relatively clean. Most of the blood would have pooled beneath the body prior to its removal.

Methodically, Harry checked the dead man's pockets. In one, he found a pair of white gloves, neatly folded. In another, a white linen handkerchief, equally pristine. The inside breast pocket yielded a small notebook, which Harry extracted carefully.

Flipping it open, he frowned. The pages were filled with what appeared to be some sort of code—columns of letters and numbers arranged in no immediately recognisable pattern.

"Did you supervise the movement of the body yourself, Mr Glenwood?" Harry asked, slipping the notebook into his own pocket.

"Yes, sir. I watched the two men pick it up, and bring it in, and set it down. Nothing was removed from the body in my presence."

"Did either man slip and fall?"

"No, sir. Perfectly straightforward process. The blanket was laid out alongside the body, the body was lifted onto the blanket, and both were carried upstairs and out to where you see it here."

"Did Vernon have his own room?"

"Of course, sir. All the senior staff have private quarters."

"Would he have kept it locked?"

Glenwood considered this. "I couldn't say, sir. As first under-butler, he would have had a key to his room, certainly."

"Has anyone been in Vernon's room since the death was discovered?"

"I couldn't say, sir."

Harry exchanged glances with Nigel, who had been quietly making notes. "Anything you want to do here?" he asked his nephew.

Nigel shook his head. "I've seen enough. The Canterbury men can take the body now."

Harry nodded to the mortuary attendants. "You can take him away, gentlemen." Then, turning back to Glenwood: "I'd like you to take us to Vernon's room immediately."

The head butler led them back into the main castle and up two flights of stairs to the servants' wing. The corridor was quiet, most of the staff presumably awaiting their interview in the Minstrel's Hall. Harry noted a passage leading to another wing, but it was closed off by a heavy oak door.

"What's down there?" Harry asked, nodding toward the sealed area.

"The military gentlemen occupy that area, sir," Glenwood replied stiffly. "I can't say more."

They arrived at Vernon's door, which Glenwood opened without need of a key. Inside, the room was neat and orderly—almost unnaturally so. The bed hadn't been slept in, its counterpane smooth and unwrinkled. A silver tray atop the dressing cabinet held a key and some loose change.

Harry glanced around the spartan quarters. A wardrobe stood against one wall, a small writing desk against another. The room spoke of a man who valued order and precision, but revealed little of his personal life.

Picking up the key from the silver tray, Harry motioned for the others to exit, then shut the door behind them and tested the key. It fit perfectly, locking with a satisfying click.

"The staff will await you in the Minstrel's Hall," Glenwood said, his tone suggesting they should proceed there directly.

Harry pocketed the key to Vernon's room. "First," he said, "I want to use that red telephone booth we saw in the entry hall."

Glenwood's marble features betrayed the slightest flicker of surprise, but he nodded. "Of course, sir. This way."

As they descended the stairs, Harry's mind was racing. A coded notebook, an unused castle keep within sight of the Pilgrim's Way, military personnel in a sealed-off wing, and a murdered butler who apparently kept meticulous records.

Where was the pattern?

Chapter 12
Evie

Evie lay flat on the floor beside the bed, listening to the sounds of clinking pots and pans downstairs in the kitchen. Gerda must be cooking supper for herself and Hans. Evie had already eaten the toast and drunk the tea on her own supper tray, having decided that she hadn't much choice but to take Gerda's word for it that the food wasn't drugged. She couldn't last without food and drink indefinitely, and she'd stand a much better chance of escaping if she wasn't weak or faint from hunger. Besides, the more naïve that Gerda and Hans thought her, the better.

The older woman seemed to have been telling the truth, though. So far, Evie hadn't felt any ill effects from the food.

Now she strained her ears, trying once again to translate the muffled German words she was overhearing as Gerda and Hans spoke together.

"— orders are orders," she heard Gerda say in what sounded like a snappish tone, as though she were quelling an argument.

"Perhaps. But it still seems like a lot of trouble to me." That was Hans, his voice grumbling.

"Far more trouble if we are discovered here. Herr Siegfried is wise to insist that we move our base of operations every three days."

"The woman will make it more complicated tomorrow." Hans still sounded irritable.

"Only if you let her," Gerda snapped. "Really, Hans, anyone would think you had never dealt with a prisoner before."

"I can do what must be done," Hans growled back.

Something clattered as though Gerda had just dumped a pot or a pan into the sink. "Then prove it by going upstairs and collecting her dishes so that I may do the washing up."

Hans didn't answer, although Evie caught the faint creak of protesting wood, as though he'd just heaved himself up from whatever chair he was sitting in. She sprang up, her mind racing with what she'd just overheard.

Siegfried— Paul— had instituted a policy of moving every three days. That was undoubtedly good spycraft; staying in one spot made you more likely to attract notice from inquisitive civilians. Even if this place was as isolated as Gerda had claimed, there was still always the chance that a stray passer-by might prove too curious for comfort. But it was bad news for her. Even if Harry or Nigel or anyone else from Crofter's Green managed to track her here, she would already be gone by the time they arrived. And she couldn't even think of a way to show that she'd been here, some clue she might leave behind if they came looking after Gerda and Hans had dragged her to wherever their next location happened to be—

Evie caught the sound of Hans' heavy footsteps mounting the stairs. Her heartbeat kicked into higher gear and her mind scrambled through a rapid assessment of her possible courses of action.

Pretend to be sleeping.

Try to get him to talk, as she had Gerda.

In the end, though, she caught up the thin metal tray on which Gerda had brought her food and stepped beside the doorway, so that she was behind it when the panel swung open. Hans entered, and Evie stepped smoothly behind him and brought the metal tray down with a ringing crash on the back of his head.

Hans let out a yell of mingled surprise and rage, but the metal was too thin to even stun him, much less knock him unconscious. He spun around, making a grab for Evie's wrist. She blocked him with the back of her arm, knocking his fist aside and at the same time stepping in close so that she could stamp hard on the bridge of his foot.

Hans let out another yell, hopped, and then made another grab, this time managing to close his hands around Evie's throat.

Hans wasn't a big man, but he was stronger than he looked, and right now his movements were fuelled by rage. Bright flecks of colour danced in front of Evie's vision as his grip tightened.

Then she heard Gerda cry out and the thump of her running footsteps coming up the stairs.

Evie shut her eyes and let all her muscles go entirely limp, as though she'd fainted. Hans staggered under her sudden dead weight, then let her go.

Evie forced her muscles to remain limp and boneless, even as she crumpled and struck the hard wooden floor. She did manage to land nearly face down, with her right hand folded under her, so that her head didn't strike the floorboards.

Gerda arrived on the scene, panting, and Evie continued to lie absolutely still.

"What happened?" she heard Gerda ask.

"Nothing." Hans, too, was out of breath. "Herr Siegfried told the truth when he said that she would not be easy. She tried to get past me. But I handled it. As I said that I would. She gained nothing but bruises."

Evie pictured Hans looking down at her in satisfaction and willed her muscles not to tense. She wouldn't be at all surprised if he kicked her to emphasise his point.

But then Gerda said, in an impatient tone, "Pick up the supper things and come away, then."

Hans must have decided to obey her, because Evie heard his retreating footsteps, followed by the shutting of the door. The bolt slid shut, and she heard Hans and Gerda descending the stairs.

All the same, Evie lay still for a count of thirty before she cautiously sat up, careful to make no noise that could be heard from down below. She might not have got past Hans, but she hadn't intended to. What grappling with him had accomplished for her was the chance to pick his pocket.

Hans wasn't a tidy man. His pockets had been a jumble of loose change and odds and ends, such that she was fairly sure he either wouldn't miss anything stolen or would assume it had been misplaced.

Evie opened her right hand, examining the two items she'd managed to extract from Hans' coat pocket: first, a crumpled pound note and second a small round cork from a bottle. Again, not much. But they were two more items to add to her stub of pencil, and she already had a plan for the pound note, at least: one that made a few bruises a small price to pay.

Chapter 13
Harry

The Minstrel's Hall evoked images of medieval times, with oak-panelled walls, a high vaulted ceiling crossed by massive wooden beams, and tall windows that caught the late afternoon sunlight. Centuries earlier, Harry imagined, travelling musicians would have entertained nobles here with tales of chivalry and romance. Today, it would host a different kind of performance—one of careful questioning and watchful observation.

The staff of Clarion Castle stood assembled in neat groups, their hierarchy evident in how they positioned themselves. The indoor and outdoor staff maintained a visible separation, with the more senior house servants standing ramrod straight at the front, while the groundskeepers and stablehands clustered uncertainly near the back. Harry could identify the housemaids by their identical black dresses with white aprons and caps, the footmen by their formal livery, and the outdoor staff by their work clothes and weather-beaten complexions.

Glenwood had taken a moment earlier to point out key staff members to Harry, ensuring he knew who was who among the extensive household. The retired inspector had also overheard Fenton speaking to Cooper about moving the body, the Irishman's distinctive lilt unmistakable. Harry had noticed Cooper's missing fingers when the young man had nervously adjusted his collar while waiting.

Harry stood on a slightly raised dais at one end of the room. He'd made his call to Crofter's Green and worked out the plan. In the morning, Alice would be in the neighbourhood, and Blake and Katherine would arrive here at the Castle. He'd get Walker's cooperation for that little ruse in the morning, he was certain.

Now Harry faced his audience, with Nigel positioned to his right, notebook open and pencil ready. Walker had taken a seat to Harry's left, his unnaturally pale eyes surveying his assembled staff with his expression of perpetual inquiry.

"Thank you all for gathering here so promptly," Harry began, his voice carrying easily in the high-ceilinged room. "I'm retired Inspector Harry Jenkins, and this is Inspector Nigel Brewster from the Ashford and Crofter's Green police. I expect you've all heard about the unfortunate event that occurred in the wine cellar last night."

A ripple of nods and murmurs passed through the assembly.

"I've already met Mr Glenwood and Mr Graves," Harry continued, nodding toward the head butler and second under-butler. "And I understand that Mr Fenton and Mr Cooper helped to move Mr Vernon's body to the ice house."

The groom with the Irish lilt and the young man with the missing fingers shifted uncomfortably under his gaze.

"Mr Vernon's death was violent and deliberate," Harry said bluntly. "Someone cut his throat with a sommelier's knife from the butler's pantry. It is our duty to find justice for Mr Vernon, and to do so quickly."

He paused, watching the faces before him. Most showed apprehension or shock, but a few—including the sharp-featured secretary with the copper hair—maintained a studied neutrality.

"In view of the need for a swift resolution, Mr Walker has generously offered a fifty-pound reward for information that leads to an arrest and conviction."

A murmur of surprise rippled through the room. Fifty pounds was more than many of them earned in an entire year.

"Anyone who believes they have such information should come forward immediately after this meeting and speak with Inspector Brewster. Time is of the essence, so we'll begin interviews tonight."

As Harry made this announcement, he watched the reactions carefully. Several servants exchanged glances. The groundskeeper with the permanent stoop removed his tweed cap and twisted it anxiously in gnarled hands. The second under-butler, Graves, seemed to shrink back slightly, his scarred eyebrow twitching nervously. The others looked interested and thoughtful, clearly calculating the value of what they might know against the substantial reward offered.

"In the meantime," Harry continued, "Inspector Brewster will be taking all your names. I need hardly emphasise the importance of complete honesty. You are not just witnesses; you are also potential suspects."

Harry caught a flicker of movement—the sharp-featured secretary had glanced briefly toward a doorway where a young man in military uniform had appeared, observed the gathering for a moment, then withdrawn. Interesting, Harry thought, filing away the interaction for later consideration.

"If you believe you have information relevant to our investigation, please come forward now. The rest of you will form a queue to give your names to Inspector Brewster. That will be all for the present."

After his speech, Harry positioned himself next to Nigel at a small table that had been set up near the dais. "Those with information, to the front," Nigel called out. A small group immediately stepped forward, while the rest formed an orderly line behind them.

"Mrs Dorothy Winters, housekeeper," announced a woman in her fifties with iron-grey hair and perfect posture. The keys at her waist jingled softly as she moved. Harry noticed how she unconsciously ran her thumb over her wedding band as she waited.

"I often check all the rooms late at night, Inspector," she said, leaning forward slightly. "Two nights ago I noticed—"

"Thank you, Mrs Winters," Nigel interrupted politely. "We'll discuss all the details during your formal interview this evening. For now, we're just identifying who has information."

A gangly young man stepped forward next, his prominent Adam's apple bobbing nervously. "Timothy Clegg, sir. First footman." His ears stuck out from his head, giving him a perpetually startled appearance, though Harry detected a quick intelligence in his eyes.

"I was serving in the dining room yesterday evening when I overheard—" Clegg began.

"That's fine, Clegg," Nigel cut in firmly. "Save it for the interview, please. You'll be among the first we speak with tonight."

A plain-faced young woman with a distinctive gap between her front teeth approached the table next. Harry noticed she walked with a slight limp.

"Beatrice Slater, housemaid," she said quietly, her eyes darting toward a pretty blonde maid who was watching from across the room.

"I clean Mr Vernon's room," she stated. "There are things I found—"

"Thank you, Miss Slater," Nigel interrupted again. "We'll go through everything thoroughly during your interview this evening."

To Harry's surprise, a barrel-chested man with a dramatic horseshoe-shaped scar on his cheek pushed his way forward next. His hands were huge and muscular, Harry observed, more than capable of wielding a knife.

"Jarrett Fenton, stable master," he announced in a voice that carried across the room, followed by an unexpectedly high-pitched laugh. "I know what that knife was really used for before it—"

"Mr Fenton," Nigel said firmly, "we appreciate your eagerness, but we'll discuss all evidence during your formal interview. For now, just note that you have information to share."

Finally, a sharp-featured woman stepped up to the table. "Millicent Hartley, secretary to Mr Walker," she said primly. "I have heard your comments to my predecessors here." She was slender, perhaps thirty-five, with wire-rimmed spectacles that magnified her hawkish hazel-green eyes. "So I will merely say that I, too, have information to share."

With that, she stepped aside and nodded to the next person in line as if directing him to come forward.

After noting these five, Nigel proceeded to take down the names of the remaining staff members, as Harry observed each of them closely, searching for any telltale signs of nervousness or deception.

As the queue continued, Walker approached Harry, his colourless eyes narrowed slightly. "You've been a bit free with my money, Inspector," he said quietly.

"Would you give fifty pounds to have this settled quickly?" Harry countered.

"Of course."

"Then you have nothing to complain of." Harry smiled thinly. "You'll only pay if you receive value."

Walker's permanently arched eyebrow rose a fraction higher, but he nodded in acknowledgment.

"Tell me, Mr Walker," Harry said, changing the subject, "what exactly are the military men doing in the east wing?"

Walker's expression hardened minutely, but then relaxed. "I've spoken with Mr Brown, as you likely expected I would," he said. "He indicated I should be frank with you."

"And?"

Walker glanced around, ensuring they weren't overheard. "Come to my study," he said. "This isn't a conversation for open halls."

Chapter 14
Evie

Evie stared up at the ceiling, listening to the quiet creaks and groans of an old house settling at night. It had been an hour, at least, she judged, since she'd last heard any sounds from Hans or Gerda. Long enough that she could safely assume that they had gone to bed? She decided to risk it.

Her whole body was stiff and aching from remaining immobile for so long, but she'd wanted Gerda and Hans to believe her still unconscious, so she hadn't dared move. Now, ignoring the twinges of her protesting muscles, she reached into her shoe and extracted the pencil stub. Then she spread out the pound note she'd taken from Hans on her knee.

She was lucky that Hans and Gerda had either forgotten to turn off the single bare electric bulb that gave the room its light or simply hadn't bothered.

Evie had been thinking for the past hour about what she ought to write. She was nowhere near as good with codes as Blake was, but at the same rate, she couldn't make this too obvious, on the chance that Hans or Gerda— or worse, Paul— might find it. But she took the pencil and wrote a column of numbers in tiny print along the side of the note, as though someone had been totalling up sums to be deposited in a bank account, or maybe tallying up winnings at the racetrack.

1 pound 5 shillings
22 shillings 8 pence
3 pounds 9 shillings
5 shillings 6 pence

Then she folded the pound note as tightly as she could manage, making it as small as humanly possible.

Evie stood up, still moving slowly and carefully, testing each floorboard to see whether it would creak under her weight. She managed to reach the bed without making any noise; then she knelt down and stuffed the folded pound note into the same crack at the join of the floor and wall in which she'd found the pencil stub. It barely protruded; you had to run your hand over the crack to know that anything was there.

Would anyone bother to search the room that thoroughly after she had gone? Would Paul?

Evie climbed up onto the bed and stretched out, trying to put that thought out of her mind. She'd done what she could. The rest was up to Nigel and the others— if they came here looking for her at all.

Chapter 15
Harry

Walker's study was everything Harry would have expected from a man of his position—imposing mahogany desk, leather-bound volumes lining the walls, and a collection of impressive artefacts that spoke of wealth and influence. The late afternoon sun slanted through tall windows, casting long shadows across the rich carpet.

Walker gestured for Harry and Nigel to take seats in the leather armchairs positioned before his desk. He remained standing, moving to a sideboard where he poured himself a measure of amber liquid from a crystal decanter.

"Whisky?" he offered.

Both men declined with a polite shake of their heads.

Walker settled into the high-backed chair behind his desk, the unusual paleness of his eyes more pronounced in the directional light from the window. The light also emphasised his arched eyebrow and perpetually sceptical expression.

"I understand your concern about the military presence," Walker began, taking a measured sip of his whisky. "But first, I think it's important you understand my position."

"By all means," Harry said, his gaze drifting to the array of mementos arranged on shelves behind Walker.

Following Harry's gaze, Walker turned slightly. "Souvenirs of past accomplishments," he explained with a hint of pride. "That ribbon-cutting was the Sheffield Works, 1936. Produced the steel for the Spitfire wing spars. And that miniature ingot there—first pour from the Birmingham foundry."

Harry nodded appreciatively. "Quite a collection."

"My business ties with the government run deep, gentlemen," Walker continued, turning back to face them. "Walker Steel currently supplies approximately forty per cent of the specialised steel required for Britain's war effort. Our contracts run into the millions of pounds."

"That's a significant responsibility," Nigel observed, pencil poised over his notebook.

"Indeed." Walker's pale eyes hardened slightly. "And one I take on with the utmost seriousness. My father fought at the Somme. Lost a leg there. I grew up understanding the price of freedom."

Harry nodded. "Your patriotism is commendable, Mr Walker. But what does this have to do with the military personnel in your east wing?"

Walker took another sip of his whisky. "Patience, Inspector. Context is important." He set down his glass with precision. "The contracts I've negotiated with the government have been favourable to Walker Steel, I won't pretend otherwise. Business is business, after all."

"Of course," Harry murmured.

"As for the meeting ..." Walker's voice lowered slightly, studying them both with his unsettling pale eyes. "Let's just say we're hosting a rather significant visitor. One who rarely travels outside London these days."

"The Prime Minister?" Harry ventured.

Walker's expression betrayed mild surprise. "Sharp, aren't you? Yes, Churchill himself, with a small entourage. Supposed to be quite hush-hush."

Harry exchanged a quick glance with Nigel. "I see."

"Desperate times," Walker said, rotating his whisky glass absently. "We're in a tight spot. The Americans are still dragging their feet while we're taking it on the chin." He gave a sardonic smile. "Winston has his work cut out for him with Roosevelt."

"You seem well-informed on international relations," Harry observed.

Walker shrugged. "I've got iron and steel interests in Pennsylvania. Been working with the Americans since before the last war. When you've dined with their industrialists as often as I have, you pick things up." He gazed out the window momentarily. "Business makes for strange bedfellows."

"So the important meeting is about securing your steel contracts?" Harry prompted.

"Actually, I'm offering concessions." Walker's tone was matter-of-fact. "Cutting my margins significantly. Can't take it with you, can you? And what good is profit if we lose the war?"

Harry studied Walker's face, trying to reconcile this apparent selflessness with the shrewd businessman before him. "That's... quite generous."

"It's practical." Walker drained his glass. "My factories can't benefit me if the Germans invade, can they? This isn't charity—it's survival. For Britain and for Walker Steel."

"Which brings us back to the murder," Nigel interjected.

"Exactly." Walker's expression darkened. "This couldn't have happened at a worse time. Churchill's security man will be here to plan the visit the day before. One whiff of trouble and they'll whisk him back to London before you can say 'Dunkirk.'"

"And the military presence in the east wing?" Harry pressed, returning to his original question.

Walker set down his glass and rose to his feet. "I've decided to have you see for yourself. It will be easier to understand when you see the operation."

Harry and Nigel exchanged glances as they stood. Walker moved toward the door with surprising vigour for a man of his size and age.

"This way, gentlemen. I'll take you there personally."

They followed Walker through the grand corridors of Clarion Castle, past the imposing entrance hall with its curious red telephone box, and toward the castle's eastern wing. The hallway narrowed as they approached a heavy oak door guarded by a young corporal in army uniform.

The soldier snapped to attention at Walker's approach. "Sir!"

"At ease, Corporal," Walker said with the casual authority of a man accustomed to military deference. "These gentlemen are here at the request of Mr Brown. They have clearance to observe the operation."

The mention of Brown's name worked its magic once again. The corporal stepped aside, producing a key to unlock the heavy door.

"You'll need to maintain absolute secrecy about what you're about to see," Walker warned as the door swung open. "This installation is of vital importance to the war effort."

Harry nodded his understanding, curiosity mounting as Walker led them into the mysterious east wing of Clarion Castle.

Chapter 16
Harry

The east wing corridor was narrower than the grand hallways of the main castle, with lower ceilings and fewer windows. Harry noted the strategic placement of blackout curtains over the few windows they passed—clearly designed to prevent any light from escaping after dark.

Walker led them down the corridor, past several closed doors, until they reached a large room at the far end. A pair of guards flanked the entrance, standing at attention as Walker approached.

"Afternoon, gentlemen," Walker said briskly. "These visitors have clearance from Mr Brown."

The guards saluted and stepped aside. Walker pushed open the door, revealing a scene that immediately explained the mysterious military presence at Clarion Castle.

Before them was a listening post—a compact yet efficiently arranged radio intelligence operation. Two uniformed servicemen sat at radio sets positioned against the far wall, both wearing headphones and focused intently on their work. They were transcribing Morse code onto notepads, their pencils moving in swift, practised motions across the paper. Harry noticed stacks of sharpened pencils next to each man, ready for immediate replacement when their current ones wore down.

The radio sets themselves looked to be new equipment, with dials, meters, and switches labelled "send" and "receive." Both were currently set to "receive." The operators adjusted frequencies occasionally, their movements precise and methodical.

At a side table sat another man in a commander's uniform, grey at the temples and wearing wire-rimmed glasses that gave him a scholarly appearance. He was reviewing a stack of transcribed notes, occasionally tapping out a transmission on a telegrapher's key switch. A wire ran from the key to a socket built into the grey-painted wood skirting just above the floor.

The room smelled of coffee, cigarettes, and the faint ozone scent given off by electronic equipment. Maps covered one wall, with pins marking various positions in the English Channel and North Sea. On the wall immediately to Harry's left was a small window, and alongside it a partially open door revealing a tightly curved staircase. The atmosphere was one of quiet intensity—the silent battlefield of intelligence work.

"Gentlemen," Walker announced, "a moment of your time."

The commander looked up from his work and removed his spectacles as he rose to greet them. The radio operators remained at their posts, duty-bound to their listening tasks.

"Captain Richard Marlowe," Walker introduced the commander, "head of this operation. And that's Lieutenant James Foster and Corporal Samuel Bartlett at the radios."

Captain Marlowe stepped forward, offering a firm handshake. "Gentlemen," he said with crisp military efficiency. His methodical military bearing matched his neatly organised workspace, Harry thought.

Lieutenant Foster turned briefly, offering a charming smile that didn't quite reach his cold eyes. "Welcome to our humble outpost," he said, before returning to his work. His dark hair was perfectly combed, and he maintained an air of casual competence at his station.

Corporal Bartlett merely nodded nervously, his ink-stained fingers and cigarette-yellowed teeth visible even from across the room. He appeared younger than the others, perhaps twenty-five, and seemed uncomfortable with the interruption to their routine.

"This is retired Inspector Harry Jenkins and Inspector Nigel Brewster," Walker explained. "They're investigating the unfortunate incident with one of my staff. Mr Brown has authorised them to know about the operation."

"I see," Marlowe said, his expression carefully neutral. "How can we assist?"

"Perhaps you could explain the operation to them," Walker suggested. "I'll let you cover the details you deem appropriate."

Marlowe nodded and gestured for Harry and Nigel to come closer to the radio equipment.

"We're a forward listening post," Marlowe explained, his voice low. "There are six others on staff, for a total of nine men covering three eight-hour shifts. We maintain round-the-clock monitoring."

"What exactly are you monitoring?" Harry asked, though he had his suspicions.

"Enemy transmissions," Marlowe replied succinctly. "We dial the radios to frequencies the Jerrys are known to prefer. Sometimes there's traffic, sometimes not. But we must be on duty and ready at all times to receive it."

"Berlin and the U-boats, primarily," Foster added without looking up from his work. "Hunting for fleet movements, attack coordinates, operational instructions."

"And once you've transcribed these transmissions?" Nigel inquired.

"We edit the transcriptions, clean them up," Marlowe explained, gesturing to the papers before him. "Then we send them back, in code of course, exactly as they were received, via that telegraph key. It's connected to a secure land line so the Germans won't know we're transmitting their own messages."

"I won't tell you where it's going," Walker interjected.

"Somewhere to be decoded, I expect," Harry said mildly.

Both Marlowe and Walker remained impassive, neither confirming nor denying Harry's assessment.

"No comment, Inspector Jenkins," Walker said with the hint of a smile.

Harry's mind was racing. He was picturing the coded fragments they'd found at the abbey ruins, the fragments that formed the word "Clarion."

"I'd like to interview the three of you as soon as you come off duty," Harry said, "and the other six as soon as they're ready." He gestured towards the partially opened door alongside the window. "Are they sleeping up there?"

"That's just a storage attic," Walker said. "Sleeping quarters are downstairs."

"Understood," Harry said. "No need to wake them now. We just want to see if anyone heard or saw anything relevant to our investigation."

"Happy to help," Foster said smoothly, glancing up from his radio.

"We will all cooperate," Marlowe said. "Where should we report for these interviews?"

"Use my study," Walker offered. "That's where you should interview all the staff as well. Quiet in there."

As they prepared to depart, Harry watched the three men, now back at their work.

Outside in the corridor, as Walker led them back toward his office, Harry and Nigel exchanged meaningful glances. Harry felt sure they had found the major clue they'd been waiting for—the definite reason to link "Clarion" with the operation here.

Had this top-secret installation been betrayed, and the secret revealed to the Germans by the now-dead Vernon?

Had Vernon uncovered the traitor, and been killed for it?

Harry tapped his jacket pocket, where Vernon's notebook rested securely. He was sure that somewhere in this web of espionage and murder was the key to finding Evie. The answers might be so very close at hand, literally within his grasp. But how would they decode whatever Vernon had written?

When they neared the study, Harry could see several of the staff were already waiting for their interviews.

Harry shook off a wave of light-headed excitement, mingled with fatigue. "Thank you, Mr Walker," he said. "Just one request. Could you have the cook send up some coffee to your study?"

"I'll tell her to add some sandwiches as well," Walker said. "Likely you'll be having a long night."

Chapter 17
Harry

Harry settled into a comfortable leather armchair in the small study that Walker had designated for interviews. The room was intimate but well-appointed, with bookshelves lining one wall and a small window opposite, overlooking the east gardens. Nigel sat at a writing desk nearby, notebook open and pencil poised.

"Send in Mrs Winters first," Harry instructed the footman who stood by the door.

The housekeeper entered with a measured stride, keys jingling softly at her waist. Her iron-grey hair was impeccably arranged, and her posture remained ramrod straight even as she took the seat opposite Harry.

"Thank you for coming, Mrs Winters," Harry began. "You mentioned you check the rooms at night?"

Mrs Winters nodded, her thumb unconsciously moving across her wedding band. "Every night at eleven, Inspector. It's been my routine for twenty years."

"And two nights ago you noticed something unusual?"

"Indeed, sir." She leaned forward slightly. "I was making my final rounds when I passed Mr Vernon's room. His light was still on, which wasn't unusual—he often worked late. But as I passed by, I heard voices. He was arguing with someone."

Harry's interest sharpened. "Could you make out what was being said?"

"Not precisely, sir. The voices were hushed, though heated. But I distinctly heard Mr Vernon say, 'I won't be part of this.' Then something about 'telling Mr Walker.'"

"Did you recognise the other voice?"

Mrs Winters hesitated, her fingers now working at her wedding band more intensely. "I believe it was Mr Graves, sir. I can't be absolutely certain, but the cadence was familiar."

"What time was this?"

"Just after eleven, sir. My rounds are very regular."

"And after that?"

"I continued my rounds. When I passed back twenty minutes later, the light was out, and all was quiet."

Harry nodded thoughtfully. "Did you see anyone else moving about the house at that time?"

"Miss Hartley—Mr Walker's secretary—was working late in the library. And I glimpsed one of the military gentlemen heading toward the east wing. I believe it was the lieutenant, the handsome one."

"And did anything else strike you as unusual in the past few days? Any changes in routine or behaviour among the staff?"

Mrs Winters considered this carefully. "Well, Miss Hartley was out of the castle with Mr Graves. That was unusual."

"How?'

"I saw Mr Graves get into one of the staff cars last night. Miss Hartley was driving. Then about ten o'clock I saw them return."

"In the same car?"

"Yes. They drove around back. It was unusual because the two of them wouldn't normally socialise. She is his superior on the staff, after all. Though I would think they are of about the same age."

Harry caught her small smile of satisfaction, as if she'd uncovered a romantic weakness in Miss Hartley. "Anything else?"

"Well, besides Miss Hartley, Mr Vernon had been more reserved lately. He's usually quite sociable at staff meals, but the past week he kept to himself. And..." she hesitated again, "he was making notes in a small book he kept. Very secretive about it."

Harry exchanged a glance with Nigel, thinking of the coded notebook they'd found in Vernon's pocket.

"Thank you, Mrs Winters. That's very helpful." Harry rose, signalling the end of the interview. "We may have additional questions later."

As the housekeeper departed, her keys jingling softly, Harry turned to Nigel. "Clegg next, I think."

Timothy Clegg entered nervously, his prominent Adam's apple bobbing as he swallowed. The young footman's ears seemed to stick out even more prominently under Harry's scrutiny.

"You have information for us, Mr Clegg?" Harry prompted once the footman had taken his seat.

"Yes, sir." Clegg's voice cracked slightly, and he cleared his throat. "Last evening before supper, I was serving drinks in the library. Mr Walker was meeting with Miss Hartley—his secretary—and they didn't notice me clearing the side table."

"What did you overhear?"

"They were discussing the guest list for tomorrow's gathering. Miss Hartley mentioned that 'the Prime Minister's representative' would require special accommodation. Mr Walker corrected her rather sharply, saying she should refer to him only as 'the cabinet minister' even in private conversations."

Harry nodded encouragingly as Clegg continued.

"Then Miss Hartley asked about 'security arrangements for the gentleman in question' and whether the military presence would be sufficient. Mr Walker told her that was not her concern." Clegg's Adam's apple bobbed dramatically. "Then Mr Vernon entered with the wine selection for approval, and they stopped talking immediately."

"How did Vernon seem at that moment?"

"Perfectly normal, sir. Professional as always. Although"—Clegg frowned slightly, his quick intelligence evident in his thoughtful expression— "Miss Hartley seemed unusually interested in Mr Vernon's wine selections. She asked him several questions about which bottles would be served from which cellar racks. Never known her to take an interest in such things before."

"What time was this?"

"Around seven in the evening, sir. Dinner was at eight."

"Did you serve at dinner as well?"

"Yes, sir. Nothing unusual there, except Mr Graves seemed rather distracted. Dropped a spoon, which isn't like him at all."

Harry made a mental note of this. "Thank you, Mr Clegg. Anything else?"

"Just one thing, sir. Later in the evening, around ten, I saw Mr Vernon heading toward the east wing. The military wing. Carrying some papers."

This was an interesting detail. "That's most helpful. Thank you."

After the footman departed, Harry was grateful to see housemaid Beatrice Slater arrive with a tray of coffee and sandwiches. Roast beef, Harry noticed. Clearly, Walker's status and wealth meant he wasn't nearly as troubled by wartime rationing as most of the country.

"I stopped by the kitchen and Mrs Finch was looking for someone to bring you this," she said, her words tumbling out in a rush, "and of course I was coming here anyway to tell you things, so I told her I'd do it." The gap between her front teeth showed briefly as she gave a nervous smile before setting the tray down on one of the tables. "I can wait outside, if you like."

Nigel was already lifting the silver coffee urn.

"Not necessary," Harry said. "If you don't mind, we'll just carry on with the questions while we have our supper."

He waited while Nigel poured out coffee and took a sandwich back to his own chair. Then Harry poured for himself, noting the scalding heat of the brew, and the blue castle motif, an outline of Clarion Castle, emblazoned on the mug. "Miss Slater," he began, after taking a cautious sip, "you clean Mr Vernon's room, I understand?"

"Yes, sir. Every day except Sundays."

"And you found something?"

Beatrice nodded, glancing quickly toward the door as if worried about being overheard. "Three days ago, while changing his linens, I found letters hidden between his mattress and bedsprings. Foreign letters, sir. The writing wasn't English."

Harry raised an eyebrow. "German, perhaps?"

"I couldn't say, sir. Never learned languages. But there were stamps I didn't recognise. And photographs."

"What kind of photographs?"

"Of the castle, sir. Different angles. The old keep especially. And maps with markings on them. They gave me an uneasy feeling, so I put them back where I found them."

"Did you tell anyone about this?"

"No, sir." She hesitated, then added, "But I think Miss Hartley saw me leaving his room that day. She asked me what I was doing in there so early."

"How did Vernon behave toward you after that?"

"Same as always, sir. He barely noticed me. But yesterday I went to clean as usual, and the letters and photographs were gone." Beatrice twisted her hands nervously in her lap. "And later, I saw Mr Vernon talking to Miss Hartley in the corridor. Looked serious, it did."

Harry nodded thoughtfully. "When was the last time you saw Mr Vernon alive?"

"Yesterday afternoon, sir. About four o'clock. He was heading toward the wine cellar with Mr Graves. They didn't look friendly."

Harry thanked her and called for Jarrett Fenton next. The stable master filled the small study with his presence, the horseshoe-shaped scar prominent on his weathered cheek.

"Mr Fenton," Harry began, "you mentioned something about the knife?"

"Aye, Inspector." Fenton's booming voice contrasted with his unexpectedly musical laugh. "That fancy wine knife wasn't just for bottles. Last week, I saw Vernon using it out by the old keep. He was scraping at something in the stonework. Hiding something, if you ask me."

"The old keep?" Harry's interest was immediately piqued. "What time of day was this?"

"Dusk, sir. I was walking back from the stables when I spotted him. Curious behaviour, I thought. When he saw me, he pocketed the knife quick-like and made some excuse about checking the mortar condition for Mr Walker."

"Did you believe him?"

"Not a word of it." Fenton's large, shovel-like hands gestured expressively. "The next day, I went to look. Found a loose stone that had been recently disturbed. Mortar picked away. But whatever he might have hidden there was already gone."

"The loose stone—where was it?"

"Outside, of course. Old keep's padlocked, y'see. Can't get to the inside."

Harry leaned forward. "Did you mention this to anyone?"

"Mentioned it to Cooper when we were moving the body. He said Vernon had been acting strange lately. Always wandering around the grounds after dark. Sometimes meeting with one of those military gentlemen."

"Which one?"

"The lieutenant. Handsome fellow with cold eyes."

Harry exchanged another meaningful glance with Nigel. "Mr Fenton, when you and Cooper moved Vernon's body, did you notice anything unusual about it, or about the scene in the wine cellar?"

Fenton's expression grew serious. "The blood was all smeared about, sir. And Vernon had something in his hand."

"Something in his hand? What happened to it?"

"Mr Glenwood took it. Bent down and put it into his pocket, he did."

"Did you see what it was?"

"Looked like a scrap of paper, sir. Nothing more than that. Glenwood tucked it away quick."

Harry thanked the stable master and dismissed him. When the door closed, he turned to Nigel.

"Interesting threads emerging," he said quietly. "Vernon seems to have taken a great deal of interest in the military presence here."

"You think he was a spy?" The tone of Nigel's voice said that the possibility had already occurred to him.

"It's one possible explanation, isn't it?" Harry said. "He tried to be friendly with Foster in hopes of getting information about the operations in the Tower wing."

"And he visited the old keep in order to pass that information on by leaving a message behind a loose stone he'd dug out?"

"It's a possible explanation," Harry said again. He wasn't willing to commit himself fully until they learned more, but the facts so far made a suspiciously suggestive picture.

"So who killed him?" Nigel said. "Someone on our side, who'd found out he was spying and wanted to stop him?"

"Or someone on his side," Harry said. "If he was in the pay of the enemy."

"You think there could be another traitor here."

"I think it's a possibility we can't ignore," Harry said grimly. "We already know there's one bang-up secret that Vernon or another traitor here at the Castle might have passed on. One that might even have the potential to win this war for the Germans."

"Churchill's visit." Nigel, too, looked grim. "Kill the Prime Minister, and our government would be thrown into chaos."

"The whole country would be thrown into chaos," Harry said. "Not that I mean to downplay the role of the rank and file fighting this war. The men fighting over there in France or the RAF men flying missions night after night. But they need a strong man in charge of it all, and Churchill has been that."

"Good for morale, too," Nigel said. "I doubt Londoners would have made it through the Blitz without his radio talks."

There was a moment's silence, during which Harry felt the weight of all that was at stake settle like an almost-physical pressure on his shoulders.

"So where are we?" Nigel asked.

Harry roused himself. Sitting here with coffee and sandwiches wasn't going to accomplish anything. As Churchill himself had said in a speech last year, *I have nothing to offer but blood, toil, tears and sweat.*

"We're at the point," Harry said, "Where I go back to the red telephone box and make another call for reinforcements."

Chapter 18
Harry

Weak morning light filtered through the windows of Clarion Castle's small dining room. It did little to brighten Harry's mood. After a night of seemingly endless questioning of the staff members who hadn't volunteered, and the indifferent signal corps men who kept aloof from the servants, he'd learned precious little. And Miss Hartley, who'd claimed to have information, had never appeared. Neither had Mr Graves, the sleek-haired under-butler who'd acted so nervous when Harry had seen him from the wine cellar.

Still, Harry had managed a few hours of fitful sleep before dawn.

The dining table, set for six, had been laid out with a full English breakfast spread that normally would have delighted Harry. Silver chafing dishes on the sideboard held heaps of crisp bacon, sausages glistening with fat, scrambled eggs of perfect consistency, grilled tomatoes, and mushrooms sautéed with herbs. A covered dish kept a stack of toast warm, while jars of marmalade, honey, and preserves stood nearby. A silver teapot steamed gently beside fine bone-china cups.

Plainly, Mr Walker's estate also enjoyed immunity from rationing rules for breakfasts. Harry wondered if the household staff partook of the abundance.

He had asked for coffee, which Clegg, the footman, had just gone into the kitchen to fetch.

Despite the array of tempting dishes, Harry found himself picking at his food, his mind trying to sift through the interviews they'd completed. He had to admit it: he was tired. Yesterday had been a long, long day.

Across the table, Nigel looked equally worn as he mechanically buttered a piece of toast.

"What are we going to do about Evie?" Nigel asked suddenly, his voice low enough that Clegg, now bringing Harry's pot of coffee, couldn't hear.

Harry waited until Clegg had retreated to a discreet distance before answering. "I'm hoping Alice will turn up something in the neighbourhood. Or Katherine will coax something helpful out of someone who knows the local gossip."

"The listening post changes everything," Nigel murmured. "If Vernon passed on information about its existence to the Germans, Siegfried's bound to know."

Harry nodded grimly. "And to be around here. Maybe to blow it up."

Nigel took a sip of tea. "How do we proceed?"

"We go back to yesterday's witnesses, and probe a little harder. At the end of the day we check in with our reinforcements. Alice should already be walking on the Pilgrim Way by now."

"And Blake and Katherine?"

"Should be here late morning," Harry replied, checking his watch. "Blake's arranged for credentials as a newspaper reporter here to cover—"

The door to the dining room swung open, and Bradford Walker strode in, his pale eyes sharp in the morning light.

"Gentlemen," Walker said, taking a seat without invitation. "I trust you slept well?"

Harry met the steel magnate's gaze. "As well as could be expected, Mr Walker."

"Excellent. Then I'll trouble you for a progress report." Walker helped himself to tea from the silver pot. "I presume you've made an arrest?"

"Not yet," Harry replied carefully. "We don't have enough evidence to charge anyone, though there are certain lines of inquiry that show promise."

Walker's teacup clattered against its saucer. "Don't give me that old claptrap, Jenkins. What have you got?"

Harry maintained his composure, sipping his coffee before responding. "I'm not at liberty to incriminate anyone without sufficient evidence, Mr Walker. It wouldn't be fair."

"Fair?" Walker's tone sharpened. "You know what's not fair? Having a murder in my home practically on the eve of the most important meeting of the war effort—for me at least. The Prime Minister arrives tomorrow, and you're wasting my time by talking about fairness?"

"There could be something far more dangerous at play if we arrest the wrong person and let the real murderer go free," Harry countered.

Walker's eyes narrowed. "Who would you arrest, if you had to choose right now?"

"I won't arrest anyone without proper evidence," Harry replied firmly. "That's not how justice works, even in wartime."

Walker leaned forward, his voice dropping. "With Churchill practically on his way, we are cutting it rather fine, wouldn't you say? What makes you think you can solve this in time?"

Once again, Harry couldn't commit or reveal what he knew. He played his best card. "I'm optimistic because two of our best people are arriving at the castle today. They'll take undercover roles and learn what they can."

"Undercover?" Walker's eyebrow arched impossibly higher. "What sort of undercover?"

"My colleague Blake Collins will be playing the role of a newspaper reporter, here to cover architectural features of the castle for a historical piece. And Katherine Chapman will be posing as a rare book librarian, cataloguing your collection."

Walker's face darkened. "Absolutely not. I won't have spies wandering about my home when the Prime Minister is here."

"They'll be discreet," Harry assured him. "And may well help us resolve this matter before any... unpleasantness occurs."

After a long moment, Walker gave a reluctant nod. "Very well. But they have to be out of the way when the PM arrives."

Chapter 19
Alice

After her first five miles on the trail, Alice Greenleaf reached a hilltop and stopped to rest.

She adjusted her modest cloche hat against the August sun, grateful for the wide brim that shielded her face. She leaned on her walking staff—a practical hazel switch that doubled as both support and protection—taking in the rolling Kent countryside spread out before her.

The Pilgrim's Way stretched like a pale ribbon through the landscape, winding through fields golden with ripening wheat and disappearing into a patch of woodlands surrounding another hill. Here and there she'd passed hedgerows thick with blackberry brambles, their fruits still more red than black, though Alice spotted a few early ripeners that tempted her botanical instincts. Elder trees heavy with dark berries stood sentinel at intervals, their medicinal bounty nearly ready for harvesting.

She smiled at the thought of the elderberry syrup she'd be making come September—excellent for winter coughs and colds. The herbalist in her couldn't help but notice the plantain and yarrow growing at path's edge, useful for poultices and staunching blood.

True, she was here on a different mission entirely. But old habits die hard.

She set off again, taking brisk strides in the new walking shoes she'd bought for the purpose, all the while wishing she could be riding her bicycle instead.

But bicycles weren't the way of the pilgrim.

Soon she reached the small wooded section, where the slope went up again and the temperature dropped immediately. Sunlight filtered through oak and beech leaves, creating dappled patterns on the path. Wild woodruff grew in patches where light penetrated the canopy, and the subtle scent of its dried leaves reminded Alice of the sachets she made to ward off moths.

Emerging from the woods, she caught her first glimpse of Clarion in the near distance. The village nestled in a gentle hollow, its church spire piercing the sky, its medieval square surrounded by timber-framed buildings in warm Kentish colours. Beyond it, barely visible, rose the more substantial silhouette of Clarion Castle.

Alice straightened her simple linen cloak and checked her small pack. Her disguise was deliberately unassuming—a middle-aged woman of no particular note, seeking spiritual renewal on the ancient pilgrim's path to Canterbury. Her Oxford education and herbalist knowledge were carefully tucked away beneath this humble exterior.

As she approached the village, she rehearsed her story once more. The war had taken her brother (true enough, though it was the previous war, and it had been her fiancée, not her brother), and she had promised their elderly mother to make the pilgrimage to pray for his soul. The part about her mother, of course, had been entirely fabricated. Still, with the recent news of British troops fighting in North Africa, it would seem to be an appropriate time to fulfil this long-delayed promise.

The cobbled streets of Clarion were quieter than they would have been in peacetime. A few locals moved about their business, eyeing her with the natural suspicion reserved for strangers in wartime. The central square featured a small stone monument, surrounded by a plaza and several shops. Alice saw a bakery, a greengrocer, a pub called The White Horse, and a tea shop that bore the sign "Clarion Tea Rooms."

She headed for the tea shop, knowing that such establishments, like Evie's Cozy Cup, were reservoirs of local gossip. A bell tinkled as she entered, and several heads turned to examine the newcomer. The proprietress, a stout woman with greying hair pinned severely atop her head, approached with a businesslike smile.

"Good afternoon. Will you be wanting tea?"

"Yes, please," Alice replied, adopting a slight West Country accent. "And perhaps a scone if you have any. I've been walking since sunrise."

"Pilgrim, are you?" the woman asked, gesturing to a small table by the window. "Don't get many these days."

"Yes," Alice nodded, settling gratefully into the chair. "Promised my mother I'd make the journey to Canterbury. For my brother's soul."

The woman's face softened slightly. "Lost him, did you? The war?"

"North Africa," Alice said simply, letting the woman draw her own conclusions about which conflict she meant.

"God rest him." The woman crossed herself. "I'm Mrs Gibbs. I'll fetch your tea."

As Mrs Gibbs bustled away, Alice surveyed the room. Two elderly women sat in the corner, heads bent in conversation. A middle-aged man in a farmer's cap nursed a cup by the counter. At a table near the back, a young woman with a fretful baby attempted to soothe the child while hastily drinking her tea.

Mrs Gibbs returned with a teapot, cup, and a scone with clotted cream. "There we are. Don't get many walking the old path now. Too busy with the war effort, I suppose."

"Have there been any others recently?" Alice asked casually, pouring her tea. "I'd hoped to find companions for the journey."

Mrs Gibbs considered this as she arranged Alice's plate. "There was a gentleman about two weeks back. Foreign accent—said he was Swiss. Neutral country, he said." Her tone suggested scepticism.

Alice made a noncommittal sound of interest while spreading cream on her scone. "Was he alone?"

"Far as I know. Asked a lot of questions about the castle, he did." Mrs Gibbs lowered her voice. "Mr Walker doesn't like strangers poking about, especially now."

"The castle is nearby, then?" Alice asked, feigning ignorance.

"Just up the hill. Can't miss it." Mrs Gibbs gestured vaguely. "Important government business goes on there, they say."

Then, as if sensing she'd said too much, Mrs Gibbs straightened. "Will you be staying in the village tonight? The White Horse has rooms."

"I had hoped to continue on a bit further before dark," Alice replied. "Is there accommodation on the path ahead?"

Before Mrs Gibbs could answer, the bell tinkled again, and a tall man in gamekeeper's attire entered. The atmosphere in the tea room subtly shifted, conversations quieting.

"Afternoon, Tom," Mrs Gibbs called. "The usual?"

The gamekeeper nodded, his eyes falling on Alice. His weathered face betrayed nothing as he approached her table.

"You're walking the path?" he asked without preamble.

"To Canterbury," Alice confirmed. "I'm a pilgrim."

"Pilgrims usually travel in groups," he observed, his voice neutral but his eyes sharp.

"Times being what they are," Alice replied, meeting his gaze steadily. "Not many making the journey these days."

He studied her for a moment longer. "Keep to the marked path, mind. Some of the surrounding land is private. Mr Walker doesn't like trespassers."

"I'll be careful," Alice promised.

The gamekeeper nodded curtly and moved to the counter, where Mrs Gibbs handed him a wrapped package. He exchanged a few quiet words with her before departing.

"Don't mind Tom," Mrs Gibbs said, returning to Alice's table. "He takes his job seriously. Manor lands begin just beyond the village."

Alice finished her tea, paying careful attention to the snippets of conversation around her. The young mother with the fussing baby caught her eye.

"Is your little one unwell?" Alice asked gently.

The woman looked up, surprise crossing her tired face. "Just colicky. Nothing serious."

"I know a remedy for that," Alice said before she could stop herself. "Fennel tea, very weak. Just a few drops for the baby."

The woman's eyes widened. "Are you a nurse?"

"I know a bit about herbs," Alice answered, mentally chiding herself for the slip. "My mother taught me."

"You should speak with our vicar's wife," said one of the elderly women, who had been listening. "She's a dab hand at herbs and such. Always wantin' to help folks."

"Like that poor woman in Blair Cottage," said her companion. "Though she didn't get very far with that, now, did she?"

"Hush, Edith," the other elderly woman scolded. "That's not our business."

Alice's interest was immediately piqued. "Someone's ill?"

Edith leaned forward, clearly pleased to have an audience. "Young woman, taken ill just when she arrived with her parents. Fever, they say."

"The vicar's wife wanted to bring meals," the other woman added reluctantly. "But the parents said they could manage. So did her husband."

"The daughter's married?"

"Oh, aye, and the man's very protective," Edith continued. "Comes in from time to time to see her. Foreign gentleman, I believe. Belgian, he told the vicar."

Alice felt her pulse quicken. A sick woman. A protective foreign husband. Arrived recently. With parents.

"How terrible," Alice said, careful to keep her voice measured. "Is there a doctor in the village?"

"Dr Parsons comes twice a week from Canterbury," Mrs Gibbs supplied. "But I heard the husband refused his services. Said his wife had a delicate constitution and he knew best how to treat her."

Alice finished her scone and paid for her tea. "I should continue on my way if I'm to reach shelter before dark. Is there a place to stay near this Blair Cottage?"

"The Shepherd's Rest is a mile or so beyond," Mrs Gibbs replied. "Just a simple inn, but clean enough."

Alice thanked her and gathered her things. As she stepped back onto Clarion's main street, her mind was already forming a plan. The sick woman in Blair Cottage might have nothing to do with their case—or she might be Evie.

Either way, Alice Greenleaf intended to find out.

Chapter 20
Katherine

Clarion Castle was every bit as grand as Katherine had imagined it would be. Exactly the kind of place where an emergency meant running out of sherry before the servants' bell was fixed.

A stiffly polite butler had shown her into the drawing room, which was very nearly the size of Dorothy and Tom's entire cottage, and almost oppressively rich and luxurious. The tall sash windows were framed in heavy, lined curtains made of burgundy velvet. The walls were covered in dark red damask wallpaper, and edged with ornate plasterwork and decorative cornices. A grand chandelier of crystal and brass hung as a centrepiece in the middle of the high ceiling.

Katherine felt rather like Jane Eyre entering Thornfield Hall for the first time. Worse, actually. She hadn't yet spoken a single word to any of the household besides the butler, and already her insides felt cold and shaking. What on earth had she been thinking, coming here? She had wanted to help Blake and of course she wanted to find Evie. But she wasn't an actress, much less a detective. And she didn't even remember her own mother and father or a single day of all the years she'd spent in school.

How could she expect to fool an entire household into believing that she was some sort of expert in rare books?

The furniture was comfortable, at least. She was sitting on a tufted armchair in dark green brocade that had been placed in front of the carved marble fireplace. From above the mantle, a portrait of a heavyset man in the garb of the 16th century glowered down at her. A long-dead Walker ancestor? Or just a historical figure whom Katherine's brain had helpfully erased from her memories? Either way, he didn't appear to think that she belonged here, either.

"Katherine Chapman?"

Katherine stood up to greet the woman who had just entered the room and was coming briskly towards her.

"Yes." She was slightly surprised to hear that her voice sounded steady, despite the nervous squirming inside her.

"I'm Millicent Hartley, Mr Walker's secretary," the woman said.

She was a slim, sharp-featured woman of about thirty-five with wire-rimmed spectacles that magnified her sharp hazel-green eyes. Everything about her appearance was both elegant and immaculately tidy, from her smoothly combed hair to the crisp bow on her silk blouse and the string of pearls around her neck. Her copper-coloured hair was pulled into a severe bun so tight that Katherine almost felt the prickle of a headache just looking at her.

"It's a pleasure to meet you," Katherine said.

Millicent didn't actually reply with, *I assure you, the pleasure is all yours.* But her sniff and her disapproving look made it clear that she agreed with the scowling subject of the mantlepiece portrait when it came to whether or not Katherine should be here.

"Mr Walker really should have told me earlier that he had hired you to catalogue the books in the library," she said. She had a brisk, clipped way of speaking, as though she was trying to be as efficient as possible even with her words. "I would have been far better prepared for your coming."

Katherine met Millicent's disapproving look with a calm smile. She might have only faulty patches of memory up until the past year, but she had dealt with her fair share of irate doctors at St Thomas's. Wartime conditions in London, with Hitler's planes raining bombs down night after night, had meant that everyone's tempers ran high.

So she said, still smiling, "I quite understand. Mr Walker applied to our firm, requesting the service of a librarian."

Millicent had already been supplied with a card from an entirely fictional antique book auditor's firm with an address in London. There was always a chance, of course, that she or someone else here at Clarion Castle might make inquiries and find out that no such firm existed. But in addition to straining everyone's nerves, the confusion wrought by the Blitz meant that inquiries would be difficult. Countless numbers of businesses had been bombed and then had to relocate from their original address.

"I had tentatively scheduled him for next month," Katherine went on. Had she read somewhere that if you were going to lie, you ought to do it with confidence? Even if not, it seemed like sound advice. "But as it happened, I was able to finish the last cataloguing job I had taken sooner than anticipated, so I was able to come earlier. Mr Walker quite understood that our services are in high demand and that if he did not take advantage of this gap in my schedule, I couldn't guarantee when I might be able to do the job as he asked."

Millicent gave a grudging nod of acknowledgment. "Then I suppose you had better come with me to the library," she said, gesturing towards a door that opened from the back of the drawing room.

"Thank you," Katherine said.

She followed Millicent as the other woman led the way out of the drawing room and through a short hallway, then into another long, high-ceilinged room. Katherine let out a silent breath of relief as a little of the cold and shaking feeling inside her began to evaporate. Really, the library was every bit as grand as the drawing room, but here she felt at home rather than intimidated. Mahogany panelling lined the walls, broken only by towering bookshelves that stretched nearly to the ceiling. The shelves were crammed with leather-bound volumes—many with cracked spines and gilded titles that glinted in the sunlight.

A big, mullioned window at the far end of the room overlooked a small rock garden with clumps of gorse and heather planted in amongst the carefully arranged stones. Wisps of ivy hung over the window, casting shadows on the window seat, which was cushioned in faded green velvet. A pair of high-backed armchairs, upholstered in tufted leather, flanked the hearth. But most importantly of all, the air smelled of furniture polish, leather, and old books.

Katherine didn't remember the time she'd spent working at the British Museum Library, either, but even still the smell was somehow familiar and brought an inexplicable wave of peace.

Millicent clearly didn't at all share Katherine's view of the place. "I assume you have everything you need?" she asked briskly. Her tone implied that the answer had better be, *Yes*. "I really know nothing at all about the book collections, so I'm afraid that I won't be of any help."

"Thank you." Katherine was already letting her gaze travel over the shelves, trying to pick out some of the titles. She could picture coming here on a rainy afternoon, choosing a book, and then curling up on the window seat to read. Of course, that wasn't at all the reason that she was here, but just imagining it made her feel steadier and less nervous. "I'm sure I'll be quite all right."

"I'll leave you to get on with it, then," Millicent said. "I'll send Lillian, our housemaid, along in a bit so that she can show you to the room where you will be sleeping while you work here."

"Thank you," Katherine said again.

Millicent turned to go, then turned back. "Just one other thing," she said. "There's been an . . ." She seemed to pause, searching for words. "An incident here. You may see one or more police officers around the castle. Pay them no mind. They will not interfere with the job you have been hired to perform."

Her tone made it clear that she wasn't inviting either questions or comments, but Katherine decided to ignore that. "Oh? What sort of incident?" she asked.

Millicent was clearly irritated by the inquiry. Then again, she'd been irritated by nearly everything Katherine had said in the course of their conversation.

Katherine wasn't even certain that the older woman would answer, but finally Millicent said in the same clipped tone, "Our first under-butler died recently under unfortunate circumstances."

Katherine wondered whether if she'd had her full memory back, she would be able to recall a more euphemistic way to refer to a murder. She suspected not.

Before she could ask any more questions, Millicent went on firmly, "I'm certain that the matter will soon be—" she broke off with an exclamation of annoyance.

She and Katherine had been standing beside the big mullioned library window, and now Millicent's attention was fixed on something outside.

Following her gaze, Katherine saw a pretty blonde girl wearing the dark dress and starched white cuffs and apron of a housemaid. She was standing in the small rock garden outside the window and talking to a handsome, dark-haired young man in military uniform.

"Really," Millicent muttered. Twin lines of temper had appeared between her brows. "Really, these girls have nothing better to do than to make eyes at the military men." Without bothering to bid

Katherine goodbye, she swept out of the room, and a moment later, Katherine saw her walk briskly up to the blonde girl and the uniformed man. The window glass was too thick for Katherine to hear what was being said, but from her emphatic gestures, Millicent seemed to be telling the young housemaid to go back to the house and get on with her duties.

The girl obeyed, looking sulky, and Millicent walked off in the opposite direction with the dark-haired young man. But Katherine saw the look that the housemaid shot over her shoulder at Millicent's back.

If looks really could have killed, there would have been another murder— or death in unfortunate circumstances as Millicent would put it— right there outside the library window.

Chapter 21
Katherine

Katherine looked up from her notebook as the library door swung open. After Millicent Hartley had gone, she had chosen a shelf at random and begun cataloguing the contents, writing down the title, author, publisher, date, and any notes on the condition of the volume. She assumed that sooner or later, some member of the household was likely to inquire about her work and that she'd better have something to show for it. But really, this sort of corroborating detail was a pleasure.

She'd found a 1755 edition of Samuel Johnson's A Dictionary of the English Language— massive, leather-bound, and gloriously detailed— that had made her catch her breath.

Now she saw a blonde-haired girl in a housemaid's dark uniform entering the room. The same blond girl whom Katherine had seen outside a short while ago, talking to the dark-haired young soldier.

Katherine smiled. "You must be Lillian."

"Yes, miss." The girl bobbed her head. "Miss Hartley said that I was to come along and show you up to your room. They've put you in the east wing."

Seen up close like this, Lillian looked to be about twenty or twenty-one. She was pretty in a conventional way, with blue eyes and a sprinkling of freckles across her nose. Katherine had to credit her; her voice barely changed tone at all when she mentioned Millicent

Hartley's name. Which could mean that she was either exceptionally forgiving, or an exceptionally good actress.

"Thank you. Although I'm not sure that I dare to leave my work just yet." Katherine laughed just a little. "Miss Hartley seems dreadfully exacting. She'd probably try to convince Mr Walker to dock my pay if she thought I was shirking my duties."

While working at St Thomas's, Katherine had found that most people— if they really disliked someone— would jump at the opportunity to talk about that person behind her back. Most of the hospital staff were willing to pull together and work under difficult circumstances, but that hadn't stopped the occasional flare of resentment cropping up between the certified nurses and the VAD girls or between the surgeons and the chemists.

Lillian was no different than the VAD girls had been. She tossed her head. "Don't worry about old Hartless. She likes to try and boss everyone around because she's Mr Walker's private secretary. Thinks she's a cut above the rest of us. But she takes her salary from him, just like we do. And we don't have to answer to her; it's Mrs Winters, our housekeeper, that's in charge of all the domestic staff."

Katherine lowered her voice. "Miss Hartley mentioned that something had happened here at the castle— something involving the police— but she didn't tell me exactly what it was."

"Oh." Lillian cast a quick look around them, although they were still definitely alone in the library. "Yes. Mr Vernon— he's our first under-butler, or he was— was murdered."

"Murdered?" Katherine drew in her breath sharply and clapped a hand over her mouth. She worried momentarily that she was over-acting, but Lillian didn't seem to notice.

"Yes. It was horrible— his throat was cut and there was blood all over. I didn't see it, of course. But our head butler Mr Glenwood did, and I overheard him telling Mrs Winters about it."

Katherine mentally filed that away in her catalogue of facts to remember. If Lillian was in the habit of eavesdropping, there might be other interesting conversations that she'd overheard. "How dreadful," she said aloud. "Have the police any idea who can have done such an awful thing?"

"Oh, the police." Lillian gave a dismissive toss of her head. "I don't know whether they know anything at all. They look rather stuffy and dull to me. But Jim thinks that it was because Mr Vernon got himself mixed up with German spies."

"Jim?"

A faint flush of colour came up into Lillian's cheeks. "Lieutenant Foster. He's part of the Signal Corps working in the Tower Wing."

"Is he the dark-haired man I saw you speaking to outside in the garden?" Katherine gestured to the window. "He's very handsome," she added with a smile. If Lillian continued after the pattern of the hospital VAD girls, she'd also welcome any chance to talk about a potential love affair.

"Yes, that's Jim," Lillian said. "Sometimes when I have a free moment during the day, I can slip out into the grounds to meet him. Unless old Hartless sees us." Her expression darkened. "Just because she wants to chase after Jim herself, she won't let me have a second alone with him if she can help it. As though Jim would look at her twice! With those glasses of hers and that awful way she styles her hair?"

Lillian cast a quick, complacent look into the gilt-framed mirror above the hearth, as though confirming that she was still far prettier than Millicent Hartley.

"Miss Hartley has designs on Lieutenant Foster?" Katherine asked.

"Yes, we all laugh about it in the servant's hall. It's pathetic, really. But I'll tell you something else." Lillian lowered her voice again. "I've heard Miss Hartley was engaged before the war to another man— a German. That just shows the sort of person she is, doesn't it?"

"Well, we weren't at war with Germany then," Katherine pointed out.

"Oh, I know. But still. A foreigner." Lillian made a face.

"What happened?" Katherine asked. "Why weren't they married?"

"I suppose it was rather sad, really," Lillian admitted. "The story I heard was that he had to go back to Germany when the war broke out. And then he was killed in a bombing raid. But I don't suppose old Hartless could really have cared about him, or else she wouldn't be chasing after Jim every chance she gets, would she?"

"Perhaps not." All this might be helpful or it might not, but they'd wandered rather far from Vernon' murder. "So Lieutenant Foster thinks that the man who was killed was a German spy?" Katherine asked.

"That's right. He said that Vernon was always hanging around the Tower Wing, making up excuses to see what they were working on."

"Has Lieutenant Foster spoken to Mr Walker about his suspicions?" Katherine asked.

"I don't think so." Lillian shrugged. "Mr Walker doesn't bother himself much with what goes on in the tower wing. He's too busy with running the estate— oh, and hunting."

"Hunting?"

"Yes, he's always going out after the deer on the estate. He bought a new rifle last month, and it was all I heard about for weeks— Mrs Winters kept telling me how I wasn't allowed to so much as dust it!" Lillian made a scornful face. "As though I don't have enough work to do that I'd want to take on extra without being asked. But we're not allowed anywhere near Mr Walker's gun cabinet. He handles all of that himself."

"So who do you think can have killed Mr Vernon, then?" Katherine asked. "One of the German agents? Or one of ours?"

Lillian looked as though that question had never occurred to her before. Her mouth dropped slightly open and her eyes rounded. "Do you mean that there might be more spies hanging about?"

Katherine was silent for a moment, letting Lillian absorb that. Maybe it would encourage her to be cautious. The housemaid struck her as a bit silly and perhaps more than a bit full of herself. But Katherine wouldn't want to see her get hurt, for all that— and it was settling on her with cold certainty that Clarion Castle could become a very dangerous place.

Chapter 22
Alice

The late afternoon sun cast long shadows across the Pilgrim's Way as Alice trudged onward. The stolid leather hiking shoes she'd chosen for authenticity were proving considerably less comfortable than her usual sensible oxfords, and her feet, unaccustomed to such prolonged walking, protested with each step.

She paused at a bend where the path crested a small rise, giving her a view of the countryside spread out below. In the distance, she could make out the weathered slate roof of her destination—The Shepherd's Rest Inn.

Unlike the main Pilgrim's Way toward Canterbury, this branch of the ancient path had fallen into disuse. Grass and wildflowers encroached from both sides, leaving only a narrow track down the centre. In peacetime, the route would have seen a steady trickle of pilgrims, but war had reduced foot traffic to almost nothing.

Alice adjusted her hat and tightened her grip on her walking staff. Her pack, containing herbal medications, a change of clothes, and her identification papers, felt increasingly heavy as the day wore on. But it wasn't physical discomfort that concerned her—it was time. Somewhere nearby, if her suspicions were correct, Evie was being held against her will.

The Shepherd's Rest emerged fully into view as Alice descended the slope. It was a rambling, half-timbered structure that had clearly seen better days. The whitewash on its walls had faded to a dingy grey, and several roof tiles appeared to be missing. A weathered sign creaked gently in the breeze, its painted shepherd namesake barely discernible.

As Alice approached, she noticed a small Victory Garden to one side, the neat rows of vegetables incongruous against the general air of neglect. A thin wisp of smoke rose from one of the inn's three chimneys, suggesting at least some level of occupancy.

The door groaned in protest as Alice pushed it open. The interior was dim, with low beams that forced her to duck slightly. A stone hearth dominated one wall, though it held only the faintest glow of embers despite the evening chill. The floor was uneven flagstone, worn smooth by centuries of pilgrims' boots.

"Hello?" Alice called, her voice echoing slightly in the empty common room.

After a moment, a curtain behind the small bar parted, and a woman emerged, wiping her hands on a faded apron. She was perhaps fifty, with grey-streaked hair pulled back in a practical bun and a face lined by weather and worry.

"Good evening," the woman said, surprise evident in her voice. "Don't get many travellers these days, especially not pilgrims."

"Good evening," Alice replied, adopting her West Country accent. "I'm hoping for a room for the night, if you have one available."

The woman gave a short, humourless laugh. "Have my pick of rooms, I do. War's taken care of that." She gestured around the empty common room. "Used to be bustling, this place. Now it's just me and my nephew running it, and half the time not enough custom to afford keeping the fire lit properly."

"I'm sorry to hear that," Alice said sincerely. "It must be difficult."

"We manage," the woman replied with the stoic resignation that had become characteristic of wartime Britain. "I'm Mrs Hadley. You can have the room at the top of the stairs, first on the right. Two shillings, including breakfast."

"Thank you," Alice said, counting out the coins from her pilgrim's purse. "I'll be continuing on the path tomorrow. Are there many houses along the way where I might ask for water? It's a warm day for walking."

Mrs Hadley set down the coins in her apron pocket. "Not many, I'm afraid. There's Blair Cottage about a mile on, but I wouldn't trouble them if I were you."

Alice raised her eyebrows in question, and Mrs Hadley leaned in conspiratorially, clearly welcoming the chance for conversation after what must have been a lonely day.

"New tenants," she explained, lowering her voice. "Foreign gentleman and his wife. Keep to themselves."

"Oh? I'll be sure to avoid disturbing them, then."

Mrs Hadley sniffed. "Probably for the best. My nephew—he helps me run this place—said he was out hunting rabbits three nights ago and heard the most peculiar commotion from there. A man crying out and a woman calling after him."

"Goodness," Alice said. "An argument?"

"That's what Archie thought. He's a good lad, worried it might be serious, so he went to check. Foreign gentleman came to the door, calm as you please, said his wife was just helping him through a bad dream about the war." Mrs Hadley's expression suggested she didn't entirely believe this explanation. "Made it quite clear visitors weren't welcome. Almost threatening, Archie said."

"How strange," Alice murmured, her heart racing.

"Strange indeed. And that's not all." Mrs Hadley glanced toward the window, as if checking for eavesdroppers. "Lights at odd hours.

Strangers coming and going. Not the usual sort we get around here at all."

"I'll certainly keep my distance, then. Thank you for the warning," Alice said. "I was wondering, though—is there a telephone I might use? I promised to let my sister know I'd arrived safely."

Mrs Hadley's eyebrows rose slightly. "Modern pilgrim, aren't you? There's one in the back room. Cost you thruppence for a local call."

"Actually, it would be to Clarion Castle," Alice explained. "I have friends working there who are expecting my call."

At the mention of the castle, Mrs Hadley's expression grew more guarded. "Grand connections for a pilgrim," she observed. "That'll be sixpence, then."

Alice nodded, following the innkeeper through the curtain behind the bar and into a small private sitting room. A black Bakelite telephone sat on a side table, looking oddly modern against the room's worn furnishings.

"I'll give you some privacy," Mrs Hadley said, moving toward the door.

When Mrs Hadley had departed, Alice lifted the receiver and gave the castle's number to the operator. After a series of clicks and whirs, the line connected.

"Clarion Castle," came a measured voice that Alice assumed was Glenwood's.

"Good evening," she said. "This is Miss Greenleaf. Could I speak with Inspector Jenkins, please? He's expecting my call."

"One moment, miss."

There was a pause, then Harry's familiar voice came on the line. "Alice? Where are you?"

"At The Shepherd's Rest Inn, about a mile from Blair Cottage," she replied, keeping her voice low. "Harry, I think we're on the right track.

The innkeeper just told me there have been 'strange goings-on' at the cottage—lights and strangers at odd hours, coming and going. And someone heard a commotion—a man crying out and a woman calling after him."

"Could that be Evie?" Harry's tone was cautiously hopeful.

"Not sure, but a man with a foreign accent claimed his wife was helping him through a bad dream about the war."

Harry was silent a moment. Alice could almost see his furrowed brow. Then he said, "There are two ways we could go about this. One, we could march in there at once— tonight— with guns blazing, and demand that whoever's in Blair Cottage open up and let us see who's inside. If I tell Nigel about any of this, I can nearly guarantee that's what he'll want to do."

Alice had been envisioning the possible scene at Blair Cottage that Harry described, but was momentarily distracted. "Has he told Evie how he feels about her, do you know?"

Harry made a sound that was midway between a grunt and an exasperated exhale of breath. "I'm not sure Nigel's even admitted to himself how he feels about her. It takes older, experienced eyes like ours to see it's plain as the nose on his face he's in love with her."

For a moment, they were both quiet. They were separated by miles, and yet Alice felt they were sharing a brief moment of mutual understanding, two people with age and experience who were now able to view the heartaches and yearnings of the young with the clear-eyed view wrought by greater distance.

Then she said, "You obviously don't think that forcing our way into the cottage tonight is the right thing to do, though."

A part of her— the part of her that was desperately worried about Evie— would have liked to do just that. But she went on, "And you're quite right, of course. If Siegfried is the one holding Evie at Blair cottage, he's both clever and ruthless. If he so much as suspects that police are closing in on him, he might well decide to kill Evie so that he can flee without encumbrance."

"Exactly," Harry said. "Our second option is to be more cautious. Wait until we can orchestrate a visit that won't rouse anyone's suspicions."

Alice twisted the telephone cord around her finger. "I shall visit the cottage first thing tomorrow morning."

"Be careful, Alice. Siegfried is dangerous."

"I'll just be a pilgrim asking for water," Alice assured him. "Nothing suspicious about that. I'll see what I can observe without raising any alarms."

"Good. Call again tomorrow if you can."

"Any progress on your end?"

"Blake and Katherine have arrived. They're working on decoding a notebook we found on Vernon's body—the murder victim," Harry explained. "We're hoping it might contain something useful."

"Clues to Evie's disappearance?" Alice murmured.

"Possibly. But we still don't know for certain."

"I'll let you know tomorrow," Alice promised. "I should go now—the innkeeper is hovering."

Indeed, Mrs Hadley had reappeared in the doorway, making a show of straightening a picture frame.

"Take care, Alice," Harry said before disconnecting.

Alice replaced the receiver and thanked Mrs Hadley, who led her upstairs to a small, clean room with sloping ceilings and a narrow bed. The window overlooked the inn's back garden and, beyond it, the dark silhouette of woodland that surrounded Blair Cottage.

As she unpacked her few belongings, Alice's mind raced with possibilities. If Evie was indeed at Blair Cottage, what was happening there?

The story about nightmares seemed dubious at best. And who was the man with the foreign accent? Siegfried himself, or another German agent?

She leaned on the windowsill, staring out at the darkening landscape. Somewhere out there, Evie might be held prisoner. Tomorrow, Alice hoped, she would find out more.

As night fell over the countryside, Alice prepared for bed, methodically organising her belongings for a quick departure the next morning. Her pilgrim's disguise had served her well thus far. She hoped it would continue to do so when she reached Blair Cottage—and whatever secrets it held.

Chapter 23
Evie

The first thing Evie saw when she opened her eyes was Paul's face. She'd fallen asleep after hiding the pound note under the bed last night, and now Paul was leaning over her, his face just inches away from her own.

Evie's heart jolted hard against her ribcage and she couldn't suppress her gasp of shock.

"Sorry. Didn't mean to frighten you," Paul said. His tone was light, but she didn't miss the cold hardness of his gaze or how closely he was watching to see how she would respond.

Evie laughed and sat up. "I know it's been months since France, but I'm still used to waking up ready to defend myself. You're lucky I didn't punch you in the nose."

Paul smiled, too, and she thought the watchfulness of his gaze might have relaxed just a fraction. The coldness, however, remained the same. "I'm sorry to wake you, but we don't have much time. Hans and Gerda are making all the arrangements to move to a new safe house."

"Move?" Evie tried to inject the proper note of surprise into her tone.

"Yes. Standard protocol." Paul grimaced. "And then some of the local folk have been getting a bit too curious about us."

Evie's heart leapt at that, then squeezed itself into a cold clump. Were the local folk just neighbours? Or did that mean that Nigel and the others from Crofter's Green were actively looking for her? Either way, if anyone, friend or neighbour, had already been here, it wasn't likely that they would come back, unless Gerda and Hans had somehow roused their suspicions.

She couldn't let any of what she was thinking show, though, so she cast a look around the dingy, windowless little room and said lightly, "Well, I suppose anywhere else has to be better than this place."

"Yes, not too cheery, is it?" Paul agreed. "I'm sorry about that, darling."

"Oh, I don't mind," Evie said. She drew her feet up, hugging her knees. "If it will help."

"I knew you'd see it like that. You always were game for anything—ready to tackle any problem head-on. By the way, I hear that Hans' headache this morning is thanks to you."

Paul grinned down at her again, and this time, Evie would have sworn that just for a brief flicker, there was genuine affection, or at the very least admiration in his blue-eyed gaze.

For some reason, that flicker of affection made her stomach twist and her whole body flash even colder than his detached scrutiny had done.

She smiled back. "I had to make it look as though I were at least trying to escape. If they know anything about me at all, they'd never believe I would just sit here without a single attempt to get away. Hans should be grateful I wasn't actually trying; otherwise he'd have worse than a headache to complain of this morning."

Paul laughed. "True enough."

"What can I do now?" Evie asked. "There must be something; otherwise you wouldn't have risked coming back here again. Gerda said you were called away; that you were at work on a critically important mission."

She added the last just in case Gerda had already told him of their conversation. She had to be open, Evie told herself. Completely guileless, as though she trusted Paul as implicitly as she would have done during their time as a married couple in London.

Paul nodded. "Yes, there's a job not far—"

"Don't tell me!" Evie interrupted. "You can't give me any details at all. What if I talked in my sleep and Gerda and Hans were to overhear that I knew more than I ought? Or what if they drugged me and I accidentally let something slip? Then they'd know that you confided in me. It would be only one step from there to knowing that you're a double agent!"

"You're wonderful, Evie!" Paul's voice was fervent. "And you're right, of course. I'm just so thankful to be able to see you— speak to you— again that I forget to be cautious."

Evie didn't believe that for a second. But she did think that the taut, watchfulness in Paul's expression had relaxed just a little more. Which meant his seeming slip in beginning to tell her about his mission had been a calculated test. One that she had— apparently— passed.

"So what do you need from me?" Evie asked.

"Well." Paul's expression took on an apologetic look. "I'm afraid my handlers— my German handlers, that is— will be expecting me to get information out of you. Not that I'll tell them the whole truth, of course," he hastened to add. "But if you could give me something— something about what you know of the top brass officials in the SOE, for example— that would give me material to work with. You know how the game works: include just enough truth that your enemy swallows down the convincing lie."

Evie did know. She knew, in fact, that cloaking a lie with a bit of truth was exactly what Paul was doing with her, now. But she kept her bright smile in place. Open. Guileless. "Of course! What would you like to know? Let me see. I met with a man who called himself Mr Brown, although I'm sure that's not his real name. I don't know that— or anything else about him, except that he had a covert office in Threadneedle Street. I can give you the address to that, of course. Although I'm afraid that by this time, he may have moved on to somewhere else. I don't think it was a permanent address."

Paul nodded. "Yes, that's a start. I mean—" he caught himself. "That gives me something to report. How did you first get in touch with Mr Brown?"

This was stepping onto shaky ground. Evie had met with Mr Brown thanks to the intervention of an SOE agent named Diana Lovecraft. Her stomach sickened at the thought of giving Diana away to Paul. But Diana was no longer in Crofter's Green. Evie wasn't even sure that she was still in England. She had been called away on another SOE assignment, and if Diana was any good at her job—which she undoubtedly was— she would have covered her tracks well and would be firmly established with a new cover identity by now, one that Paul and his Nazi friends would have a good deal of trouble in tracking down.

"In Crofter's Green, Lady Hawthorne had an old friend from school staying with her," Evie said with barely a second's pause. "Her name was Diana Lovecraft. Although I'm not actually sure whether that was her real name. I mean, so far as I know, she really had been at school with Lady Hawthorne, but I think she'd made up a fictional married name for herself, to use while she was there. And I never knew what her maiden one was."

Paul nodded with barely concealed impatience. "Is she still there now?"

"No. Mr Brown told me that he'd called her away for another assignment. Of course, he couldn't tell me what it was. I'm sorry I can't be more helpful." She rubbed her forehead. "I think maybe the chloroform is still making me a bit groggy. But I might be able to remember more about Diana. I did have several conversations with her— just about trivialities, really. But maybe there's something I'm forgetting for now that will come back to me later."

Paul nodded again. Evie could still see the tightly masked frustration simmering under his smiling expression. Frustration, and a flicker of something that it took Evie a moment to identify, because it was so completely foreign to Paul's nature: nervousness.

Before this, she would almost have laughed at the very idea of the word being applied to Paul. He was so supremely confident always, so utterly self-assured. But now, without question, he was definitely worried, maybe even uneasy.

The stakes for which he was playing must be high indeed, or else he wasn't quite as securely in the good graces of his Nazi handlers as he'd have liked.

Before he could ask her any further questions, though, Hans' voice came from downstairs. "We are ready."

Paul's lips thinned, but he said, "Yes, we must go now, before it's daylight. Less chance of anyone seeing us." He paused, then his expression took on a look of apology once again. "I'm sorry about this, but I'm afraid I'll have to ask you to take this. To keep up appearances with Hans and Gerda."

Reaching into the pocket of his coat, he drew out a small stoppered glass vial, filled with some clear liquid. A sleeping draught. Chloral, probably.

Or something to make her sleep permanently?

Evie snapped off that thought and thrust it far out of her mind. She couldn't let any hint of anxiety or mistrust creep into her expression or voice. "Of course. I understand. They have to believe that you'd take every precaution to stop me from trying to escape during the journey." She put out her hand for the vial, and when he'd handed it over, she uncorked it and raised it unhesitatingly to her lips. "Will you be there when I wake up?"

Paul smiled as she took the first sip. The taste was the harshly bitter, soapy flavour of chloral, mixed with the syrupy sweetness of sugar that was in theory supposed to make it more palatable. If there was poison in the mixture, Evie couldn't detect it. She drank it all off in a quick gulp, and Paul smiled at her again.

This must have been another test. He took her hand in his, and she forced herself not to shudder at the heat of his skin against her own. "I'm not sure, darling," he said. "But I promise that I'll see you as soon as I'm able."

Chapter 24
Harry

Harry and Nigel made their way through the labyrinthine corridors of Clarion Castle, bound for the records room where they'd been told Miss Hartley was working. The morning sun slanted through tall windows, casting long shadows across the ornate rugs.

"She said she had information," Nigel murmured. "Why do you suppose she failed to appear last night with the others?"

Harry nodded, a familiar tightness in his chest. Ever since Evie's disappearance, each interview felt like walking a tightrope—he had to balance the urgency of finding her against the methodical pace needed to solve Vernon's murder. He straightened his tie, willing his racing thoughts to settle.

"Let's ask her."

They found the door to the records room ajar. Inside, Millicent Hartley was arranging documents with methodical precision. Her sharp, angular features were accentuated by the harsh overhead light, and her copper-coloured hair was still tightly pulled back. Behind wire-rimmed spectacles, her hawkish green eyes scanned the papers before her with unwavering focus, as if searching for discrepancies amid the columns of figures.

"Miss Hartley," Harry said. "We'd like a moment of your time."

She glanced briefly in their direction, her expression impassive. "I'm rather busy preparing for tomorrow's important visitor."

"This won't take long," Harry assured her, closing the door behind them. He felt a flutter of anticipation. From the time he'd first met Miss Hartley, something about her manner had struck him as not quite right. "You said you had information for us, but then you didn't appear. Why was that?"

She sighed, closing the file drawer with a sharp click. "I was occupied with pressing matters."

"Such as?" Nigel opened his notebook.

"Our upcoming governmental visit, of course. I'm sure Mr Walker has told you."

Harry nodded. "So you've been busy."

At her nod, Harry continued, "Although you had time to take Mr Graves for a ride the night Mr Vernon was killed."

A flicker of recognition told Harry that Millicent had been ready for the question. Her reply came only a moment later. "Yes. I drove him into town and back to the castle afterward." Her tone was clipped, each word measured out with careful economy. She offered nothing more.

Harry waited, letting the silence stretch, but Millicent simply stared back at him, arms folded across her leather-bound appointment book. Harry had used this technique countless times in his years at Scotland Yard—the power of uncomfortable silence to draw out information. His patience had often been rewarded by nervous confessions. Yet Millicent's composure didn't crack, and a prickle of unease crept up Harry's spine.

"Why did you drive Mr Graves into town?" he finally asked.

"He was upset. I thought a change of scenery might calm him." Her answers remained tersely minimal.

"Upset about what?"

A flicker of annoyance crossed her features. "Inspector, I have significant responsibilities, particularly with tomorrow's visit. I've told you what you asked—I drove Mr Graves to town and back. Beyond that, I have nothing to add."

Harry felt his jaw tighten with frustration. Each evasive answer reinforced his growing suspicion that Miss Hartley was hiding something crucial.

"Did you see Mr Vernon when you returned?"

Her eyes narrowed slightly. "No."

"Are you certain?"

"I said no, Inspector." She adjusted her spectacles with one precise movement. "Now, if you'll excuse me, I really must finish these preparations."

Harry studied her face carefully, suppressing the urge to press harder. Years of experience had taught him when to retreat tactically. "Did you know that Mr Vernon had recently discovered something hidden in the old keep?"

For just an instant—a moment so brief Harry might have imagined it—Millicent's composure faltered. But her voice remained steady. "I know nothing about that."

The momentary lapse sent a jolt of satisfaction through Harry. A chink in her armour, however small.

"Were you aware of any connection between Vernon and the military personnel in the east wing?"

"Certainly not," she replied, perhaps too quickly. "Mr Vernon had no reason to interact with those gentlemen. Their presence here is quite... compartmentalised."

"I see." Harry nodded thoughtfully. "Thank you for your time, Miss Hartley."

As they left the records room, Nigel murmured, "She wasn't exactly forthcoming."

"No," Harry agreed, a grim smile playing at the corners of his mouth. "But her reluctance tells us something."

They made their way toward the butler's pantry, where they hoped to find Glenwood. Nigel flipped through his notes as they walked.

"Housekeeper Mrs Winters heard an argument between Graves and Vernon the night before the murder. Footman Clegg saw Vernon listening when Walker was discussing the Prime Minister's arrival. Apparently, Miss Hartley showed unusual interest in the wine cellar inventory."

"I ought to have asked her about that." Harry tried to arrange these puzzle pieces.

"And Beatrice Slater saw photographs of the castle and German letters in Vernon's room that later disappeared," Nigel added. "After which, she saw Vernon and Miss Hartley having a serious discussion."

It was all a muddle, Harry thought. How was he ever going to make sense of this jumble of events?

"Then there's Fenton's claim about Vernon using the sommelier's knife at the keep," Nigel continued. "And that paper Vernon was clutching when they found him."

Harry's pulse quickened at the mention of the paper. So many threads seemed to lead back to that mysterious note, and they were about to confront the man who had made it disappear.

They found Glenwood in his pantry, meticulously polishing a silver tureen. The room was a shrine to pristine order—shelves lined with gleaming flatware, glasses arranged by size and type, starched linens stacked in perfect alignment.

"Mr Glenwood," Harry began without preamble, "Tell me about the piece of paper you took from Mr Vernon's dead hand in the wine cellar."

The butler's deep-set eyes widened slightly—the first genuine surprise Harry had seen him display. The polishing cloth froze mid-motion.

"I beg your pardon, sir?"

Harry felt a surge of triumph at the reaction. After all the hours of carefully maintained façades he'd endured, this unguarded moment was refreshing.

"Mr Fenton mentioned seeing you remove something from Vernon's hand before the body was moved," Harry pressed. "A scrap of paper."

Glenwood's thumb moved unconsciously across his ring finger. "I... that is to say... it was merely a wine notation, sir. Nothing of consequence."

"I'll be the judge of that," Harry said firmly. "Why did you remove it?"

"Force of habit, I suppose. Maintaining order, even in... difficult circumstances." The butler's military bearing faltered slightly. "It seemed inconsequential, given the nature of the tragedy."

"We'll need to see that paper, Mr Glenwood."

"Of course." Glenwood carefully set down the silver tureen and the polishing cloth. "I shall endeavour to find it in my quarters immediately."

"And if you see Mr Graves, please ask him to wait for us in the small library."

As the butler departed, Harry examined the meticulously organised pantry, a knot of anticipation forming in his stomach. If his instincts were correct, they were about to discover something significant.

"He certainly values order," Nigel observed.

"Perhaps too much," Harry replied. "Removing evidence from a murder scene goes beyond professional tidiness."

When Glenwood returned minutes later, he handed Harry a small envelope. "Here is the item you requested, sir. As I said, it appeared to be merely a wine notation." His expression showed genuine embarrassment. "Mr Graves is waiting in the small library as requested. He seems... agitated."

Harry's fingers tingled with anticipation as he withdrew a small folded paper. Written in a neat, precise hand was:

VINTAGE SELECTION - SPECIAL GUEST
BOLLINGER RESERVE 1941 - ARRIVAL 4/8 - DECANT 19:35

"Is this in Vernon's handwriting?" Harry asked, studying the paper carefully.

"Yes, sir," Glenwood confirmed. "He was very particular about his penmanship."

Harry nodded, recognising the same neat script he'd seen in Vernon's coded notebook. A quiet thrill of discovery coursed through him.

"Thank you, Mr Glenwood. That will be all for now."

As the butler departed, Nigel leaned forward to examine the note. "Looks innocuous enough. Just wine preparation instructions."

"But it's not," Harry mused, his mind racing ahead, connecting dots. "Why else would Vernon hold this so tightly in death? And why would Glenwood remove it?"

"I see now," Nigel said. "'Special Guest'— that has to be Churchill. 'Arrival 4/8.' Tomorrow's August 4th. And 19:35—that's 7:35 in the evening."

Harry's expression grew thoughtful as he folded the paper carefully and placed it in his pocket. "So this says Churchill arrives tomorrow at 7:35 p.m. Which is highly classified information. Where did Vernon learn that, do you suppose?"

"And why did he write the note?" Nigel murmured. "Who was he going to give it to?"

"We'd only be speculating at this point," Harry said. "Let's see what Mr Graves can tell us."

Five minutes later, they stood in the doorway of the small library, exchanging concerned glances. The room was empty. Harry felt a cold weight settle in his stomach.

"I thought Glenwood said Graves was waiting here," Nigel said, scanning the shadowy corners between the bookshelves.

Harry frowned, a sense of foreboding washing over him. "He did."

"Perhaps he stepped out for a moment?"

A quick search of the adjoining corridor and rooms yielded nothing. Simon Graves had vanished. Harry's jaw clenched as he fought back a wave of frustration.

Chapter 25
Dorothy

Working first at the King's Arms and then at the Cozy Cup had given Dorothy a knack for reading people. She'd been able to look at a group of men and peg the one that would turn out to be a nasty drunk, even before she'd served him so much as a pint of ale. She could also usually tell which of the ladies who came in for a cup of tea would be the agreeable sort and which would be the complainers.

But she'd never had quite as bad a feeling as she had this morning, as a man she'd never seen before came through the Cozy Cup's front entrance.

She wasn't even sure why the man made her feel that way. On the outside, he didn't look like the sort to turn nasty. He was somewhere around forty, of middle height and neither fat nor thin. He was wearing a tweed suit and a grey felt hat, and his face, too, was just ordinary. Not handsome, but certainly not ugly, either. He was clean-shaven, with brown eyes and a slightly cleft chin.

And yet Dorothy's skin started crawling from the moment he set foot inside the tea room. He stood in the doorway a second or two, letting his gaze travel over the customers who were already seated and drinking their tea. There weren't many. It was only nine o'clock, and most of the Crofter's Green women who were out and about were still doing their marketing. Between ten and eleven was usually the Cozy Cup's busiest time.

Right now, though, there were only Mrs Benton and a couple of her friends at one table, talking over the latest village gossip— which so far as Dorothy had overheard involved a rumour that Mrs Ellison's blackout curtains weren't quite up to standard, and a report that the vicar's niece had signed on to be a land girl and was now wearing trousers and driving a tractor.

The stranger seemed to dismiss all of them with a cursory glance. He sauntered over to the counter where Dorothy had been restocking their array of cakes in the glass bakery case. Rationing forced her and Evie to be creative with the baking side of the business, and today she'd made an eggless sponge cake, oatcakes, and what their government-issued recipe book called a 'wartime tea loaf.' The loaf was sweetened with dried currants and sultanas soaked in tea instead of sugar, and it had smelled surprisingly good while baking, so with any luck it would go down all right with today's customers.

"Can I help you?" Dorothy asked the stranger.

His gaze flicked over the selection of baked goods in the case, although Dorothy could tell that he didn't actually care what was inside. His brown-eyed gaze might just be the coldest she'd ever seen. Maybe that was what was making her skin crawl.

"I'll take one of those." His voice wasn't unpleasant, exactly. He didn't growl or snarl, but it had an oddly flat quality. He pointed to one of the oat cakes.

Dorothy took one of the cakes out, wrapped it in waxed paper, and set it on the counter. "That'll be tuppence, please."

The man dug in his pocket and produced the coins. Then he suddenly leaned an arm against the counter and smiled. The smile made Dorothy feel even more uneasy than his cold-eyed stare. It was as though he'd quickly and deliberately put on a mask that would let him pretend to be friendly. "I drove past a grand-looking stone house on the way here. Would you know what it's called?"

Dorothy couldn't think of a good way to avoid answering. She might be wrong about the stranger, and even if he was up to no good, she'd only put herself and everyone in the tea room in danger if she let him know that she was onto him. "That would be Hawthorne Manor," she said.

"Hawthorne Manor?" The man's smile remained firmly fixed in place, though it didn't come anywhere close to his eyes. "Do you know, I believe I know someone who was staying there earlier this year. Diana Lovecraft, her name was."

Dorothy was startled. "Yes. Mrs Lovecraft is a friend of Lady Hawthorne's." She couldn't imagine why the man should be asking about her, though. Or rather, she could think of a reason, but it wasn't a sinister one. Diana Lovecraft had always seemed willing to bat her eyelashes at any male under ninety.

Maybe she'd been wrong about the stranger? Goodness knows, she was worried enough about Evie these days. Maybe that worry was making even perfectly ordinary people seem threatening.

The next moment, though, Dorothy was certain she hadn't made a mistake. The man rested his hand on the counter, trying to look casual, but Dorothy could tell he was feeling anything but. "Is Diana still staying up at the hall?" he asked.

"No. She went back to London a few months ago, or so I heard from Lady Hawthorne."

"London? I don't suppose you'd happen to have her address?" the stranger asked. "I'm on my way there now, as it happens. I'd love the chance to look her up."

Dorothy shook her head. "No, I haven't got her address." And if she did, she certainly wouldn't give it to this man.

The stranger's brow furrowed as though he were trying to remember something, but the expression was about as convincing as his smile had been. "What was her last name, again, before she married Mr Lovecraft?" he asked.

"No idea, I'm afraid," Dorothy said. "I hardly knew her."

"Ah well. Thank you anyway." The man took his oat cake, tipped his hat, and walked out.

There was a brief hush of the ladies at the table as he passed them by, and then, when the door had shut behind him, Mrs Benton said, "That fellow is up to no good."

It was about the only time Dorothy could think of when her own opinion entirely matched Mrs Benton's. The question was: what was she going to do about it? She thought fast. Then she quickly untied her apron strings at the back and hung the apron on the hook behind the counter.

"Mrs Benton, can you mind the shop for me for a little while?"

Mrs Benton was a heavyset, matronly woman with stiffly permed grey hair and a determined chin who looked like nothing on earth short of a hurricane would move her. But she actually looked flustered at that.

"What, me?"

"Yes." Dorothy spoke quickly. "I'm afraid you're right. That man was asking too many questions. I'm going to go after him and see that he doesn't cause any harm."

"I— I—" Mrs Benton looked even more flustered. "Well, of course, but do be careful—"

"I will be; don't worry." Dorothy didn't know whether the stranger would still be within sight of the tea room's front entrance, so she ducked into the kitchen, where she could go out the back door and keep out of sight of the main road.

Back in the tea room, she could hear Mrs Benton and her cronies already gasping and exclaiming and murmuring that they hadn't at all liked the look in the man's eye and that his expression had definitely been sinister.

Well, if nothing else came of today, at least they'd have fresh news to talk over for weeks after this and could give the subject of the vicar's poor niece a rest.

Chapter 26
Alice

A cool morning mist clung to the hedgerows as Alice stepped outside The Shepherd's Rest, wincing slightly. Even after a night's rest, her sturdy walking shoes were no less stubbornly stiff and chafing. She'd broken the cardinal rule of long walks—never wear new footwear—and her feet protested vigorously. If only she'd brought her comfortable old oxfords instead. But she'd thought the walking shoes would look more authentic for her role as a pilgrim bound for Canterbury.

Alice had mixed feelings about her 'pilgrimage.' Though raised in the Church of England tradition, her scientific education had led her to a more questioning stance on matters of faith. Still, she couldn't deny the historical significance of the tradition. For centuries, countless souls had trodden this path seeking spiritual solace or miraculous healing at the saint's shrine. But she was taking this journey with an entirely different purpose—seeking only to find her friend. The pretense of piety made her feel somewhat uncomfortable.

"Will you be returning for another night, miss?" Mrs Hadley called from the doorway, wiping her hands on her apron.

"I'm not certain," Alice replied, adjusting her modest hat. "I'll let you know by midday."

The innkeeper nodded. "If you do stay, we'll have shepherd's pie tonight. My sister's recipe—won first prize at the village fête three years running before the war."

"That sounds lovely," Alice said with genuine enthusiasm.

"Mind yourself if you pass Blair Cottage. Strange folk, as I told you."

Alice smiled noncommittally and set off down the narrow unpaved road. The morning air was crisp against her face, but the cloudless blue sky promised warmth later. Dew sparkled on spiderwebs strung between blackberry brambles, and birdsong accompanied her laboured steps.

She passed a small roadside shrine—a weathered stone niche containing a faded statue of St James, patron saint of pilgrims. Someone had recently placed wildflowers at its base. Even in wartime, old traditions persisted in this timeless corner of Kent.

The village of Clarion was just visible in the distance, its church spire rising above the morning mist. Smoke curled upwards from cottage chimneys, and on the ground Alice could see tiny figures moving about—women hanging laundry, children walking to school, the routines of village life continuing as they had for generations.

Despite her discomfort, Alice felt a surge of determination. Somewhere ahead, Evie might be held captive. Every minute could matter. She quickened her pace, ignoring the protests from her feet.

The road showed recent tire tracks—two distinct sets, one wider than the other. A car and perhaps a motorcycle, Alice guessed. Both appeared fresh, cutting through the softer parts of the dirt road where morning dew had dampened the surface.

Around a bend, a rickety gate, with a faded sign that read 'Blair Cottage,' hung from its hinges at the entrance to a flagstone path. At the end of the path was a modest stone structure with a slate roof and small windows, set back from the road. On either side of the path was an untended garden now overgrown with summer wildflowers.

Alice approached cautiously, her senses alert for any sign of movement. The cottage stood silent; no smoke rose from its chimney. The curtains in the front windows hung limply, and the door stood slightly ajar.

"Hello?" she called. "Might I trouble you for some water? I'm a pilgrim on my way to Canterbury."

Only silence answered her.

With a quick glance around to ensure she wasn't being observed, Alice pushed the door open wider. It creaked on its hinges, the sound unnaturally loud in the morning stillness.

"Hello?" she called again, stepping inside.

The cottage was deserted. The front room was sparsely furnished with a worn sofa, a small table, and two wooden chairs. A fireplace dominated one wall, a dusting of cold ashes in the grate. Everything was tidy—too tidy, as if someone had carefully removed all personal traces.

In the adjoining kitchen, Alice found cupboards standing open and empty. A kettle sat on the cold stove, and a single mug rested upside down on the still-damp draining board. Whoever had been here had cleared out thoroughly and recently.

A narrow staircase led to the upper floor. Alice climbed it carefully, each step creaking beneath her weight. The upper floor contained a tiny bathroom and two bedrooms. Both bedroom doors stood open, revealing three iron bedsteads, two in one and a single in the other. All were stripped of bedding. The mattresses were bare, and the small wardrobes stood empty.

In the larger of the two bedrooms, Alice noticed faint rectangular marks on the wall—pictures or maps recently removed. The smaller bedroom showed signs of hasty departure: a drawer partially open, a scrap of paper on the floor. She stooped to pick it up, but it was blank.

The bathroom yielded nothing beyond a bar of soap and a worn-out toothbrush.

Alice descended the stairs, her initial hope deflating with each step. If Evie had been here, she was gone now—taken elsewhere, perhaps to another hiding place. The thought sent a chill through her despite the warming day.

Outside again, Alice noticed an elderly man tending to a vegetable patch in the neighbouring field. She approached him, adopting her pilgrim's demeanour.

"Good morning," she called. "Might I ask you a question?"

The man straightened, one hand pressed against his lower back. "Mornin'," he replied, eyeing her curiously. "Don't see pilgrims much these days. Used to be dozens passing through come summer, before the war. Heading to St Thomas's shrine, were you?"

"Yes," Alice nodded, automatically touching the pilgrim's badge she wore, an imitation of the small metal ampullae medieval pilgrims would have carried to collect holy water from the shrine. "Though I was hoping to find the people at Blair Cottage first. I need water for my journey, but the house seems empty."

"Gone," the man said, nodding. "Heard a car before dawn, I did. Woke me up—not many vehicles about at that hour." He squinted at the sun. "Must've been around four this morning."

"The people who were staying there—did you meet them?"

"Foreign gentleman and his wife," the man said, leaning on his garden fork. "Kept to themselves, they did. Barely saw the wife—ill, the gentleman said. Though..." He paused, lowering his voice. "Funny sort of illness that lets you argue loud enough to wake the neighbours."

Alice's pulse quickened. "Arguments? When was this?"

"Two nights back. Terrible row, sounded like. Then quiet, like someone had clapped a hand over a mouth." The old man shrugged. "Not my business, mind you. Name's Wilkins, by the way. George Wilkins. Been tending this patch since before you were born, I reckon."

"A pleasure to meet you, Mr Wilkins. I'm... Agnes," Alice replied, using her pilgrim alias. "Have you lived in Clarion long?"

"All my life. My father was born in that cottage there," he gestured toward a small stone building farther down the lane. "Village hasn't changed much, thank the Lord. Though we've fewer young men about now, with the war."

"Of course," Alice agreed. "Thank you for the information. Is there a telephone nearby? I need to let my sister know I won't reach Canterbury today after all."

"Shepherd's Rest has one," the man said. "Or the post office in the village. Mrs Potter runs it—opens at nine sharp, never a minute early or late. Makes excellent seed cake too, if you're peckish."

Alice thanked him and hurried back to the inn, her mind racing. Her feet protested with every step, but her disappointment outweighed the pain. If only she'd come to the cottage last night instead of resting! She might have found Evie still here, might have been able to help her.

As she walked, she passed a farmer driving a cart pulled by an ancient Shire horse, the massive animal plodding patiently along the lane. The farmer tipped his cap to her, a gesture of country courtesy that warmed her heart despite her worries.

At The Shepherd's Rest, she paid for the telephone call and waited impatiently as the operator connected her to the castle, and then as the butler went to bring Harry.

"Miss Greenleaf?" Harry's voice came through after an eternity of moments.

"Harry, I'm at The Shepherd's Rest. Blair Cottage is empty—completely cleared out. A neighbour heard a car leaving before dawn this morning."

Harry's exclamation was muffled, as if he'd turned away from the receiver. Then, clearly: "Any sign of Evie?"

"I didn't find any. Two bedrooms, both stripped. But there's evidence of a couple staying there—neighbours mentioned an ill wife and arguments. It could have been Evie and someone posing as her husband."

"Sit tight, Alice. Nigel and I will be there as quickly as possible. There might be something we can use."

"Harry, I'm sorry," Alice said, unable to keep the disappointment from her voice. "If I'd gone to the cottage last night instead of waiting—"

"You did exactly right," Harry interrupted firmly. "Going alone at night would have been dangerous. We'll be there within the hour."

As Alice replaced the receiver, Mrs Hadley hovered nearby, poorly disguising her interest.

"Everything all right with your sister, then?" the innkeeper asked.

"Yes, thank you," Alice replied, remembering her cover story. "I'll be staying another night after all. My... brother-in-law is coming to meet me."

"Well, that's nice," Mrs Hadley said, bustling about straightening the small sitting room. "Family should stick together, especially in times like these. I'll put out some fresh scones when he arrives. Made them this morning—old recipe from my grandmother. She used to feed the pilgrims who came through, back when the shrine was more popular. Said it was good luck to help a pilgrim on their journey."

As she waited in the inn's small sitting room, Alice couldn't shake the feeling that they'd missed something crucial by mere hours. Evie had been so close—and now she was gone again, taken to some new hiding place.

But where?

Chapter 27
Dorothy

Dorothy pushed open the back door to her own cottage and called out, "Hello? Tom?"

She'd run all the way home from the Cozy Cup, taking the back lanes and cutting across fields. She'd had to crash through a couple of hedgerows and leap over a ditch. She was out of breath and had one foot covered in mud, and she had burs in her hair. But she'd covered what was usually a ten-minute walk in probably less than five minutes. She hadn't seen the brown-haired stranger on the road, either. If she was guessing right, he'd be heading in the opposite direction right now, straight towards Hawthorne Manor.

Tom didn't answer, though.

Her kitchen was empty, the curtains fluttering a little in the hot summer breeze, the breakfast dishes that Tom and Tommy must have used neatly stacked in the draining board by the white porcelain sink.

Dorothy tried again. "Tom?"

Then the door to the kitchen swung open and Dorothy's mother appeared.

"Are you looking for Tom, dear?"

Dorothy's mum was a small woman, delicate and more than a bit frail looking, with a cloud of white hair surrounding her blue-eyed face. She suffered terribly with rheumatism, but this must be one of her good days because she was up and dressed, wearing a navy cotton print dress with a blue cardigan over top.

"Don't you remember?" Mum asked Dorothy now. "He's working at the Bainbridges' in the mornings this week. He walked Tommy over to school and then went straight over there."

That's right. Dorothy's heart sank. She had entirely forgotten, but an elderly couple who lived on the other side of Crofter's Green had hired Tom to build some new cabinets for their kitchen. Dorothy was happy for Tom— thrilled, really. Tom had lost a leg while he was fighting in the war; that was why he'd been invalided home.

Dorothy would never stop being grateful that he had come through alive and was now back home safe, but she knew Tom had worried a lot about being a cripple and a burden. Him having the chance to earn a living for them again was something that she'd hoped and prayed for. Just now, though, she'd have given almost anything to have found him at home this morning.

Should she run over to the Bainbridges'? But they lived clear across the village, over near the school. By the time she could get there, find Tom, and then bring him with her up to Hawthorne Manor, it might well be too late.

"What did you need him for?" Mum asked.

"Oh, nothing much." Dorothy pasted on a smile. She didn't want Mum to worry. "I just wanted to see what he was up to this morning."

"Dorothy Ann Baker." Mum drew herself up and fixed Dorothy with the kind of look she'd given Dorothy when she was six and had been caught with her hand in the biscuit tin. "I may be old, but I've not yet lost the use of my eyes or my common sense. You're supposed to be working over at the tea room this morning, but instead you come bursting in here, out of breath and looking like you've been dragged through a hedge backwards. Tell me what's happened!"

Dorothy sometimes forgot that though Mum might be frail looking, she still had plenty of grit left in her. That was the reason she was able to carry on cheerfully, no matter how much pain she was in.

"A man came into the Cozy Cup," Dorothy said. "I can't explain everything; it would take too long. But I'm certain he's a bad lot and I'm afraid he's on his way up to Hawthorne Manor now and that he may hurt Lady Hawthorne."

"We could telephone to the police?" Mum said.

Dorothy shook her head. "I'm not even sure anyone's left at the station. Inspector Brewster and his constables will all be up at Clarion Castle looking into the murder there."

Her mind was spinning. If only she could telephone to Tom. But the Bainbridges weren't on the telephone, and the nearest neighbour who did have a telephone lived a mile down the road and was an elderly woman, besides. By the time Dorothy could get old Mrs Cope to go and give a message to Tom, something awful might have already happened—

Mum, though, didn't hesitate. She interrupted Dorothy's racing thoughts. "Then take your father's service revolver. It's in the top drawer of my nightstand."

Dorothy had always known, of course, that her dad had served in the last war. But she hadn't realised that Mum still kept his sidearm. "Do you know how to load it?"

Mum clicked her tongue. "Of course I do. Your father showed me whenever he had to be gone overnight taking the sheep to market. He didn't like to leave me alone on the farm without a way to defend myself if need be. You go and fetch the revolver. I'll telephone to the police, just in case there's anyone left on duty who might be able to help."

Chapter 28
Harry

Harry scanned the passing landscape as Nigel's little Ford Prefect sped down the narrow country lane. The familiar car had been a deliberate choice—less conspicuous than a larger police vehicle. Nigel navigated the corners with skill, but each bend in the road felt like precious seconds lost.

They were bound for their meeting with Alice, heading toward the inn where she had spent the night and from which she had telephoned this morning.

Harry glanced at his nephew's tense profile, recognising the barely contained anxiety behind his professional demeanour. Nigel had never spoken openly about his feelings for Evie, but Harry had observed enough to know.

"Are you certain we shouldn't have brought backup?" Nigel asked, slowing slightly for a farmer's cart before accelerating again.

"If Siegfried is behind this, he's likely to have informants," Harry replied gently. "The moment uniforms appear, he'll know we're onto him."

The car crested a hill, revealing a pastoral vista of rolling fields dotted with grazing sheep. In the distance, the distinctive slate roof of The Shepherd's Rest came into view.

"There," Harry pointed.

Minutes later, they pulled into the inn's small gravel forecourt. Alice was waiting on the front step, her wide-brimmed hat and pilgrim's disguise making her almost unrecognisable until she stepped forward.

"Harry, Nigel," she greeted them with visible relief. "Thank goodness you're here."

Mrs Hadley appeared in the doorway behind her, eyes widening with interest at the sight of the two official-looking men.

"This is my brother-in-law," Alice explained quickly, gesturing to Harry. "And his colleague. They've come to escort me the rest of the way to Canterbury."

"Very nice," Mrs Hadley replied, though her expression suggested she wasn't entirely convinced by this explanation. She studied their polished shoes and Nigel's precisely knotted tie with obvious suspicion. "Would your... relatives care for some refreshment before continuing your pilgrimage?"

"Perhaps later," Harry said with a polite nod. "We'd like to stretch our legs first after the drive."

Once they were safely out of earshot, walking along the lane, Alice filled them in on the details she'd discovered at Blair Cottage.

"The neighbour, Mr Wilkins, heard them arguing two nights ago," she explained. "Then sudden silence, 'like someone had clapped a hand over a mouth,' he said."

"That fits with Evie being held against her will," Nigel said, his voice tight with controlled emotion.

Harry placed a steadying hand on his nephew's shoulder. "We'll find her, Nigel."

Blair Cottage stood as Alice had described it—a modest stone structure with an air of abandonment about it. The front door remained slightly ajar, swinging gently in the breeze.

"I've gone through the main rooms," Alice told them as they approached. "Nothing obvious left behind."

Harry nodded, his eyes scanning the surroundings as they entered. Years of investigative experience had taught him that houses, like people, revealed their secrets reluctantly.

"Let's be methodical," he instructed. "Nigel, take the kitchen and front room. Alice, check upstairs again—cracks, crevices, loose floorboards. I'll examine the garden and outbuildings."

As the others set to work, Harry circled the cottage's exterior. The garden had been neglected long before its recent tenants arrived—weeds grew between flagstones, roses sprawled untrimmed, and a wooden bench had cracked and weathered to silver-grey. A small shed stood at the back, containing only garden tools thick with cobwebs. Nothing used recently.

Inside, Harry found Nigel on his hands and knees, examining the hearth with an intensity that spoke volumes about his determination to find any trace of Evie.

"Nothing yet," his nephew reported, brushing dust from his knees as he stood. "Though the ashes have been thoroughly cleaned out—not a scrap left behind."

Harry climbed the narrow staircase and found Alice examining the walls of the larger bedroom.

"These rectangular marks," she said, "were where pictures or maps hung, I think. Recently removed."

Harry nodded and stepped back into the hallway. "I'll check downstairs again. Nigel, can you take this smaller bedroom?"

"Of course," Nigel replied, moving past them into the room with the single iron bed.

Harry descended to the ground floor and resumed his methodical search. He circled the front room, tapped walls, checked behind furniture, and examined the cold hearth more thoroughly.

Meanwhile, upstairs, he could hear Nigel's footsteps moving across the floorboards, and then the creak of the bed frame as Nigel presumably checked beneath the mattress.

"Harry?" Nigel's voice called from above, a new note of excitement breaking through. "Alice? I think I've found something."

They hurried upstairs to find Nigel on his knees in the smaller bedroom, his fingers working delicately at the junction of the floorboard and wall.

"There's something wedged here," he said, producing a small pocketknife from his jacket. "Just the tiniest corner showing."

Harry watched as Nigel worked the blade into the crack with surgical precision, gently easing the hidden object free. His nephew's hands trembled slightly—not from lack of skill but from what Harry recognised as hope and fear intertwined.

"Got it," he murmured, holding up what appeared to be a tightly folded banknote.

Harry's heart quickened as Nigel carefully unfolded the paper on the bare mattress. It was an ordinary pound note, but along one edge, written in a minute hand that Harry immediately recognised as Evie's, was a column of figures:

1 pound 5 shillings

22 shillings 8 pence

3 pounds 9 shillings

5 shillings 6 pence

"It's a code," Harry said softly. "Evie left us a message."

He could see how Nigel's expression transformed at this concrete evidence of Evie's presence—relief and renewed determination washing across his features.

"But what does it mean?" Alice wondered, leaning closer.

Nigel studied the figures, his forehead creased in concentration. "Wait... the shillings. If we convert them to letters of the alphabet..."

Harry nodded encouragingly. "E is the fifth letter..."

"And V is the twenty-second," Nigel continued, excitement building in his voice. "I is ninth, and E is fifth again."

"EVIE," Alice breathed. "She signed it. She was definitely here."

"And wanted us to know it," Harry added, watching Nigel carefully fold the note and place it in his breast pocket. At least they now had confirmation that they were on the right track. Evie was alive and coherent enough to leave them a clue.

"But where is she now?" Nigel asked, his professional demeanour reasserting itself, though Harry could see the personal stake that drove his nephew's determination.

Harry moved to the window, looking out at the peaceful countryside that suddenly seemed full of hidden threats. "They must have another safe house. Somewhere else they could move her quickly."

Nigel asked, "Anything else you noticed, Alice? Any clue to their destination?"

She shook her head. "Just the tire tracks on the road—a car and what looked like a motorcycle."

"A motorcycle?" Harry's attention sharpened. "That's an unusual choice for someone moving a captive."

"Unless..." Nigel began.

"Unless they separated," Harry finished the thought. "Siegfried—if it is him—might have sent Evie with an accomplice in the car while he took the motorcycle elsewhere."

"And if he knows about Churchill's visit to the castle ..." Nigel's voice trailed off, thick with tension.

Harry checked his watch. Just past noon. They still had over thirty hours until the Prime Minister was scheduled to arrive at Clarion Castle tomorrow evening. Not much time, but perhaps enough if they moved quickly.

"Alice, can you see if you can learn anything else from your Mr Wilkins?" he asked. "Then head back to Shepherd's Rest. On your way, you might check with other cottages along this road. Someone might have seen which direction they went."

"And if no one has?" Alice asked.

"Nigel and I will be at the castle. You can telephone us there."

As they hurried outside, Harry couldn't shake the image of that pound note, with Evie's distinctive handwriting leaving them both hope and warning. She was clever, his friend—resourceful enough to leave them a message even while captive.

He glanced at Nigel, seeing the carefully controlled worry beneath his professional exterior. For both their sakes, he had to maintain an optimistic front, though his own concerns ran deep.

He only hoped Evie would remain safe until they could find her. And that they could unravel Siegfried's plot before it was too late.

Chapter 29
Dorothy

As Dorothy, circled around towards the back of the Hawthorne Manor estate, her heart was pounding like a drum, and whatever she was breathing felt too thick and viscous to be called air. The manor's spreading green lawn was backed by a wooded hillside, and she hugged the tree line, trying to stay as much as possible out of sight.

Over the past months, an entire wing of the manor house had been converted into a hospital for wounded soldiers. Originally, Lady Hawthorne had planned to live in the other wing, but the noise of the construction and the ambulances coming and going at all hours had made her decide to live in the dower house.

The dower house was a smaller place—although it was easily three times the size of Dorothy's own cottage— about half a mile from the main manor, that had been built for the original Lord Hawthorne's mother-in-law. Dorothy had debated on the way here how best to approach. Should she just go up and ring the front door?

But she didn't know what kind of a nightmare mess she might be walking into. Maybe the stranger was trying to pass himself off as a friend of Diana Lovecraft's, as he had down at the Cozy Cup, and was politely asking Lady Hawthorne civil questions.

But maybe he was even now threatening Lady Hawthorne at gunpoint, and Dorothy would be heading straight into the line of fire if she just walked in openly.

Like everywhere else around here, Hawthorne Manor had to operate with a far smaller staff than before the war. All the young men were off fighting, and even unmarried women between 20 and 30 were now being drafted into the WRENS or the WAAF or another branch of the service or the civil defence departments.

Dorothy knew that Lady Hawthorne had moved into the dower house with only her own ladies' maid and the elderly butler. All three of them were getting on in years; it wouldn't take much for the stranger to overpower them.

Of course, Dorothy could have stopped off at the manor and tried to get help from one of the doctors or staff there. But that would inevitably take time— time to convince whoever she found that she hadn't lost her marbles, babbling about German spies here in Crofter's Green. And time was what Dorothy was almost certain that Lady Hawthorne didn't have.

She stopped now, leaning against the trunk of a thick oak tree so that she could peer out towards the square, brick-built dower house. She could see windows of the sitting-room — which was surely where Lady Hawthorne would have greeted any visitor— but she couldn't see anything of what might be happening inside. The sunlight was too bright. She couldn't see anyone else about, either. Just like up at the manor, the back garden was planted with victory plots of potatoes and cabbage, but there was no sign of the gardener.

Dorothy took another painful gulp of air and then before she could change her mind, ran across the garden towards the small paved veranda at the back of the house. Her dad's service revolver was a heavy weight in her pocket, banging against her leg with every step. But she reached the veranda safely. No shouts, no one rushing out to meet her.

As she pressed herself against the outer wall, though, she did hear voices. She'd fetched up next to the tall French windows that opened out from the sitting room, and the voices were coming from in there.

First a man's voice, raised and angry— but she recognised it at once as the dark-haired stranger's.

"Don't lie to me!"

"I'm not lying!" That was Lady Hawthorne's voice, sounding as though she were near to tears. "I have no idea at all what you're talking about!"

"You can cut out the innocent act," the man growled. "Diana Lovecraft stayed here for months, posing as an old school friend of yours. You're expecting me to believe that you had no idea she was with the SOE?"

"The SOE?" Lady Hawthorne sounded as shocked as Dorothy felt. Although if Mrs Lovecraft had been an agent for the Special Operations Executive, that would explain why the stranger was so interested in her. "No! Diana and I were at school together. I—"

Her voice cut off abruptly, and Dorothy heard the sound of a ringing slap, as though the man had struck Lady Hawthorne across the face.

Dorothy's own hands curled into fists at her sides. Lady Hawthorne was gentry, born with a silver spoon in her mouth. But she was still a good sort, and she'd been through enough hardship and sorrow lately. Her husband had died less than a year ago.

"Answer me!" the man's voice was a harsh growl. "Where is Diana Lovecraft now?"

"I don't know!" Lady Hawthorne was openly weeping now, her words coming between choked sobs. "I'm telling you the truth; I haven't heard from Diana in months!"

"Stop sniffling, or I'll shoot you here and now," the man barked.

Dorothy squeezed her eyes shut. She now knew that the stranger had a gun— and he was probably a lot more skilled with it than she would be with her dad's old service revolver. Help would be nice, but none seemed to be on hand. If Mum had reached anyone at the police station, they hadn't made it up to the manor yet—

Something cold and wet touched Dorothy's ankle. She was so startled she almost let out a shriek, but managed to stop herself and look down. Bonzo, Lady Hawthorne's little Pomeranian dog, was nudging at her with his nose.

Dorothy blew out a hard breath. "You're not exactly the help I was hoping for," she muttered, "but I suppose beggars can't be choosers."

The fur around Bonzo's neck was raised and he was growling, teeth bared, at the pane of window glass. Dorothy hadn't risked looking in yet, but Bonzo could probably see the stranger there, threatening his mistress.

Now, if only the French door was open. Her heart pounding, Dorothy took the revolver gingerly out of her pocket, though she kept the safety catch on. She wasn't entirely confident she wouldn't shoot her own toes off in a struggle. Then, with her other hand, she reached out and pressed down on the handle that opened the door. It moved easily. The door swung open, and the stranger must have been too busy threatening Lady Hawthorne to notice, because he went right on, growling another demand to know where Diana Lovecraft was now.

Maybe Bonzo was all the help Dorothy needed after all, because the instant the door opened wide enough, he was off like a shot, rocketing through in a blur of russet-coloured fur. Still gripping the revolver, Dorothy followed and was in time to see the little dog launch himself forward and sink his teeth into the dark-haired man's leg.

The man let out a bellow of pain and outrage and shook his leg, trying to fling Bonzo off. But Bonzo hung on, still snarling and growling.

Dorothy sprang forward. She'd been terrified up until a second or two ago, but now she felt oddly calm. Every detail of the room seemed unnaturally clear: the big black revolver clutched in the stranger's right hand; Lady Hawthorne cowering on the sofa, with the red mark of the stranger's hand livid on her cheek.

Dorothy moved past her and struck the dark-haired man's gun hand with the grip of her own weapon.

He'd been too distracted by Bonzo to even notice her entrance. He shouted something incoherent again, but the weapon dropped from his grasp and landed with a clatter in the fireplace grate.

Dorothy pointed her own revolver at him. "Don't move," she said.

The stranger's cold, hard gaze flicked from her face to the gun in her hand. Dorothy tried not to let herself tremble as she wondered whether she could actually bring herself to shoot him. But she didn't get the chance to find out.

The man whirled around and raced for the window, leaping through the French door and out onto the veranda. The movement was so sudden that Bonzo was flung aside, although the little dog wasn't hurt. In a split second, he picked himself up and tore after the stranger, yapping and snarling and finally vanishing through the window.

Chapter 30
Blake

Blake Collins settled himself at the small writing desk by the window of his assigned guest room at Clarion Castle. Late morning sunlight slanted across the polished oak surface, illuminating the leather-bound notebook before him—the late Mr Vernon's mysterious journal.

Blake adjusted his position, stretching his right leg carefully to ease the familiar ache. The leg had improved considerably over the past weeks, thanks in no small part to Tom Baker's determined coaching during their rehabilitation sessions, but still, extended periods of sitting inevitably brought back the pain.

He reached for his fountain pen, then paused, checking his watch. Katherine would return from her exploration of the castle library in approximately forty-seven minutes—she was nothing if not punctual, even with her memory still fragmented. The thought brought a mix of emotions: gratitude that she was alive and with him again, mingled with a persistent ache that she couldn't remember their engagement or their life together before the bombing.

"Focus, Collins," he murmured to himself, returning his attention to the notebook.

Vernon's handwriting was meticulous—small, precise characters arranged in columns. Blake recognised the structure immediately. This was a simple substitution cipher.

Blake began with a fresh sheet of paper, tearing off two strips and writing the letters of the alphabet on each one. Then he took another sheet of paper and turned to the notebook. After adjusting the two alphabet strips, he began to write. A knock at the door interrupted his concentration.

"Come in," he called, not looking up from his work.

The door opened to reveal Katherine, her golden hair pinned neatly back, a stack of books in her arms. Blake felt the familiar catch in his breath at the sight of her. How many times during those bleak months had he dreamed of seeing her again?

"I thought you'd be in the library until eleven," he said, checking his watch again.

Katherine smiled—that same smile that had first captivated him four years ago at a mathematics symposium. "Mrs Cartwright arrived to catalogue the first editions. I didn't want to disturb her."

Blake nodded, understanding completely. In their cover roles—he as a journalist researching architectural features, she as a rare books expert—they needed to maintain a certain professional distance from the castle staff.

Katherine set the books down on the small table near the window and peered over his shoulder. "Vernon's notebook?"

"Yes. Harry hopes I'll find something useful."

Blake gestured to his preliminary work. The two strips of paper each contained the letters of the alphabet in order. The second strip, however, contained an additional '*a*'. Lining up the two strips with the '*a*' of one strip beneath a certain letter in the second—the key letter—would make for an easy conversion. Provided there wasn't some other twist involved.

"So, it's just a straight substitution cipher?" Katherine asked,

"I think so. But I haven't found the key letter."

"How far have you gone?"

"I'm at d." He would have gone further, of course, if he hadn't been daydreaming about Katherine, but he didn't want to tell her that.

"So, only 22 to go, then." She gave a bright smile and continued, "But, after all, the man wasn't a cryptographer. He used a simple code just because he wanted to keep his notes safe from prying eyes as he was writing them. Perhaps we can make an educated guess."

"Then guess away," Blake said, a wave of affection washing over him. This was the Katherine he'd fallen in love with—brilliant and intuitive, but completely grounded in common sense. He didn't add that her presence beside him, the subtle floral scent of her, the warmth of her arm so close to his shoulder, made concentration considerably more difficult.

"May I?" she asked, reaching for the two strips of paper.

"Please."

She lined up the two strips so that the 'a' at the end of the second strip was beneath the 'v' of the first.

Blake quickly applied the substituted letters to the first two words of the notebook text.

He read aloud, "Important visitor."

"Got it in one," Katherine said.

They worked through the journal in companionable silence, Katherine transcribing onto a clean sheet of paper while Blake dictated. This felt achingly familiar—the two of them tackling a puzzle together, minds working in harmony. As he dictated, Blake wondered if something about the process would help Katherine recover her memory.

But Katherine gave no indication of that as she wrote out the words. Finally they were done. Now it was time to see what meaning they could extract from the decoded notes.

THE MURDERS AT CLARION CASTLE 163

Katherine moved the pages she'd written closer to Blake, so that they both could see them. Once again, Blake felt the warmth of her presence alongside him.

"This is odd," Katherine said, pointing to a passage. "Vernon writes about observing 'unusual interactions' but he's frustratingly cryptic about who's involved."

Blake nodded, scanning further. "He refers to them only as 'M' and 'S.C.' throughout. And mentions a third party, designated simply as 'visitor.'"

"He was being cautious," Katherine observed. "Perhaps he wasn't certain who could be trusted. After all, he must have had some reason to use a code."

"A good reason, it seems." Blake turned the page, finding a new entry. "Listen to this: 'Have discovered messages hidden in loose stone. Copied and replaced originals. Trust no one yet, not even W.'"

"W being Walker?" Katherine asked.

"Most likely." Blake was already dissecting the implications. "Vernon was playing a dangerous game—intercepting messages but leaving them in place to avoid alerting whoever left them."

"Blake," Katherine said softly, pointing to the final entry, dated the day before Vernon's death. "Look at this."

The passage read: "S.C. showed particular interest in main tower again today. Claimed routine maintenance. Must speak with G about wine discrepancies first, then consider whom to trust with this information."

"G could be Graves," Blake murmured. "The second under-butler. He would have been familiar with the wines."

"Vernon was investigating something about the main tower," Katherine said. "But he never got the chance to follow through."

Blake nodded grimly. "We need to tell Harry what we've found."

They made their way downstairs, Blake moving with efficiency and, he thought, not showing weakness to Katherine. He was glad that the exercises with Tom had strengthened muscles long neglected.

Still, by the time they reached Harry's temporary office on the ground floor, perspiration beaded his forehead.

Harry looked up from his desk as they entered, his expression brightening. "Blake, Katherine—tell me you've found something."

"Vernon had suspicions about the staff," Blake explained, handing over his transcription. "He was tracking their activities, though he's deliberately vague about identities."

Harry's eyes narrowed as he scanned the decoded passages. "M and S.C.—any ideas?"

"Likely initials of the names he had for people," Blake suggested.

"He discovered messages hidden in a loose stone at the keep," Katherine added. "And made several cryptic references to the castle's main tower."

Harry nodded thoughtfully. "Anything about tomorrow evening?"

"Not directly," Blake said cautiously. "But Vernon's first words in the journal are 'important visitor.' That entry was made two weeks ago. If that was the date he learned about the PM's visit, it could be the reason for his investigations."

"Can you two work on what he might be hinting at—about the main tower?"

"Of course." Blake exchanged a glance with Katherine. More time with her—just what he'd been hoping for. He hoped she felt the same.

"Then I'm going to find Nigel," Harry said. "We'll take another look at that loose stone."

Chapter 31
Harry

Harry squinted up at the looming silhouette of the castle keep. What was it hiding?

Its jagged battlements towered above a high stone wall, stark against the sunlit clouds overhead, a grim and ancient sentinel no longer needed to protect the adjacent main 'castle' and elegant Victorian manor house. Today, according to the coded notes Vernon had recorded in his journal before he died, someone was using it for another purpose.

"So, the loose stone?" Nigel asked, noting his uncle's contemplative expression.

"Indeed," Harry replied, taking a glance at the immaculate lawns behind them. No one else was in sight. "Let's find it," he said.

They approached the imposing structure, Harry assessing the perimeter. The keep was a square-angled Norman tower, perhaps fifty feet tall and roughly thirty feet on each side, built of local stone that had weathered to a mottled grey-green. Unlike the main house with its ornate embellishments, this building was plain, nearly windowless, designed for practical storage and defence in a simpler age.

"Too bad Fenton wasn't specific about the location," Nigel said, consulting his notebook.

"That would have been too easy," Harry replied with a slight smile. "We'll need to do some walking."

As they circled the base of the ancient tower, Harry couldn't help noticing how the structure dominated this section of the grounds, offering excellent views in all directions, except where it was blocked by the sprawling bulk of the newer main castle.

"There's the door," Nigel said, pointing to a heavy oak entrance reinforced with iron bands. "But where's the lock? Glenwood and Fenton both said the door was padlocked."

Harry's eyebrows rose as they drew closer. The padlock that should have secured the entrance was missing, its iron hasp hanging empty.

"It appears we're not the first visitors today," Harry murmured, exchanging a meaningful glance with Nigel.

They continued their circuit of the keep's exterior, examining the stonework with careful attention. On the western face, partially concealed by a climbing rose that had been allowed to grow wild, Harry spotted what they were seeking—a section where one of the stones protruded slightly from the otherwise uniform wall.

"There," he said softly, pointing. "Near the ground."

Nigel knelt beside the area Harry had indicated. The stone in question was roughly the size of a bread loaf, and unlike its neighbours, showed signs of recent disturbance. Fresh scratch marks marred its surface, and the ancient mortar around its edges was nearly all scraped away.

"Someone's been here quite recently," Nigel observed, brushing away a remnant of mortar dust.

Harry nodded, crouching despite the protest from his knees. "Can you remove it?"

Nigel worked his fingers carefully around the edges of the stone, finding purchase where the mortar had been deliberately weakened. With a gentle tug, the block came free, revealing a dark cavity behind it.

"Empty," Nigel said, reaching inside to confirm.

"But recently used," Harry added, noting the absence of cobwebs or settled dust that would indicate long abandonment. "The question is, what was here? And more importantly, who removed it?"

A soft scrape of footsteps from the keep's open doorway caught their attention. Both men turned to see.

Simon Graves stood frozen in the entrance, his normally immaculate appearance dishevelled. The second under-butler's eyes widened at the sight of them. His scarred eyebrow twitched nervously. In his right hand, he clutched what appeared to be a small leather pouch.

For a heartbeat, the three men stared at each other, motionless.

Then Graves bolted.

He darted back into the keep with surprising agility for a man of his age. Harry was on his feet in an instant, years of police work overriding the protests of his aging joints.

Harry sped toward the keep's entrance. "Circle around the back!" Harry called to Nigel. The younger man nodded sharply, breaking into a run toward the rear of the structure where a second, smaller door might offer Graves an escape route.

As Harry entered the keep's shadow-filled interior, his eyes adjusted quickly to the dimmer light. The ground floor inside was largely empty save for a few wooden crates stacked against one wall and the remains of what might have been a medieval hearth. Shafts of sunlight streamed through the narrow wall slits where, long ago, archers would have been stationed. Dust motes danced briefly in the sunbeams before vanishing into the surrounding shadows.

The sound of hurried footsteps echoed from the spiral block staircase that led to the upper levels. Harry followed, taking the worn stone steps two at a time. The staircase wound clockwise, a defensive design that favoured right-handed defenders. Harry kept his right hand against the central column, using it to pull himself forward as he climbed.

The tower had three levels, with the staircase continuing up to a battlement walk at the top. Harry's breath came harder as he ascended, a reminder that retirement had put more years between him and his prime than he sometimes cared to admit. Still, the thrill of the chase was familiar, awakening muscle memories from decades of similar pursuits through London's back alleys and up to the rooftops of tenements.

"Stop, Graves!" Harry called, his voice echoing against ancient stone. "There's nowhere to go!"

The footsteps above faltered briefly, then continued upward with renewed urgency. Harry pressed on, and finally emerged onto the second level to find another empty chamber, this one with larger windows offering glimpses of the surrounding countryside. There was no sign of Graves, but the sound of shoe leather on stone continued above.

Harry took a moment to catch his breath, listening carefully. The footsteps had reached the top—Graves had climbed the stairs all the way to the battlements. A tactical error, Harry thought with grim satisfaction. Unless the man planned to sprout wings, he'd effectively cornered himself.

The final flight of stairs brought Harry out onto the open roof of the keep. The view was spectacular—rolling Kentish countryside spreading in all directions, the main house of Clarion Castle gleaming in the midday sun, and the distant spire of the village church rising above the trees. Under other circumstances, he might have paused to appreciate the panorama.

But Graves had to be dealt with. The under-butler stood against the far parapet, breathing heavily, his face pale with fear or exertion or both. In his right hand, he still clutched the leather pouch.

Harry positioned himself between the man and the staircase. "Nowhere to go, Mr Graves," he said. Experience had taught him that cornered suspects were at their most dangerous. "Unless you're considering a permanent exit."

Graves' eyes darted to the edge and back. Harry tensed, ready to lunge forward if necessary, but the man's shoulders slumped in defeat.

"I didn't kill him," Graves said, his voice hoarse. "I swear I didn't kill Vernon."

"I didn't say you did," Harry replied reasonably. He took a careful step forward. "Why don't you hand me whatever you're holding, and we can discuss this like gentlemen?"

For a moment, it seemed Graves might comply. Then a door slammed somewhere below, and the under-butler startled like a frightened animal. He darted suddenly to Harry's left, and made for the staircase.

Harry pivoted, years of rugby and police work guiding his movement, and he managed to catch the sleeve of Graves' jacket. The fabric held for a critical second, slowing the man's momentum. It was all the time Harry needed to step into Graves' path and use the under-butler's own forward motion to unbalance him.

They grappled briefly, Harry's experience compensating for the other man's desperate energy. He twisted Graves' arm behind his back in a standard restraint hold, careful not to apply undue pressure.

"That's quite enough of that," Harry said firmly, as footsteps pounded up the stairs. Nigel emerged onto the roof, slightly winded but moving with purpose.

"Found the back door locked," Nigel explained. "Circled back around."

"And just in time to help escort our friend here downstairs," Harry said, maintaining his hold on Graves, who had stopped struggling.

Nigel quickly took over the restraint as Harry recovered his breath. The older detective bent down and retrieved the leather pouch that had fallen during the struggle.

Inside the pouch was a padlock and a small key. The padlock looked like it might fit the empty hasp Harry had seen earlier. Also in the pouch were several folded papers—handwritten notes in what appeared to be a foreign language, possibly German.

"Interesting reading material, Mr Graves," Harry observed.

The under-butler's face was a mask of misery, his earlier defiance completely evaporated. "It's not what you think," he said weakly.

"I think," Harry replied, fixing Graves with the steady gaze that had broken many a suspect in his Scotland Yard days, "that you have quite a lot of explaining to do."

"I didn't kill him," Graves repeated, more desperately now. "Someone put that knife in my hand..."

Harry's eyebrows rose at this unexpected news. He exchanged a glance with Nigel, whose expression mirrored his own surprise.

"Perhaps we should continue this conversation somewhere more comfortable," Harry suggested. "The library, perhaps?"

Nigel nodded. His firm but professional hold on Graves' arm never wavered as they headed for the stairs.

As they descended through the ancient keep, Harry turned the small key over in his palm, wondering what lock it might open—and what secrets that might reveal. One thing was becoming increasingly clear: Vernon's murder was far more complex than a simple case of wine theft gone wrong.

By the time they reached the ground floor, Graves had regained some composure, though his customary polish remained distinctly tarnished. Harry paused by the open door and looked back at the keep's shadowy interior.

"I think we might just replace the padlock," he observed mildly.

He took the lock from the leather pouch, secured it onto the hasp, and snapped it shut. "Why did you break in?" he asked.

"I didn't break in," Graves replied, a hint of his usual precision returning to his voice. "I have a key to all the outbuildings."

"You're not in a position to bandy words, Graves. What were you doing inside?"

"When I saw you coming, I thought you might be the one who put the pouch in the outside cavity. So I wanted to hide. Then I saw it was you. And then I, well ..."

"You panicked?" Nigel asked.

Graves nodded. "I'm not very good at this sort of thing."

"And the loose stone outside?" Harry asked. "Had you just taken the pouch?"

Graves wouldn't meet his eye. "I was going to see what was inside and then put it back."

"Just like that?"

A reluctant nod.

Harry studied the under-butler with renewed interest as they walked back toward the main house, the leather pouch weighing heavily in his pocket.

They reached the library and took seats inside. "Now, Mr Graves," he said, his tone deceptively gentle, "tell us about the last time you saw Mr Vernon."

Chapter 32
Harry

Harry watched as Graves sank back into the library chair. The man's composure seemed to be crumbling further with each passing moment.

"So, the last time you saw Mr Vernon alive?" Harry prompted.

"It was the afternoon before he died." Graves swallowed hard. "He wanted to check the wines for the Prime Minister's visit. For a moment, I thought he was insinuating that more bottles were missing, but he wasn't. We parted on good terms."

"Then what happened?"

A shudder passed over him. He shook his head and lowered his gaze. "I don't want to think about it."

"Mr Graves," Harry said carefully, "We need the whole truth, and we need it now. What happened next?"

Graves stared at his trembling hands. "I'm afraid— "

But at that moment, the library door opened. Glenwood, the butler stepped inside, tall, grey and very properly deferential.

"Inspector, I apologise for the interruption. Some officials from London are here. I thought you might like to join them."

Churchill's security detail, Harry thought. "Where?"

"In the Minstrel's Hall, sir."

"Please thank them and tell them I'll join them in a few minutes."

Glenwood closed the door quietly. Harry turned his attention back to Mr Graves.

"You were saying?"

Graves lifted his head, drew a deep breath, and seemed to have gathered some courage. "I'm afraid that I killed him."

Graves' words hung in the air, stark and heavy.

Harry exchanged a glance with Nigel. "Start from the beginning."

"Mr Vernon caught me stealing wine from the cellar," Graves said, in a quavering voice. "Vintage bottles from obscure corners that I thought wouldn't be missed. He threatened to tell Mr Walker."

"Did he follow through on that threat?" Harry asked.

"No. He promised to keep it quiet if I stopped. And I did stop," Graves added hastily. "That was only three days ago."

Harry leaned forward slightly. "And then?" Harry prompted.

"That was when he brought me down to the wine cellar to check on the supply for our visiting guests. As I said, we parted on good terms."

"And then?"

"I decided to go into town, to the White Horse—to celebrate my reprieve." Graves ran a hand through his hair, disturbing its careful arrangement. "Miss Hartley drove past and offered me a lift. Said she wanted to talk."

"About what?"

"She didn't say at the time. But when we got to the White Horse and ordered drinks, it turned out that she wanted to talk about my drinking." A bitter laugh escaped him.

"She didn't approve?"

"She said it was becoming excessive. So naturally, I had another drink, and then another. Then she mentioned hearing that Mr Vernon was going to speak with Mr Walker about me after all. I felt betrayed. Furious."

Harry watched Graves carefully. "What happened when you left the pub?"

"Miss Hartley said I'd had enough. She drove me back to the castle." Graves looked up, his face pale. "Everything was fine when we left."

"She'd stopped criticising your drinking?"

He gave an ironic smile "Actually she was taking a different tack about it. She said she'd rely on me to do the right thing."

"When did she say that, exactly?"

"As she was dropping me off at the castle. I was getting out, and she was going to park the car. So just to spite her, I toasted her with my flask as she drove away. Took a good long pull, I did. Then I went in through the kitchen entrance. After that... nothing."

"Nothing?"

"I don't remember anything until I woke up in the wine cellar. I had a bloody sommelier's knife in my hand and blood on my clothes, and I was lying on the floor alongside Mr Vernon's body."

And you smeared the blood on the wine cellar floor when you got up, Harry thought.

He asked, "The flask was yours?"

Graves' brow furrowed. "Yes, of course it was."

"What did you have in it?"

"Cognac." He shook his head with another ironic smile, tinged with, Harry thought, both vanity and self-loathing. "My usual solitary tipple. I had the White Horse barman fill it while I was... using the facilities. He brought it back to the table."

"What did you do after finding yourself beside Vernon?" Nigel asked.

"I panicked," Graves said. "I got out as quickly as I could. I used my key to lock the wine cellar from the outside, made sure no one was around, then ran to the swimming pool. I dived in fully clothed to wash off the blood, then took a terrycloth robe from the pool house. I went to my room and tried to sleep, but that was impossible."

"What time was this?"

"About two AM. I have a clock in my room and I kept staring at it."

"And the next morning?"

"At breakfast, Mr Glenwood wanted some wine bottles brought up and was wondering where Mr Vernon had gone. I said I hadn't seen Mr Vernon since the previous afternoon. Mr Glenwood said well, then, he'd just have to get the bottles himself, and then..." Graves trailed off. "Then he found the body."

Harry nodded. "Mr Graves, did you know Mr Vernon kept a notebook? He documented things he observed around the castle."

"I'd seen him writing in it," Graves confirmed. "He always had it with him."

"It was found in his coat pocket," Harry said. "Did you see anyone take an interest in his notebook, or ask him about what he was writing?"

Graves thought for a moment. "Miss Hartley once. I overheard her asking what he was always scribbling about. Vernon said it was wine inventories, but I could tell he was lying."

Harry nodded. "Mr Graves, one last question. Has Miss Hartley had any unusual interactions with anyone that you've observed?"

Graves shook his head. "I haven't noticed anything. Though Vernon did mention her and the lieutenant once."

"Which lieutenant?"

"I don't know. The young lieutenant, I think he said. I didn't catch a name. He said something cryptic about how people ought to behave professionally."

Harry exchanged a meaningful glance with Nigel. "Thank you, Mr Graves. You've been very helpful."

"What happens now?" Fear returned to the man's voice. "I swear I can't remember even going into the wine cellar that night, let alone actually killing Mr Vernon. Do you believe me?"

"I believe there's more to this story than meets the eye," Harry replied carefully. "For now, return to your duties as normal. Say nothing of our conversation to anyone. We're taking a chance on you, but don't let us down, or we'll have no choice but to throw you straight into a cell."

After Graves departed, Harry opened the leather pouch and took time to examine its contents. The notes were indeed in German, and Harry couldn't read them. He'd give them to—who? He realised he didn't know who among the sleuths—other than Evie, of course—could help. Maybe Blake could. Maybe Alice. Or if not, who? Who could translate, but also be relied on?

"Knockout drops in his flask," Nigel was saying. "That would explain his memory loss."

Harry came back to earth. "Agreed," he said. "Why don't you have a chat with the barman at the White Horse."

He tucked the pouch into his inside pocket. "Meanwhile, I'll join that meeting with Mr Churchill's security team."

Chapter 33
Evie

Evie woke slowly. Her body felt heavy, as if she'd been pinned to the mattress, and a bitter, chemical taste lingered on her tongue. She swallowed against the dryness in her throat and tried to understand why, despite the dull fatigue that enveloped her, her stomach was also clenched with a feeling of urgency. She had to wake up. She had to—

What? Her mind felt like a spinning radio dial, with bursts of a broadcast coming in through loud static.

The bare, windowless room.

A glass vial of chloral.

Paul's face—

Evie sat bolt upright as the entirety of the memory landed in her head with what felt like an almost palpable thunk. Paul. And Gerda and Hans. They'd moved her during the early hours of the morning, away from wherever she'd been held captive before.

So where was she now? And exactly how long had she been unconscious?

Evie rubbed the lingering haze from her eyes, trying to clear her vision enough that she could take in her surroundings. Her previous room had been windowless and plain: four square walls and a single door. Now she seemed to be in a garret. The walls were sharply slanted, crafted of bare, dusty boards without any plaster or paint.

There was a single dormer window, though: a grimy square of glass, set high in the wall directly in front of her.

The window wouldn't do her any good as an escape route; Evie doubted anything larger than a cat could get through. But it did enable her to see that it was still light outside, with the sun just beginning to sink down towards what must be the western horizon. She couldn't see anything else, though. Just that small patch of sky.

Evie stood up, looking around for something that she could climb on. Also unlike her original prison, the garret wasn't entirely bare. It bore signs of having been hastily cleared out. There were scuff marks in the dust on the floor and bare patches where boxes and barrels must have stood until very recently. But there was an old-fashioned iron bed frame leaning crookedly against the far wall, its springs rusted and broken, and beside it, a small writing desk sat buried under a stack of yellowed newspapers. A needlepoint footstool that looked as though most of the stuffing had been chewed by mice sat beside the desk, and she could also see a few old hat boxes shoved into the shadows under the eaves.

Evie dragged the stool over to the window and stepped up so that she could peer through the glass. She still couldn't see much, but by craning her neck she was able to make out the tops of some oak trees down below her and far away in the distance a thin ribbon of road winding through what looked like wheat fields. But nothing to tell her where exactly she was. Once again Paul had found a place that seemed to be entirely isolated.

As she watched, a car drove along the road, but it was so far away that it looked like a child's toy. No chance that whoever was driving the car would hear her, even if she managed to break the window and somehow miraculously call for help without alerting either Gerda, Hans, or Paul.

Evie tried shoving at the window, but it must have been painted shut. If she had a knife or something else to use for prying, she might be able to budge it.

Then again, if she were armed with a knife, she'd use it to better advantage than just prying open a tiny window.

Evie stepped down and debated momentarily on whether to continue her search through the attic. There might be something of use in either the desk or one of the boxes. But in the end, she crossed to the door, which was another depressingly solid panel of heavy, age-hardened wood. The knob didn't turn when she tried it— not that she'd been expecting that it would.

Evie pressed her ear to the door, trying to hear anything from the other side. She assumed Gerda and Hans must be somewhere on guard down below. But was Paul still in the house, or had he gone on to wherever his important assignment was going to carry him?

She couldn't hear anything at all when she tried to listen. No voices. No footsteps. Not even a creak of floorboards. After a moment or two, she gave up and was just about to turn towards the writing desk when she felt a vibration and heard the slam of a door from somewhere down below. An outer door; the sound had come from just below the small dormer window.

Evie leapt back onto the stool and pressed her face against the glass once again. She still couldn't see anything but the trees and distant hills, but she heard a voice that was definitely Hans's say, in German, "When will you return?"

He must be standing outside the house directly below her. And Paul must be with him, because it was his voice that answered in the same language.

"Not until tomorrow or the day after. I must make sure that all the final arrangements have been made."

"I don't like to rely on someone else's weapons," Hans grunted. He sounded sullen.

"That is the beauty of the scheme," Paul said. "We need not worry about trying to smuggle anything onto the site."

Evie leaned forward. If she pressed any harder against the window glass, it was going to shatter. She willed Paul to keep going, to say more. But instead Hans asked, "What about the woman?"

Paul's answer came without hesitation. "I don't think that she can be of further use to us. She has told me all she knows."

Any slight feelings of satisfaction that Evie might have had at Paul's belief that she'd told him everything were immediately cancelled by the eagerness in Hans' voice as he asked, "Should I dispose of her then?"

"She might still have some value as a hostage," Paul said. "Let us get through these next two days. Then if all has gone according to plan, we can get rid of her."

Evie heard the slam of a car door, followed by the roar of a motor that quickly grew distant and faded. She stepped away from the window, her heart drumming in her ears. Bitterness that had nothing to do with the lingering taste of chloral rose in her throat.

She shouldn't be hurt or even shocked. She'd already known exactly what sort of man Paul really was. She shouldn't be surprised that he'd spoken of killing her with the same detached indifference that he might have used when talking about stomping on a garden grub. No. What she needed to focus on was finding a way out of here before Paul's mission—whatever it might be— was over and her time ran out.

Later she could think over the implications of what she'd overheard from Paul and Hans and try to decide whether she'd learned anything useful. Right now, she needed a plan of her own.

Evie crossed to the writing desk and started pulling out dusty drawers, though her mind was racing so hard that she scarcely registered the contents.

Tomorrow or the day after, Paul had said, when asked when he'd be back. That meant she had at least twenty-four hours in which to find a way to escape.

No. She stopped and corrected herself. She had twenty-four hours to discover just what it was that Paul and Hans were planning and then to stop them. Then and only then could she worry about trying to get free from here.

Because, so help her, she wasn't going to let Paul succeed, not even if the price to stop him was her own life.

Chapter 34
Harry

Harry's mind still churned over Graves's story as he approached the Minstrel's Hall. Should the man be arrested? He hoped Nigel would learn something useful from the barman at the White Horse.

For now, though, any decisions about Graves would have to wait.

Harry had this meeting with Churchill's security team to contend with. What suspicions ought he to disclose? Or should he disclose anything at all? It was hard to see how the murder of an under-butler could connect with a plot against Britain's most important citizen.

Except that, if there was such a plot, and if Vernon had learned of it, that definitely would have been cause to kill him.

As Harry reached the ornate double doors, Clegg, the young gangly footman, stepped forward to announce him.

"Inspector Jenkins, sir," the young man said, swinging the door open.

Three men were standing by the fireplace at the far side of the enormous room. They all turned as Harry entered.

Mr Walker stood in the centre, his pale eyes catching the late afternoon light, that characteristic arched eyebrow rising slightly in acknowledgment. To his right stood a thin, austere man in a charcoal suit that Harry immediately marked as a Whitehall official. But it was the third man who drew Harry's attention—a towering figure with broad shoulders and an unforgettably stoic expression.

"Walter Thompson," Harry said, a smile warming his face despite the gravity of circumstances. "It's been some years."

The tall man's impassive features softened slightly. "Jenkins. Still with that deceptively friendly old Dutch uncle look about you."

"And you still could pass for a cigar-store wooden Indian," Harry returned. Both were referring to the barbs they'd endured during their days at Scotland Yard.

A flash of genuine warmth crossed Thompson's face, gone as quickly as it appeared. "The years have been kind to you, Harry. Retirement suits you."

"Some of us know when to put our feet up," Harry replied with a pointed glance. "Others insist on following bulldogs across continents."

Thompson's mouth twitched—the closest he ever came to a smile in professional settings.

Walker cleared his throat. "Inspector Jenkins, this is Mr Hargreaves from the Prime Minister's office. We were just finalising the arrangements for tomorrow evening."

Hargreaves extended a thin hand. "Inspector. I understand you've been assisting with a local matter here at Clarion."

"A matter that has grown rather more complicated than it first appeared," Harry replied, measuring his words.

"Indeed," Hargreaves said, his tone carefully neutral. "I trust it won't interfere with the Prime Minister's visit?"

"That's precisely what I want to ensure," Harry said, meeting the man's gaze steadily.

Walker gestured to the nearby seating arrangement. "Gentlemen, please. We have details to confirm."

They settled around a low table where a map of the castle grounds had been spread. Walker produced a silver fountain pen and indicated the main driveway. "We thought this would be the appropriate point of entry. I'll have the gatehouse attendant open up as soon as we see your arrival."

"Which will be at precisely 7:35 tomorrow evening. The PM will be in his armoured Rolls," Thompson stated, his voice deep and authoritative. "I will be in the vehicle with him, as will his valet, two guards, and, of course, the chauffeur. A second car will follow with secretaries and other officials."

"A dozen in total," Hargreaves added. "Including myself."

"And the dog," Thompson said with the faintest hint of resignation. "The Prime Minister's poodle accompanies him everywhere these days."

Walker nodded. "All arrangements have been made for their comfort. We've prepared the west wing bedrooms, and Mr Churchill will occupy my suite. I'll be moving into the east gatehouse for the night."

A generous show of hospitality, Harry thought. He wondered if the sacrifice was part of Walker's negotiating strategy.

"The Prime Minister will wish to freshen up before dinner at eight," Hargreaves continued. "The following morning will be dedicated to discussions regarding steel contracts. After luncheon, we depart for Dover."

Harry noted something in Thompson's expression—the slightest tightening around the eyes when Hargreaves mentioned Dover. There was more here than was being shared.

"Mr Thompson," Harry said carefully, "I imagine you'll want to inspect the rooms before the Prime Minister's arrival?"

"Tomorrow, my two guards will precede us into the castle," Thompson confirmed. "They'll conduct a thorough search of every room the Prime Minister is expected to enter. However, I'd like to take a preliminary look, if Mr Walker permits."

"Of course," Walker said. "Inspector Jenkins can accompany you, if you wish. He knows the castle well by now."

"That would be helpful." Thompson heaved his massive frame up from the chair.

"I'll remain to discuss the list of steel contract points with Mr Walker," Hargreaves said, removing a slim leather portfolio from his briefcase.

Harry led Thompson into the grand entrance hall. As they climbed the main staircase, Harry observed his old acquaintance with a policeman's eye. For more than two decades, Thompson had been Churchill's bodyguard—a position requiring unwavering vigilance and absolute discretion. Those qualities were evident in his careful scanning of each doorway, each corridor.

"So, Jenkins," Thompson said as they reached the landing. "Tell me about this murder you're investigating."

"My nephew is handling the official investigation," Harry replied. "I'm just an advisor."

Thompson gave a short, unconvinced nod. "You were always a poor liar, Harry. What's really going on here?"

They had reached Walker's suite, where the Prime Minister would be staying. Harry paused before the door, weighing his next words carefully.

"There's evidence to suggest the man's murder may be connected to something larger. Possibly involving German intelligence."

Thompson's expression didn't change, but Harry detected the slightest hesitation before he reached for the door handle. "Show me the rooms first. Then we'll talk."

They proceeded through the suite—a spacious sitting room with a writing desk, tall windows overlooking the grounds, a bedroom with a massive four-poster, and a modern bathroom with fixtures that had been specially imported from America.

Thompson inspected everything with methodical care—testing the windows, examining the fireplace, checking beneath furniture.

"This will do," he finally said. "Now, about these German connections."

Harry provided a concise summary of the evidence—Vernon's coded notebook, the mention of the 'important visitor,' the German communications found in the keep, and the suspicious activities of Mr Graves. He deliberately omitted any names, watching Thompson's reactions carefully.

Thompson listened without interruption, his face revealing nothing. When Harry finished, the tall man walked to the window and gazed out at the magnificent grounds.

"I can't tell you everything, Harry," he said finally, his voice lower than before. "But I'll say this—we've received intelligence suggesting a possible threat to the Prime Minister during this visit. Nothing specific, mind you. Just enough to put us on heightened alert."

"Walter," Harry said carefully, "if there's any way I can help—"

"We'll handle the Prime Minister's security," Thompson interrupted, turning from the window. His expression once again might have been carved from wood. "You focus on your investigation. If either of us feels there's a connection, we can talk further."

There it was—that strange detachment, as though Thompson was holding something back. Harry had known the man long enough to recognise the signs.

"He won't be negotiating steel contracts all morning, will he?" Harry ventured.

Something flickered in Thompson's eyes. "The Prime Minister's schedule is confidential, Harry. You know that."

"I also know he rarely rises before noon if he can help it," Harry replied mildly.

Thompson's mouth twitched—almost a smile. "Some things never change, indeed."

As they returned to the grand staircase, Harry felt that much remained unsaid between them. Whatever Churchill's true purpose in visiting Clarion Castle might be, Thompson wasn't sharing it. And he was relying on Harry to unravel whatever secrets might connect the murder of Mr Vernon with the PM's visit.

Harry had less than twenty-four hours to unravel those secrets before Churchill's motorcade wound its way up the castle drive.

Chapter 35
Harry

Harry met Blake at the top of the terraced south garden. The mathematics teacher was leaning on his cane, studying the castle's façade, the ornate features casting complex shadows in the late-afternoon sunlight.

"What have you found?" Harry asked without preamble.

Blake waved his cane to point upward, towards the east wing. "That tower has a direct line of sight to the entry drive. Anyone inside would have an unobstructed view of arriving vehicles."

Harry followed Blake's gaze. The tower stood prominently at the corner of the east wing, its narrow windows like watchful eyes surveying the grounds.

"And so?" Harry asked.

"So it's the perfect vantage point for someone monitoring arrivals and departures. Or for someone with more sinister intentions."

Harry understood. "You're thinking of Vernon's notebook. His suspicion of 'S.C.'"

"Which likely means the occupants of that very tower. The Signal Corps."

Harry nodded. "I might mention this to Walter Thompson—though he's no doubt already aware of the tower's position. Pity he's left the castle for London."

"The Prime Minister's bodyguard?" Blake asked.

"An old colleague from my Scotland Yard days, gone on to a far more important role." Harry patted his pocket where he'd tucked Thompson's London telephone number. "At least he left a way to reach him if necessary."

A breeze rustled through the hedgerows, carrying the scent of roses from the nearby garden. Harry glanced around to ensure they weren't being overheard before continuing.

"By the way, Blake, do you read German?"

Blake shook his head. "Afraid not. Mathematics is my language of choice." A slight frown crossed his face. "But Katherine does— or rather she did. She studied in Vienna before the war."

Harry could see the indecision in the other man's face. "Do you think she might be able to read some notes written in German?"

Blake seemed to debate momentarily, then nodded. "It's worth showing her to see. She hates feeling like a failure when she can't remember something. But we're short on time and there's clearly a very limited circle of people we can trust to ask for a translation."

"Good man." Harry reached into his coat and extracted the leather pouch they'd taken from Graves. "Can you see that Katherine gets this, then?"

Blake tucked the pouch carefully into his jacket. "Consider it done. Anything specific I should tell her to look for? Always assuming that she can translate it, of course."

"Military communications, coded messages—anything that might indicate a threat to the Prime Minister's visit."

Blake nodded, his expression grave. Then he paused, seeming to weigh his next words. "There's something else, Harry. Something about the way the castle was renovated to accommodate the Signal Corps. The modifications seem... excessive for a temporary installation."

"How so?"

"I saw new electrical wiring throughout the east wing. Reinforced flooring in the tower. All the renovations looked far more robust than needed for a few radio sets." Blake tapped his cane against the ground, a habit Harry had noticed that meant the man was deep in thought. "It suggests permanence."

Harry filed this observation away for later consideration. "Let's discuss that when we know what's in those notes."

Blake nodded and took his leave, moving with gratifying agility.

After a moment, Harry turned his attention back to the castle, particularly the east wing tower. With the glare of sunlight reflected from its windows, he couldn't see if anyone was watching from within.

Harry made his way back inside, heading for the east wing corridor. The Signal Corps had been given a suite of rooms adjacent to the tower, converted from what had once been guest accommodations. Harry had noted during his earlier explorations that the officers maintained a duty roster posted outside the main operations room.

Now, he saw no one in the corridor. Perfect. He studied the list of names. Lieutenant Foster was scheduled at the listening post when the Prime Minister was expected to arrive—7:30 to 10:30 PM tomorrow evening.

"Convenient timing," Harry murmured to himself.

He examined the rest of the schedule. Three men on duty at all times in the listening post, rotating shifts. If Foster harboured ill intentions toward Churchill, he would have two witnesses to contend with. Not impossible to work around, but certainly more complicated.

"Finding anything of interest, Uncle Harry?"

THE MURDERS AT CLARION CASTLE

Nigel's voice startled him. His nephew had approached silently, a skill Harry had helped him develop during his early days at Scotland Yard. Nigel's expression was thoughtful, bordering on troubled.

"You look like a man who's discovered something, Nigel," Harry said.

"Indeed I have." Nigel glanced around, then lowered his voice. "From the barman at the White Horse."

"And what did our friend behind the bar have to say?" Harry asked, as they walked toward a quiet alcove beneath the stairs.

Nigel flipped open his notebook. "According to the barman, Graves and Miss Hartley arrived together around eight o'clock. She ordered a sherry, and he had a brandy."

"As Graves reported," Harry nodded.

"Yes, but there's more." Nigel tapped his pencil against the page. "After his second drink, Graves handed his flask to the barman to be filled with brandy, then excused himself to use the facilities. The barman filled the flask as requested, but—and this is what's interesting—he didn't return it directly to Graves."

Harry's eyebrows rose. "He gave it to Miss Hartley?"

"No, that's just it. He simply set it on their table, then went to serve other customers. When he next looked over, Graves had returned and was speaking with Miss Hartley. The flask was no longer visible."

"So that suggests she may have taken it while Graves was absent," Harry concluded. "Plenty of opportunity to add something to it."

"Precisely my thinking," Nigel agreed. "The barman also mentioned that while Graves was gone, Miss Hartley appeared to be writing something in a small notebook."

"Any idea of the contents?"

"Impossible to say. But she concealed whatever she was writing when other patrons passed by."

Harry absorbed this information. "Did the barman observe anything else unusual?"

"Only that Miss Hartley seemed quite keen to leave once Graves returned. According to him, she 'practically dragged' Graves out, though he'd intended to stay for another round."

Harry rubbed his chin thoughtfully. "This all supports Graves' account of the evening. His memory loss would be consistent with being drugged, though he didn't explicitly suggest that. Anything else?"

"The barman recalled one more thing. He saw Lieutenant Foster earlier in the evening, though he'd left well before Miss Hartley and Graves arrived."

"Interesting." Harry's gaze drifted toward the east wing. "Foster is scheduled at the listening post during Churchill's arrival tomorrow—7:30 to 10:30 PM."

"Convenient timing," Nigel observed.

"My thought exactly. But with two other Signal Corps men present, anything sinister would be difficult to accomplish."

"Unless they're all involved," Nigel suggested.

"Three conspirators rather than one? Possible, but it multiplies the risk of exposure." Harry shook his head. "Still, I think we should pay a visit to the listening post. Perhaps put the wind up whoever might be contemplating treachery."

"If there's a traitor at all," Nigel added.

Harry nodded. "Indeed. This could all be an elaborate coincidence—Vernon might have stumbled upon something entirely unrelated to Churchill's visit."

Neither of them believed that, Harry knew. The timing was too perfect, the words 'important visitor' too suggestive.

"Blake's hoping Katherine can translate the German notes," Harry continued. "If she can, we might see this puzzle more clearly."

Nigel glanced at his watch. "It's nearly six. We have two hours before dinner, and I understand Mr Walker is hosting a final staff briefing afterward to prepare for tomorrow's festivities."

"The staff briefing might prove illuminating. We should watch Miss Hartley, and see if Lieutenant Foster puts in an appearance on some pretext or other."

They began walking toward the main staircase, still keeping their voices low.

"What's your assessment of Graves now?" Harry asked. "His story about the memory loss?"

"The barman's account certainly supports the possibility he was drugged," Nigel replied. "And Miss Hartley could have helped him down to the wine cellar, and then laid him out once he was unconscious. Maybe she lured Vernon down there on some pretext—likely that his underling was dead drunk—and killed him."

"A tidy solution to two problems," Harry observed. "Eliminating Vernon and providing a convenient scapegoat. But she was upstairs working till late, she says."

"We need to check with the rest of the staff. See who saw her and when."

"And why would she need to kill Vernon?"

The question hung in the air unanswered. They reached the landing.

Harry's mind turned to the following day and Churchill's arrival. The castle was like a chessboard now, with pieces moving into position for some final gambit.

"Twenty-six hours, Nigel," Harry said quietly. "That's all we have before Churchill's motorcade comes up that drive."

"And where is Evie?" Nigel asked. "Have we heard from Alice?"

Chapter 36
Evie

Evie lifted the lid of a hat box, trying not to sneeze at the cloud of dust that rose into the air. She'd already searched through the drawers of the writing desk and amassed a small pile of potentially useful objects, which she'd hidden underneath the mound of stuffing that the mice had spilled out of the gnawed-on footstool.

So far, those objects included such incredibly useful treasures as a spool of thread, a felt pen wiper, a picture postcard from Lyme Regis, and a yellowed newspaper clipping entitled, *How to preserve new potatoes*.

She shut her eyes briefly. In the past, she would have tried to imagine Paul with her at a moment like this, pictured what he might say. Now, it was Nigel's lean, angular face that popped into her mind, looking at her with what she thought of as his official police expression: the one with the cold, hard gaze that gave absolutely none of his private thoughts away.

Wonderful. Even her imaginary version of Nigel disapproved of her.

Evie tried to replace the picture with her other memories of Nigel, the times when he'd shown that he was human after all: romping with his niece and nephew, affectionately teasing his elderly mother.

Promising her that he'd be with her at all times on a dangerous assignment, even if he had to keep out of sight.

Evie stared unseeingly at the contents of the hatbox, wondering whether Nigel— or anyone else— was searching for her, and whether they'd found the message she'd left behind on the folded pound note.

If they had found it— if they'd deciphered her message and confirmed that she had indeed been a prisoner there— then there was just a chance that they might still manage to track her down to wherever she was now being held.

Paul had driven off in a car, which meant presumably that was how she'd been transported here. So someone might have seen them on the road.

But that didn't help her now. She needed to send out some sort of message to Nigel and the others. Although if she could only get the window open—

Whoever had cleared out the attic before locking her in had clearly done a hasty, slap-dash sort of job, which meant that there was at least a chance there might be something of value in here, even if she hadn't found it yet.

Evie tipped the contents of the hatbox out into a pile on the floor and sorted rapidly through them. An old scrap of lace, two hair ribbons, three buttons, a woman's hairbrush . . . and a small manicure set of the kind that came in a white kid leather pouch.

Evie's pulse rate picked up as she started to unfasten the clasp on the pouch, but before she could open it, she heard heavy footsteps coming up the stairs that must be just outside of the attic door.

Hans.

She debated momentarily on whether to try speaking with him and see if she could learn anything useful. But after their scuffle the day before, Hans would be on his guard— and what was more, carrying a grudge.

Her heart still hammering, Evie slid the manicure set into the pocket of her skirt. Then she lay back down on the bare floorboards, praying that she was in roughly the same location as she'd been when they'd left her. She shut her eyes. The hinges on the door creaked as it swung open, and Hans' heavy footsteps plodded into the room, then stopped.

Evie kept her breathing shallow and even, although the seconds seemed to drip by even more interminably than the last time she'd feigned unconsciousness this way. She could feel the weight of Hans's gaze on her. Did he suspect that she wasn't asleep?

Or had he noticed that the lid was off the hatbox over in the corner? Evie felt a sickening clutch under her ribcage as she realised that she might have hidden the manicure set, but she'd forgotten to put everything else back. There was every chance that the stacks of papers on top of the writing desk weren't as they'd originally been, too.

"Hans!" Gerda's voice came from somewhere downstairs. "Come here! I need to finish the fitting of your uniform!"

For a moment, Evie wondered whether she'd translated the words correctly from the German. But uniform was one of those words that was almost identical in both German and English, and heaven knew she'd heard it often enough when speaking of the Nazi patrols in France.

She was liking this less and less. She didn't know why Hans would need any sort of uniform, but the answer couldn't possibly be a good one.

There was a metallic clink as Hans set something down on the floor, and then the door swung shut once more. Evie heard the scrape of a key turning in the lock.

She sprang up. Hans, she saw, had deposited a tray for her with a cup of water and another piece of dry toast. But she ignored those for now. Working as quickly and as quietly as she could, she bundled the assortment of items back into the hatbox and replaced the lid, then set the hatbox back in its original place. Only then did she take out the manicure set and unfasten the clasp on the kid leather pouch with shaking hands.

The set was complete. Tweezers, nail files, and not one but two sharp pairs of scissors were arranged neatly in their proper spots. Evie pocketed the scissors. She could try to work out a better hiding spot for them later, but for now she wasn't sure how much time she might have to accomplish her aims. She took out the sturdiest of the nail files, carried the stool back over to the dormer window, and set it down carefully, trying not to make any tell-tale thumps that might be heard from down below.

When she'd taught school, she'd often read her students the story of how King Richard the Lionheart had been captured while returning from the Third Crusade and imprisoned by Emperor Henry VI. His exact location became a mystery, and a large ransom was demanded for his release. According to the legend, his friend and minstrel Blondel set out to find him, travelling from castle to castle across Europe, singing a song that only he and Richard knew — a duet they had composed together.

At one remote castle, Blondel sang the first verse, and — miraculously — a voice responded from a window, singing the second verse. And thus was Richard the Lionheart discovered and freed from prison—or so legend would have it.

Evie didn't know any minstrels, and what was more it was highly unlikely that anyone searching for her would be humming a tune. What she did have, though, was a window, if only she could use it to send a signal to the outside world.

She climbed onto the stool and slid the nail file into the gap under the window pane, trying to loosen the layers of paint that had glued it shut. It was hard, tedious work, and several times Evie was certain that she would snap the nail file in half before she'd managed to open the window— or that Hans would come to check on her again.

But at last she felt the window shift in its frame, and when she gave it a hard shove with the heel of her hand, it shot upwards with a screech that sounded to her over-wrought nerves as loud as an air-raid siren.

Evie froze, ready to leap off of the stool if she heard anyone coming from downstairs. She had the scissors, which meant that she wasn't entirely unarmed. Two pairs of nail scissors might not be an entirely equal match for the German-issue guns that Hans and Gerda undoubtedly had, but they were all the weaponry she had, so they would have to do.

No one came, though. After silently counting to thirty inside her head, Evie released a slow breath, then stopped to consider.

If Paul were anywhere in the house, she wouldn't even attempt this. But Hans was clearly far less observant. He hadn't noticed the disturbed hatbox or the disarranged writing desk. And Gerda?

Gerda's observation skills were still an unknown factor, but Evie could at least be reasonably sure that the German pair would be staying indoors as much as possible, out of sight of anyone who might pass by.

She went back to the hatbox, lifted the lid, and took out one of the hair ribbons— a length of ivory coloured satin that had begun to yellow with age. She fed it through the open window and then carefully pushed the window back down, holding her breath as she braced herself for another screech.

But the window moved more easily this time, pinning the end of the ribbon in place. When Evie stood on her toes and peered out, she could see the length of ivory satin fluttering a little in the breeze like a tiny pennant.

Would anyone passing by notice it and think it out of the ordinary?

Evie stepped down and returned the stool to its former place. She'd done what she could. The rest was up to chance— and maybe to Nigel and the others from Crofter's Green.

Chapter 37
Dorothy

Dorothy peered anxiously through the window of the big Daimler car. The afternoon sun was just beginning to sink lower on the horizon, tingeing the wheat in the surrounding fields with golden summer light. "Do you see anything?"

Tom was in the driver's seat, scanning the road through the wind-screen. "Not yet. But it's entirely possible that Bonzo would just cut through the fields or the hedgerows and not stick to any kind of road."

After Bonzo had disappeared, running after the man who'd threatened Lady Hawthorne, her ladyship had nearly had hysterics with worrying about what would happen to the little dog. Dorothy didn't blame her for that; a good part of the hysterics were probably delayed shock from being knocked about and threatened with a gun. That sort of violence didn't at all fit in with Lady Hawthorne's orderly and perfectly manicured way of living.

Dorothy had offered to go with Tom in search of Bonzo, since he was the most promising way they had to find the brown-haired man again.

And maybe Evie? Dorothy was trying not to get her hopes up, but she couldn't help wishing desperately that the stranger might be headed to wherever it was that Siegfried was keeping Evie.

Lady Hawthorne had immediately offered them the use of the Daimler when Dorothy had spoken of going after Bonzo. She'd offered to loan them her chauffeur, too, but Dorothy had told her that Tom could drive. She'd rather not put anyone else in danger if they did happen upon the brown-haired stranger.

Now Tom was steering the car along the narrow, rutted lane that would eventually lead them the six miles to Clarion Castle, and Dorothy, despite her worry, almost smiled. "We'd better not tell Tommy about this. If he hears that we both got to ride in as grand a car as this one, he'll never forgive us for leaving him with Mum."

Tom grinned briefly, but then braked with a suddenness that made Dorothy put her hand out to brace herself against the dashboard.

"What is it?" she asked.

"Motorcycle tracks." Tom pointed to narrow wheel marks in the dirt road up ahead, overlaying the marks left by cars and wagons and farm carts.

Dorothy eyed them. "Not many other vehicles can have passed by since the motorcycle; the tire marks are right on top of all the rest."

Tom glanced at her sideways, his hands still on the wheel. "It might not mean anything."

"Maybe not. But there aren't many motorcycles on the roads around here; this is all farm country. No one has a need for a motorbike. Or the extra petrol coupons to run it." Dorothy gestured to the fields around them and the crofters' cottages in the distance.

"Shall we follow them, then?" Tom asked.

The motorcycle tracks turned down a narrow lane that led off between a thicket of trees and vanished. Dorothy felt a trickle of ice slide down her spine at the thought of coming face to face with the dark-haired man again. This time, he'd be bound to have some of his friends with him, too. But she nodded. "Let's see where they go."

Tom turned the Daimler onto the narrow lane and they set off, bouncing along the rutted and muddy track. The woods around them thickened, and the road twisted and turned so often that Dorothy lost all sense of direction. The motorcycle tracks went on, though, leading the way.

Finally, after what must have been a quarter of an hour at least, the lane came to a dead end stop in front of a wicket gate that seemed to lead through into a farmer's wheat field.

Dorothy's heart sank. "What now?" Clearly, they'd come as far as they were able, and there were no houses, no signs of Evie or any other humans— and for that matter, no trace of Bonzo— in sight. "Do we give up and turn back the way we came?"

"Let's have a look around first." Tom applied the brake, switched off the engine and got out. He didn't look nearly as discouraged as Dorothy felt, but she did see him check the service revolver which was now in the pocket of his trousers. She'd gladly handed it over to Tom to take charge of at the start of this journey.

Tom pointed to something on the ground. "Look there. See that patch of oil? At least, I think it's oil." He couldn't crouch down easily, not with his prosthetic leg, but he pointed to a small darkish puddle on the ground near the gate.

Dorothy bent and studied it more closely, sniffing. "You're right— it is oil. That was well spotted."

Tom's sober expression lightened in another brief grin. "You don't think they made me a captain in the army because I know how to whistle, do you?" His gaze swept the ground once again. "You see what this means. Whoever was riding the motorbike had it parked here. Look, you can see the marks in the grass there, where the tyres sank in."

Dorothy nodded. She could see the crushed blades of grass and the slight depressions in the ground. "And that means that whoever was riding the motorbike must have come from somewhere within walking distance of this spot." She turned in a circle, surveying the field and the woods that surrounded them on three sides, her flicker of excitement waning as she saw just how dense the forest was and how vast a swath of countryside they were facing. "Although we don't have anything to give us a hint on which direction we'd need to go before we find that somewhere."

And the sun was sinking lower, the first purple shadows of dusk beginning to fall between the trees. They didn't have more than an hour at most before it would be fully dark.

"We don't have anything to give us a hint yet," Tom corrected. "Come on, let's keep looking."

It was Dorothy who found the marks, after about five minutes of kicking through the fallen leaves and brambles that covered the ground. "Tom!" she called out. "Look here!"

Tom came at once to her side, and she pointed. There, on a muddy patch of ground between two leaves, was the clear imprint of a small dog's paw.

Tom looked at her. "Bonzo?"

"I hope so." Dorothy's chest felt tight with just how much she hoped that the paw print had been left by the brave little dog.

Tom leaned over a little to study the print. "It looks like he was heading in this direction." He pointed off through the trees, away from the wheat field.

They set off, winding their way through the forest, stopping every few feet to inspect the ground. The air grew damp and chillier, and Dorothy felt a tug of foreboding gather inside her. The woods were still, save for the occasional rustle of a squirrel or a bird in the trees, and somehow the silence felt menacing. But the ground was damp enough to show the paw print marks of a small dog in several places, and so they kept on.

Finally the woods began to thin. And, raising her head, Dorothy saw a small stone cottage silhouetted against the last crimson bands of sunset.

The place looked innocent enough, and yet she froze, instinctively putting her hand out to catch hold of Tom's arm. Neither of them spoke as they studied the place in silence. Then Tom murmured, "Do we go up and knock on the door so that we can get a look inside? We could claim our car's out of petrol and we're hoping to telephone to the nearest garage."

As excuses went, it was a perfectly plausible one, but Dorothy shook her head. "Not yet, anyway. Do you see any signs that Bonzo's been here?"

They both scanned the ground, although it was difficult to see anything in the gathering dark, and after a few moments, Dorothy shook her head again and said, "Let's see if we can get a little closer."

They moved through the trees, approaching the stone cottage from the front. Dorothy could tell from the stiffness of Tom's gait that his leg was hurting him. She knew the artificial leg chafed if he walked on it for too long, but she also knew that he'd never complain.

The cottage windows were already covered with the usual blackout curtains. Tom raised an eyebrow, glancing at Dorothy. "Either whoever lives there is extra careful about the blackout regulations . . ."

"Or else they don't want anyone getting a look inside," Dorothy finished for him. She was about to say something more, when she suddenly froze. A man in a dark suit was striding through the woods off to the right of the cottage, where a narrow dirt lane led towards the front door. He was still at least five hundred yards away, but Dorothy still recognised him at once.

"That's him!" she breathed to Tom. "That's the man who threatened Lady Hawthorne!"

Tom didn't move, but his whole posture tensed and hardened somehow, and his expression turned a shade darker. He didn't talk much about his time over in France, but right this moment, Dorothy got a glimpse of the Tom who'd been to war and had to fight for his own life and the lives of the other men in his company.

He took an instinctive half-step forwards, but Dorothy caught hold of his arm again. "You can't tackle him here. I know you could take him on, but we don't know how many others are in the cottage, just waiting to come out and back him up if they hear a row from outside."

"You're right." Tom's stiff muscles relaxed a fraction, and he eyed the stranger, a furrow gathering between his brows. "We need a way to draw him off, away from here."

In Dorothy's experience, some ideas crept up on you slowly, while others struck all at once, with the force of an icy gust of wind. The plan that jumped into her head now was one of the icy-gust kind, and it took her breath away just as thoroughly.

"I have an idea," she whispered to Tom. "Fair warning, though, you're going to hate it."

Chapter 38
Dorothy

Dorothy took a breath and softly cleared her throat in hopes that her voice wouldn't shake. Her throat felt dry and her palms were clammy, but she wasn't actually nervous for herself so much as for Tom. She didn't have any doubt that Tom would protect her with his life— and that was exactly the problem. She couldn't let this turn into a situation where Tom sacrificed his own life to save hers.

Yet they had to find Evie and stop Siegfried, and Dorothy had to act now, right away, before the dark-haired man got any closer to the cottage. Otherwise this plan was doomed before it had even begun.

She opened her mouth and called out in the sing-song voice of someone calling to a favourite pet, "Bonzo! Bonnn-zo!"

The dark-haired man stopped in mid step, turning at the sound of her voice, squinting into the shadows of the trees. Dorothy spun quickly away. She couldn't let on that she'd seen him or knew that he was there. Her job was to be the bait. The silly, oblivious bait that would draw the dark-haired man away from any friends he might have inside the stone house.

"Bonzo!" She took a few steps forward, crunching through leaves and dry bracken, deliberately making as much noise as she possibly could. She just had to hope that it was enough to draw the dark-haired stranger, yet not so much as to alert anyone who might be inside. "Here boy! Bonnn-zo!"

She heard the dark-haired man's steps behind her long before she let herself spin around to face him. If she'd thought she was nervous before, it was nothing to the wave of fear that swamped her now. She couldn't control her gasp or her instinctive jerk backwards at the sight of his face.

"You!"

The dark-haired man's upper lip curled back, sneering. He'd recognised her, as well, despite the fading light. "Did you actually follow me all the way here on account of that wretched dog?"

A spark of anger cut right through Dorothy's fear. "Yes, I did. And you'd better not have hurt him!"

The man barked a short laugh at that. "The dog's going to be the least of your—"

He didn't get the chance to finish, though. Tom slammed into him in a flying tackle from behind that carried them both to the ground. Dorothy jumped back, trying to stay out of the way. Trust Tom. She had to trust him. Even with one leg missing, he was bigger and stronger than the stranger—

The dark-haired man was fighting like a man possessed, though, thrashing and kicking as he tried to break free of Tom's grip. Dorothy's heart almost stopped as she saw something metallic flash in the stranger's hand. A knife. Somehow, he'd pulled out a knife.

Tom either saw or sensed the threat, though, and grabbed hold of the other man's wrist, slamming the knife hand hard against the ground, trying to break the stranger's grip on the knife hilt.

Dorothy couldn't stand it another second. She bent, seized up the biggest fallen branch within reach, and darted forwards, bringing the hefty wooden stick down on the stranger's head with a crash. He dropped the knife, which gave Tom the opening to deliver a sharp uppercut punch to his jaw.

The stranger groaned and collapsed, lying motionless.

Tom got up slowly— although not before he'd pulled up the stranger's eyelid to check whether he was really unconscious and not just shamming.

"All right?" he asked Dorothy.

"I'm not the one who was just wrestling with a German spy!" Now that it was all over, Dorothy was having a hard time not shivering. "Are *you* all right?"

"Fine." Tom drew off his belt, using it to bind the stranger's hands behind his back. Then he used the dark-haired man's own belt to do the same with the man's ankles. "We need to let Harry and Nigel know about this, though. I can go and try to fetch Alice. If—"

"I'll stay," Dorothy said at once. "We can drag him into the bushes so that we'll both be hidden."

"You're sure?" Tom asked.

"It'll be dark soon. I'll be perfectly safe. If there is anyone inside the cottage, I doubt they'll bother coming out here into the woods—" Dorothy stopped abruptly. She'd been looking once more up at the small stone cottage, and something had caught her eye.

There was a narrow dormer window in the upper story, just under the thatched eaves . . . and from it, something white fluttered, highlighted by the very last rays of the sinking sun.

"Evie!" she gasped.

"What?" Tom looked round, puzzled.

"No, I don't mean I've seen her. But do you see that ribbon?" Dorothy pointed. "I'll bet anything that Evie put it there for us to spot."

Tom's gaze followed where she was pointing, and he nodded, but his expression was a bit more cautious. "It's possible, of course," he said. "But we can't know for sure that she's inside."

"She is." Dorothy couldn't entirely explain her utter certainty that they'd found Evie at last, but she felt it all the same. "I know it. Go and find Alice, Tom, and then get her to telephone Harry up at the castle."

Chapter 39
Alice

Alice Greenleaf paused, leaning against a moss-covered milestone to ease the weight from her aching feet. Ahead of her, red-gold rays of the late afternoon sun slanted through ancient oaks, casting long shadows across the Pilgrim Way. The cool forest air carried the scent of damp earth and wild thyme.

But Alice found little comfort in nature's offerings at the moment. Her new shoes—acquired for her disguise as a pilgrim—were still playing havoc with her blisters.

'*Thanne longen folke to goon on pilgrimages*' she murmured, recalling Chaucer's words from The Canterbury Tales. What a difference, she thought, between her solitary quest and the one undertaken by those merry medieval travellers nearly six centuries ago! They had companionship, horses to bear their weight, and most importantly, certainty of destination. Canterbury Cathedral awaited their journey's end, its spires a promise of spiritual renewal.

Alice, on the other hand, had only questions and growing unease. The cottage where she'd believed Evie was being held had proven empty, the kidnappers having moved their prisoner before dawn. Each fork in the path presented a painful choice—might she be walking farther from her friend with every step?

She adjusted her herb pouch, fingers brushing against the dried lavender and chamomile she'd gathered earlier. The herbs wouldn't guide her to Evie, but their familiar textures grounded her in this moment of doubt.

"Pilgrims must have faith," she told herself, though the words rang hollow in the fading sunlight. The Pilgrim Way stretched before her like a riddle without answer, branching into paths as numerous as possibilities in a game of chess.

A sudden rustling from a nearby hedgerow broke her reverie.

Alice tensed, her hand moving instinctively to the small knife concealed in her belt—a precaution she'd taken after her discoveries at Blair Cottage. The rustling grew more frantic.

Then a small, dirt-covered ball of fur burst through the undergrowth.

"Bonzo?" Alice exclaimed, recognising the tan and white Pomeranian despite his bedraggled state. The dog's usually pristine coat was matted with mud and studded with burs, his bright eyes wide with exhaustion and relief at finding a familiar face.

Alice knelt, ignoring the protest from her tired knees, and gathered the trembling creature into her arms. Bonzo licked her face frantically, his entire body quivering with the force of his wagging tail.

"What are you doing here, little one?" she whispered, examining him for injuries. "Hawthorne Manor is nearly five miles away."

Had he been running from something? Or someone? The dog's presence so far from home suggested circumstances beyond a simple escape through an unlatched gate. Alice stroked his head, noticing how he calmed at her touch, his trembling gradually subsiding.

Unscrewing her thermos, she poured water into her cupped palm, watching as the small pink tongue lapped gratefully. After Bonzo had drunk his fill, Alice set about removing the worst of the burs from his coat, using the small comb she carried to coax petals or pollen from plant specimens.

As the shadows deepened around them, Alice confronted the decision before her. The practical herbalist within urged return to The Shepherd's Rest before complete darkness fell. The seeker in her heart protested abandoning the search for Evie.

"You can't find her in the dark," she reasoned aloud, her words meant as much for herself as for the dog. "And now I'm responsible for you, too."

She studied Bonzo thoughtfully, remembering how he had once tracked Evie to a church when given the command she'd taught him. Worth trying, at least.

"Bonzo," she said firmly, kneeling to look into his bright eyes. "Find Evie."

The Pomeranian's ears perked up at the familiar words. He turned in a circle, nose to the ground, then looked back at Alice with a whine of confusion. He pawed at the earth, clearly understanding what was asked but finding no trail to follow.

Alice sighed. "No scents here, are there? I suppose it was too much to hope for."

Straightening, she made her decision. "Let's live to fight another day," she told Bonzo, gently tucking him into the crook of her arm.

As she retraced her steps along the Pilgrim Way, Alice found comfort in the warm weight of Bonzo against her chest. Perhaps faith, she reflected, wasn't about blindly believing in predestined outcomes but in recognising the unexpected blessings that appear along the journey—even when they arrive in the form of a dirty, burr-covered Pomeranian.

The analytical part of her mind began calculating the possibilities. If Bonzo had travelled this far from Hawthorne Manor, what had driven him to flee? And more importantly, what might his presence here signify about Evie's location—if anything? These questions would need to wait until she reached the inn, but Alice felt the first stirrings of hope. In her experience, such seemingly random encounters often proved to be the thread that, when pulled, unravelled even the most complex mysteries.

The way seemed shorter with company, even such small company as Bonzo. The distant profile of The Shepherd's Rest Inn appeared between the trees, a temporary sanctuary lit by the setting sun. Tomorrow would bring renewed searching, but tonight required rest and strategy—and a telephone call to Harry at the castle. Perhaps he and the others had made discoveries that would guide her next steps.

As they approached the inn, Alice felt Bonzo stiffen in her arms.

He was staring fixedly at something ahead.

Following his line of sight, she noticed a figure slipping between the shadows near the inn's stable yard. Something about the furtive movement triggered her instincts.

"Curious," she murmured, instinctively dropping into a crouch behind a thicket of hawthorn. Bonzo sensed her tension and remained perfectly still in her arms, his earlier excitement replaced by watchful silence.

The figure—tall and lean, clad in dark clothing that would soon blend into the deepening dusk—paused briefly, head turning as if scanning for pursuers. Though the fading light obscured any distinguishing features, there was something vaguely familiar about the figure, a certain military precision that reminded Alice of the commando trainees she'd encountered nearly a month ago. Yet something else nagged at her. There was a hesitation in the way the man moved.

Logic dictated that she should continue to The Shepherd's Rest, telephone Harry, and report her findings. That would be the prudent course—the safe course. Yet Alice had learned long ago that safety rarely walked hand-in-hand with discovery.

"What do you think, Bonzo?" she whispered. "Shall we see where our mysterious friend is headed?"

The Pomeranian offered no objection beyond a quick lick to her wrist. Alice took it as assent.

Setting Bonzo gently on the ground, she secured his makeshift lead—fashioned from the length of twine she carried for bundling herbs. "Stay close and quiet," she instructed, though she doubted the instruction was necessary. The little dog seemed to understand the gravity of their impromptu surveillance mission.

Alice moved warily, each footfall placed with deliberate care to avoid crackling leaves or snapping twigs. The figure ahead kept a steady, though somewhat irregular pace, along a barely discernible trail that veered away from the main pilgrim path.

The rational portion of Alice's mind catalogued possibilities: a local resident taking a shortcut home, another pilgrim seeking solitude, or—more ominously—someone connected to Evie's disappearance. The latter seemed increasingly probable as the figure followed a route that grew progressively more obscure, eventually departing from any path Alice recognised from her previous explorations.

After nearly twenty minutes of careful pursuit, she noticed the woods had begun to thin. Ahead, silhouetted against the last crimson bands of sunset, stood a small stone cottage Alice hadn't encountered in her previous searches. Smoke curled from its chimney in a thin grey ribbon, suggesting recent occupation.

Then she realised that the figure she'd been following had vanished. Had it gone into the cottage? No, she hadn't seen that. Then where?

Alice settled behind the trunk of a massive beech tree, close enough to observe but far enough to avoid detection. Bonzo sat beside her, his small body alert but calm.

"Well," she whispered, "perhaps we've found something interesting after all."

From her vantage point, she could make out fragments of movement through the cottage window—shadows stretching and contracting across the uneven glass. One silhouette appeared, then another, shorter than the first, and Alice's heart quickened. Was there something in the set of those shoulders, the tilt of that head?

No. The second silhouette turned in the window frame, and she saw a profile. Definitely not Evie's.

She nearly jumped out of her skin as a familiar voice came from behind her: "Alice?"

She whirled round and saw the shadowy figure.

Relief and recognition swirled through her in simultaneous waves.

She'd been following Tom Baker, Dorothy's husband.

Chapter 40
Katherine

Katherine was in the library, adding a copy of Edward Gibbon's, *The History of the Decline and Fall of the Roman Empire* to her catalogue when a movement outside the library window caught her eye. Looking out, she saw a man she recognised as Mr Walker, striding away from the house with a shotgun over his shoulder. His long strides covered the lawn in scarcely any time at all, and he vanished into the thick forest that surrounded the castle on all sides.

"Katherine?"

Katherine started at the sound of Blake's voice from behind her. She'd been so lost in thought that she hadn't even heard him come in.

She smiled. "Sorry— I was wool-gathering."

Blake studied her expression. "Is something wrong?"

"Not really. I was just wondering how trustworthy Mr Walker is. Whether Harry believes that he truly does have Britain's interests at heart in this war."

She spoke a little hesitantly, not knowing whether she was being overly suspicious or fanciful. Another delightful side effect of having amnesia was that she didn't automatically trust her own mind, even when memories weren't in play. But Blake seemed to take the question seriously, considering it with a slight furrow between his brows.

"I would assume that Mr Churchill's staff would have thoroughly vetted him and looked into his antecedents before allowing the Prime

Minister to journey here. Why? Do you have a reason to think that he might be a traitor?"

"Nothing like that, not if we're speaking in terms of concrete proof," Katherine said. "But I saw him go off into the forest just now to go hunting. According to Lillian— she's the housemaid, or one of them— he's a keen sportsman, always going off to shoot deer. But it occurred to me how easy it would be for him to hide a weapon somewhere on the grounds, under the guise of going off on another shooting expedition. Somewhere, say, with a good vantage point of the drive along which Mr Churchill will approach the house."

Blake nodded slowly. "And then someone else could come along at the right moment and use it to take a sniper's shot at the Prime Minister's motorcade."

"It's possible, isn't it?" Katherine found herself wishing that Blake could have dismissed her fears after all. She didn't at all like the possibilities that this line of thinking opened up. "If there is a traitor here— someone passing on secrets from the Signal Corps in the north tower— then Mr Walker would be ideally placed, wouldn't he? Because he's the master here. Everyone might not quite assume that he's above suspicion, but they'd be used to accepting his orders and authority."

"You're right, and it's something we ought to talk over with Nigel and Harry," Blake said. "First, though—" he stopped, seeming to hesitate.

"What is it?"

"Harry's given me some notes written in German," Blake said. "He's hoping we might be able to translate them."

"You mean with a dictionary?" Katherine frowned a little as she studied the library shelves. "I don't think I've seen a German dictionary here, but I haven't had time to look through all of the books."

"Not exactly." Blake took a breath. "Harry was actually hoping you could translate them because you speak German."

Katherine stared at him. "I speak German?"

If it were anyone other than Blake, she would have suspected that this was some sort of joke. But he was looking at her in the way that meant he was worrying he had said the wrong thing. "I'm sorry. Maybe I should have told you more . . . more gradually somehow?"

Despite herself, Katherine smiled. "There are a limited number of ways in which you can tell someone that they speak a foreign language, none of which are particularly conducive to tact. It's all right. I just—" she rubbed her forehead. "I just sometimes feel that I'm getting reacquainted with myself, and then some new fact jumps out of hiding and shouts, Boo! Like a child's game of hide-and-go-seek. Can you tell me why I speak German?"

"You studied in Vienna before the war," Blake said.

Katherine eyed him a little nervously. "You're not going to tell me that I was training for the opera or anything like that, are you?"

Blake shook his head. "No. You were doing a course in languages at the University of Vienna."

"Well, that's a relief, at any rate." A course in languages was less at odds with what she knew about her former self. "And now Harry wants to know whether I still remember German well enough to be able to translate something?"

"Yes. But it's all right if you can't," Blake said quickly. "You don't have to feel as though you've let him down if it doesn't come back to you."

He was so kind, Katherine thought. So kind and truly good. Even with the fate of the country and maybe even the outcome of the war at stake, he was still trying to reassure her and consider her feelings.

And but for the chance meeting with Dorothy at the hospital that had led her to Crofter's Green, she might never have found him again. The thought gave her the resolve to say, "Of course I'll try."

Blake drew a small notebook out of his pocket and handed it over to her. Katherine shut her eyes for a moment, trying to empty her thoughts of any doubt or uncertainty. Just because she couldn't think of a single word in German at this particular moment didn't mean that she never would.

Katherine blew out a breath. Eliminating her own doubts didn't seem to be working very well, so she opened her eyes and looked down at the page that Blake had found for her.

"*Warnung.* That means warning." She heard her own voice speak the words, but they came as a complete surprise to her all the same, so much so that she actually dropped the notebook. She looked up at Blake, feeling her eyes going wide. "Did I really just say that?"

"You did." Blake squeezed her hand. "You can do this. But I always thought that *achtung* was the German for warning?"

Katherine shook her head. "That's generally just for a shouted command. For a written warning, it's, *warnung*."

She was once again caught off-guard by how readily the answer came to her lips, without any conscious thought. But it was slightly less disconcerting than the last time. She picked up the notebook again. "I'll read, if you'll write the translation down?"

When they'd finished, Katherine looked down at the page on which Blake had jotted down everything she said:

> Warning: Local police inspector (N. Brewster) investigating under-butler's death. Retired Scotland Yard inspector (H. Jenkins) assisting. Both asking questions about keep and east tower. Vernon's note-

book missing. Graves situation handled. Awaiting further instructions regarding compromised assets.- Nightingale

Update: Churchill security detail expected tomorrow for preliminary inspection. Six rooms East Wing designated for PM's use. Schedule confirmed - arrival two days 19:35, dinner 20:00, departure following day after lunch. Steel contract negotiations scheduled for morning session.- Nightingale

Alert: Jenkins and Brewster have questioned staff about Vernon's death. Have maintained cover story effectively. Will report any complications immediately.- Nightingale

"Nightingale?" she frowned. "What do you suppose that means?"

"Some sort of code name?" Blake said. "I'm not sure, but we'd better get this to Harry straight away."

He stopped, though, before picking up the paper, and smiled at her. "Well done."

Chapter 41
Harry

Harry Jenkins carefully slid the leather pouch back into the crevice behind the loose stone in the ancient wall of Clarion Castle's keep. The long shadows of approaching twilight made the task more difficult than it should have been. Also, he couldn't help but worry he was late. He wished he'd thought to replace the messages earlier.

After finding them, he'd simply handed them straight to Blake for Katherine to translate, never considering the importance of returning the originals promptly. He could have made copies, kept those for translation, and returned these German notes immediately.

He told himself there was no use wasting energy on things he couldn't control. Besides, odds were that whoever collected these messages did so after dark, when fewer eyes might spot someone lurking near the keep. It wasn't even proper twilight yet.

So he should be in plenty of time.

But if he wasn't?

The thought had unsettled him more than he cared to admit. His fingers, still nimble despite the occasional arthritis that plagued them on damp mornings, made quick work of putting the pouch into place. He hoped it appeared undisturbed—or at least that any disturbance wouldn't be discernable in the dark.

The smell of damp stone and moss filled Harry's nostrils, along with something else—a faint metallic tang that reminded him of approaching rain. The sounds around the keep seemed unnaturally amplified —the whisper of wind through ancient arrow slits above him, the distant caw of rooks returning to roost, the soft scuffing of Nigel's shoes on gravel.

His nephew stood beside him, keeping watch on the entry door and its heavy padlock.

As he nudged the stone into place, hiding the cavity, Harry found himself wondering if someone might be observing from afar, perhaps with binoculars or a telescope trained on this very spot. He paused to scan the horizon, searching for the telltale glint of waning sunlight reflected off a lens.

Nothing. Just the rolling countryside gradually dissolving into evening shadows.

"There," Harry murmured, giving the stone a gentle pat.

"Too bad we can't wait to see whoever comes to collect," Nigel said.

Of course they couldn't, Harry knew. Too much risk they'd be spotted, even in the dark. The collector would stay away, and maybe try a backup location that Harry and Nigel didn't know about.

They walked away from the keep in companionable silence. The sun hung very low now, casting their elongated shadows across the courtyard. Before them, Clarion Castle loomed against the darkening sky.

"Those notes worry me," Nigel said finally, his face set in grim lines. "Churchill's exact arrival time, the exact rooms set aside for him, even the dinner schedule—it's all laid out."

Harry nodded, instinctively scanning the grounds as he walked. "Someone high up is a traitor."

"So this Nightingale writing the notes," Nigel mused, his voice low. "Could be anyone who knows Churchill's schedule."

"Which narrows it a bit, but not enough," Harry replied, making sure they wouldn't be overheard by the gardener trimming hedges nearby. "Starting from the top, there's Walker himself."

"And there's Millicent, his secretary," Nigel added thoughtfully. "And then there's Glenwood, and the housekeeper, and her staff, who would have to know which rooms were assigned and when to prepare them. And the cook, who would have to know the timing of the meals and the number of guests."

"The notes were printed, not handwritten," Harry observed. "A deliberate choice to conceal identity."

The castle loomed before them now, its stone façade taking on a reddish glow in the fading light. Harry couldn't help but admire the grandeur of the place, even as he puzzled through the web of conspiracy within its walls.

"Something else troubles me," he continued as they approached the main entrance. "The reference to Vernon's notebook being missing. Who would know that?"

Nigel's stride faltered slightly. "Someone who knew Vernon always kept it with him, for one thing. But that would include all the staff. They'd seen him keeping tabs on their work."

"But they'd need to have had access to the body, after it left for the police mortuary." Harry placed a hand on his nephew's shoulder. "Or access to the medical report. Maybe you can look into that?"

Nigel nodded.

They entered through the grand entrance, not taking time to knock, their footsteps echoing on the marble floor of the entry hall. Then came the sharp ring of a telephone, coming from the red phone box, Walker's whimsical installation in the far corner.

With his typical silent efficiency, the silver-haired butler Glenwood came into the hall to answer it.

Harry watched as Glenwood listened briefly. The man's eyes flickered toward Harry before he covered the mouthpiece with one gloved hand.

"It is for you, Inspector Jenkins," Glenwood announced, his tone revealing nothing of the call's nature or his thoughts about a retired Scotland Yard inspector receiving telephone calls at Clarion Castle.

Harry crossed to the phone box, aware of Nigel's questioning gaze following him. He took the receiver, noting the slight tremor in his own hand. Thirty years of police work had taught him that unexpected telephone calls rarely brought good news.

"Jenkins here," he said.

"Harry, it's Alice." Her voice came through clearly, though pitched low, as if she were concerned about being overheard.

"Hello, Alice."

"I've just seen Dorothy and Tom," Alice said. "We've found her. At least we've reason to hope we have."

A jolt of adrenaline snapped through Harry's spine. He turned slightly away from Glenwood, who had retreated to a respectful distance but remained within earshot.

"Where?" he asked carefully.

"A cottage in the woods, off the Pilgrim Way. Tom and Dorothy found the cottage," Alice replied, "They stayed behind to keep watch while I came here to call. The three of us saw Evie in an upstairs window. She's put out a distress signal."

Harry's eyes met Nigel's across the hall, and he gave a slight nod. His nephew immediately understood, moving closer to hear what he could of the conversation.

"You're at The Shepherd's Rest now?" Harry asked, remembering the small inn where Alice was staying.

"Yes, with an unexpected companion. A certain small dog has joined my expedition."

Harry's eyebrows rose in surprise. "Bonzo?"

"The very same. He appeared in the woods, quite far from home." Alice's voice held a note of significance that Harry didn't miss. "I believe our friends have been busy on multiple fronts."

"Stay where you are," Harry instructed, his mind already calculating distances and timing. "We'll join you within the hour. Don't go anywhere."

As he replaced the receiver, Harry was keenly aware of Glenwood watching him with polite but unmistakable interest. The butler's expression remained impassive, yet Harry couldn't shake the feeling that their conversation had been carefully monitored.

"We need to go," he told Nigel quietly as they moved away from the phone box.

Nigel nodded, understanding. "I'll get the car."

As his nephew strode toward the door, Harry glanced up at the grand staircase and caught a glimpse of Bradford Walker, dressed for dinner, but headed for the corridor that led to his bedroom suite. The steel magnate's distinctive pale eyes and arched eyebrow were visible for just a moment before he vanished from sight.

Chapter 42
Harry

Harry sat in the passenger seat of Nigel's Ford, his focus entirely on the dark-haired man handcuffed in the back. The car was parked just off the road and within the tree line, far enough from the cottage and the road that they wouldn't be easily spotted. Harry hoped he was close enough to see anyone going towards, or from, the place where Evie was most likely being held captive.

Twenty minutes ago, Dorothy and Tom had departed in Lady Hawthorne's borrowed Daimler, taking Alice and Bonzo back to The Shepherd's Rest Inn. Harry had wanted Alice safely away from whatever might unfold here, and Dorothy had insisted on going with her. Tom, ever protective of his wife, wouldn't hear of letting her make the journey without him.

That left Harry alone with their prisoner while Nigel conducted a careful reconnaissance of the cottage.

Dusk was settling rapidly now, the forest growing darker by the minute. Shadows stretched long and ominous between the trees, and the temperature had begun to drop, bringing with it the distinctive earthy scent of an English woodland at twilight. A distant owl called twice, the sound carrying clearly in the still air.

"Let's try this again," Harry said, keeping his voice low. "Who are you working for?"

The dark-haired man—who had refused to give his name—remained stubbornly silent, his features barely visible in the gathering darkness. Harry could just make out the tight set of his jaw and the calculating gleam in his eyes. The man's wrists were now secured by Nigel's police-issue handcuffs, but that hadn't made him any more cooperative.

Harry's patience, considerable after years at Scotland Yard, was wearing dangerously thin. Every minute that passed was another minute Evie remained in danger—another minute Nigel spent creeping closer to the cottage where enemy agents might be waiting.

"You realise your position is untenable," Harry continued, his tone matter-of-fact. "Lady Hawthorne will identify you as the man who threatened her. That alone would see you imprisoned. Add assault with a deadly weapon, and you're looking at a considerable sentence."

The thug smirked, clearly unimpressed by the threat of legal consequences.

"I'm a patriot," he said finally, the words dripping with contempt. "Something you wouldn't understand."

"A patriot who threatens elderly ladies?" Harry asked mildly. "Curious definition."

"This is war, old man. There are no civilians anymore."

Harry leaned forward, deliberately crowding the man's space. "I've taken the precaution of closing all the windows," he said softly. "No one would hear if our conversation became... less civilised."

It wasn't Harry's usual approach to interrogation, but these weren't usual times. The war had changed everything, even the rules by which he'd conducted his professional life. The thug's eyes flickered briefly, registering the threat, but his smirk remained firmly in place.

"I've dealt with police before," he said. His accent was educated, nothing like the rough criminal element Harry had often encountered during his years at the Yard. "You're Scotland Yard. You don't operate that way."

"Retired," Harry corrected him. "And these are extraordinary times."

He studied the man's hands, noting the way he was subtly working against the handcuffs, testing for weaknesses. Earlier, Harry had discovered him nearly free of the makeshift bonds that Tom had fashioned. That was when he'd retrieved Nigel's handcuffs from the glove compartment, securing the prisoner properly despite his violent resistance.

The resulting struggle had left the thug with a split lip and Harry with scraped knuckles—small injuries that somehow made the current tension between them sharper, more personal.

"Why Diana Lovecraft?" Harry asked, watching carefully for any reaction. "What's your interest in her?"

The thug's eyes narrowed slightly—a tell Harry might have missed if he hadn't been watching so closely.

"Never heard of her," the man replied, but his voice lacked conviction.

"Strange. You seemed quite intent on getting information about her from Lady Hawthorne."

"The old woman was confused. Senile, probably."

Harry nodded thoughtfully. "And yet you risked breaking into her home and threatening her with a gun—all for someone you've never heard of."

Silence stretched between them, thick with unspoken hostility.

"Let's try a different approach," Harry said. "You've been to Clarion Castle, haven't you?"

The thug's face remained impassive, but Harry caught the slightest tensing of his shoulders.

"I don't know what you're talking about."

"I think you do." Harry leaned back, affecting a casualness he didn't feel. "Interesting place, Clarion. Quite the hive of activity lately."

"If you say so."

"I do." Harry smiled thinly. "And I think you know exactly why."

The man shifted in his seat, a barely perceptible movement that nonetheless told Harry he'd struck a nerve.

"You're wasting your time, old man."

"Perhaps." Harry glanced briefly toward the cottage, where Nigel was somewhere in the gathering darkness. "But your associates aren't. They're quite busy, from what we've gathered."

The thug laughed, a short, harsh sound. "You don't know anything."

"We know about Vernon," Harry said, watching the man's face carefully. "We know he was killed because he discovered something he shouldn't have."

A flicker of surprise crossed the thug's face, quickly suppressed. "I don't know any Vernon."

"No? Pity. His death might have warned you how dangerous it is to cross paths with certain people." Harry paused. "People like those you're working for."

"I work for England," the thug insisted, a touch of defiance creeping into his voice.

"So you say. And yet you're hampering an official investigation. One might almost think you were working against England's interests."

The thug's lips tightened. "You don't understand the bigger picture."

"Then enlighten me," Harry suggested.

"Some sacrifices have to be made. For the greater good."

"Sacrifices like Diana Lovecraft?"

The man's eyes hardened. "She's a traitor."

"To whom, exactly?" Harry asked, sensing he was finally getting somewhere.

"To England. To everything we're fighting for."

Harry studied him in the gathering darkness. "You seem very certain of that."

"I am."

"Based on what evidence?"

The thug fell silent again, clearly having said more than he intended.

"Who told you she was a traitor?" Harry pressed.

"People who know. People who see the whole picture, not just the bits and pieces you're fumbling with."

"These people have names, I presume."

"None that would mean anything to you."

Harry felt a chill that had nothing to do with the evening air. "Try me."

The thug smiled suddenly, a cold expression that didn't reach his eyes. "Why don't you ask your policeman friend? He should be back by now, shouldn't he?"

Harry kept his face impassive, though the man's words sent a jolt of worry through him. Nigel had been gone longer than planned. In the deepening twilight, time seemed to stretch and compress by turns, making it difficult to judge exactly how long had passed, but Harry knew it had been too long.

"Nigel is quite capable," Harry said, maintaining his calm demeanour. "I'm not concerned."

"You should be," the thug said quietly.

The smug certainty in the man's voice made Harry's blood run cold. He glanced toward the cottage again but could see nothing in the gathering gloom.

"What do you know?" Harry demanded, grabbing the man's collar.

The thug didn't resist, didn't pull away. Instead, he smiled. "Listen."

At first, Harry heard nothing beyond the natural sounds of the forest at dusk—the rustle of leaves in the gentle breeze, the distant call of a bird. Then it came—the faint but unmistakable sound of a motorcycle engine, somewhere in the distance but drawing steadily closer.

"Who is that?" Harry demanded.

The thug's smile widened. "Someone you don't want to meet, old man."

"A name," Harry insisted, his grip tightening.

But the man merely leaned back, a look of anticipation spreading across his face as the motorcycle sound grew louder, cutting through the stillness of the evening.

Harry released him and turned toward the window, straining to see through the darkness. The motorcycle was still out of sight, but the engine noise was louder still, coming from the direction of the main road.

"They'll be dealing with you," the thug said softly. "All of you."

The motorcycle engine roared louder, now unmistakably heading toward the cottage. Harry reached for his revolver, the weight of it both reassuring and terrifying in his hand. Somewhere in the darkness, Nigel was still out there, possibly in danger, while Harry sat in a car with a handcuffed prisoner, listening to the approaching sounds of what could only be more trouble.

The motorcycle drew closer, its headlamp not yet visible through the trees but surely soon to break through the darkness. Harry's mind raced with possibilities, none of them good. Was this Siegfried himself, coming to check on his operation? Or another agent, arriving with new orders?

Either way, Nigel was out there alone, and Harry was stuck here with a prisoner he couldn't abandon. The sound of the motorcycle engine filled the forest now, drowning out the evening's natural chorus, bearing down on them like the harbinger of some inevitable doom.

Chapter 43
Evie

The last red-orange rays of the sunset were fading from the sky and the garret was rapidly growing dim with shadows as Evie crouched with her ear pressed to the floorboards underneath the dusty old writing desk. For the most part, she couldn't hear anything from Hans and Gerda downstairs. But for lack of anything better to do, she'd been experimenting all afternoon, and she'd discovered that in this particular spot she could occasionally catch a word or two.

Now she heard Gerda say, sharply, "Come away from the window. Do you want someone to see you?"

"Who is there to see?" Hans grunted. "Except for Boris, and he is late."

Gerda's reply was indistinguishable, and although Evie waited for a few more minutes, she heard nothing more. Her German captors must have moved into a different part of the house. At least she now had acquired one more tiny scrap of information to add to her pile of knowledge about whatever Paul was planning: a man called Boris was somehow involved, and whoever he was, Gerda and Hans were clearly expecting him to arrive here tonight.

Now he was late, though. Evie let her mind flip through a few possibilities for what could have delayed the unknown Boris's arrival. But without further information, it was pointless to speculate.

She straightened, stretching out her cramped muscles, and acknowledged that she coped much better with fear than with simple boredom—and the kind of tense, helpless boredom she was experiencing now was particularly unpleasant. She'd already eaten the toast and drunk the cup of water left by Hans earlier. She was still hungry, but there was nothing left for her to do except debate whether pacing back and forth across the garret would make her feel better, or only alert Gerda and Hans to the fact that she was awake and moving around.

She scarcely noticed the light tapping sound at first, her unconscious mind dismissing it as the nighttime settling of an old house at night or maybe the rap of a tree branch against the roof. Only gradually did it dawn on her that the tapping sound was extremely rhythmic and steady for a tree branch . . . and that it was coming from the dormer window.

Evie whirled around, drawing the pair of nail scissors out of her skirt pocket and holding them in her clenched fist, ready to stab if this was the unknown Boris or some other underling of Paul's who'd spotted her ribbon signal outside.

She was just in time to see the window slide up, and Nigel's face appear in the resulting gap.

For a second or two, all Evie could do was stare, wondering whether his appearance was some sort of strange hallucination brought on by hunger, worry, and the effects of chloral on top of chloroform. Then he raised an eyebrow at the nail scissors in her hand.

Evie lowered her arm. "All right, not the most deadly of weapons, I admit." She spoke in a whisper.

Nigel's mouth twitched briefly. "If I were a scrap of yarn or a piece of string, I'd be quaking in my boots right now." His spoke in his usual tone of voice: level, detached and slightly ironic. But there was an expression of wondering, astonished relief in his eyes as he stared back at her.

At least, she thought there was. In the rapidly fading twilight, it was difficult to tell, and the next moment, he spoke in an urgent whisper. "What can you tell me about whoever's downstairs? Dorothy saw your ribbon in the window, so I waited until dark and climbed up the ivy on the outside walls. This window's small, but at least it's not hard to access. There's a porch roof just below it to stand on."

Which explained why he was able to stay here at the window without danger of falling.

"I didn't want to risk trying to get a look at the occupants of the place before I'd confirmed you were actually here," Nigel said.

"So far as I know, there are only two of them," she whispered back. "Gerda and Hans. Both German, although they've been passing themselves off as English. And they're expecting a third man, Boris, to arrive any minute."

Which meant that Boris would almost certainly see Nigel as he approached the house.

Nigel, though, shook his head. "That's all right. I'll wager Boris is the unpleasant character whose current headache is thanks to Dorothy and Tom. He won't be going anywhere tonight."

"Dorothy and Tom were here?" Evie was still struggling to take in the fact of Nigel's presence. She'd put the ribbon in the window, of course—but really, she had been bracing herself to either escape due to her own efforts or else die according to Paul's carelessly issued command. Rescue was something she'd scarcely let herself hope for.

"And Alice," Nigel said. "But the whole story can wait. Are Hans and Gerda armed?"

"Hans has a gun, I know," Evie said. "At least one. Probably more. I can't imagine that Paul would have left them here without adequate weaponry."

"Paul?" Nigel frowned.

"That's right." The haze of shock that had descended on Evie began to dissolve as she realised just how much Nigel didn't yet know. "Paul is Siegfried."

From the expression on Nigel's face, he was wondering whether imprisonment had somehow altered her wits.

"I've not gone crazy," Evie said quickly. "Paul's not dead at all. The report of his plane crash in enemy territory was all a fake."

Nigel's expression changed, disbelief warring with dawning understanding. "You're saying that your husband Paul—"

"Is Siegfried," Evie said. "Still alive, and he's been an agent working for the Germans all this time— even from before I married him."

"I'm sorry, Evie." Nigel's voice was quiet.

"Don't be sorry, help me to stop him!" Evie broke off as the last of the shock vanished and sudden reality slapped her in the face. "I can't leave with you."

"What?" Nigel was back to looking at her as though she'd lost her mind.

"Listen," Evie whispered urgently. "Paul is planning something— some sort of espionage mission that will strike a significant blow at Britain's defences. I don't know the details yet, only bits and pieces. But don't you see? My being here, inside the enemy's camp, so to speak, is our best chance for learning exactly what it is that he's planning."

"You think he's just going to walk in here and explain his plans to you?" Nigel said.

"He might— if he comes back here before the operation begins. He trusts me. Or rather, he thinks that I trust him. I have him convinced that I still have faith in him— that I think he's a double agent working on our side," Evie said.

Nigel's face had gone stony hard; she couldn't at all guess what he was thinking. At last he said, "Tell me what you've found out so far."

"Not terribly much," Evie admitted. "I overheard Gerda speaking of Hans wearing a uniform. So I assume that whatever his role is to be, it involves masquerading as some sort of military or police officer. And then I also overheard Hans saying to Paul that he didn't like the idea of relying on someone else's weapons. And Paul saying that was the beauty of the scheme, that they didn't need to worry about smuggling anything onto the site. I think that's all." Evie leaned forward a little. "But whatever it is that they're planning, it's bad, Nigel. Catastrophically bad. I know it is."

Again Nigel was silent for what seemed a long moment. Then he said, almost unwillingly, "There was a murder at a place not far from here called Clarion Castle. Harry and I were sent to investigate. Because the Prime Minister is going to arrive there in—" he checked his wristwatch. "Something less than sixteen hours."

"Winston Churchill is coming . . ." Evie's voice trailed off. An icy hand had wrapped around her chest and was squeezing tighter with every passing moment. "But that's—"

"Catastrophically bad," Nigel finished. His mouth has flattened into a grim line.

Evie shook her head, as though she could physically dislodge the spinning chaos that had taken the place of rational thought in her mind. "Don't you see, though? That makes it all the more urgent that I find out what Paul is planning. If he and the others are part of a plot to assassinate the Prime Minister, then we need to find out exactly how they intend to make the attempt so that Mr Churchill's staff can be warned and put on guard."

"Mr Churchill's staff can be put on guard without your staying here as a prisoner," Nigel said. "We can take Gerda and Hans into custody tonight and interrogate them about Paul's plans."

"Maybe. But in order to fully eliminate the threat, we need to capture Paul— and I don't know where he is right now. I'm not sure that Hans and Gerda do either. Even if you do arrest them and interrogate them— and even if they are willing to talk, which is a horribly big if— they certainly don't know as much as Paul does about the workings of Paul's espionage ring." Evie stopped and took a breath. "We already know that Siegfried doesn't trust any of his underlings with that sort of information. If I leave with you tonight, he'll find out I'm gone and he'll just disappear. He might even give up on the assassination scheme, or at least postpone it for another time when Mr Churchill is forced to travel away from 10 Downing Street. We'll lose our best chance at trapping Paul and ensuring that he never gets another chance to strike a blow for Germany."

"I can put men on surveillance here, surrounding the cottage—" Nigel began.

Evie interrupted. "No, you can't. Paul would spot them in a moment from a mile away. He's expertly trained at what he does, Nigel, and he's had time to study the terrain around here. Put even one lookout here, and I can guarantee that Paul will vanish long before your man spots him, and then all the same arguments apply."

Nigel didn't speak. Evie could tell from his expression that he could see the truth in every argument that she'd just made. Of course he did; Nigel was nothing if not intelligent. All the same, he shut his eyes briefly and said, "I don't want to leave you here, Evie." His voice had turned husky, a tone she'd never heard from him before.

Evie's own throat tightened, hot pressure building behind her eyes. She stepped closer to the window, standing on tiptoe so that she could reach up to touch Nigel's cheek. "You're a good man," she said softly. "Whatever happens, I'm thankful to have known you—"

"Evie." Nigel's eyes had fluttered shut again at the touch of her fingers against his cheek, but at that he looked back at her, drawing in a ragged breath. "You're drastically over-estimating just how good of a man I am. If you say another word, I'm going to break down the door of this place and carry you out, no matter the consequence."

"Then I'll stop." Evie took a step back and swallowed hard, forcing away the sting of tears in her eyes. When she was certain that she could trust her voice not to shake, she said, "Can you give me a weapon of some kind? I may have to stay here, but that doesn't mean I wouldn't prefer to be armed with something better than nail scissors."

"Take this." Nigel drew out a revolver and handed it in to her through the window. For a moment, as Evie took the gun, their fingers touched, and the warmth of Nigel's skin seemed almost to burn into hers, as though an electric current had passed between them. Then she drew back.

"Thank you."

Nigel didn't move back from the window at once, though. Finally he said, "I know we just agreed not to exchange last speeches. But all the same, I want you to know that you're the bravest woman I've ever met."

"That's funny." Evie's eyes stung all over again. "I'm not feeling especially brave right now."

But Nigel's gaze remained steady on hers. "You don't need to feel it for it to be true."

Chapter 44
Harry

The sound of the motorcycle had barely faded when Harry caught movement at the edge of the tree line. A familiar figure emerged from the shadows, moving with the careful precision of a man trying to remain unseen. Nigel's silhouette was unmistakable, even in the fading light.

Harry felt a wave of relief wash over him, though he kept his expression neutral. The dark-haired thug in the back seat didn't need to know how worried he'd been.

Nigel approached the car quickly, his face half-hidden in shadow. When he reached the passenger window, he didn't speak but made an urgent gesture for Harry to get out. Something in his nephew's expression sent a fresh jolt of concern through Harry's veins.

With one last warning glance at his prisoner, Harry opened the door and stepped out, closing it firmly behind him. If the man in the back seat decided to shout, the thick forest would swallow the sound before it reached the cottage. Besides, with those handcuffs secured tightly, there wasn't much mischief he could accomplish in their brief absence.

Nigel led Harry several paces away from the car, where the deepening shadows beneath the trees offered additional concealment. The forest smelled of damp earth and pine needles, the scent intensifying as evening dew began to settle. Somewhere in the distance, an owl called, the sound eerie and forlorn in the gathering darkness.

"What's happened?" Harry asked, his voice low. The forest seemed to absorb his words, muffling them even as he spoke.

Nigel glanced back at the car. "Our friend in the back seat is named Boris. He's waiting for Siegfried."

"How do you know that?" Harry asked, surprised.

"Evie told me. She overheard the name." Nigel ran a hand through his hair, a gesture Harry recognised as a sign of his agitation. "And yes, I've seen her. But there's more. The man we know as Siegfried is actually Evie's husband. Paul."

If Harry had been surprised a moment ago, it was nothing to the stunned disbelief with which he stared at Nigel now.

"Yes, I know," Nigel said. "My response was similar when Evie told me. But it's quite true. She's actually seen and spoken to the man."

"How is Evie?" Harry asked.

"She's coping." Just for a moment, Nigel's expression lightened in a brief, grim smile. "Really, Siegfried's the one who should be worried, assuming we all get through this alive. I wouldn't want to be in his shoes when he has to face Evie again."

A career at Scotland Yard had trained Harry in adjusting his viewpoint quickly to accommodate new ideas. Now he filed Siegfried's real identity away in a category to be dealt with later, and returned to the question most immediately at hand.

"So Evie's captors were expecting our prisoner? Do they know what's become of him?"

"According to Evie, they don't. We've another problem, though." Nigel's voice was tight with tension. "A man went by on a motorcycle as I was coming out to the road. He passed the lane to the cottage.

I heard the sound of the engine die away in the distance. Then it stopped."

Harry felt the hairs on the back of his neck rise. "Siegfried?"

"It's possible, isn't it?" Nigel said. "Evie said that the couple he'd left guarding her weren't expecting him back so soon. But his plans may have changed."

"And now he may be walking back," Harry said, his eyes scanning the dark forest around them. The trees now seemed filled with potential threats, the shadows between them perfect hiding places for a man intent on harm. "Did he see you?"

"I don't know. Possibly."

Harry could tell that Nigel's thoughts were as grim as his own. "If he saw you— and if he's on his way back to Evie—"

"I know. But Evie says she's convinced him that she's on his side. If that's the case, then the worst thing we can do for her is to go anywhere near that cottage tonight. She says she needs to stay till she learns what they're planning." Nigel's jaw clenched. "I hate that, but she's right."

She was. Harry, too, hated the thought of Evie facing the man who'd betrayed both her and their country, especially if that man suspected that Nigel might have been searching for her. But there was nothing to do but trust that she would be more than a match for Siegfried if and when that meeting occurred.

A gentle breeze rustled through the trees. Harry pulled his coat tighter around him, feeling every one of his years in the chill that settled into his bones.

"Do you want to wait here?" he asked, though he already knew the answer.

"We can't. Siegfried would be bound to spot us." Nigel shook his head. "I told Evie how to get to The Shepherd's Rest. She'll come there when she's ready."

The thought of leaving Evie behind made Harry's stomach knot with worry, but he recognised the cold logic of Nigel's decision. Sometimes the most difficult choice was the correct one.

"And in the meantime..." Nigel gave a significant glance at the Ford, and the shadowy figure visible through the rear window. The moonlight caught the gleam of handcuffs as the thug shifted position, clearly still working to free himself despite the restraints.

"We need to do something about our friend Boris," Harry said, his voice grim.

"I've been thinking about that." Nigel's expression hardened in a way that reminded Harry powerfully of himself in his younger days. "We might take him to Ashford Station, but that's a bit far, and there's bound to be a lot of paperwork. Same goes for the station at Crofter's Green."

Harry nodded, understanding the implications. Official channels meant reports, questions, delays—none of which they could afford with Siegfried possibly returning and Churchill's visit to Clarion Castle mere hours away.

"So I have another idea," Nigel continued. "We'll need to blindfold our friend."

Chapter 45
Evie

After Nigel had gone, Evie allowed herself exactly ten seconds to stand still, her eyes burning and her chest aching with the wish that she could have gone with him. Then she wiped her eyes with the heels of her hands and ordered herself to think. She wasn't going to sacrifice her own life for nothing.

Well, ideally, she wasn't going to sacrifice it at all. But if she was going to make her decision to stay locked up here worthwhile, she had to find out Paul's plan.

Was he going to make an attempt on Mr Churchill's life? A part of Evie wanted to believe that even Paul wouldn't be bold and reckless enough to take on so difficult a mission. But she already knew that wasn't true. Paul was more than conceited enough to think that he could strike such a devastating blow all by himself. And besides, the puzzle pieces fit only too well.

Evie's thoughts were interrupted by the distant sound of an engine, coming from outside. For a moment or two, she thought it was an aeroplane engine— an all-too familiar sound by now, whether it was a German bomber or a British fighter flying out to defend the Channel.

But this was no aeroplane.

The breath scraped in Evie's throat and fear sliced inside her like blades as she realised that what she was hearing was the approaching roar of a motorbike.

Paul? It almost had to be. Hans and Gerda hadn't mentioned that they were expecting anyone besides Boris, and Dorothy and Tom had dealt with him.

If this was Paul, returning before he'd told Hans he'd be back . . . if he'd seen Nigel somewhere on the road—

Almost as though in answer to her question, the motorbike roared past the cottage, the sound fading into the distance. Evie didn't even let herself hope that the motorcyclist was just a random stranger, though, someone unconnected to her and this place. She drew out the revolver Nigel had given her, her mind flipping through and almost instantly discarding ideas. She couldn't just shoot her way out of here and flee; everything she'd said to Nigel about Paul simply postponing his mission in that case still applied. No, she needed to somehow ensure that even if he'd seen Nigel on the road, Paul would leave here feeling entirely confident . . . victorious . . .

Evie's breath went out in a rush as she stared down at the gun in her hand. A fully formed plan had just appeared in her mind with all the sudden force of a bombing strike.

She'd need luck to be on her side to an almost ridiculous degree, so much so that the idea was arguably an insane one.

In her head, she could almost hear Nigel's commentary: *All your ideas are arguably insane.*

But she could also see Nigel, framed in the window just minutes ago. *I want you to know that you're the bravest woman I've ever met.*

To carry out the plan she had in mind, she would need to be.

Chapter 46
Harry

Fifteen minutes later, Harry peered through the windscreen as they approached the entry gate of Fort Hardwick.

The low buildings of the military training facility were barely visible in the darkness. The perimeter fence had faded into the twilight. In accordance with strict blackout regulations, the checkpoint was illuminated only by a heavily shielded lamp that cast a small pool of dim light downward, barely enough to identify approaching vehicles.

A sentry stepped forward, rifle at the ready, his face a pale blur in the carefully contained illumination. Recognition flickered in his eyes as the car stopped and Nigel and Harry got out. Once more, Harry shut the door on their prisoner.

"Inspector Brewster," the young man said, a note of surprise in his voice. "And Mr Jenkins. Wasn't expecting to see you gentlemen again so soon."

"Urgent business, Sergeant," Nigel replied. "We need to speak with Colonel Merriweather immediately."

The sentry's eyes darted to the back seat, where Boris sat blindfolded and silent. Since they'd secured a handkerchief over his eyes, he hadn't uttered a word—a silence Harry found more unnerving than any threats or protests might have been.

"Right away, sir." The sentry stepped back and signalled to his companion to open the gate. "Drive straight to headquarters. I'll telephone ahead."

The gravel drive crunched beneath the tyres as they proceeded through the compound. They passed the buildings Harry had seen before—barracks, training facilities, and storage sheds that testified to the urgent need to expand Britain's commando forces. Finally they arrived at the main building that housed the officers' quarters and administrative offices.

Moments later, they stood outside the car, facing Colonel Merriweather in the shadows. Harry was struck, as always, by how Merriweather seemed to dominate any space he occupied. The colonel had the air of a man who could swagger even when standing still—a quality that had been both impressive and occasionally irritating during their work together on the Judas Monk case.

In the dim light provided by a carefully shielded lamp above the entrance, Harry could see that Merriweather looked much the same as he had a month ago—still solid as a man half his age, with broad shoulders, a thick chest, and muscular arms that strained against the fabric of his combat fatigues, which were somehow crisp and starched even at this, the end of the day. His close-cropped hair, shot through with steel-grey, only emphasised the severe angles of his face, and that cleft chin still jutted forward assertively, as though challenging the world to defy him.

The commander's steely blue eyes—sharp as ever—assessed Harry and Nigel with the same clinical precision Harry remembered. If anything, Merriweather looked even more formidable in the shadowy half-light, his rigid posture and precisely arranged medals a reminder of the disciplined force he commanded.

Flanking him were four powerfully built men in combat fatigues, their faces impassive, their stance alert despite the late hour. Two positioned themselves on either side of the car, their very presence a silent warning to the man inside.

"Jenkins, Brewster," Merriweather nodded curtly, his gravelly voice cutting through the night air. "My sergeant tells me you've brought us a visitor."

"Indeed we have," Harry replied, feeling a strange comfort in the colonel's unchanging demeanour. In a world turned upside down by war, there was something reassuring about Merriweather's immutable presence. He indicated the blindfolded and handcuffed figure in the back seat. "We had a run-in with this fellow at Hawthorne Manor. He was threatening Lady Hawthorne, demanding information about a woman named Diana Lovecraft."

Merriweather's expression remained unchanged, but Harry caught the slight narrowing of those steely blue eyes at the mention of Lovecraft's name.

"We also know he's a German spy," Harry continued. "Just before we detained him, he was on his way to meet the man you and I watched from a distance at Dover Beach."

The colonel spoke only one word. "Siegfried."

At that, a ripple of tension passed through the assembled commandos, invisible to the untrained eye but clear as day to Harry's experienced gaze.

"His name is Boris, and he's been most uncooperative," Harry said.

"So we need someplace secure to hold him," Nigel added. "Somewhere not on any official record."

The colonel nodded.

"We need to go now," Harry said.

The colonel nodded once more.

"So you'll take care of him, then, Colonel?" Harry asked, confident he already knew the answer.

A long, slow grin spread across Merriweather's face, transforming his stern features into something almost predatory. The muscles in his jaw flexed visibly—a tell Harry remembered.

"Oh yes, we will," he said, his voice dropping to a near whisper. "Oh, *hell* yes."

At the colonel's nod, one of the commandos opened the car door. Boris flinched at the sound but said nothing as strong hands grasped his arms and pulled him from the vehicle.

Harry felt no pity.

Chapter 47
Evie

Evie lay with her ear pressed hard against the floorboards in the one spot where she'd been able to overhear what went on down below. She was trying to imagine what Paul would do, knowing him as she did.

Attack Nigel? Shoot him in cold blood?

She remembered the steely note in Paul's voice when he questioned her about Nigel a few days ago, and felt a fresh throb of fear that churned in the pit of her stomach like sickness. But rationally she doubted Paul would do it. He'd know that shooting Nigel might draw attention, and attention was exactly what he'd want to avoid just now. He'd wait to kill Nigel until after his mission was complete.

So what would Paul be doing? He'd want to draw attention away from the cottage, so he wouldn't simply drive the motorbike up to the front door. No, he'd park it somewhere not too far off and walk back—

Down below her, she felt the faint tremor of a slammed door through the floorboards, and then she heard Hans' startled voice. "Mein Herr!"

Paul answered, also speaking in German. "Pack everything into the car; we must leave now. At once!"

"Certainly, if you wish." Evie could hear the surprise in Hans' voice. "But why?"

"Because I have just seen that policeman, Inspector Brewster, on the road!" Paul barked. "If he has not been here already, he will be here soon."

"The woman?" Hans asked.

"Pack up first," Paul said. "Then take care of her. I must get back to meet our contact before daybreak if I am to get into position in the tower."

Hans said nothing more, but Evie could hear a flurry of activity taking place downstairs. She stood up. Really, the only surprise was that Paul didn't want to take care of her, as he put it, himself. But that meant she had only one possible course of action. If Paul had come up here alone, she might have tried to leverage the element of surprise in her favour. In a match of close physical combat, he would always overpower her, but he wouldn't be expecting her to have a gun.

Now, though, she crossed to the door of the garret and quickly, before she could let fear creep in and try to change her mind, she aimed and fired directly at the lock. Wood splintered and the bullet ricocheted . . . somewhere.

Evie didn't wait to find out. She shoved the now-unlocked door open and ran down a narrow flight of wooden stairs. She saw a landing, and what looked to be a couple of bedrooms, but since they were dark and empty, Evie didn't pause to investigate but continued on her headlong flight to the ground floor.

The staircase opened onto a shabby, sparsely furnished sitting room, dimly lit by the flickering glow of a single oil lantern. Hans and Gerda had been packing what looked like the components of a short-wave radio and some assorted weapons into a couple of leather satchels that lay open on a central table. The German pair had clearly heard the shot, though, and had halted what they were doing, drawing aside to allow Paul to run for the stairs.

All three of them froze at Evie's entrance, Paul stopping short in the centre of the room. Hans and Gerda's expressions were almost comically slack with astonishment, but Paul's brief moment of shock gave way almost at once to a sneer.

"So." Paul wore dark trousers and a leather driving coat, belted around the waist. His gaze focused on the revolver in Evie's hand. "Courtesy of your friend Brewster, I assume?" He took a step towards her, his expression hardening. "I wondered whether your starry-eyed belief in me was quite sincere."

"That's far enough." Evie aimed the gun at him. "And no— you didn't wonder. You were perfectly ready to believe that I was still your adoring wife. That's always been your downfall, Paul. You've far too high an opinion of yourself, and therefore you assume that others must share that opinion."

"You—" Rage shivered in Paul's face, but was instantly quelled. Evie saw his hands flex, but when he spoke his voice was grating but calm. "Be reasonable, Evie. You're not going to be able to shoot your way out of here. You might take a shot at me, but the instant you pull the trigger, either Hans or Gerda will fill you with bullet holes."

Unfortunately that was all too true. Evie had already seen both Gerda and Hans reach for the weapons on the table. Now Hans was aiming a snub-nosed pistol at her while Gerda held a Colt 45.

"What's the alternative?" Evie demanded. She let her voice rise. "Do you really think I'm just going to wait quietly upstairs until Hans comes up to introduce me to the afterlife? If you think that, Paul, you don't know me at all. But then, you always were really rather stupid. Nigel is far more intelligent. He didn't have any trouble at all in finding me here."

Paul's face radiated such angry colour and twisted fury that Evie hardly recognised him. He looked not like himself, not even like a man anymore, but like some raging wild beast. "Hans!" He barked. He put out his hand in clear demand for the German man to toss the pistol over to him.

"No!" Evie shouted. She didn't entirely have to fabricate the edge of hysteria in her voice. Her heart was pounding hard enough that her vision shivered, and her palms were clammy. "I'm not going to give you the satisfaction of killing me, either, Paul. If I'm going to die tonight, it will be by my own hand!"

She turned the revolver around, pressing the barrel against her own breast. Then she shut her eyes for a brief instant and pulled the trigger.

Chapter 48
Evie

Through a throbbing haze of pain, Evie lay where she'd fallen at the foot of the stairs. The deafening sound of the gunshot still rang in her ears, and she could feel the hot ooze of blood down her side. At the last second, she'd shifted the barrel of the revolver so that she shot through the upper part of her arm rather than her chest, but even in the dim lamplight, Paul would have to see actual blood to be convinced.

Her eyes were closed, but she heard him cursing fluently. Evie held her breath. Even worse than the gnawing, fiery pain was the fear that Paul might come closer to examine her and see whether she really was dead. If he'd been thinking clearly and had been in full control of himself, he certainly would have done, but she'd deliberately goaded him, provoking and enraging him. Still, that might not be enough—

The night stillness was broken by the noise of a car engine. Evie couldn't tell from which direction it came, but it wasn't too far off.

Paul swore again. "Move— now!" he barked at Gerda and Hans. "We must be gone from here."

Evie forced herself to lie perfectly still, forced herself not to grit her teeth as the pain chewed through her every nerve. She heard a scuffle of movement as they picked up weapons and satchels, then footsteps, followed by the slam of a door. More slamming of car doors, and then the roar of another engine coming to life. When at last the growl of the car had died away and faded into the distance, Evie opened her eyes and sat up, looking down at herself. Her head swam and there was a far more sizable pool of blood under her than she'd been expecting.

No wonder Paul and the others had been convinced.

Holding onto the newel post at the foot of the stairs, she managed to stand upright, though the effort left her with stars dancing across her field of vision. Evie shut her eyes, fighting a wave of nausea from the pain. This was one part of her plan that she hadn't fully accounted for: if this was how awful it felt to simply stand up, how would she manage to walk out of here— and potentially for miles further on?

Go on, stop feeling sorry for yourself, it's not as though you have any other choice. Evie locked her jaw, ordering herself to take a step. She swayed, almost fell, and then caught her balance and kept moving.

One step at a time.

Chapter 49
Katherine

Katherine woke before dawn, her mind restless with the German translations she and Blake had completed for Harry. The decoded messages from "Nightingale" had troubled her deeply—evidence of a spy at Clarion Castle with intimate knowledge of Churchill's impending visit.

Despite this worrisome discovery, however, she found herself oddly comforted by how easily the German language had returned to her. Perhaps her other memories weren't completely lost, just hidden behind some mental curtain she couldn't yet draw aside.

Rather than lying in bed watching the ceiling gradually brighten, she decided to get up. Fresh air might help her organise her thoughts. She dressed quickly in a simple skirt and blouse, then slipped quietly from her room in the east wing.

The corridors of Clarion Castle were silent at this hour, save for the occasional creak of floorboards under her feet. A grandfather clock in the main hall chimed five as she passed—heavy, sonorous notes that seemed to reverberate through the empty spaces. Katherine paused at a side door that led out to the gardens, drawing in a deep breath before stepping outside.

The morning air was cool and sweet with dew. Tendrils of mist hovered above the lawn, giving the formal gardens an otherworldly quality in the pearl-grey light that preceded sunrise. Birds were already active, their morning songs creating a cheerful counterpoint to the stillness. A robin hopped boldly along the gravel path ahead of her, pausing to cock its head as if considering whether she might be a source of breakfast.

As she walked, Katherine found her thoughts drifting to Blake. Their work on the translations had brought them closer, reminding her of something she couldn't quite grasp—a sense of partnership and intimacy that felt both new and achingly familiar. The way he'd looked at her when she successfully read the German text, pride mingling with tenderness in his eyes, had stirred emotions she was still learning to interpret.

Was it always like this before? she wondered. The uncertainty was maddening. Sometimes she felt as though she was acting a role in a play where everyone else knew the script while she improvised, hoping to strike the right note. Yet with Blake, the performance fell away. There was something solid and true in their connection that transcended her fractured memory.

Katherine followed the path that wound between neatly trimmed boxwood hedges and past stone urns overflowing with summer flowers. The groundskeepers at Clarion Castle clearly took pride in maintaining the gardens to their pre-war standards despite the shortages of labour. Off to her right, she could see the rose garden—its entrance marked by an ivy-covered trellis arch that framed the path.

The perfume of roses grew stronger as she approached, a heady mixture of scents from dozens of varieties. Morning light was beginning to touch the tops of the castle towers, painting them in pale gold, though the gardens still lay in soft shadow. Katherine remembered reading once that roses released their strongest fragrance at dawn, when the essential oils were most concentrated in the cool air.

She paused, hand lightly touching the trellis. This was a memory she could trust—a fragment of botanical knowledge not tied to her personal history. These small certainties had become precious to her, islands of confidence in the sea of uncertainty that was her past.

As she passed beneath the trellis, she noted how the gardeners had arranged the beds to create a peaceful sanctuary. Stone benches were positioned at strategic intervals along the gravel paths, inviting contemplation among the blooms. Katherine found herself drawn to a particularly lovely display of pale pink roses near the centre of the garden. Their delicate colour reminded her of ballet slippers.

She was about to turn away when something caught her eye—a splash of darker pink among the pale blooms that seemed out of place. At first she thought perhaps it was another variety of rose intermingled with the pale ones, but something about the shape wasn't right. Katherine moved closer, her footsteps crunching on the gravel.

A gardening basket lay tipped on its side. Pruning shears and twine spilled onto the path. Odd that someone would leave their tools out overnight, especially when the groundskeepers seemed so meticulous.

She took another step forward and felt her heart stutter in her chest.

A hand. A human hand, pale against the dark earth, partially concealed by the rose bushes.

"Hello?" Katherine called, her voice sounding unnaturally high. "Are you all right?"

No response came save the continued chorus of birdsong.

Katherine forced herself to move around the rose bed for a clearer view, though every instinct screamed at her to turn and run back to the castle. What she saw made her press her own hand against her mouth to stifle a cry.

Lillian, the young and pretty housemaid, lay on her side among the roses, her blonde hair spread out like a fan across the dark soil. Her blue eyes were open, staring at nothing, and her face held an expression of mild surprise. She was still wearing her uniform, though the starched collar was askew, revealing a single dark mark across her throat.

For a terrible moment, Katherine simply stood frozen, unable to process what she was seeing. Then her experiences volunteering at St Thomas's Hospital took over. She'd seen enough during the London air raids to recognise death, even if she couldn't recall all the details of those chaotic nights. She knelt beside the body, automatically reaching to check for a pulse at Lillian's wrist, though she already knew what she would find. The skin was cool to the touch, with none of the pliancy of life.

"Oh, Lillian," she whispered.

The girl looked as though she'd been carefully arranged, almost posed—her hands folded over a single rose placed on her chest, her skirts smoothed neatly around her legs. It gave Katherine a chill that ran deeper than the morning air could account for. This wasn't a spontaneous act of violence but something calculated and deliberate.

Katherine's mind raced. What had Lillian told her just yesterday about Foster, the Signal Corps man she was so obviously sweet on?

The words came back: "Jim says Mr Vernon was always hanging around the Tower Wing, making up excuses to try and get a look."

Lillian had seemed curious about what Mr Vernon had been doing at the Tower Wing. Had she been too curious?

A twig snapped somewhere in the garden beyond, and Katherine's head jerked up. Was someone watching her? The murderer could still be nearby.

She rose quickly, backing away from Lillian's body. She needed to tell someone—Blake first, then Harry and Nigel. The translations she'd completed took on an even more ominous significance now.

As Katherine hurried back toward the castle, the sun finally crested the horizon, casting long shadows across the lawn. The dew on the grass sparkled like scattered diamonds, a beauty that now seemed heartless in contrast to what lay in the rose garden. She tried not to run, not wanting to draw attention if anyone hostile was watching, but her pace was brisk enough that she was slightly out of breath by the time she reached the side door.

The castle was beginning to stir. She could hear distant sounds from the kitchen—the clatter of pots and pans as the day's meals were prepared. A maid passed at the end of the corridor carrying fresh linens, glancing curiously at Katherine's flushed appearance but continuing on her way without comment.

Katherine climbed the main staircase two steps at a time, her heart still pounding. Blake's room was on the second floor in the west wing—the farthest possible location from her own quarters. As she hurried along the portrait gallery that connected the wings, she felt the painted eyes of generations of previous inhabitants following her progress.

The irony wasn't lost on her—here she was, in need of Blake at the most basic, human level, just as she'd needed him to give her confidence for the translations. Her missing memories hadn't prevented her from doing important work yesterday, and they wouldn't prevent her from handling this crisis either. Perhaps that was the key—focusing on what she could do rather than what she had lost.

She slowed as she approached Blake's door, suddenly aware of how she must look—dishevelled, agitated, possibly with garden soil on her skirt from kneeling beside Lillian. Taking a moment to smooth her hair and collect herself, Katherine drew a deep breath.

Then she knocked firmly on Blake's door, three sharp raps that seemed to echo down the hushed corridor.

Chapter 50
Harry

Squinting at the direct rays of the early morning sun, Harry nearly stumbled on the path to the rose garden. He was following Nigel. They'd both dressed hastily, after Blake had pounded on their doors with news of Katherine's grim discovery. Harry hadn't even bothered with his tie, and Nigel's hair was still mussed from sleep.

Long shadows streamed across the dewy grass that lay before them.

"How long has she been there?" Harry asked, his mind already shifting into the familiar routines of an investigation, despite the unusual setting.

"Katherine found her just before dawn," Blake replied, walking a few paces ahead. "She came straight to me, and we thought it best to wake you both immediately. Her name's Lillian. One of the housemaids."

The sweet scent of roses grew stronger as they approached the trellis arch. In any other circumstance, Harry might have appreciated the beauty of the morning—the golden light filtering through the mist, the birdsong that continued its cheery chorus, oblivious to human tragedy. But not today. Not with a dead girl waiting for them.

Katherine stood at the entrance to the rose garden, her arms wrapped around herself as though warding off a chill despite the mild morning air. She looked pale but composed, and Harry felt a surge of respect for her steadiness. Not every civilian could discover a body and maintain such self-possession.

"This way," she said quietly, leading them along the gravel path to the centre of the garden.

Harry saw the girl immediately—a splash of darkness amid the pale pink roses. Lillian lay on her side, blonde hair fanned out across the soil, blue eyes open and unseeing. Someone had placed a single rose on her chest, and folded her hands neatly over it. The sight sparked a rush of indignation within him. He'd seen many deaths during his years with Scotland Yard, but the staged quality of this one struck him as particularly cruel.

"The rose," he said, kneeling beside the body but careful not to disturb anything. "It seems like mockery."

"It looks almost... ceremonial," Nigel observed, his voice tight. "As though the killer was performing a ritual rather than covering up a crime."

Harry glanced at the overturned gardening basket nearby, pruning shears and twine scattered across the path. The arrangement seemed deliberate, too perfect in its disarray. "This looks false," he said, gesturing toward the tools. "She wouldn't have been gardening here at night, and surely she would have been reported missing if she hadn't returned to her quarters."

"Which means she was either killed elsewhere and brought here, or..." Blake didn't finish the thought.

"Or she sneaked out to meet someone," Harry concluded. "Did she have a boyfriend? Someone she might have arranged to meet in secret?"

Katherine cleared her throat. "She had aspirations above her station." She glanced at the castle, lit up by the sunrise as if by golden floodlights. "The very pinnacle of stations around here, if you catch my meaning."

"What?" Harry looked up sharply. "Mr Walker?"

"Yes," Katherine nodded. "She was Mrs Walker's housemaid, but since Mrs Walker's away, she's been quite attentive to Mr Walker."

"How attentive?"

"I don't really know. That's just gossip I've picked up. Also, I saw her with one of the Signal Corps men yesterday. She referred to him as Jim. She said Jim thought Mr Vernon had been killed because he'd got mixed up with German spies."

Harry sighed, running a hand through his hair. "The naïve young girl." What had she seen—the same thing Vernon had seen? Or something different?

He forced himself to study the body more carefully. The mark on her throat was consistent with strangulation, or with a direct blow to the girl's exposed throat, perhaps. The medical examiner would clarify that. Her uniform was relatively undisturbed, which suggested the primary motive hadn't been assault. Her expression was one of surprise rather than terror, and that might indicate she'd known her killer. Or at least that she hadn't perceived an immediate threat until it was too late.

"Nigel," he said, standing up, "can you go back to the lodge and telephone the police mortuary? And the photographer? We need to document everything."

Nigel nodded. "What about footprints? Should I ask them to bring someone who can make casts?"

"Yes, good thinking." Harry gazed around the garden. The gravel paths would make footprints difficult to distinguish, but the soft earth of the flower beds might hold some evidence. "We need to determine if she was killed here or elsewhere. Tell Glenwood to have the area roped off. Nothing is to be touched until the photographer is finished."

"I'll stay here until you've done that," he added. "Then I'm going to call Mr Thompson. He needs to be told. Maybe they'll want to postpone the visit."

As Nigel hurried back toward the castle, Harry turned to Blake and Katherine. "I'll need statements from both of you later. Every detail you can remember about Lillian—her behaviour recently, anyone she might have been afraid of, anything unusual she mentioned."

Katherine nodded. "She seemed... excited yesterday. As though she knew something important."

"Or thought she did," Blake added grimly.

Harry glanced back at the dead girl, so carefully arranged among the roses. Death always angered him, but there was something about this particular tableau that tightened his chest with fury. A young life cut short, and for what? What secrets could possibly be worth this?

Chapter 51
Alice

Alice trudged up the worn path back to The Shepherd's Rest, Bonzo trotting faithfully at her heels despite his obvious fatigue.

Disappointment weighed heavily on Alice's shoulders. She'd risen before dawn, hopeful that the cover of early morning might allow her to approach the cottage where Evie had been taken. But when she'd arrived, the place seemed deserted—no guards visible, no movement inside. She'd circled the perimeter, the stillness only deepening her anxiety. Had they moved Evie elsewhere? Or had something worse happened?

But she'd seen no clues, and Bonzo had picked up no scents. The little Pomeranian had given his all this morning—nose to the ground, ears perked for any sound—but their search had yielded nothing. No sign of Evie anywhere.

"Come on, boy," she murmured, pushing open the weathered oak door of the Shepherds's Rest. "Let's get you some water."

The common room was empty save for Mrs Hadley, who looked up from behind the counter where she appeared to be tallying accounts. The innkeeper's face brightened at their arrival.

"There you are, Miss Greenleaf! I was beginning to wonder."

Alice forced a smile, though

"Any messages for me?" Alice asked, though she already knew the answer from Mrs Hadley's expression.

"None at all, I'm afraid." The older woman wiped her hands on her faded apron—a habitual gesture Alice had noticed before. "But I've kept your breakfast warm, though it's almost eleven and really nearly lunchtime."

"That's very kind of you." Alice bent down to scoop up Bonzo, who was panting slightly. "This little soldier has earned his rest, haven't you?"

She'd tried her last resort—the "Find Evie" command they'd practised a month ago. Bonzo was clever and had succeeded once before, but without a recent item of Evie's to refresh his memory, and with the morning breeze carrying scents in unhelpful directions, even his keen nose had been thwarted.

Mrs Hadley came around from behind the counter, her grey-streaked hair pulled back in its practical bun, her weather-lined face softer with concern than Alice had seen it before.

"Is there anything I can do to assist you?" she asked, her voice lowered though they were alone in the room. "I couldn't help overhearing some of your telephone conversations..." She hesitated, then pressed on. "You're looking for someone, aren't you? A friend?"

Alice studied the woman carefully. The innkeeper's eyes held genuine concern, though Alice also recognised the practical consideration that would motivate any business owner in these lean times.

"Will you be wanting a room for your friend as well, when you find her?" Mrs Hadley asked, confirming Alice's assessment. "I could prepare the blue room—it gets the morning light. Quite cheerful."

Despite her exhaustion and worry, Alice felt a surge of warmth toward the woman. The war had affected everyone—not just those in uniform or in the direct path of bombs. Here was Mrs Hadley, whose livelihood depended on travellers and pilgrims who no longer came, offering what help she could while trying to keep her business afloat.

Bonzo, who was typically wary of strangers, wagged his tail hopefully at Mrs Hadley. Another point in her favour—the little dog had good instincts about people.

"Thank you," Alice said sincerely. "Yes, I'd love whatever breakfast is still available and some strong coffee, if you have it." She set Bonzo down gently. "And perhaps some meat scraps and water for my friend here. We'll be going out again soon."

"Of course." Mrs Hadley nodded, already moving toward the kitchen. "I'll bring it right out. You sit down and rest those feet. You've been walking since first light, if I'm not mistaken."

Alice settled at a small table near the window, where she could watch the road while still keeping an eye on the telephone near the staircase. Bonzo curled up at her feet, his warm little body a comforting presence.

She rubbed her eyes, fighting both fatigue and frustration. The cottage had appeared deserted from her distant vantage point—no smoke from the chimney, no movement at the windows. But that didn't mean Evie wasn't still inside. On the other hand, she might have escaped, only to become lost in the unfamiliar woods. Alice didn't want to think of the other alternatives. Every hour that passed was another hour Evie remained in danger, either in Siegfried's custody or alone somewhere in the countryside.

The uncertainty was almost worse than knowing. At least if she could confirm Evie was still at the cottage, she'd have a target. As it stood now, Alice's imagination conjured a dozen scenarios, each more troubling than the last.

Alice pushed the dark thoughts away. She needed to focus, to plan her next move. Perhaps she could approach from the north after dark, using the ridge as cover. Or maybe...

Mrs Hadley returned with a tray laden with food—eggs, bacon, toast, and a small pot of coffee that sent a reviving aroma through the room. She set it down before Alice, then produced a small bowl of chopped meat scraps and another of water, which she placed on the floor for Bonzo. The Pomeranian gave a soft bark of appreciation before diving in.

"You eat up now," Mrs Hadley instructed, sounding momentarily like the mother Alice had lost too young. "Can't help your friend if your tummy's empty, now, can you?"

As the innkeeper turned to go, Alice impulsively reached out to touch her arm.

"Mrs Hadley... thank you. For everything."

The older woman's face softened. "We all do what we can in these times, don't we? Some fight abroad, some keep the home fires burning." She glanced down at Bonzo, who was enthusiastically finishing his meal. "And some of us just try to keep a roof over our heads and help where we can."

With that, she returned to her ledgers, leaving Alice to her breakfast and her thoughts. As she ate, Alice mentally mapped the countryside surrounding the cottage. There had to be a way to get closer, to find a weakness in Siegfried's security—if, in fact, Siegfried and his men were still there.

She would find Evie. She had to. And when she did, perhaps they really would need that cheerful blue room Mrs Hadley had mentioned. The thought gave her a flicker of hope as she sipped her coffee.

Then from outside the inn came the sound of tyres on gravel, and a car engine switching off. Moments later, Alice looked up and saw Dorothy Baker.

"Tom and I came to help," Dorothy said.

Chapter 52
Harry

The red telephone booth was stuffy, and Harry had to stoop slightly to fit comfortably inside.

Before making this call, he'd waited until the police photographer had finished and the medical examiner had arrived. They'd readily acknowledged Nigel's authority in the matter, which was a positive development. At least Harry and Nigel didn't have territorial squabbling to contend with.

He dialled the number for Thompson's office in London, tapping his fingers impatiently against the wooden panel as he waited.

"I'm sorry," a coolly competent young woman's voice came through after he'd explained who he was and where he was. "Mr Thompson isn't available at the moment."

Harry gritted his teeth. "Then tell him to call me at Clarion Castle, urgently. There's been a murder here—the second in a week. He needs to know about this immediately."

There was a pause on the other end of the line. "I'll... I'll make sure he gets the message, sir."

"As soon as you can. Thank you," Harry replied, and hung up with perhaps more force than necessary.

He stepped out of the booth into the small antechamber off the castle's main hall, where Nigel was waiting.

"Any luck?" Nigel asked.

Harry shook his head. "Thompson wasn't available. A young woman promised to pass on the message."

"Do you think they'll cancel the visit?"

"I don't know. They should—two murders in a week, a spy sending signals about the PM's plans... it's too dangerous." Harry ran a hand over his face, suddenly feeling the fatigue of the early wake-up call. "But Churchill's not known for backing down from danger. Quite the opposite, in fact."

"What's our next move?" Nigel asked.

"We need to talk to Foster—this Jim fellow Lillian was sweet on. Find out what he knows about Vernon and these supposed German spies." Harry straightened his shoulders. "And we need to look more closely at everyone who had access to the castle in the last forty-eight hours. Whoever did this is either still here, or has been coming and going without drawing attention."

Like Siegfried, Harry thought.

Nigel caught his eye. "Coming and going on a motorcycle, perhaps?"

"Got it in one," Harry said, feeling a surge of pride for his nephew's quick insight. "But we can't just assume that."

Nigel nodded grimly. "I'll ask Glenwood to arrange a list of all recent visitors."

"Good." Harry gazed out the window toward the gardens, where police were still working around the rose beds. He noticed that Nigel appeared more composed now that he'd had a chance to properly dress and comb his hair. "Let's go have a chat with Mr Foster. He should be on duty now, yes?"

Nigel consulted his notebook again. "Started at eight this morning in the Tower Wing."

"Right," Harry said, heading for the door.

They were halfway across the great hall when a booming voice stopped them in their tracks.

"Inspectors! Gentlemen! A word, if you please!"

Harry turned to see Bradley Walker striding toward them, his face flushed with anger. Harry wondered how the owner of Clarion Castle would react to this second murder.

Harry braced himself. "Mr Walker," he acknowledged.

"Is it true?" Walker demanded, lowering his voice only slightly as he drew near. "Another death? One of my housemaids?"

"I'm afraid so, sir," Harry confirmed. "We're investigating it now."

Walker shook his head, moustache quivering with barely contained emotion. "This is intolerable. Absolutely intolerable. First Vernon, now this girl."

"We're doing everything we can—" Nigel began, but Walker cut him off.

"And now my hunting rifle is missing from the gun room, along with my new crossbow." He glared at them both. "I was going to show them to the Prime Minister. Churchill appreciates fine weapons, you know."

Harry felt a new weight settle in his stomach. "Your rifle and crossbow are missing? When did you notice this?"

"Just now. I went to clean the rifle in preparation for the Prime Minister's visit. The cabinet was unlocked and both weapons gone." Walker's eyes narrowed. "I want them found, Inspector. Immediately."

"When did you last see them?" Harry asked, his mind already racing through the implications. A killer with access to firearms was significantly more dangerous.

"Yesterday afternoon," Walker replied. "I was showing the crossbow to Lord Harrington—it's a new model, quite powerful."

"We'll look into it right away," Harry assured him, exchanging a meaningful glance with Nigel. "But first, we need to speak with one of the Signal Corps men."

Walker's expression darkened further. "You think one of them is responsible?"

"We're not jumping to conclusions," Harry said carefully. "But Lillian had connections to one of them that we need to explore."

Walker studied him for a long moment, during which Harry wondered just how much the death of Lillian meant to the steel magnate.

Then Walker gave a curt nod. "Very well. But I expect to see results, Inspector. This meeting is too important to be derailed by some... some maniac running loose on my property."

"We understand the significance of the meeting, Mr Walker," Harry replied evenly. "But with all due respect, two people are dead. And now weapons are missing. The safety of everyone at Clarion Castle has to be our priority."

"Just find my rifle and crossbow," Walker insisted. "And catch whoever is responsible for these deaths. Before Churchill arrives."

"Yes, sir," Harry said, watching as the steel magnate turned and stormed off toward his study.

Nigel waited until Walker was out of earshot before speaking. "Missing weapons. That complicates things."

"Considerably," Harry agreed grimly. "Let's talk to Foster first; then we'll organise a search for those weapons. The last thing we need is an armed killer roaming the grounds."

They resumed their path toward the Tower Wing, Harry's earlier fatigue forgotten in the face of this new, unsettling development.

Chapter 53
Alice

The slanting afternoon light cast long shadows across the countryside as Alice made her way back to The Shepherd's Rest. Her shoes had softened somewhat, but her feet still ached, and discouragement sat heavy on her shoulders. Another day nearly gone, and still no sign of Evie.

Dorothy and Tom had joined the search that morning, dividing the area around the cottage to cover more ground. Alice had been grateful for their help, especially since Tom had insisted his leg was up to the task.

"Been walking miles every day for my recovery training," he'd said firmly when she'd expressed concern. "There's no reason I can't walk for miles around here. Especially for something this important."

They'd separated at midday—Dorothy and Tom heading west through the woods while Alice took the path that curved east and eventually led back toward the village. They'd arranged to meet at the inn by sundown, but Alice was returning early, her instincts telling her they were searching in the wrong place.

Bonzo trotted dutifully alongside her, occasionally sniffing at interesting scents but always returning to heel. The little Pomeranian had been tireless all day, despite the disappointment of their efforts. Alice glanced down at him affectionately.

"At least one of us still has energy," she murmured.

They were less than a quarter mile from The Shepherd's Rest when Bonzo suddenly froze. His ears perked forward; his body went tense as a bowstring. Before Alice could react, he bolted ahead, barking furiously.

"Bonzo!" she called, alarmed by the sudden change. "Bonzo, wait!"

But the little dog was already dashing through the tall grass beside the path, his barks growing more insistent. Alice broke into a run, following the sound. Had he found a rabbit? A fox? Or...

Her heart leapt as another possibility surfaced.

"Evie?" she called. "Evie!"

Bonzo's barking led her to a dense thicket just off the path. As she drew closer, Alice could see him pawing at something half-hidden among the brambles. She dropped to her knees, pushing aside the tangled growth, and felt her breath catch in her throat.

"Evie! Oh dear God, Evie!"

There, crumpled on her side in the shadow of the thicket, was Evie. So close to The Shepherd's Rest, yet concealed from any casual glance. Her face was pale beneath smudges of dirt, her eyes closed, her breathing shallow and irregular.

Alice quickly checked for injuries and found a wound in Evie's upper arm. It looked as though the bullet had gone straight through, and she'd clearly lost an amount of blood. The surrounding fabric of her blouse was stiff with it.

"Evie, can you hear me? It's Alice. I'm going to get you to safety."

Evie's eyelids fluttered. "Al ... ice?" The word was barely audible.

"Yes, it's me. Don't try to talk. We're very close to shelter."

With strength born of urgency, Alice managed to lift Evie and help her stand, supporting her weight as best she could so that Evie could take slow, halting steps. Bonzo circled them anxiously, occasionally nudging at Evie's dangling hand with his nose.

"Good boy," Alice told him, her voice thick with emotion. "You found her. Good, good boy."

The short distance to The Shepherd's Rest seemed interminable with Evie's weight leaning against her, but Alice pressed on, her mind racing. How long had Evie been lying there? How had she escaped from Siegfried? And the wound—a knife? A bullet?

Mrs Hadley was emptying a bucket of wash water behind the inn when Alice staggered into view.

"Help!" Alice called. "Please, I need help!"

The innkeeper dropped the bucket with a clatter and rushed forward. "Good heavens! Is this—"

"My friend. She's hurt. Please, can you help me get her inside?"

Between them, they managed to manoeuvre Evie into the inn and up to the blue room Mrs Hadley had mentioned earlier. As they lowered her onto the bed, Evie's eyes opened again, more lucid this time.

"Alice," she gasped. "They—"

"Save your strength," Alice soothed, but Evie clutched weakly at her arm.

"Get Nigel," she whispered. "Tell him... tell him..." But whatever message she had for Nigel was lost as her eyes rolled back and she slipped into unconsciousness.

"Evie!" Alice patted her cheek gently, but there was no response. She turned to Mrs Hadley. "Do you have any medical supplies? Bandages, iodine, anything?"

The innkeeper nodded. "I keep a good first aid kit. War preparations, you know. And I've got brandy if you need it."

"Thank you. And warm water, and clean cloths." As Mrs Hadley hurried away, Alice reached for her own satchel, which she'd dropped by the bed, and felt a surge of relief that she'd thought to bring along her essential supplies. She quickly located what she needed—a small tin of yarrow powder to help staunch bleeding, and a vial of her own tincture made from nettles and yellow dock root, excellent for replenishing blood.

As Mrs Hadley returned with the first aid supplies, Alice set to work removing Evie's soiled blouse. Her skin was blistered and singed around the wound. Clearly, the shot must have been fired from very close range, although at least the bullet had exited rather than becoming lodged inside the arm, which would have made infection more likely. Had Evie been grappling with one of her captors, wrestling for control of the gun when it had gone off? Or had someone tried to execute her and very nearly succeeded?

Together they cleaned the wound, Alice carefully applying the yarrow powder before bandaging. She then mixed her blood-replenishing tincture with a little water and coaxed it between Evie's lips. To her relief, her friend swallowed reflexively.

"Now we need to telephone the castle," Alice said, rising. "She asked for Nigel specifically."

At the telephone in the downstairs hall, Alice dialled with trembling fingers. A maid answered, and Alice fought to keep her voice steady.

"This is Alice Greenleaf. I need to speak with Nigel Brewster immediately. It's an emergency."

There was a pause, then: "I'm sorry, miss. Mr Brewster isn't here at present. Nor is Mr Jenkins. They left about an hour ago."

"Where did they go? When will they be back?"

"I couldn't say, miss. There's been quite an uproar today, what with the murder and all."

Alice felt her stomach drop. "Murder? Who was murdered?"

"One of the housemaids, miss. Lillian. Found in the rose garden this morning. The police have been here all day."

Alice leaned against the wall, momentarily stunned. Another death? What was happening at Clarion Castle?

"Please," she said finally, "when Mr Brewster returns, tell him Alice Greenleaf called. Tell him we've found Evie, and she's asking for him. He'll understand. It's urgent."

She hung up, frustration and worry battling within her. Of all the times for Nigel to be away from the castle...

Of all the times for there to be a second murder...

Upstairs, Evie seemed to have regained some colour. She stirred as Alice entered the room, her eyes opening to focus hazily on Alice's face.

"You're safe," Alice told her, taking her hand. "You're at The Shepherd's Rest in Millfield. I've tried to reach Nigel, but he's away from the castle right now."

Evie seemed to want to speak, but could only manage a weak squeeze of Alice's hand before taking a deep, shuddering breath and slipping back into unconsciousness.

Alice sat beside her, watching the slow rise and fall of her chest, feeling helpless and frustrated. She'd found Evie—or rather, Bonzo had—but now what? She couldn't move her in this condition, and whatever urgent message Evie had for Nigel remained locked within her unconscious mind.

The sound of voices from downstairs interrupted her thoughts. She recognised Dorothy's concerned tones, followed by Tom's deeper response, and then rapid footsteps on the stairs.

Dorothy burst into the room first, her face alight with hope and worry. "We heard Bonzo barking! Mrs Hadley told us—"

She broke off at the sight of Evie's pale form on the bed. Tom appeared behind her, his expression sobering as he took in the scene.

"You found her," Dorothy whispered, moving to the bedside. "Oh, Alice."

"Bonzo found her," Alice corrected, giving the little dog a grateful glance where he sat vigilantly at her feet. "In a thicket not far from here. She's been wounded, lost a lot of blood."

Tom approached the bed, looking at Evie with concerned eyes. "Good bandaging. What's her level of consciousness been?" he asked, his tone reflecting the practical nature he'd developed during his rehabilitation.

"In and out. She asked for Nigel—that's all she's said. I tried calling the castle, but apparently there's been a murder there this morning, and Nigel and Harry are away investigating."

Dorothy gasped. "A murder? Who?"

"A housemaid named Lillian," Alice replied. "I don't know the details."

They all looked down at Evie, questions hanging in the air between them. What had happened to her? What did she know that was so urgent she needed to tell Nigel?

"We'll go to the castle," Tom said decisively. "Find Nigel and Harry, bring them back here."

Dorothy nodded. "Yes, we should go immediately. We'll take the Daimler."

Relief washed over Alice. "Thank you. That's exactly what's needed. I'll keep trying to reach them by telephone, and I'll stay with Evie to be here if—when—she wakes again."

As Dorothy and Tom prepared to leave, Alice returned to Evie's side. She smoothed a strand of hair from her friend's forehead, noting the slight improvement in her colour. Though still pale, Evie's breathing seemed steadier now.

"You rest up, dear," Alice whispered. "Get all the rest you can."

She settled into the chair beside the bed, Bonzo curling up at her feet. She heard the sound of Dorothy's car starting up outside, then fading as it began its journey toward Clarion Castle. All she could do now was wait, and hope that Evie would wake soon with answers to the questions that multiplied with each passing hour.

Chapter 54
Dorothy

Tom steered the Daimler down the narrow country lane that would lead them back to Clarion Castle. The road here was really little more than a single ribbon of tarmac— which gave way to gravel, in some places— hemmed in closely by thick hedgerows and overhanging trees. Beyond, Dorothy could see fields of wheat and barley ripening under a golden sun, and the occasional flutter of swallows diving through the blue sky overhead.

Tom was driving with the same calm, level-headed competence that he had when pounding in a nail or sanding a piece of wood. But Dorothy, glancing at him, could see a faint, underlying shadow of regret in his expression.

"You're wishing we could do more," she said.

Tom glanced at her with a brief smile. "Maybe. I suppose getting mixed up in these mysteries of yours has given me a taste for excitement. But I can't see there's anything left for us to do besides alerting Nigel and Harry to what's been happening. Evie's safe; that's the main thing."

"As for guarding Mr Churchill," Tom went on, "that's something best left to the professionals. I'm sure his security detail's top notch; they don't need me getting in the—"

He broke off, stomping hard on the brake as a green Lagonda Two-litre shot out ahead of them from a side lane, careened around the curve almost on two wheels, and then roared off down the road in a cloud of dust and gravel.

"What the dickens—" Tom began.

With petrol rationed, there were few other cars out, and so far the only other traffic they'd seen on the roads had been a couple of farm carts. An expensive car like the Lagonda almost had to be coming from the castle.

Dorothy sat up straighter as something caught her eye. "Tom, we need to go after whoever that was! Get as close as you possibly can!"

Tom knew her well enough that he didn't ask any questions. He spun the wheel, turning the car around in a tight turn that almost ran them into the ditch. Then he pressed hard on the accelerator.

At least catching up to the Lagonda wasn't a problem, even as fast as it was. The big Daimler leapt forward, engine roaring, eating up the yards between them and the other car in a bare handful of seconds.

Dorothy leaned forward on the edge of her seat, straining her eyes to see through the glare of the afternoon sun and the dust that clouded the windscreen. "Tom, look. There, in the back window!"

Tom let out a wordless exclamation, and Dorothy knew that he'd seen it, too. Framed in the rear window of the Lagonda was a pair of man's booted feet— which might have been a bit comical, under normal circumstances. But there wasn't anything funny at all about the rope that clearly bound the man's ankles together, or the way he was kicking against the window with desperate, pounding strikes of his boots against the glass.

"Whoever's driving has got someone tied up in the back," Tom said.

"And he's trying to break free— or attract attention," Dorothy said. Her own chest hurt at the thought of the terror that the man in that car must be feeling right now.

Tom glanced at her. "Still got your dad's revolver?"

Dorothy nodded, reaching into her handbag. "Yes, but I'd still feel a lot better if you were the one doing the shooting."

Tom was focusing on the road and the car ahead of them. The driver of the Lagonda had seen the Daimler and put on a fresh burst of speed, trying to draw ahead. They roared over a slight dip in the road, landing with a thump that snapped Dorothy's teeth together. But Tom took his eyes briefly away from the road and squeezed Dorothy's hand.

"You can do it, I know you can."

Dorothy tried to squelch any feelings of doubt or fear. "You've got a plan?"

Tom nodded, pressing his foot to the accelerator once again. "We need to stop them. Roll down your window, and when I tell you, you're going to shoot at their back tyres."

Chapter 55
Harry

"Satisfied, gentlemen?" Captain Marlowe gestured around the tower's upper chamber with a slightly impatient sweep of his arm.

Harry suppressed a sigh as he completed his inspection of the cramped storage room at the top of the main tower. The space was dusty but orderly, with crates of supplies neatly stacked against one wall, spare radio equipment on shelves along another, and a small table beneath the single window that offered a panoramic view of the castle grounds.

"Everything seems to be in order," he admitted, exchanging a glance with Nigel. Both of them had hoped to find something—anything—that might connect this tower to the suspicious signals or to Lillian's murder. But there was nothing obviously amiss.

The window that faced the main drive was securely locked from the inside, its latch showing no signs of tampering. While it offered an excellent view of anyone approaching the castle, accessing it would require climbing the narrow spiral staircase past the Signal Corps station on the floor below.

"As you can see," Marlowe continued, his military posture never wavering, "unless someone manages to climb these stairs undetected, there's no security concern. With my men on duty round the clock monitoring transmissions, and two guards posted at the base, I'd say the risk is nonexistent."

Harry nodded, though he wasn't entirely convinced. His years at Scotland Yard had taught him that "nonexistent" risks had an uncanny way of materialising at the worst possible moments.

"Where is Foster?" he asked abruptly. "He was supposed to be on duty this morning, according to the roster."

A flicker of annoyance crossed Marlowe's face. "Foster swapped shifts with Simmons. A common enough practice among the men, provided their duties are covered."

"And where is he now?"

Marlowe turned to one of the guards who had accompanied them up the tower. "Cromwell, check Foster's quarters, would you?"

The guard saluted crisply and departed down the spiral staircase. Harry moved to the window, gazing out at the grounds below. The rose garden was visible in the distance, and beyond, the gravel drive leading to the tall entry gates was in plain view.

"Foster mentioned something to the housemaid Lillian about Vernon," Nigel said to Marlowe. "Did he report any concerns about Vernon to you officially?"

"Certainly not," Marlowe replied, his tone suggesting he found the very idea absurd. "If any of my men had security concerns, they would report directly to me. And I would have passed that information to you immediately."

Harry turned from the window. "What about Vernon himself? Did he ever try to access this tower, as Lillian suggested?"

"He had no reason to be here," Marlowe said firmly. "And my men have strict orders about unauthorised personnel."

Before Harry could press further, the guard returned, slightly out of breath from his quick ascent.

"Foster's not in his quarters, sir," he reported. "His roommate says he sometimes goes for a walk after a late shift. Helps him sleep, apparently."

Harry felt a familiar prickle of suspicion at the base of his skull. Two murders, cryptic German messages about Churchill's visit, and now a missing Signal Corps man who had connections to at least one of the victims.

"Thank you, Captain," he said, moving toward the stairs. "We've seen enough here. Nigel, let's check the other tower as well."

As they descended the spiral staircase, Nigel kept his voice low. "You think Foster's disappearance is significant?"

"I think everything is significant until proven otherwise," Harry replied. "Especially when it involves someone who apparently had information about Vernon's activities before his death."

They emerged into the great hall, the afternoon light slanting through the high windows and casting long shadows across the stone floor. A maid approached them, bobbing a quick curtsy.

"Telephone call for you, Mr Jenkins. From a Miss Greenleaf."

Harry followed her to the telephone alcove off the main hall, Nigel close behind.

"Jenkins here," he said, taking the receiver and holding it slightly away, so that Nigel could hear.

"Harry, it's Alice." Her voice sounded tired but relieved. "I've found Evie—or rather, Bonzo found her. She's safe, but she's been wounded and she's mostly unconscious."

Harry felt a surge of relief. After days of worry, at least this was good news. "Where are you? How badly is she hurt?"

"We're back at The Shepherd's Rest. She has a bullet wound in her arm—treated and bandaged now, and I want to let her sleep. But she did wake briefly and she asked for Nigel."

Harry glanced at Nigel, who was watching his face intently. "Nigel's right here with me."

"Dorothy and Tom are on their way to tell you in person," Alice continued. "They should be arriving soon."

Nigel took the receiver. "Alice? It's Nigel. We may not be here when Dorothy and Tom arrive. If Evie needs to rest, let her. We'll be along as soon as we can."

He handed the receiver back to Harry. Now that he knew Evie was safe, his thoughts were already turning to the other tower they still needed to check, and the missing Foster, who seemed increasingly important to their investigation. Alice was talking, but he missed what she had said. "I didn't quite catch that. Are you there, Alice?"

Alice raised her voice slightly. "I said the maid who answered before said you've had another murder."

"I'm afraid so. We're waiting for a call from the PM's security man, in fact."

"Oh dear, well then I'd better get off the line," Alice said quickly. "I'll keep watch on Evie. If she has more to tell us, I'll call right away."

"Do that," Harry agreed.

Nigel took the receiver. "And Alice—be careful. With everything that's happening, none of us should take any unnecessary risks."

He hung up and turned to Harry. "I heard everything. We shouldn't wait for Dorothy. Shall we check the other tower?"

They crossed the great hall toward the main entrance, Harry's mind already planning their next steps. The tower of the ancient keep had been empty when they'd found Graves there, but that was no proof that it had stayed empty.

They had just reached the massive oak entry doors when he heard the maid calling them again.

"Mr Jenkins! Another telephone call for you, sir!"

Harry turned back with a frown. "Who is it?"

"A Mr Thompson, sir. He says it's urgent."

"I'll take it," Harry said, returning to the telephone alcove.

He picked up the receiver, conscious of Nigel hovering nearby. "Jenkins here."

"Thompson." The voice was clipped, authoritative. "I need a full status report. Meet me outside the White Horse Inn immediately."

Harry blinked in surprise. "The White Horse? That's in the village. When did you arrive?"

"I'm on my way now and I don't have time for questions. Just get over here. Now."

The line went dead before Harry could respond. He slowly replaced the receiver, frowning.

"Thompson wants to meet us at the White Horse," he told Nigel. "Right now."

Nigel looked as surprised as Harry felt. "Why not come directly to the castle?"

"That's what I'd like to know." Harry strode toward the doors, his earlier intentions forgotten in the face of this new development.

Chapter 56
Dorothy

Dorothy leaned out the Daimler's side window, clutching her dad's service revolver with both hands. The road was uneven and rutted enough that she was terrified she was going to drop the gun every time they went over a bump. The whistling air whipped her hair back, dust stung her eyes so that she could scarcely see, and the roar of the engine drowned out even the pounding of her own heart. Tom was keeping the accelerator pressed nearly to the floor, trying to draw as close to the green Lagonda as he possibly could.

As the car ahead of them rounded a curve in the road, Dorothy caught just a quick glimpse of the driver: a middle-aged woman with copper-coloured hair, hunched over the steering wheel.

The Daimler rounded the curve after her, and Tom managed to draw up so that they were just an arm's width away from the Lagonda's back fender.

"Now!" he shouted.

Dorothy took aim as best she could at the other car's rear outside tyre, said a quick prayer, and then squeezed the trigger. The gun kicked in her hands so hard that she lost her balance and slammed back into her seat, banging her shoulder against the window rim. But the prayer must have worked, because there was a loud bang! and the Lagonda swerved violently.

Through the windows, Dorothy could see the driver was clutching the steering wheel, trying desperately to wrestle the car back under control, but she couldn't manage; she'd been going too fast. The Lagonda veered, careening wildly, spun, and then plunged nose-first into the irrigation ditch on the side of the road.

Tom slowed, stopped, and parked the Daimler just behind the Lagonda's spinning back tyres.

Dorothy put the revolver into Tom's hand before he climbed out of the driver's seat. She might by some miracle have managed to hit the other car's tyre, but there was still no question which one of them had more experience with firearms.

Tom motioned for her to stay back as he approached the Lagonda with the revolver at the ready. Through the windows, Dorothy saw the woman driver, now slumped over the steering wheel. Dead? Or only knocked unconscious by the crash?

Still keeping the revolver raised, Tom yanked open the driver's side door and hauled the woman out. She didn't fight back. As soon as Tom had her up out of the ditch and let go of her, she collapsed onto the tarmac. But she glowered up at Tom, despite the blood that was trickling from a cut on her forehead.

"You've absolutely no right to wave that gun in my face!" Her voice was strident, nearly hysterical. "I'll have you up before the authorities for assault and reckless driving, and—"

"You do that," Tom interrupted. Unlike the woman driver, he sounded completely calm. "They might have a thing or two to say to you about kidnapping. Dorothy? Can you see if the fellow in the back is all right?"

Swallowing, Dorothy nodded and approached the Lagonda, glad that Tom was continuing to keep the revolver trained on the red-haired woman. If looks could really have killed, Tom would be pushing up the daisies right now.

Dorothy opened the side door and found a man sprawled across the floor of the back, where he'd clearly rolled off the seat during the crash into the ditch. His ankles were bound, his hands were tied behind his back, and someone had used what looked like a dirty old rag as a gag for his mouth. His eyes were open, though, and alert, and when Dorothy slipped the gag off him, he rasped out, "She was going to kill me!"

"Who is she?" Dorothy asked.

"Millicent Hartley." The man spat the name out as though even the words were poisonous. "She's Mr Walker's private secretary up at Clarion Castle."

"And you are?" Tom still had one eye on Millicent, but he shifted his gaze to give the other man a quick look, too.

"Simon Graves." The man drew a ragged breath. "Under-butler."

Dorothy looked a question at Tom. He nodded, so she set to work untying Simon Graves's hands and feet.

"Why would Miss Hartley have been planning to kill you?" Tom asked.

"Because I saw her up at the Tower and followed her, that's why!" Graves shot out. "Didn't want the police pinning a charge of murder on me, so I went back up there to have a look around."

Dorothy had managed to get his bonds untied, and he sat up with a grunt of effort, jerking his hand at Millicent, who was still sitting in the road. "I saw her there— looking furtive, like she was up to no good. So I decided to follow. She must have known I was there, though, because she got behind me somehow and clubbed me over the back of the head." Wincing, Graves touched the back of his skull. "Next thing I knew, I was trussed up like a turkey and riding along while she drove like all of Hitler's armies were on our heels."

If what Dorothy suspected was true, Millicent wouldn't have been nearly as frightened of the German army as Graves. But the other woman didn't say a word, only continued to glower at them all in stony silence.

"What should we do?" Dorothy asked Tom.

"Only thing we can do," Tom said. "Take them both back to the Castle and hand them over to Harry and Nigel."

Chapter 57
Evie

Evie jolted awake with a strangled gasp, her body snapping upright as if pulled by invisible strings. Her heart pounded in her chest, thunderous and erratic, drowning out every other sound, and the taste of metal filled her mouth. She couldn't remember where she was, but she knew there was danger—possibly close at hand.

The sour throb of pain in her upper arm hit her next. Her hand flew instinctively to the wound, and encountered . . . bandages.

A hand touched her shoulder and a gentle voice from somewhere close by said, "It's all right, my dear. You're quite safe, now."

Evie blinked the shimmering darkness away from her eyes and saw Alice's familiar face leaning over her. "How—" her voice came out raspy, a cracked whisper.

"Drink this." Alice pressed a glass to her lips. "It will help."

Evie took an obedient swallow, then coughed as a bitter, astringent taste like menthol mixed with grass clippings filled her mouth. "Ugh."

Alice smiled faintly. "Yes, well, I didn't promise that it would taste agreeable, only that it would help."

Looking around, Evie saw that she was in a small but scrupulously clean room with knotty pine floorboards and age-darkened beams. The four-poster bed on which she lay was of dark carved mahogany, and an old-fashioned brass washstand with a blue basin and pitcher stood over in one corner.

"Where are we?"

"At the Shepherd's Rest Inn." Alice placed the glass she'd given Evie back on the bedside table. "Do you remember anything at all from last night?"

Evie frowned, trying to think past the burning pain in her arm as fragmented memories flashed through her mind's eye: Nigel. The motorbike. Paul.

She remembered leaving the cottage, and then the seemingly endless journey through the woods. She'd tried to staunch the bleeding in her arm by wrapping it with her cardigan, but it had soon soaked through. Every step had felt as though she were moving through a quagmire, her muscles slowly turning to lead, and in the nearly pitch black, she'd started to wonder whether she was only going around in circles, exhausting herself to no purpose.

She couldn't remember collapsing, but she supposed she must have done, because the next memory fragment that she could call up was of lying on the ground amidst the bracken and dead leaves. And then—

Evie looked up at Alice. "Bonzo? Was Bonzo actually out there in the woods last night, or was I hallucinating?"

"Oh yes, he was there." Alice stooped, picking up the little dog from where he must have been lying beside the bed. "You may even owe your life to him. He led me straight to you; I'd never have found you otherwise."

Before Evie could answer, Bonzo bared his teeth and growled in Evie's direction. He might have saved her, but clearly his overall opinion of her remained unchanged. Then again, whenever Evie turned up, the humans he most cared for tended to run into danger, so maybe Evie couldn't blame him for his low opinion.

"Who shot you?" Alice asked. "Was it . . ." She seemed to hesitate, then said, in a quiet voice, "Was it Paul?"

"You know about Paul?" Evie asked. At the moment, she cared less about that than the fact that if Alice knew, then Nigel must have told her— which meant that Nigel must still be alive.

"I'm afraid so." Alice's china-blue eyes were filled with sympathy.

Evie, though, struggled to sit up, ignoring the fresh throb in her arm. "It wasn't Paul who shot me. I did it myself— to convince him that I was dead, so that I could get away. I'll explain more later, but Alice—" Evie had just realised with a fresh jolt of panic that the sunlight slanting in through the windows wasn't the pale gold of early morning as she'd first thought, but the deeper orange glow of approaching sunset. "Alice, what time is it?"

Alice glanced at the delicate gold wristwatch she always wore. "Nearly six o'clock."

"Harry and Nigel?" Evie asked.

"They've gone to meet Churchill's motorcade," Alice said. "To warn him."

"Warn him?"

Alice's lips compressed. "There was another death this morning— a young housemaid was killed at Clarion Castle. Harry and Nigel have gone to inform Mr Churchill's security detail of the possible danger."

Evie struggled to throw off the blankets, one-handed. "Help me. Please, Alice. We need to get to Clarion Castle right away!"

Chapter 58
Dorothy

"They're not here?" Dorothy stared at the stiffly correct, silver-haired butler who had just delivered the news.

"I'm afraid not, ma'am."

They were standing on the steps of Clarion Castle: she, Tom, and Mr Glenwood the butler. Mr Graves was waiting in the parked Daimler, which they'd left on the gravel drive. Millicent Hartley was currently tied up in the back. They'd used the same ropes with which she'd bound Graves, and before they'd come halfway back to the castle, Dorothy had wished they'd stopped her mouth with the gag, as well. Millicent had kept up a stream of furious abuse and threats all throughout the drive.

Now Mr Glenwood's face was so calm and politely expressionless that Dorothy's hands balled up into fists at her sides. "As I understand it, both Inspector Brewster and Mr Jenkins have gone to meet the Prime Minister's motorcade."

"The Prime Minister is still coming, then? Despite the danger?" Dorothy asked.

Mr Glenwood looked down his long nose at her. For a moment, she thought he was too offended even to answer, but he finally— with the air of doing her a tremendous favour— deigned to say, "Inspector Brewster and Mr Jenkins inspected the Tower Wing as well as the rest of the grounds most thoroughly. And they have posted some twenty-five police constables on guard, both on the grounds and inside. I believe they were satisfied that our premises are as secure as we can make them."

But now that Nigel and Harry were gone, Dorothy wouldn't be able to tell them anything about Millicent and Graves.

"What about Alice and Evie?" Dorothy asked. "Alice Greenleaf and Evelyn Harris?"

"I'm afraid that I am not familiar with either of those names." Mr Glenwood's expression was still as impassively calm as though he'd been offering a dish of mint jelly to go with the roast leg of lamb at the dinner table.

"Mr Walker?" Dorothy asked. She'd never met the owner of Clarion Castle, but she was willing to try to make him understand the events of the morning, if that was what it took to make sure Millicent Hartley got what she deserved and Winston Churchill remained safe.

Mr Glenwood drew himself up once again. Now he looked like he'd just found a fly swimming in the mint jelly. "Quite out of the question," he said. "Mr Walker is going over important documents relating to his upcoming meeting, and has given strict instructions that he not be disturbed in any circumstances."

The way Dorothy felt right now, she'd have been happy for Tom to force his way past the butler at gunpoint. But that would probably only get them arrested, or at best hopelessly delayed while they tried to explain. Without Nigel and Harry, they didn't have any kind of authority here.

She glanced at Tom. "What should we do? Go after Harry and Nigel, do you think?"

Tom frowned, but finally shook his head. "Too much chance that we'd get cut off by Churchill's motorcade and not get to see them at all." He turned, focusing on Mr Glenwood. "Do you have somewhere secure? A place where a prisoner could be locked up until the police can take charge?"

Dorothy had the slight satisfaction of watching a flicker of surprise pass across the butler's stiff, perfectly controlled features. "A prisoner, sir?"

Dorothy would have enjoyed watching Tom tell Mr Glenwood that Mr Walker's private secretary was a German spy who'd just tried to kill Mr Graves. But he never got the chance.

A small blue Ford came racing up the driveway, screeching to a halt beside the Daimler. The driver was a middle-aged woman whom Dorothy didn't recognise, but she released a breath as she saw the passengers. "That's Alice," she said. "And she's got Evie with her!"

Chapter 59
Evie

"I'm all right," Evie promised Dorothy.

That statement depended heavily on one's definition of 'all right.' Evie's arm was hurting furiously, the pain only mildly dimmed by Alice's herbs, and her vision had a slight tendency to go shimmery at the edges. But she was ignoring both of those things for now.

"Where are Nigel and Harry?" she asked.

"Gone." Dorothy's cheeks were pale, and even Tom, who was usually unflappably cheerful, was looking grim around the mouth. The two of them had come running over to meet Evie and Alice the moment they'd alighted from Mrs Hadley's car, and now they were all four standing on the gravel drive in front of the massive structure that must be Clarion Castle.

"What?" Evie felt a lurch under her ribcage. She hadn't even known how much she'd been counting on finding Nigel here— on telling him everything that she suspected— until the word left Dorothy's mouth.

"They've gone to meet the Prime Minister's security team, apparently," Dorothy said. "We just arrived here ourselves. Tom and I caught Millicent Hartley— she's Mr Walker's private secretary— on the road just a short while ago. She had the Castle's under-butler in the back seat, and was planning to kill him, or so he claims. And I don't see any reason to doubt it. Tom and I ran her car off the road and then brought her back here."

"I see." Evie blinked. Even with Nigel and Alice's briefing on the earlier murders here, this was quite a bit to take in. But she didn't have time to ask Dorothy for the full story. "I need to tell Nigel and Harry everything I overheard—" she caught herself before she could say, Paul. She also didn't have time for those explanations. "Siegfried. He's planning to assassinate the Prime Minister." She tilted her head, looking up at the huge edifice of the castle. "I overheard him say he needed to get into position in the tower before Mr Churchill arrived."

Tom frowned. Dorothy shook her head. "I don't think he could have meant this tower here. According to Mr Glenwood the butler, Nigel and Harry inspected the tower before they left. And they left constables on guard, besides. I don't see how Siegfried could hope to get past them."

Evie pressed her eyes shut. Had she got it wrong? Somehow misheard what Paul had said? She could almost feel the minutes before Winston Churchill's arrival slipping away, and she still didn't know for certain what Paul had planned—

"This Millicent Hartley," she asked Dorothy. "You said she's Mr Walker's private secretary?"

"That's right."

"I need to speak to her." Evie swung around, moving towards the Daimler.

Alice had been quiet until now, but touched her arm lightly. "Not that I wish to dissuade you, my dear. I fully understand the stakes. But you are not perhaps at your strongest just now—"

"I know." Evie did know. She currently didn't feel as though she had the strength to intimidate a mouse. But she had to try. "Just let me talk to Miss Hartley."

Nodding, Tom crossed to the Daimler and opened the rear door, revealing a thin, sharp-featured woman with red hair. Her hands and feet were bound with rope, and she had the beginnings of a spectacular bruise and a smear of blood on her forehead. But she seemed more or less alert. Dazed, and perhaps a little rattled, but that was all to the good for Evie's purposes.

She glowered at Tom as he opened the door and snapped, "I demand that you untie me at once!"

The Daimler's other passenger was a tall, middle-aged man who also looked rumpled and somewhat the worse for wear. But he glanced at Miss Hartley and said, "Give it up. Everyone here knows you killed poor old Vernon— and then you tried to pin it on me!"

"That's a lie!" Millicent Hartley interrupted. "I never killed anyone, it was—" she cut off speaking abruptly, clamping her mouth shut as though realising she'd been on the verge of saying more than she'd meant to.

"Siegfried, were you going to say?" Evie asked. "Or does he have someone else on the payroll here?"

Millicent Hartley drew in a sharp breath at the mention of Siegfried's name and her face went a shade paler, but she didn't speak.

Evie leaned forward, trying to make her voice sympathetic. Approachable. Friendly tactics in an interrogation sometimes produced faster results than hostile ones, especially if your subject was already on the verge of cracking. "Listen to me. Whatever you're mixed up in, you're not in so deeply that you can't get back out again. The penalty for treason is death. But if you tell us what Siegfried is planning, you still have a chance to save yourself—"

"I don't want to save myself!"

Millicent's voice rose, gaining an edge of hysteria, and she spat the words as though they were bullets. "I don't care, do you hear me?

I was engaged to a man I loved before the war. And do you know what happened? He was forced out of the country— sent back to Germany— and then one of our British planes dropped a bomb on him and killed him. So go ahead— have me arrested and tried and then shot for treason! I don't care— I've done what I could to avenge Carl's death, and I'm glad, I tell you, glad!"

Evie shook her head. "Do you really think you can make your Carl's death less unjust and unfair if you let Hitler's armies march through Britain? How will ensuring that more innocent civilians are killed make up for what you've lost? Do you really think it will help you if thousands more women lose their husbands and sweethearts, and suffer as you have?"

Just for a flicker of a second, Evie thought she saw something like uncertainty wavering in Millicent's gaze. But then her expression hardened. She turned her head away, her mouth once more shut and her jaw locked. She might, in time, be coerced or threatened into speaking, but that would take hours— hours that they couldn't afford.

Alice spoke quietly from Evie's side once again. "Is that all you overheard?" she asked. "Just that the would-be assassin would be in position in a tower?"

"And that the plan was to use weapons that I think were to be stolen from the castle," Evie said. "Yes."

She was trying to recall whether she could remember anything— even a tiny fragment of conversation between Paul or Gerda or Hans— that might give them more to go on, when Mr Graves cleared his throat.

"There's another tower here," Graves said.

Evie wheeled around. "What? What do you mean?"

Mr Graves looked slightly nervous at her intensity, but he licked his lips and said, "Well, I don't know if it's what you're after. But there's the abandoned keep on the grounds. That is, the remains of the old castle that was pulled down to build the new one. It's mostly tumbled down, but the tower's still standing. That's where I saw her." He jerked his head at Millicent. "Just before she knocked me out."

Evie's heart was beating fast and hard. If she was wrong about this—

But she wasn't wrong. This had to be right, it just had to be. She drew in a breath and faced Graves. "Tell me how to get there."

Chapter 60
Harry

The late evening sun cast long shadows across the village square as Harry pulled the car to a stop outside the White Horse Inn. The amber glow through the centuries-old windows suggested warmth and conviviality within—a stark contrast to the tension that had settled in his chest during the short drive down the Clarion Castle entry drive and across the wide pavement of the square.

"Almost seven," Nigel remarked, checking his watch as they exited the vehicle. "If Churchill's schedule remains unchanged, he'll arrive at the castle in half an hour."

Harry nodded grimly. "Assuming Thompson doesn't convince him otherwise after our report."

The White Horse Inn was a sixteenth-century coaching inn with timber frames and whitewashed walls. Its sign—a prancing white horse on a navy background—creaked gently in the evening breeze.

As they pushed through the heavy, dark-stained oak door, the hum of conversation and clinking glasses washed over them. The public house was doing brisk business, filled with locals and a few faces Harry didn't recognise—perhaps journalists or curious onlookers drawn by rumours of the Prime Minister's impending visit.

The interior was low-ceilinged with exposed beams darkened by centuries of smoke from the large stone fireplace that dominated one wall. Though the summer evening was mild, tradition kept a small fire burning, more for atmosphere than warmth.

Thompson was seated at a table in the back corner, partially obscured by a jutting stone column. His back was to the wall, giving him a clear view of the entire room and both entrances. The positioning was not coincidental, Harry noted—it was the instinctive choice of someone accustomed to assessing security threats.

"Jenkins. Brewster." Thompson acknowledged them with the barest nod as they approached. His face remained as impassive as ever, giving away nothing of his thoughts. "Sit down."

There was no sign of Churchill or any obvious security personnel, though Harry suspected several of the seemingly casual patrons scattered around the room might be part of the Prime Minister's protection detail.

"I've been trying to reach you all day," Harry said as they took their seats, keeping his voice low. "There's been another murder at the castle."

Thompson's expression didn't change, but Harry noticed a slight tightening around his eyes. "Details."

For the next several minutes, Harry provided a succinct account of Lillian's murder, the missing weapons, and the decoded notes from Vernon's diary. Thompson listened intently, checking his watch twice during the report. The second time, Harry noted it was precisely seven-fifteen.

"Your conclusion?" Thompson asked when Harry had finished.

"The notes seemed to indicate an assassin planning to use the main castle tower, which has a direct view of the entry drive," Harry explained. "But we've checked the tower thoroughly. It's empty, with Signal Corps men inside and guards posted at the entrance."

Thompson absorbed this information, his wooden expression betraying nothing. "And the suspicious transmissions? Any progress there?"

"Captain Marlowe claims his men have detected nothing unusual," Nigel said. "But Foster—the Signal Corps man who might have had information—is currently unaccounted for."

Thompson drummed his fingers once on the wooden tabletop—the most overt display of emotion Harry had seen from him. "Your recommendation?"

Harry exchanged a glance with Nigel before answering. "Given the circumstances—two murders, missing weapons, evidence of German intelligence about the visit, and these unresolved security concerns—I would strongly advise postponement."

"Does the Prime Minister want to postpone?" Nigel added.

Thompson's lips thinned slightly. "I think I already know the answer, but I'll check with him directly. Follow me."

He stood abruptly and led them back toward the door. As they passed through the crowded room, Harry noticed several men shift subtly, their eyes tracking Thompson's movement. Definitely security personnel, he thought.

Outside, the town square was bathed in the golden light of early evening. The shadow of the church spire stretched across the cobblestones like a sundial marking the approaching hour. Thompson set a brisk pace up the hill toward the large Norman church that overlooked the village.

"Churchill is here? Now?" Harry asked, lengthening his stride to keep up.

"Security precaution," Thompson replied without elaboration.

They rounded the church to a paved area behind it, partially hidden from the village below by a stand of ancient yew trees. Two gleaming

Rolls-Royce limousines awaited, their polished surfaces reflecting the sunset in shades of crimson and gold. Several men in dark suits stood vigilantly around the vehicles.

In the rear of the first Rolls, the unmistakable silhouette of Winston Churchill was visible through the open window. A cloud of cigar smoke hovered around him, and Harry could see the small form of Rufus, the Prime Minister's miniature poodle, perched on his lap. Churchill was engaged in conversation with several aides clustered around the car, their voices a low murmur as they reported information and received directives in return.

Thompson approached the vehicle and bent slightly to speak through the window. After a brief exchange, he beckoned Harry and Nigel forward.

Up close, Churchill appeared both more human and more formidable than Harry had expected. His round face was set in lines of determination, his eyes sharp and assessing as they took in the two men.

"These are the security officers from the castle?" Churchill asked, his voice a gravelly rumble.

"Yes, sir," Thompson confirmed. "Jenkins and Brewster. They've been investigating the incidents at Clarion Castle."

Churchill's gaze fixed on Harry. "Thompson tells me you think I should cancel my appearance."

"Given the circumstances, sir, postponement would be the prudent course," Harry replied evenly.

Churchill stroked Rufus absently, the dog's curly coat gleaming in the fading light. "Is there a crowd at the castle gate?"

The question caught Harry off-guard. "There wasn't one when we left the inn to come up here. That was about ten minutes ago, sir."

"And the square below? People about?" Churchill pressed.

"Yes, sir. The inn has a good business tonight, and there are villagers in the square."

Churchill nodded, seemingly satisfied with this information. He glanced at his watch—seven twenty-five. "Then no," he declared firmly. "No postponement. We must go forward."

Thompson didn't seem surprised by the decision. "Very well, sir. We'll proceed as planned."

As Churchill's aides made final preparations, Thompson gestured for Harry and Nigel to join him at the lead car.

"We'll walk ahead of the Prime Minister's Rolls," he instructed.

The small procession began moving down the hill toward the village square, Thompson and Harry in front, with Nigel falling in beside one of Churchill's security men. Behind them came Churchill's Rolls-Royce, windows still open despite the security concerns, followed closely by the second vehicle containing additional staff and security.

As they entered the village proper, people on the street began to notice.

Initially, there were just curious glances, but as recognition dawned, excitement spread visibly. Soon there was a gathering crowd.

"It's Churchill!" someone exclaimed, and suddenly people were streaming from doorways and side streets, rushing to get a glimpse of the Prime Minister.

Harry watched with growing concern as onlookers pressed closer to the slow-moving vehicles. Some began to follow the procession, while others rushed ahead, going into the White Horse, presumably to spread the news. Moments later, as the procession reached the town square, the inn's door burst open and patrons spilled out, adding to the rapidly growing crowd.

"Why the exposure to the crowds?" Harry asked Thompson quietly. "Given the security threats, wouldn't it be safer to minimise public contact?"

Thompson's expression remained neutral. "The Prime Minister always seeks out the crowds. The news of two murdered servants doesn't frighten him."

"Still, with what we know—"

"Churchill," Thompson interrupted, "has been known to stand on the rooftop of 10 Downing Street during a bombing raid, watching the German planes. After the raids, he walks the streets with crowds everywhere. This—" he gestured to the village scene around them, "—is nothing unusual."

Harry shook his head slightly. "Must be a nightmare for you, protecting him."

Thompson's shoulders lifted in a small shrug. "So far, so good."

But there was something in Thompson's tone—a slight tightness, perhaps—that made Harry glance sharply at the security man's profile. Thompson's face remained impassive, but Harry couldn't shake the feeling that the man was holding something back.

The crowd continued to grow as they approached the castle gates, people calling out greetings and waving. Churchill, far from being concerned, seemed to draw energy from the attention, occasionally raising his hand in his signature V-for-victory salute. Rufus remained perched on his lap, surveying the scene with canine dignity.

Then Nigel said, "Look over there—it's Dorothy and Alice. But where's Evie?"

The two women were standing with Tom, alongside the big Daimler, on the far side of the village square. Alice was holding Bonzo.

Suddenly Nigel was running. Harry followed.

Chapter 61
Harry

"There's Alice, but I don't see Evie!" Nigel's voice was tight with concern as he broke away from the procession.

Harry followed close behind, weaving through the gathered villagers toward the Daimler parked on the far side of the square.

The late afternoon sun still bathed the cobblestones in warm light, the sky a darkening blue that would turn to indigo when the twilight came. Harry hurried after Nigel, quickening his pace as they crossed the square. Even from behind, Harry could read the urgency in Nigel's movements, his usual measured stride replaced by something more desperate.

Dorothy's expression was grave as they approached, and Alice clutched Bonzo tighter to her chest, the little dog unusually subdued in her arms. Tom stood slightly apart from the women, his weight resting heavily on his good leg, fatigue evident in the slump of his shoulders.

Movement inside the Daimler caught Harry's attention. Through the window, he could make out two figures in the back seat. He stepped closer, and recognition hit him like a physical blow.

"That's Millicent," he said sharply. "And Graves."

The under-butler—who Harry had allowed to go free, despite his suspicious behaviour—sat rigidly in the back seat beside Walker's personal secretary. Millicent's face was pale, her hands clasped tightly in her lap.

"What's happened?" Harry demanded, his instincts immediately on alert.

"Long story," Tom said, his voice weary but urgent. "But I can tell you where Evie is. She's on her way to the old castle."

"The keep tower," Alice added, her eyes darting toward Clarion Castle's imposing silhouette. "She insisted on going. Said there wasn't a moment to lose."

"She'd overheard someone saying the assassin would be in position in a tower," Alice continued, her voice low but clear. "And that the plan was to use weapons stolen from the castle."

"Graves had a key, and she took it with her," Dorothy said. "In a great hurry. We couldn't stop her."

A cold sensation spread through Harry's chest, as if someone had replaced his blood with ice water. The keep tower. He'd padlocked it yesterday, but he hadn't checked it since. In their rush to meet Thompson, they hadn't gone back. Hadn't even stopped off for a quick walk-around.

Didn't even know whether the padlock was still in place.

Harry hadn't thought it through. If Graves had a key to the padlock, someone else could also have one.

The implications cascaded through his mind in a terrible sequence: the missing German messages he'd hidden in the loose stone, Foster's disappearance, Walker's stolen rifle and crossbow, the cryptic notes about an assassination attempt from a tower with a view of the entry drive...

Behind him, he could hear the growing murmur of the crowd as Churchill's procession moved toward the castle's main gate. The purr of the Rolls-Royce engine mingled with the excited murmurs of the crowd. The polished metal exterior gleamed in the low-angled sunlight. Harry turned to the castle entryway, his heart hammering against his ribs.

The heavy iron gates were beginning to swing open, their ancient hinges groaning in protest. Churchill's car would pass through in moments. In a stately processional, it would follow the sweeping drive that led directly to the castle's grand entrance.

How much of the drive was visible from the keep tower's battlements?

The angle of fire might be acute, sharper than the view from the main tower. But a practised assassin wouldn't need a perfect angle.

Harry turned to Nigel to voice the warning—but Nigel was already moving, his expression transformed by the same horrific realisation.

Without a word, Nigel broke into a run, sprinting toward the castle gates where Churchill's car was about to enter. His police credentials were already in his hand, held high above his head as he shouted for attention.

Harry paused only long enough to bark orders at Tom and Dorothy: "Stay with them," he instructed, gesturing toward the Daimler where Millicent and Graves sat. "Don't let them leave."

Then he was running too, his legs pumping hard as he chased after Nigel across the cobblestones. The crowd had thickened around the entrance gates, faces turned eagerly toward Churchill's approaching vehicle. Harry dodged between villagers, his lungs burning as he pushed himself faster.

Ahead, he could see Nigel waving frantically at Thompson, who stood just inside the gate. Churchill's Rolls-Royce continued its stately progress towards the gateway, the Prime Minister visible through the open window, still offering that confident V-sign to the cheering onlookers.

Time seemed to slow, each second stretching painfully as Harry ran. He was too far away to hear what Nigel was shouting, but he could see Thompson's face change—the wooden expression finally cracking as understanding dawned.

Harry's gaze lifted instinctively to the keep tower, its ancient stone stark and imposing in the bright afternoon light. From this angle, he couldn't see the battlements at the top, couldn't tell if someone waited there, rifle aimed through one of the medieval archer's embrasures.

The certainty that they had missed something crucial all along hardened into a cold knot in his stomach as he ran, jolting and breathless, toward what felt increasingly like an imminent disaster they had failed to prevent.

Chapter 62
Alice

Alice clutched Bonzo tighter as Churchill's Rolls-Royce approached, the little Pomeranian sensing the excitement in the air and squirming against her chest. From her position beside the Daimler, she had a clear view across the village square to the castle gates, where the crowd had swelled to several rows deep.

"Stay still," she murmured into Bonzo's silky fur, but her attention was divided between the wriggling dog and the drama unfolding before her. Harry and Nigel were moving through the crowd outside the gate, their urgency palpable even from this distance. Something must have gone terribly wrong, though she couldn't quite piece it together from the fragments of conversation she'd caught.

"Should we follow them?" Dorothy asked.

"Harry said to stay here," Tom reminded her, his gaze fixed on Millicent and Graves in the backseat of the Daimler. "To make sure these two don't leave."

Alice nodded, though her instincts were screaming for action. If Evie had gone to the keep tower, if there truly was an assassin waiting there...

She swallowed hard, trying to focus on what she could control in this moment. Bonzo wriggled again in her arms, his small body tense with excitement. The Prime Minister's gleaming Rolls-Royce glided forward along the cobblestones of the square, moving at a stately pace that seemed perversely calm given the urgency of Harry and Nigel's departure.

Churchill was clearly visible through the open window, his round face pink with pleasure as he waved to the cheering villagers. He seemed utterly unconcerned, a man accustomed to adulation and no doubt also to danger.

Then Alice spotted a second, smaller figure at the window beside Churchill—a miniature poodle with curly brown fur, its alert face taking in the scene with what appeared to be aristocratic interest.

Bonzo saw the other dog at exactly the same moment. His entire body went rigid in Alice's arms, and then he erupted into a series of high, sharp barks, his tail wagging furiously.

"Bonzo, shh!" Alice tightened her grip, but the Pomeranian was fixated on the other dog, straining toward the passing limousine with single-minded determination.

The poodle—Rufus, Alice presumed, having heard that Churchill rarely travelled without his beloved pet—turned its head at the sound of Bonzo's barking. Its ears perked up, and it placed its front paws on the window ledge, nose twitching with interest.

In that moment of canine connection, Bonzo gave an almighty wriggle and, before Alice could react, slipped through her arms and dropped to the ground.

"Bonzo!" she cried, taking an instinctive step forward, then stopping herself. Harry's instructions had been clear; she was to stay with the Daimler and not allow Millicent and Graves to leave.

She watched in helpless dismay as Bonzo raced across the cobblestones, darting between startled onlookers, a creamy tan-coloured blur heading straight for Churchill's limousine.

"Should I go after him?" Dorothy asked, half-rising from her position.

Alice shook her head, keeping her eyes fixed on her dog. "We'll stay here. I have to trust him to come back." Her voice was steadier than her racing heart.

The motorcade continued through the gates, which had been thrown open to their fullest extent. From her vantage point beside the Daimler, Alice could see the uniformed guards standing at attention, and beyond them, the sweeping curve of the castle's circular driveway.

The Rolls-Royce came to a stop short of the main entrance, where a reception line had formed—the castle's owner, Alice assumed, at the front, flanked by what appeared to be castle staff and local dignitaries.

Bonzo had reached the limousine now, standing on his hind legs beneath the open window and pawing at the car door, still barking up at Rufus, who was barking in return, paws propped on the window ledge.

Alice watched as Churchill glanced down at the commotion, his stern features softening into what, even from the distance, appeared to be a smile. He seemed to say something to his poodle, who was trying to climb over his master's considerable girth to get a closer look at Bonzo.

The security personnel seemed momentarily unsure how to react to the canine intruder. One moved toward Bonzo, but Churchill waved him off with a gesture Alice could see even from her distance.

"He's making friends with the Prime Minister," Tom observed dryly.

"It's Rufus he's interested in," Alice replied, her fingers twisting anxiously in the fabric of her skirt. "He's always loved other dogs."

The driver's door of Churchill's limousine opened, and a uniformed chauffeur stepped out, circling around to the passenger side. Alice could see the castle's owner step forward, his chest puffed with importance, ready to greet the most powerful man in Britain.

At the same time, she caught sight of Harry and Nigel reaching Thompson at the gate. Though she couldn't hear their words, the security man's face transformed from impassive to alarmed in an instant. All three men were now looking toward the keep tower, its ancient stone battlements looming against the blue sky.

Alice followed their gaze, her breath catching. Was someone up there right now, taking aim? Was Evie in danger?

The passenger door of Churchill's limousine began to open. Bonzo was still capering around the vehicle, exchanging excited barks with Rufus. Alice's hands tightened on the edge of the Daimler, torn between her duty to stay put and her desperate wish to retrieve her dog.

Her gaze darted between Bonzo, the opening car door, and the ominous silhouette of the keep tower as Churchill prepared to step out into the late afternoon sunlight.

Chapter 63
Evie

Evie stood behind one of the massive oak trees that ringed the ancient castle keep, trying to catch her breath. After running all the way here, her lungs were burning almost as badly as the bullet hole in her arm.

She gazed up at the abandoned tower. Was Paul really inside? The place looked utterly deserted, but then if he had selected this as his base of attack, he'd have taken pains to hide any visible trace of his presence.

The door to the keep was closed and fastened with a heavy padlock, although that wasn't a problem. After he'd told her about the abandoned keep, Graves had given her a key. He had found Mr Vernon's keys when he'd been locked in the wine cellar with the man's body.

Luckily for Evie, Millicent Hartley had been too panicked to search Graves's pockets after she'd knocked him out. She'd just tied him up and bundled him into the back of one of the Clarion Castle Lagondas.

Now Evie was acutely aware that the sun was slowly sinking towards the horizon. Within a quarter of an hour— maybe even less by now— Churchill would be arriving at the castle and for those few crucial moments would be vulnerable to an attack. She couldn't rush this, though, for the same reason that she'd refused to let Alice or any of the others come with her.

If Paul was here, he was bound to have posted at least one lookout to watch for anyone who might approach, and Evie was fairly sure

THE MURDERS AT CLARION CASTLE

who that lookout would be. She needed first to spot him and then get close enough to disable him before he could sound an alarm. And there was a far greater chance that she would be able to accomplish both of those things alone. One person would always be able to move more silently and covertly than many or even just two. So she stood absolutely motionless, scanning the trees and the tumbled down stones that surrounded the abandoned keep.

A flash of movement several yards away caught her eye and made her heart jolt, but it was only a sparrow, startled out of a tree and flying to the branches of another. Below the sparrow, though—

Evie's eyes narrowed as she focused on the patch of shadow beneath the tree's spreading branches. Then she drew what felt like the first full breath she'd taken since leaving Alice and the others. Standing there in the shade of another oak was Hans, dressed in the blue, brass-buttoned tunic and trousers of a police constable's uniform.

Got you.

Evie scanned her surroundings once again, this time searching for a way to approach Hans without being seen. She had to admit that this was clever of Paul. If Hans was spotted by anyone in authority, he could easily pass himself off as one of the local constabulary, posted here to secure the area in preparation for the Prime Minister's visit.

At the moment, Hans's attention seemed to be fixed on the tower door. He hadn't— yet— glanced in her direction.

Evie took a cautious step back and sideways, screened by the shelter of the trees and small bushes, circling around the keep so that she could approach Hans from behind. She'd learned during operations in France how to move silently, how to roll her feet so as not to dislodge any stray pebbles that could give away her presence.

Still, she felt as though there would have been time for Churchill to make ten visits to Clarion Castle in the time she took to move into position.

At long last she found herself staring at the back of the tall domed helmet that was part of Hans's disguise.

Evie shut her eyes briefly, willing the pain from her wound to leave her, so that she could concentrate on her next moves,. She still had the revolver from Nigel, but that would make far too much noise. She had one chance— exactly one chance— to get this right; otherwise Hans would raise enough of an alarm to alert Paul and any reinforcements he had with him up in the tower.

Another piece of luck in her favour: Hans wasn't a big man. He stood barely an inch or two taller than she did. She gathered herself; then in a single, swift movement she sprang forward to close the distance between them and seized hold of the blue felt-covered helmet. Then she pulled with all of her strength. Hans's breath went out in a strangled, choking gasp as the helmet's strap jerked hard against his windpipe, but he couldn't cry out.

He twisted, clawing at the leather strap, trying desperately to break Evie's hold, but she hooked a leg around his ankle, sweeping his right foot out from under him. Hans staggered and fell hard, still choking and gasping for air. From there, Evie delivered a hard, sharp kick to his temple. Hans's eyes rolled back and he went limp. Unconscious.

Evie straightened, released a slow breath, and drew out the key to the tower that Graves had given her.

Chapter 64
Evie

Slowly and with painstaking care, Evie eased open the heavy wooden door to the tower roof by a fraction of an inch, then a little more. She was still winded by her climb up the steep circular stone steps, but there was no time to catch her breath. She had to move now.

And she had to move silently. She couldn't let Paul or anyone else inside notice the door being opened; the element of surprise was one of the few advantages she had.

When at last the crack was wide enough to peer through, she applied her eye to the gap and, with a fresh lurch under her ribcage, saw Paul. He was positioned on the opposite side of the circular room, hunched over the telescopic sight of a rifle on a tripod positioned at one of the archer's escarpments that interrupted the stone wall at regular intervals.

Evie opened the door just a fraction more and saw a second man with dark hair and broad shoulders standing near to Paul. The dark-haired man was also looking out through an escarpment, but instead of a rifle, his hands gripped a crossbow.

Between the two men was the gap that separated the two battlements and escarpments.

As Evie stood watching Paul and the second man, she heard the dark-haired man say, in a tone that was tense with frustration, "The door is open but no one's getting out."

Paul said nothing, remaining fixated on the telescopic sight on his rifle. He'd be watching Churchill's limousine below, Evie knew, wondering why Churchill hadn't left the car.

Evie didn't know the reason either, but through the hectic pounding of her own heart, she silently willed the Prime Minister to refrain from alighting for just a few moments more. She gripped the handle of her revolver more tightly.

A plan. She needed a plan guaranteed to neutralise both Paul and the second man as threats. If she shot one, the other still might manage to get off a fatal shot at Winston Churchill.

From far below and off in the distance, Evie could hear what sounded like excited, high-pitched barking.

Paul growled under his breath. "Cursed dogs. Keep steady, Foster. Wait until my signal."

The other man— Foster, his name must be— muttered, "He's got to show himself any second now."

Evie's gaze lighted on an irregular stone protrusion near the battlement edge, just beside the place where Paul stood. Her breath caught in her throat. She had her plan, now, although she'd once again need an almost preposterous degree of luck to make it work.

And she couldn't let either Paul or the second man know that she was armed. If she was going to succeed, Paul had to dismiss her as a threat.

With shaking hands, Evie slid the revolver into the pocket of her skirt. Then she flung the door open with a shove hard enough that it banged against the stone wall.

The man Paul had called Foster spun around, the crossbow still in his hands, and Paul's head jerked reflexively in her direction.

For a brief, satisfying instant, Evie saw the look of utter and complete astonishment cross Paul's face as he recognised her.

"Yes, I'm alive," she said. She kept her hands loose at her sides. "I suppose you could say that we're even, now. I thought you were dead, and you thought I was dead. The only difference between us is that you've lost and I've won."

"Won?" An angry sneer replaced the shock in Paul's expression. He glanced at Foster. "Shoot her and let's get on with this."

He didn't even wait to see whether his order would be obeyed, only spun back to stare once more through the scope of his rifle. Waiting for the chance to take his killing shot.

Evie could feel the beating of her heart all the way out to the tips of her fingers as for what seemed another brief eternity, her eyes met the cold blue gaze of Paul's accomplice.

Foster took aim, and Evie saw his hand start to tighten on the trigger of the crossbow.

In a flash, she threw herself to the right and in the same moment, drew the hidden revolver out of her pocket. "I don't bloody think so."

She squeezed off a shot and saw Foster stumble back, hands clutching at his chest. The crossbow clattered to the stone floor, but Evie didn't see where it landed.

She was already in motion, charging across the tower, straight at Paul.

Paul had looked up at the sound of the gunshot, but Evie's charge still caught him off guard.

She slammed into him with a force that sent a fiery jolt of pain through her wounded arm and made bright flashes explode across her vision, but she didn't stop or pull back. The momentum of their collision knocked Paul away from the rifle and the escarpment, toward the open space between the rooftop battlements.

They careened towards the low wall. Evie felt the jolt reverberate through her own body as Paul's legs slammed into the stones, and then they tumbled over.

Evie flung out her hands, grabbing hold of the stone protrusion at the last possible second. The wrench almost pulled her arms out of their sockets, but she hung, her legs dangling in the air. Then she heard Paul land, far, far below her, with a dull, heavy thud.

Chapter 65
Evie

Evie didn't dare look to see where Paul had fallen. She struggled to cling onto the stone outcropping and dug her feet against the tower wall, trying to find enough traction to pull herself back up and over. But her fingers were slick with sweat, and her wounded arm was nearly useless. Even the muscles in her good arm were cramping with fatigue. She could feel her grip slipping. She couldn't pull herself up, still less hold on much longer.

She'd probably land right beside Paul, dashed to bits against the paving stones far below—

Strong hands closed around her wrists. Evie felt herself being hauled upwards until she landed on the top of the tower, staring up into Nigel's face.

Nigel was breathing hard as though he'd sprinted all the way here, and he looked paler and more shaken than Evie had ever seen him.

"Evie—"

Evie interrupted. "Paul!" she gasped. "He went over. But he was a pilot— he had parachute training in how to survive a fall." She couldn't get breath for any more, but Nigel understood. Without another word, he spun for the tower door, and together they raced down the spiral stairs and burst out into the ruins of the castle keep down below.

Evie saw Paul at once, lying about twenty feet from the foot of the tower. One of his legs was bent at a stomach-twisting angle, but he was still alive. At the sound of their approaching footsteps, he managed to wrestle himself up to his knees.

In this moment, Evie scarcely recognised him. His once handsome face was transformed, twisted with defiant fury so that he looked more like a rat caught in a trap than the man Evie had married.

Her lungs aching, her heart pounding, her arm and shoulder muscles still burning, Evie stared at him and felt . . . nothing.

All the hurt, all the anger and betrayal had somehow dropped away, stripped from her in the moment when Nigel's hands had pulled her back from certain death.

Fast as a slithering snake, Paul's hand moved towards his jacket pocket.

"Evie!" Nigel shouted a warning, but Evie had already seen the snub-nose pistol Paul had drawn. She stepped forward, and in a single kick, knocked the gun out of Paul's hand, sending it clattering away. Paul tried to scramble after it, but he was hampered by his broken leg, and Evie got there first.

She picked up the gun and levelled it at Paul. "Don't move."

Paul's lips drew back in a snarl. "You're not going to shoot me. You haven't got the nerve."

"You don't think so?" Evie flicked the safety catch off the pistol.

"Evie—" Nigel's voice still held a note of warning.

From somewhere in the distance, Evie could hear footsteps running in their direction. Reinforcements, no doubt, led by Harry and coming to take charge.

Paul's face was still twisted in a mask of defiant fury. But looking down at him, Evie still felt . . . she felt as though a sunlit door had opened beside her. Paul was the past, and through that other door was the future.

She shook her head. "It's all right; I'm not going to shoot him," she told Nigel. "He's not worth it. Although it is lucky he survived the fall. This way he can be tried for treason, and forced to betray his network of spies."

Chapter 66
Harry

At the small writing desk in his Crofter's Green cottage, Harry Jenkins paused to review the letter he had written to his sister, Mrs Joan Brewster.

20 August 1941

Dear Joan,

For reasons that will become obvious, you will not be reading the full details of the Prime Minister's visit to Clarion Castle in the newspapers— and neither am I entirely free to speak of what occurred— but I can say without reservation that your son acquitted himself well and was instrumental in saving Mr Churchill's life.

A certain Pomeranian dog also played his own part, and has already received a reward—a package con-

taining one pork chop. The package label bore the return address of Number 10 Downing Street.

What you may have seen in The London Times is the news that Churchill had left England the week before to journey to Placentia Bay, Newfoundland, to meet with U.S. President Franklin Roosevelt. Apparently, during several days aboard the U.S.S. Augusta the two men worked out and signed the mutual declaration of their two nations known as The Atlantic Charter.

We don't know exactly what effect, if any, their meeting will have on the war. But having seen the great man in person, I find myself with a renewed sense of hope and faith in our British government— which, as I can almost hear you say, is somewhat remarkable for a cynical old policeman.

To return to the Clarion Castle affair, though, we have arrested two traitors who were working within the castle: a signal corps officer by the name of Foster and a woman called Millicent Hartley. Both are to be charged with treason, as well as with the murders I spoke of in my last letter.

> *Nigel also had the satisfaction of netting three members of a spy ring: two Germans and another man, the leader of the ring, who as it turned out was Paul Harris, the husband of our mutual friend Evie.*

> *I know you will be as grieved as I was to hear that news. But I don't believe you need worry about Evie's state of mind. Paul Harris is currently undergoing interrogation, after which he will without doubt be hanged for treason along with the other two German spies and the traitorous Foster and Hartley.*

> *Evie, however, appears to me entirely at peace. She bears the look of someone who has passed through a trial by fire and yet not been burned.*

Harry finished considering what he'd written, briefly resting the top of his pen against his upper lip. Finally he added,

> *As for Evie and Nigel, only time will tell. But I find myself with a renewed sense of hope and optimism as regards the two of them.*

> *Yours as always,*

Harry

THE END

We hope you've enjoyed this fifth adventure in our Homefront Sleuths series. More adventures are coming!

To find out what fate has in store for Evie, Nigel, and all the other Sleuths in a new thrilling tale of espionage, murder, and moral choices in wartime Britain, you can preorder *The Harvest Festival Murders* here:
[link]

In the meantime, we hope you'll consider the other adventures penned by Anna and Charles, listed in the 'Also by' section that comes at the end of this book.

Chapter 67
Historical Notes

This is a work of fiction, and the authors make no claim whatsoever that any historical locations or historical figures who appear in this story were even remotely connected with the adventures and events recounted herein.

However, we can provide a few historical tidbits that we hope you'll enjoy...

1. The Atlantic Charter, which plays a background role in our story, was indeed issued on August 14, 1941, following historic meetings between Winston Churchill and Franklin D. Roosevelt aboard the U.S.S. Augusta in Placentia Bay, Newfoundland. This joint declaration outlined the two leaders' vision for a post-war world and became one of the foundational documents for the United Nations. Churchill braved U-boat-infested waters to reach this meeting—a testament to his well-documented willingness to place himself in harm's way when duty called!

2. As readers will have gathered from Harry's letter to his sister, the fates of Siegfried, Hans, Foster, Millicent, and Gerda were sealed when they faced justice under the Treachery Act

of 1940. On May 23, 1940, Parliament passed this legislation outlawing any conduct "designed or likely to give assistance to the enemy," and carrying just one sentence: death. Between 1940 and 1946, nineteen actual spies and saboteurs were executed under this Act, most at Wandsworth Prison.

3. In our story, Churchill's visit to Clarion Castle for negotiations regarding steel contracts is, of course, entirely fictional. We took inspiration from the famous British deception operations of World War II, including Operations Mincemeat and Fortitude, which were designed to conceal the true targets of the Allied invasions of Sicily and Normandy. These elaborate ruses involved planted documents, double agents, and false information deliberately leaked to confuse German intelligence. Churchill was a great enthusiast for such "special means" of warfare, famously establishing the Special Operations Executive with instructions to "set Europe ablaze" through sabotage and subversion. While we've invented our particular deception—the abbreviated visit to the castle that masked the PM's departure for Newfoundland—the use of cover stories and decoys was very much part of the actual wartime playbook!

4. Speaking of Churchill, his beloved miniature poodle Rufus was a genuine historical figure in his own right. The Prime Minister was seldom separated from his canine companion and was known to share his meals with Rufus, who enjoyed a privileged place at the dinner table. Sadly, the original Rufus was killed in a road accident in 1947, after which a heartbroken Churchill acquired Rufus II.

THE MURDERS AT CLARION CASTLE 335

5. We drew inspiration for Clarion Castle from the magnificent Chilham Castle in Kent, which was built on the site of medieval ruins, part of which—the keep tower—still stands as a dramatic reminder of the past. The Jacobean mansion that now constitutes the main castle was begun in 1616 and has been home to a colourful cast of residents through the centuries, including King Henry VIII. Today, the Castle's website notes that it's available for overnight guests who fancy experiencing a taste of the grandeur we've depicted in our story.

6. The White Horse Inn has been operating since the 16th Century, still located on the Chilham Village square, across from the entrance to the Castle. Our Shepherd's Rest Inn is inspired by the Woolpack Inn in Chilham Village, which dates back to the 15th century and continues to welcome weary travellers with hearty fare and local ales.

7. The Pilgrim Way does indeed wind through Chilham Village and has done so for centuries, since the time Geoffrey Chaucer immortalised it in "The Canterbury Tales." Chaucer's pilgrims would have passed directly through Chilham's picturesque square, dominated by the Castle's ancient keep tower.

8. During World War II, many stately homes throughout Britain were requisitioned for military purposes, including intelligence operations and planning. While we've invented the secret intelligence work at Clarion Castle, country houses did indeed serve as locations for clandestine activities. Bletchley Park, where the Enigma code was broken,

is perhaps the most famous example, but numerous other estates played vital roles in the war effort, their grand rooms transformed into map rooms, radio stations, and command centres. Our fictional listening post was inspired by the Y Station in Kent, located in a residential home on Abbot's Cliff, overlooking the English Channel and just 23 miles from the coast of France.

9. The Signal Corps mentioned in our story was a real branch of military communications, responsible for maintaining the vital flow of information between commands. Their work was often unheralded but absolutely essential to the war effort—though we hasten to add that there's no historical evidence of any Signal Corps member moonlighting as an assassin!

Chapter 68
A Note to Readers

Thank you for reading ***The** Murders at Clarion Castle*. We hope you've enjoyed it!

As you probably know, reviews make a big difference! So, we also hope you'll consider going back to the Amazon page where you bought the story and uploading a quick review. You can get to that page by using this link:

https://geni.us/xOePs

You can also sign up for our Sherlock and Lucy mailing list and get a FREE download of four new classic-style Sherlock Holmes adventures and audiobooks:

dl.bookfunnel.com/o56982auvp

If you continue to the next few pages, you'll see a list of all our adventures with links to order – they're all FREE if you have Kindle Unlimited.

Chapter 69
Also by Anna Elliott and Charles Veley

OUR NEW WEBSITE
https://thehomefrontsleuths.com/

THE HOMEFRONT SLEUTHS SERIES PAGE ON AMAZON

https://geni.us/95ICC

THE HOMEFRONT SLEUTHS MYSTERIES
THE BLACKOUT MURDERS
https://geni.us/GBOBggM
THE SPECTRE OF HAWTHORNE MANOR
https://geni.us/xOePs
THE SPITFIRE MURDERS
https://geni.us/piK3ljC
THE JUDAS MONK MURDERS
https://geni.us/G0cvg3
THE MURDERS AT CLARION CASTLE

https://geni.us/5NSX
THE SHERLOCK HOLMES AND LUCY JAMES MYSTERIES

The Sherlock and Lucy series page at Amazon:

tinyurl.com/37are7m7

The Last Moriarty

(geni.us/1vItn)

The Wilhelm Conspiracy

(geni.us/VIK8rxg)

Remember, Remember

(geni.us/w5n7)

The Crown Jewel Mystery

(geni.us/4Xf4JR)

The Jubilee Problem

(geni.us/KaiX)

Death at the Diogenes Club

(geni.us/BBeq)

The Return of the Ripper

(geni.us/Sqydk)

Die Again, Mr Holmes

(geni.us/SzaJS)

Watson on the Orient Express

(geni.us/txthZq)

Galahad's Castle

(geni.us/hs0Mjz)

The Loch Ness Horror

(geni.us/a1ZwfBr)

The Adair Murders

(geni.us/D0m6no)

The Cornwall Mermaid

(geni.us/ItWT)

Miss Nightingale's Gala

(geni.us/xZkBHK)

The Affair of the Coronation Ball

(geni.us/Fygm3iL)

THE SHERLOCK AND LUCY SHORT STORIES AND NOVELLAS

Flynn's Christmas

(geni.us/05rfH)

The Clown on the High Wire

(geni.us/wuaCNZE)

The Cobra in the Monkey Cage

(geni.us/Vww7n)

A Fancy-Dress Death

(geni.us/aupJEYh)

The Sons of Helios

(geni.us/hHmxk8)

The Vanishing Medium

(geni.us/964s6)

Christmas at Baskerville Hall

(geni.us/wkLFDTo)

Kidnapped at the Tower

(geni.us/hAhF)

Five Pink Ladies

(geni.us/65MWaN0)

The Solitary Witness

(geni.us/c8QLom)

The Body in the Bookseller's

(geni.us/8ZBD)

The Curse of Cleopatra's Needle

(geni.us/kBowMn)

The Coded Blue Envelope

(geni.us/aDhPW0h)

Christmas on the Nile

(geni.us/gHBvFG4)

The Missing Mariner

(geni.us/EptP)

Powder Island

(geni.us/8J1H)

Murder at the Royal Observatory

(geni.us/zvWXvcD)

The Bloomsbury Guru

(geni.us/sYBCW)

Holmes Takes a Holiday

(geni.us/WFvz)

Holmes Picks a Winner

(geni.us/UP9Ax)

THE COLLECTED STORIES

Season One

(geni.us/MBK65F3)

Season Two Volume I

(geni.us/Wl8q)

Season Two Volume II

(geni.us/JBHTr8)

Season Three Volume I

(geni.us/r7pGlK)

Season Three Volume II

(geni.us/B5kG)

THE BECKY & FLYNN MYSTERIES by Anna Elliott

Guarded Ground

(geni.us/V68jco)

Hidden Harm

(geni.us/1HQOFo)

Watch and Ward

(geni.us/wnNkN)

Safe You Sleep

(geni.us/SvHX4)

Star-Sown Sky

(geni.us/SNAqd)

The Becky & Flynn series page at Amazon:

tinyurl.com/bdcnbhdj

AUDIOBOOKS

The Sherlock Holmes and Lucy James series (Audible):

tinyurl.com/4fnds4p2

The Becky and Flynn series (Audible):

tinyurl.com/227xeabr

FOLLOW US

AMAZON

Anna Elliott

(tinyurl.com/ys2u2m2s)

Charles Veley

(tinyurl.com/3rbap8ya)

GOODREADS

Anna Elliott

(tinyurl.com/2udr75dk)

Charles Veley

(tinyurl.com/46993kp8)

BOOKBUB

Anna Elliott

(tinyurl.com/mwh46rm5)

Charles Veley

(tinyurl.com/yc6w25c)

AUDIBLE

Anna Elliott

(tinyurl.com/227xeabr)

Charles Veley

(tinyurl.com/27aduhjj)

Printed in Dunstable, United Kingdom